THE VINTAGE VILLAGE BAKE OFF

JUDY LEIGH

Boldwood

First published in Great Britain in 2023 by Boldwood Books Ltd.

Cover Design by Debbie Clement Design

Cover Illustration: Shutterstock

A CIP catalogue record for this book is available from the British Library.

Paperback ISBN 978-1-78513-223-0

Large Print ISBN 978-1-78513-219-3

Hardback ISBN 978-1-78513-218-6

Ebook ISBN 978-1-78513-216-2

Kindle ISBN 978-1-78513-217-9

Audio CD ISBN 978-1-78513-224-7

MP3 CD ISBN 978-1-78513-221-6

Digital audio download ISBN 978-1-78513-215-5

Boldwood Books Ltd
23 Bowerdean Street
London SW6 3TN
www.boldwoodbooks.com

To my family.

Cooking is love made visible.

— UNKNOWN

PROLOGUE

FORTY-NINE YEARS AGO

'In the presence of God, Father, Son and Holy Spirit, we have come together to witness the marriage of Harriet and Geoffrey, to pray for God's blessing on them, to share their joy, and to celebrate their love.'

The vicar smelled of something muddy and a strong whiff of aniseed. Hattie wondered if he'd just finished a quick burial outside. He must have rushed into the vestry to dust the soil from his hands and swig a swift glass of Pernod before starting the marriage service. She squinted at Geoffrey, sombre in his grey suit, through the dense net of her veil. She should have arranged for her father to lift it before the vows so that she could see properly, but Geoffrey had said he wanted to be the one to do it afterwards. Hattie had accepted his decision, as she'd accepted that he wanted her to wear white and that they'd have a one-tier cake with plastic figurines because it made sense economically, even though it was her father who was paying for the reception. She was used to doing things as others wished.

She'd never really liked the wedding dress. Right now, she hated it. It let in the cold; it was uncomfortable and stiff, it rustled and creaked like a ghost when she moved. Bunty had said she should wear red velvet. Geoffrey had suggested she should choose a sensible frock that would look appropriate next to him. In the end, she'd settled for a traditional satin gown. She'd let her mother have the final say. The brocade around the neck itched and left a red mark; it made her think of Anne Boleyn, just before her execution.

She peered at Geoffrey again. He wasn't looking at her. She needed a smile, some encouragement from someone, anyone. On a girl's wedding day, wasn't she supposed to be excited, beautiful, tingling with anticipation? Hattie felt cold and alone. The church was draughty and the sleeves on her dress were transparently thin. The truth was, so far, the marriage wasn't as she'd hoped.

The wedding service was hardly a celebration of eternal love. Incessant rain battered against the stained-glass windows from washed-out skies. Everyone in the church had wet feet and looked miserable. Hattie's mother wore a crumpled peach suit, a wide-brimmed hat, and a blank face. She stood grimly between Aunt Maud and Aunt Dorothy, who sported matching sour faces, pillar-box-red lipstick and jackets with fur collars that looked as if rats had died simultaneously around their necks. Hattie wished her mother were the sort that sobbed into a tissue, heartbroken at the loss of a dear daughter, but she was simply compliant about everything: life, love, death, marriage. It was all the same continued theme of drudgery. Harriet wondered if she'd inherited her mother's submissiveness. She hoped not.

The vicar was talking to the congregation about comfort in marriage and honour in love. Hattie had no idea what that meant. Geoffrey's face was expressionless; he was clearing his throat. It was a sound that she found a little irritating; it meant that he thought he was about to say something important. He trotted out his vows, his voice like the rattle of a machine gun. She glanced around for her siblings, for a bit of reassurance. Robert was in the pew to the left, inspecting his shoes. Without checking, Harriet knew they'd be highly polished and conventional, just like Robert. He was a schoolteacher, studious and serious. Hattie had always wanted to be a nurse, one of those carefree romantic women with bouffant hair she read about in cheap paperbacks. She'd smile a lot, wear a pristine uniform and fall for a handsome young doctor who saved children's lives. Instead, she'd studied shorthand typing and now she was a sensible secretary who spent hours each day sitting on a hard chair.

Behind her, Bunty was fidgeting with the straps of her bridesmaid's dress, looking stunning in the pink silk she'd insisted on, making eyes at the best man, or any man who glanced her way. Bunty was always bored, on the lookout for fun. She'd be centre stage at the reception, dancing and showing off by herself, all eyes on her performance. She'd end up snogging the DJ from Clive's Groove-to-Go Disco. That was typical of Bunty. Hattie thought it was depressing that both daughters had inherited their mother's serial acquiescence: Hattie did as she was told and Bunty craved approval. Nurture had a lot to answer for. Her heart had started to thump: the vicar was talking to her, the reek of aniseed on his breath.

'Harriet, will you take Geoffrey to be your husband? Will you obey him and serve him, love him, comfort him, honour and protect him and, forsaking all others, be faithful to him as long as you both shall live?'

Hattie's lips were suddenly glued together; her mouth wouldn't move. But her mind was bursting with so many thoughts: Geoffrey was the perfect husband for her. Her father had said so. He was sensible, authoritative, strong. He looked smart in a suit. He was wise about things that mattered, money, firm decisions, organising. He wasn't frivolous. Her mother repeated that her priority was to find a man who'd provide a home.

Hattie thought for a moment that it might be nice to meet a man who provided some laughter. Suddenly, her legs were jelly.

'I will,' she said, surprised by the sound of her own voice.

The vicar addressed the congregation in a mourning tone, muttering about pouring blessings everywhere. Hattie wasn't listening. Behind the veil she had a fuzzy view of the congregation: her family, awkward friends in ill-fitting clothes, the dour in-laws-to-be, their arms folded, faces like grim reapers. She noticed the vicar's greasy hair combed to one side, Geoffrey's long face, his pale eyes. He mumbled more words without looking at her: one of them was love. Hattie thought about the meaning of love – was it passion, devotion, kindness or routine? She'd believed she loved Geoffrey but now, standing in a cold echoing church wearing a thin dress she didn't like much, she wasn't so sure. For a moment, she wished she were perched at the church organ, belting out one of her favourite tunes. Or walking in the park by herself in sploshing rain, hoping the sun would come out.

The vicar was frowning, urging her to speak; there was silence as the congregation waited.

Hattie said in one breath, '... from this day forward, for better, for worse, for richer, for poorer, in sickness and in health, to love and to cherish, till death us do part...'

And that was it.

A ring was clamped on her finger, the veil was lifted. Geoffrey kissed her with cold lips and somebody behind her clapped and cheered. It was probably Bunty. Hattie waited to feel lifted on a cloud of intense happiness, but instead the draught from beneath the wooden church door seeped through the nave and chilled her skin. There were hushed voices, the congregation praying for the couple, their words sombre.

But Hattie's only thought was that she was a wife now. No longer Hattie Parkin. She was Mrs Geoffrey Bowen, and with it would come so many changes. They'd move into the bungalow, sleep in the same bed; she would make his packed lunch every day, four slices of white bread, ham and lettuce, a thin sliver of tomato.

The service was almost over. The reception would begin soon, and there would be music, speeches, cutting the cake. Champagne would fizz in glasses, music would play and the dancing would start: The Osmonds' 'Love Me for a Reason'. The Who, 'Won't Get Fooled Again'. Perhaps then the party would explode into life and the sensation of euphoria would take over.

Hattie hunched her shoulders and took Geoffrey's stiff arm as he led her down the aisle and out into the dripping rain, considering how marriage would change her life.

1

THE PRESENT

Hattie crept across the living room with her shoulders hunched. She'd moved that way since the first day of her marriage to Geoffrey almost fifty years ago, and she still edged her way around the bungalow almost a year after he'd left her for a woman from the bowling club. If she closed her eyes and thought about it for a moment, Hattie could imagine him sitting in the armchair grumbling, 'What's wrong with you, woman? You're always hovering. You're neither use nor ornament. Why don't you go and do something useful, like the washing-up?' They were divorced now, just: it had been quick, uncontested on both sides. All his belongings had been removed from the bungalow; photographs, clothes. But despite his absence, his influence seemed to stay.

Standing in front of the piano, hesitating again, she thought about playing her favourite piece. She hadn't played properly for a long time. Her hands still shook with fear, even after all these years. She'd been good once, very good. But Geoffrey would have listened to the first dramatic chord, covered his ears during the tentative notes that followed and said in a blustery voice, 'Oh no, not that damned awful racket again. For God's sake, woman, I'm trying to read my paper.'

She stretched her fingers. She'd play it now, perfectly. Hattie tried the first chord, Chopin: *Fantaisie-Impromptu* Op. 66. The notes that followed were strong, dynamic. She was a talented pianist. Then her fingers tightened, she'd made a mistake, a discordant clang on the notes. She could almost hear Geoffrey's scornful laugh. 'You're out of practice, Hattie – the old fingers aren't as nimble as they were. You're past your sell-by date, love.' Then he'd snicker in that mean way he had, and she'd feel sad, go back to her armchair and pick up a magazine on homecare. She recalled Geoffrey telling her she wasn't much of a homemaker either.

She touched the old photograph in its shiny plastic frame, the only one on the top of the piano. Light streamed through the window onto the glass, revealing a film of dust. No, she was no homemaker, Geoffrey had been right. Everything in the bungalow was past its best. Hattie sighed. The picture and piano were relics of the 1950s; they had seen better days. The magnolia walls were dingy, the colour of grime. The piano was her mother's, battle-scarred, the wooden frame scuffed, rings from many forgotten teacups making stubborn circles on the veneer. And the discoloured piano keys, like bared ancient teeth, made a jangly, slightly out-of-tune sound when played, even though it was regularly tuned. Hattie wondered whether it was time to get rid of it, but Geoffrey would have liked that. So she'd keep it, for now.

The black and white photo had faded. The three children in the foreground posed for the camera, and Hattie caressed each face in turn with a fingertip. Robert John Parkin, the oldest, blonde curls flopping over his eyes, a pale, serious face. Her brother was a dreamer, he'd always be lost in his own thoughts. In the middle was

Bunty, slim, oblivious of everyone else, tousled dark hair, a smile filling her small face, all teeth. Christened Elizabeth after the Queen, she was the youngest, the spoiled one. And on the left side, a little apart from the others, stood solemn Harriet Anne Parkin. Hattie. The middle child, the invisible one, the one who mattered least. She had allowed her insignificance to continue throughout her marriage to Geoffrey Bowen, and afterwards, throughout her life.

'Shit,' Hattie muttered to herself, a moment of realisation that she had wasted too many moments thinking of Geoffrey. That happened a lot. She wondered if she should try to play again. Geoffrey was gone – he couldn't criticise her any more. So why, as she stood at the piano, did she feel her shoulders tense? It was as if he were sitting behind her, his face filled with the familiar contemptuous sneer. She heard his miserable voice saying, 'You'll never be any good, Hattie. You don't have the skills. Mediocrity is your middle name.' And Hattie would think in her head, 'No, it's Anne – my middle name is Anne.' But she'd never dared to say it aloud.

When Geoffrey had taken up with Linda from the bowling club almost a year ago, it was a blessed relief. It was as if gates had opened wide, allowing her to walk free, breathe new fresh air. But she hadn't reconnected with Robert and Bunty as much as she'd have liked. Geoffrey's meanness had kept them away for years, and her siblings were set in their ways. Hattie had always believed she was closer to Robert than to Bunty, despite her sister's effusive texts about how they were sisters forever. But when Robert had moved to Devon five years ago, Hattie had cried for days. She hadn't understood why he wanted to live so far away, why he'd leave her alone with Geoffrey. She'd visited him twice in his new home, both times with grumbling Geoffrey in tow. Robert's little village was not far from Dawlish, where the train tracks rolled by close to the sea, and Hattie had thought it beautiful. She ought to visit him again.

Hattie's fingers slid lightly over the dull ivory keys, trying a tentative note. Her fingers shook as they hovered. She rested both hands on the keys, then she tried a phrase or two, again, Chopin: *Fantaisie-Impromptu* Op. 66. She played the chord perfectly, her fingers floating easily across the notes, and, for a while, beautiful sounds filled the air. She made a crashing mistake, a raucous sound that echoed like a fairground tune, and stopped dead. The silence rang. She didn't practise enough. She could have been good. As a fifteen-year-old, she'd dreamed of being a concert pianist. But it was too late now.

'Shit,' Hattie muttered again, wondering why she was speaking so quietly. Immediately, she saw Geoffrey's pinched face looming in front of her; she heard his irritated voice.

'Swearing is uncouth, Harriet. There's no place for it in this house.' He was a hypocrite. He swore all the time, but she never mentioned it.

She tried again, out loud, but her voice was still shaky. 'You can go to hell, Geoffrey.' She imagined his bloated cheeks reddening, she could hear the sneer in his tone.

'Whatever's wrong with you, woman? What's the matter?'

'Shit,' Hattie said again, then she said it louder. 'Shit, shit, shit, shit!'

Hattie placed both hands firmly on the keys and banged them down with a discordant, resounding clang. 'Shit.' She said it with more feeling. It didn't matter how many times she said it, her life was still empty. She'd been released from fifty years of prison after the marriage from hell, but now her world was filled with missed opportunities, and the present was a dull routine that repeated itself on a daily basis.

Hattie decided it was time for a cup of tea. It was what she did when there was a gap in her day: she'd wake up, have breakfast, wash, clean her teeth, brush her hair, check the post, then she'd have a cup of tea. She stared at her hands, plain hands, no wedding ring now. She was alone in a small modern bungalow on a small housing estate in Bodicote, Oxfordshire, and the silence screamed at her from each corner like a ghoul. She made for the warmth of the little kitchen and the temporary security of tea for one.

When the brew was suitably strong, she hauled out the teabag, adding a modest glug of milk. There was a rapping of knuckles against the window. She glanced up and felt fretful and optimistic at the same time. It was Glenys from next door, not Geoffrey. He seldom visited now, but he probably had a key – the thought of him entering her home with it made her nerves jangle in the same way they had for years.

Hattie smiled a welcoming grin; Glenys Edwards was a good sort. She was in her early sixties, full of energy, always dressed in her best, married to Bill, who sorted letters at the post office in Banbury.

Glenys liked to check on Hattie regularly, 'To make sure you're still alive and kicking.' Hattie instinctively liked her, and that was a dilemma too. She'd invite her in, and Glenys would sit at the table over a cooling cuppa and talk for over an hour. Hattie was pleased to have company, but she was relieved when Glenys left. That was the problem with being lonely: you were no good alone and you weren't any good in company either.

'Hello, Glenys,' Hattie said. 'What can I do for you?'

'It's about what I can do for you, my lovely,' Glenys enthused. She was already inside the kitchen, bustling towards the table, waving a piece of paper she'd cut from a newspaper. 'I bring tidings of great joy.' She glanced at Hattie's full cup. 'Cuppa going spare, is it?'

Hattie moved to the kettle, wondering if her sigh had been audible, but Glenys seemed not to have noticed as she flourished the clipping. 'It's half-price day at Cloud Nine tomorrow. I thought it would be an opportunity. You could get yourself a good pampering.'

Hattie frowned. 'Pampering? I don't usually pamper myself...'

'Well, it's about time you did. There's a beauty therapist there, Nikki she's called, she's in her early twenties but she's properly on-trend with all the treatments – she does wonders for the older woman. I mean, look at me...'

Hattie looked. Glenys seemed no different from how she usually looked. Hattie squinted. 'Ah, I see.'

Glenys put her hands on her hips, did a little wiggle and batted her lashes. 'I get *everything* done there.'

'Everything?'

'Oh yes, brow lamination, lash lift and tint, hydra facial... and her chemical peel is to die for.'

Hattie had no idea what Glenys was talking about. 'It's probably not for me.'

'Oh, but it is, it is,' Glenys insisted. 'I booked an appointment for myself tomorrow and Nikki said if I bring a friend, I can get extra discount for us both, so I've booked you in.'

'What for?' Hattie shook her head anxiously.

'Well, maybe it's time you got your mojo back, you know,' Glenys said confidentially. 'Come out of the seventies with your look and bring on something a bit more modern and racier.'

Hattie didn't know. 'Such as?'

'A facial maybe, you know, jazz yourself up a bit, get a younger style. Maybe lash extensions or—'

'Oh, you mean beauty treatments?' Hattie finally cottoned on. 'Oh, no, it's not really me. I don't go anywhere much.'

'Then maybe you should,' Glenys said. 'Give yourself a special treat for once instead of being cooped up here staring at the same four walls.'

Hattie paused. Maybe Glenys had a point – perhaps she should take more care of herself. What was the word she'd used – pampering? Hattie imagined herself lying on a sunbed, warm oil poured on her shoulders, enjoying a light massage. She'd breathe out all her anxieties as tension was pressed from aching muscles. She tried a smile. 'Well, maybe I could have a manicure perhaps?'

'Right, that's sorted.' Glenys accepted the steaming cup of tea Hattie offered. 'That's good, then. We'll have a talk about what options you want to pick when we arrive tomorrow at one o'clock. But there's laser hair removal, injectable hyaluronic acid lip fillers, micropigmentation.'

Hattie looked at her chipped nails and imagined her hands, neatly manicured, playing the piano beautifully. It might encourage her to start practising again. She smiled. 'Well, maybe a pearly varnish.'

'Bring it on.' Glenys slurped happily. 'I can't wait for you to meet Nikki. She'll discover the real vamp in you and get rid of the fuddy-duddy side. You won't know yourself when she's finished with you, Hattie, you wait and see.'

2

The next morning, Hattie sat at the breakfast table staring into her bowl of dry muesli. She was definitely feeling down in the dumps. It was to do with what Glenys had said yesterday while they'd shared a cup of tea. Hattie knew she ought to do something about her stuttering life, but she wasn't sure a beauty treatment was the answer to the bigger problem. She lifted a magazine Glenys had left behind, filled with glossy photos of famous actresses whom Glenys had declared 'are all your age, seventies – and look at them. They are gorgeous.' Hattie flicked the pages. Smiling women gazed back, poised and glamorous, almost faultless apart from attractive laughter lines. Meryl Streep, Helen Mirren, Joanna Lumley, Cher, Grace Jones. Hattie flicked the pages. Jane Fonda, Joan Collins, much older and positively glowing. She stared down again at the chipped nails, the dry wrinkled hands that hesitated over the piano keys. A manicure would be good.

'It's just the tip of the iceberg,' Hattie said as Joan Collins smiled back from the magazine.

Something wriggled in Hattie's mind, the two words Glenys

had used, repeating themselves like scurrying ants – fuddy-duddy, fuddy-duddy. She could hear Geoffrey saying it, his laugh full of mockery. 'You've turned into a fuddy-duddy, Hat. A stuffy old woman.'

She needed someone to talk to about how dejected she was, but there was no one she could turn to, not really. There were people she met at yoga once a week, she knew them all by their first names, but she had no one to confide in. She needed someone, and only one person came to mind. She picked up her mobile and turned it over. The age spots and a blue vein stood out on her hand. Hattie pressed a button and listened to the ring. It beeped continuously – she counted – ten times, and just as she thought it would ring out, a dry, tentative voice said, 'Hello?'

Hattie's heart leaped. 'Robert. Is that you?'

There was a pause, as if he was not sure. Then he said, 'Hello, Hattie. I've been in the garden. I was collecting the first of the marrows. They make nice jam. With ginger and lemon.'

'Ah.' Hattie wondered what to say next. 'Right.'

'Is everything OK, Hat? I mean – are you well? Or is it Bunty?' Something in Robert's voice sounded as if he was expecting the worst.

'Oh, Bunty's fine – as far as I know.' Hattie gave a little laugh and wondered why she'd done it. 'I mean, yes. I just wanted – a chat.'

'A chat?' Robert repeated. 'About what?'

'Oh, this and that.' Hattie said. 'You know, we could catch up, talk.'

'What do you want to talk about?' Robert's voice was quiet; Hattie could hardly hear him.

'The weather's nice here. Well, I mean, it's been nice. June was nice. July's a bit miserable. It rained yesterday.'

Robert paused for a moment then he said, 'Is everything all right? You seem a bit...'

'A bit what?'

'A bit odd.'

'Don't you ever feel—?' Hattie's eyes filled with tears. She swallowed hard. She didn't want to sound upset – Robert only had her voice to go on. 'Do you never feel a bit lonely?'

'No, I have the garden, the goats, the chickens – I keep myself busy.'

'Oh.' Hattie gulped. 'That's nice.'

'What's bothering you?' Robert asked quietly. 'Do you need to come down and stay for a bit?'

She took a breath: she had to ask the question. 'Do you think I'm a fuddy-duddy, Robert?' That was it. The two words were out.

'A what?'

Hattie had to say them again. 'Fuddy-duddy. My neighbour said I needed to get rid of the fuddy-duddy side of me.'

Robert laughed affectionately. 'You've always been a fuddy-duddy, Hat. Ever since you were a child.'

'In what way?' Hattie heard the indignation in her words.

'Well.' Robert was quiet on the other end of the phone, thinking. 'You were old beyond your years when you were six. And ten and twelve. And fifteen. You know, a bit conventional – in your dress and... manners.'

Hattie said nothing, allowing him to dig a hole for himself. Then she whispered, 'I had no idea.'

'Oh, it's not a bad thing, being a bit of a fuddy-duddy,' Robert muttered. 'I suppose I'm the same, stuck in my ways. I mean, we're not like Bunty now, are we, all razzamatazz and all that jazz?'

Hattie had no idea what Robert meant exactly but, for a moment, she felt that having some razzamatazz and all that jazz was the most exciting thing in the world. And the opposite of that was to be a fuddy-duddy. A deep sigh escaped from somewhere near her heart. 'Well, thanks, Robert. You've cleared that up.'

'Have I?' Robert asked. 'Oh well, that's good. I have to feed the chickens. I'm using their eggs to make a Victoria sponge.'

'Oh, you're eating cake?' Hattie was only half listening.

'Well, not just for me. The people at the gardening club are very partial to my cakes. Susan Joyce said so. I thought I'd perfect my recipe.'

'Right.' Hattie gritted her teeth. 'Is she a fuddy-duddy too?'

'Who?'

'Susan Joyce?'

'No, she's quite nice.' Robert paused, realising what he'd said. 'I mean she's quite ordinary... not really a fuddy-duddy...'

'Thanks, Robert. And what does that make me?' Hattie's teeth were clenched.

'Not that you're not ordinary too, Hat – I mean, you *are* ordinary – ordinary is not bad – it's better than fuddy-duddy – I mean, not better – just different.'

'Were you so diplomatic with all those parents when you were a head teacher, Robert?' Hattie said.

'Oh, I didn't need to be. I mean, it was a long time ago.'

'It certainly was – long before you became a fuddy-duddy too.'

'Pardon?' Robert was confused.

'Oh, never mind. I'm sorry, Robert. I'm just having a moment.'

His voice came back to her. 'Are you all right? I've never heard you sound this way. A bit – I don't know – not quite yourself. Why don't you pop down to me for a visit in Devon, Hat? Stay for a day or two? You could meet the gardening club and have a slice of cake?'

'Oh no – I can't do that – I'm far too busy.' Hattie heard the new determination in her own voice. 'I'm off for a facial this after-noon – some pampering, maybe a bit of laser hair removal, injectable hyaluronic acid lip fillers, micropigmentation.'

'Oh?' Robert had no idea what she was talking about.

'The new me. The one with razzamatazz and all that jazz. A bit of liposuction here and there, then I'll be really down with the kids. There'll be no more being a fuddy-duddy for yours truly, oh, no – I'll be just like Joan Collins.'

'Hat, are you all right?'

'Never been better.' Hattie pushed the bowl of muesli away and stood up. 'Sorry, Robert, I've got to go. I'll leave you to your marrow jam and your Victoria sponge and – and the village gardening club. I'm off for an important appointment – with my Botox surgeon.'

Hattie ended the call and took a deep breath. All was quiet now, but her thoughts raced like a charging cavalry. Her eyes filled with tears again. She knew the truth of it – she'd been a fuddy-duddy child and grown into a fuddy-duddy adult, and life had led her to this place where she was so set in her ways that she didn't recognise herself any more. Marriage to obnoxious Geof-frey had been penal servitude, a life sentence, and she'd emerged from the other side of the harrowing experience as the same dull, shrinking violet that she'd always been. That had been a mistake. Hattie frowned. Things had to change. It was about time. She'd visit the beautician – Nikki – and she'd ask for something dramatic, something life-changing. At least, she'd ask for a mani-cure with scarlet fingernails. She had to start somewhere.

* * *

The woman with the scarlet fingernails sat in the railway carriage staring through the window as the train pulled out of Liverpool

Lime Street. The journey would take three and a half hours, two changes. She gazed around to see if there was anyone interesting in the carriage to talk to. The man opposite, a balding business type with the sweet plump face of a cherub, was busy on his laptop. She imagined him to be in his thirties, a chirpy wife, a child, maybe two young boys. The woman across the aisle chattering into her phone was talking to someone who wanted to end the call. The woman's face was determined, her voice desperate to be listened to; she was interrupting, gabbling. They were always signs of loneliness. She glanced at the scarlet nails and decided she was good at working people out just from looking at them. Then she placed a hand over her smile – so why had she made so many mistakes over the years?

Uncomfortable in the hard seat, she crossed her legs, thinking that she probably looked like a young Elizabeth Taylor. In her seventies – just – she could pass for ten, fifteen years younger, she was sure. She glanced at the hefty suitcase at her feet, stuffed with her best clothes, hurriedly packed. She wouldn't go back now. She'd be in Banbury by late afternoon. Then she'd start a new life.

She wondered if she should text Hattie and tell her that she was on the way. Or perhaps she'd turn up, stand on the doorstep of the little bungalow on the small housing estate, yell, 'Surprise, surprise,' and they'd fall into each other's arms, drink tea, eat cake, and she'd tell her sister all about it. Hattie would understand. She was set in her ways, she always had been, but she had a kind heart. Besides, her bossy husband had taken away any exuberance Hattie had possessed long ago. It had been too long since they'd seen each other, they'd grown apart. That was the problem. One of many.

She felt her phone vibrate in her bag and she reached in crimson-tipped fingers and pulled it out. It was Sean, calling again. How many times had he called since she stepped on the boat? Fifteen? She cut the call once more; she had no intention of replying. She wouldn't look back.

She reached for a magazine from her bag and stared at the pictures for a while, flicking the pages disinterestedly. Gossip about royals. Something about Brad Pitt's daily workout plan, his fitness regime. She thought fleetingly that Brad Pitt was her type. Rich, handsome, a little wild. Sean had been like that once.

The horoscope page was near the end of the magazine and she glanced down the list of star signs until she came to her own: Aries, the ram. Her birthday was late March. Apparently, her characteristics were courageous, honest, energetic, generous. The article went on to say that the negative side of these traits was that a typical Aries could be reckless, tactless, overbearing and impulsive. That was her, to a tee. She scanned the page for news about how her day would unfold.

Autonomous, wilful and determined, Rams are very good at flying solo, and that's your best strategy. It's a good day to hit the road (or treadmill or track – pick your own pavement) and discover what you really really want. Then go after it with determination and guile, as only you can. Time alone will make you energised and strong. Put your head down and barrel through on your lonesome, without anyone to slow you down. This is your time.

A sigh came from beneath her smart jacket. How right the stars were. She was going it alone now. Sean O'Connor wouldn't be in her life any more. She was looking forward, on her way to Banbury on a train, to see her sister. She hesitated: she wasn't sure at all. Sean had been her rock, her soulmate. They'd been through so much together – and there was the one thing they never talked about, which drove a wedge between them. For a moment she felt the ache of separation, sadness. Tears came and she wiped them. She'd done it now – there was no looking back.

Her phone pinged again and she opened a message, smiling. Of course, she wasn't completely on her own. That was part of the plan. That was why she'd left Sean. The message read:

Stay in touch and let me know when you arrive, gorgeous.

Her grin widened as she thumbed the reply.

Can't wait. See you soon, handsome.

Then she closed the magazine and leaned back in her seat, closing her eyes, letting a daydream pull her into the centre. It was very close now; soon, she'd be living a new life. She hoped she'd done the right thing.

3

Hattie turned up at Cloud Nine in the high street at three minutes to one, feeling nervous. She wished she and Glenys could have gone together, but her neighbour had left earlier to call on a friend. It had taken her ages to find space in a car park and she was already tense. She was even more anxious when she saw Glenys, dressed in leather trousers and a red puffer jacket, looking very much the trendy woman about town. By her side, with her growing-out grey bob and her light beige mackintosh, Hattie suspected she looked like a bag lady. The wind buffeted down the high street; despite being July, it was cold as any October day, the skies ditchwater dull. Glenys's smile was bright.

'You came.' She beamed, as if she hadn't expected Hattie to arrive. Hattie wasn't sure she wanted to be there at all.

'Just a manicure.'

'Oh, you're booked in for two hours. We both want the works,' Glenys said. Hattie thought she looked momentarily insane. 'Pampering – it's what we need.' Glenys's laugh was wild abandon. 'My Bill doesn't know I come here. He believes it's all as nature intended. But we girls have to have some secrets.'

Hattie had no secrets at all and she hadn't been a girl for well over sixty years. She stared at the windowpane, the gold neon sign proclaiming Cloud Nine, an illuminated raincloud with a flashing purple 9 in the centre. The window was full of pictures of beautiful young women and words that Hattie didn't understand. Microdermabrasion and Browtox. She wondered if a chemical peel was something to do with oranges. She imagined a delightful citrus smell as a tangerine-scented cream was applied to her face. She groaned inwardly. She was here now: she'd make the best of it.

Inside, a young woman in a white coat with a blonde ponytail was seated at a desk, staring at a computer screen. She looked up. 'Glenys, bang on time. And this must be your friend – Harriet Bowen.'

The sound of Geoffrey's surname still had the ability to turn Hattie's shoulders to concrete. She said, 'Just a manicure, please.'

'I'm Nikki,' the blonde woman said. 'Glenys is having some microdermabrasion today. Lovely.'

'And a body peel.' Glenys grinned. Hattie couldn't help pulling a face as she imagined poor Glenys's skin red and excoriated, just like a Rembrandt painting she'd once seen. It might have been called *The Anatomy Lesson* and it depicted a man on a slab being cut open. In Hattie's imagination, Glenys was lying on a slab, smiling and chattering while Nikki sliced her flesh with a scalpel and talked about her new boyfriend and what she was doing at the weekend. Hattie shuddered, and then she realised that Nikki was speaking to her.

'... will be out for you in a moment, Mrs Bowen.'

'Hattie,' Hattie interrupted, shaking her head. She had missed the first bit of Nikki's words and hoped she'd repeat them. Nikki waved towards one of the treatment rooms, where the white doors with gold knobs were ominously closed.

'Follow me, then, Glenys. She won't be long, Hattie.'

Hattie was about to ask, 'Who won't be long?' but Nikki was on her way into one of the white rooms, Glenys scuttling behind her, muttering, 'Enjoy,' with a wink before she disappeared.

Hattie wondered if the word 'enjoy' was a secret phrase that meant she wouldn't enjoy it; all the treatments were painful. Her heart was thumping more than it should. She glanced at her hands, imagining red talons. It wasn't her, not really. Then a woman was standing in front of her. 'Mrs Bowen?'

'Hattie, please.' Hattie looked at a woman who might have been in her forties, her intensely black hair pulled back severely. She was very slim, wearing a white coat. Her expression was without humour, making Hattie think of a prison warden. She wondered if she had time to sprint for the door and make a getaway. Instead, she bleated, 'Manicure – just a pale pink.'

'I have you booked in for the whole self-care package – two hours,' the woman replied without a smile. 'I'm Yvonne. Would you like to follow me?'

Hattie stood up nervously, feeling like Joan of Arc on the way to the stake. She took a breath, wondering what to say, how to minimise the ordeal. Yvonne led the way into a white-walled room and Hattie stared around. There was a table, a sink, lots of bottles and in the corner a tall electric machine with a headpiece that wouldn't have looked out of place on death row. Yvonne said, 'I'll give you five minutes.'

Hattie frowned. 'To calm down?'

'To get undressed.'

'Undressed?' Hattie hadn't realised she'd need to take her clothes off. It was like going to the doctor's.

Yvonne managed a half-smile. 'Down to your panties, then slip into the robe.' She indicated a white fluffy dressing gown hanging on a gold hook behind the door. 'Then pop onto the bed.'

Hattie glanced nervously at the table. It *was* just like the doctor's. She recalled smear tests, and the angiogram she'd had at the well woman clinic she'd attended a year ago. She winced. Yvonne had gone. Then music began to leak through the speakers, slow and sonorous, as if someone had died. Hattie thought of the music played in the crematorium when her father passed away.

Hattie struggled out of her clothes and into the robe, wondering who had worn it before and what had happened to them. It seemed freshly laundered; perhaps that was to remove the blood of the last victim. Hattie reprimanded herself – she was being silly. This was pampering, not torture. Then it came into her head that the loud music that sounded like whales swimming underwater was there to muffle Glenys's screams next door. Or her own.

There was a light knock on the door, and a gentle voice said, 'Are you ready?'

'Mmm.' Hattie gritted her teeth and sat on the edge of the bed. Yvonne came in and approached her.

'So what were you thinking of today?'

'A facial?' Hattie blurted hopefully – it seemed the least likely to hurt.

'If I might suggest...' Yvonne leaned over and started to touch Hattie's face in a way she thought a little forward. 'We could do a nice aromatherapy face, neck and shoulder massage for rejuvenation, but first we could tidy up the straggly brows and get rid of this excess facial hair.'

'Facial hair?' Hattie was horrified. She hadn't noticed.

'Just a few broom handles. A quick wax, and you'll be smooth for weeks. Then a nice brow tint. You won't believe the difference when you walk out of the salon, you'll be a new woman.'

'Will I?'

'Although if I could suggest one thing.' Yvonne gave a low cough. 'You have great cheekbones and your skin has a natural sheen to it. You remind me of Helen Mirren. So...'

'So?' Hattie felt ready for anything now. She was about to be waxed and plucked, although she had no idea what that entailed. Yvonne seemed to know what she was doing though.

'The hair is all wrong. It's doing you no favours and when you come out of here, the rest of you will look bang-on.'

'Bang-on?' Hattie closed her eyes. Yvonne had wiped her face with something that smelled like industrial cleaner. Now she was smearing something above her upper lip, onto her chin.

'When you leave here, pop into Dye Hard up the road from here and ask for Michelle. She's a junior stylist and they do walk-ins today. She'll fit you in, do a nice pixie cut, get rid of the dull grey and give you a proper sheen. Okay?'

'Ouch!' Hattie yelped. Yvonne had ripped something from her top lip, like a plaster. It stung and she heard Yvonne's breathy laugh. 'Nearly done. The pain is worth the wonderful smooth skin you'll have.'

'Ow!' Hattie shrieked. More liquid was applied to her face; it smelled floral. The music filled her ears, whale sounds beneath the sea surface. Hattie sighed.

'Time to relax,' Yvonne said, her voice light as a sigh. 'Enjoy.'

'I'll try,' Hattie muttered.

'Mr Bowen won't know you when you get home. He'll be so impressed though.'

'There is no Mr Bowen,' Hattie said quickly. 'I'm divorced now.'

'Oh, I'm sorry,' Yvonne began.

'Not at all,' Hattie said, her eyes still closed. 'My marriage was nearly fifty years of non-stop misery. Then he went off with a woman from the bowling club. She's welcome to him. Good riddance.' She was surprised at the strength of her own words.

'So it's just you?' Yvonne said.

'Just me,' Hattie repeated.

'I'm on my own too.' Yvonne sighed. 'Two kids, both teenagers. My ex is no help. I'm with you on that one. Good riddance.'

'Exactly,' Hattie said, feeling the warmth of female bonding as Yvonne's smooth hands slid around her face and neck. 'This feels nice.'

'Oh, your skin will benefit,' Yvonne agreed. 'It's so good to pamper yourself. And I can see you're a strong woman. Time to put yourself first.'

'Indeed.' Hattie could feel her eyelids becoming heavy. Her nose was filled with the calming scent of lavender and all around her the sound of happy whales cooed calmly from the speakers. 'I'm strong – I put myself first...' She sighed. It was her new mantra, and it was good. Hattie felt herself drift into a dream where she was at the centre, glamorous in a pink fitted dress and long gloves. She was Marilyn Monroe singing 'Diamonds Are a Girl's Best Friend', surrounded by handsome beaux in suits who gazed at her adoringly. Then she was asleep, snorting through pursed lips while Yvonne massaged her shoulders with pungent oil.

* * *

It was past five when she parked the silver Nissan Micra in the drive. She wondered if she should change it for something sporty – a Mazda MX5, perhaps. She'd heard they were racy and she was determined that the words fuddy-duddy would never be used about her again. She stepped from the Micra, her face gleaming, proud of her newly cut silver pixie style, clutching several bags of shopping from a trendy clothes shop. Geoffrey had always told her she should have sensible clothes: skirts, blouses, flat shoes. 'Ordinary clothes for an ordinary woman. You don't want to stand out from the crowd, Hattie.' But that was in the past. So she'd bought a jumpsuit, jeans, a flowing dress and – Geoffrey would never have believed it possible – kinky boots. She had no idea what kinky boots were, in truth, but these were long and black and had a zip and a heel, and she imagined herself wearing them over jeans, looking kinky. Or slinky. Or sexy – something she hadn't felt for fifty years. Hattie felt powerful and strong for the first time ever. She was determined not to be boring and staid or the two words she'd never speak aloud again.

No, Hattie had reinvented herself. She'd made another appointment the following week at Cloud Nine for a hot stones massage. She decided that Yvonne was nice; in fact, she was rather good fun. Next time, she'd tell her about what a domi-neering pig Geoffrey was throughout their marriage, how nasty he could be and how she'd put up with him without argument for a quiet life. Hattie would listen to a story about Yvonne's horrible ex, Ryan, and then she'd say, 'How awful. And you can't imagine how hard it was to live with Geoffrey. For example, one Christmas he said the turkey was undercooked and I was trying to give him Campylobacteriosis, whatever that meant, and he called me Batty Hattie and hurled the whole plate of food against the wall. I spent Christmas afternoon washing lumps of gravy from the anaglypta...'

Hattie found that she was smiling. It hadn't been funny at the time. She'd cried all the way through the Queen's speech and well into the repeat of *The Morecambe & Wise Show*. But she saw the funny side of it now, in slow motion, like a cartoon. He was abusive, idiotic and thankfully gone forever. She was the new Hattie, the glamorous one who had radiant skin and a cute hairdo and a new wardrobe. And kinky boots.

She approached the front door and the smile froze. Someone was sitting on a suitcase, wearing sunglasses, staring at her. Hattie stared back. 'It can't be.'

'I could say the same about you.' Bunty leaped up and flung her arms wide. 'I've been waiting for ages. The taxi dropped me off hours ago. But I can see you've been out having fun. You look great. I hardly recognised you.'

Hattie was surprised to feel herself enveloped in muscular arms, almost lifted from her feet. Bunty was several inches taller and much curvier; Hattie couldn't breathe for a moment. Then she recovered her wits and said, 'I wasn't expecting you. You didn't ring or text to say you were coming.' She examined Bunty's face, looking hard for a reason. 'Where's Sean?'

'Ah—' Bunty gulped, then smiled. 'Sean's in Ireland, in Ballycotton.'

'Does he know you're here?' Hattie was immediately suspicious.

'Not really.'

'Does he or not?'

'I've left him.'

Hattie put down her bags and folded her arms. 'Left him as in – for a short holiday?'

'Left him as in – forever.'

Hattie shook her head to process the new information. 'Why?'

'I don't know. It was time.'

Hattie understood – she should have called time after the first year of her marriage. Earlier. She nodded. 'Fair enough. You'd better come in.'

'I thought you'd never ask.' Bunty stood up, rubbing her aching hips. 'I thought it would be warm in Oxfordshire but it's even colder than Ireland.'

Hattie jangled the keys in her hand. 'So, do you want to stay with me for a bit? Until you have worked things out?'

Bunty bustled inside. 'There's nothing to work out. I'm not going back. It's over.'

'And you want to stay with me...?' Hattie left her sentence unfinished, waiting for her sister to say something time-related, such as 'for a week or two' or 'until I get myself my own place'.

Bunty said, 'Yes, please,' and tugged off her sunglasses, gazing around the kitchen, her face shining with new delight. 'This place is so cosy. I'm dying for a cuppa. Shall we have coffee? I need a coffee after sitting on that smelly train for so long. Strong, please, black, one sugar. And I'm starving, Hat. I've only had a sandwich since breakfast and that was cheese and onion. What's for dinner? I don't suppose you have any chicken? I'd love a curry. That's my favourite. Do you know how to cook a tikka? And do you have any wine? Or Prosecco? Both.' She gripped Hattie's shoulder. 'Oh, we'll have such fun, Hat, me and you. Sisters together, reunited, living the life. It's just so nice to be home...'

4

A very English gentleman in a pale shirt, jacket and trousers and a panama hat knelt in the garden, squatting between the rows of neatly spaced vegetables. He pushed the round metal glasses back on his sun-pinked nose, muttering to himself. A small cat, black with a white ruffle and white socks, crouched down beside him and looked up inquisitively. The man met the cat's green eyes. 'Chard, runner bean, broad bean, early potato, rhubarb, radish, rocket. Hmmm. All coming on very nicely.' He reached out and plucked a groundsel shoot. 'We don't want you here, do we, Mr Weed?' His voice was light, without malice. 'All good. Let's have a look at the fruit bushes now, shall we, Isaac?'

The cat recognised her name and followed Robert Parkin, who was agile for his years, mid-seventies. He moved on lean legs as if he had all the time in the world. He reached the fruit bushes and knelt down again. Isaac Mewton settled beside him dutifully. Despite her male name, she was a neutered female, four years old, whom Robert had rescued as a kitten, changing her name from Peanut, which he thought lacked dignity.

Robert reached out long fingers and touched the fruit, abun-

dantly crammed on the bushes. 'Strawberries, currants, raspberries and gooseberries... ready to harvest. We should get a huge
crop again, Isaac. We'll make a few batches of jam and freeze a lot
of the fruit. That reminds me, the shoots on the pear trees are
getting a bit woody. We'll give them a bit of a prune. I'll put that
in my diary, in the to do section...' Robert glanced at Isaac, who
had raised a paw. 'All right, yes, there's no time like the present.
Let's pop into the kitchen now and I'll write it down. I suppose it's
time for your biscuit ration.' He held out a palm and Isaac
bumped her head against his fingers. He ruffled her fur affectionately. 'And an afternoon cup of tea, I think. Then we'll feed the
goats and the chickens.'

Robert pushed his metal spectacles up the bridge of his nose
and repositioned the panama hat, before walking steadily up the
winding paved path towards the house, a neat three-bedroomed
cottage dating from the 1800s, with an extended kitchen and an
oak conservatory, where Robert liked to relax with a book.
Beyond were the field and orchards, the goats and the chickens.
The front door was ajar and he stepped inside, feeling the cool-
ness of the hall. He was looking forward to a cup of tea. July had
been a little cool, and there had been a lot of rain. He was sure
the weather would improve; they were due some sunshine. He
turned in the doorway and waited for the cat. She was squatting
down, eyeing a flitting sparrow. 'Isaac, no. Leave the birds alone.
It's time for a biscuit,' Robert said kindly and Isaac trotted obedi-
ently behind him into the house, then he closed the door.

Inside, Robert picked up a small leather-bound diary and
wrote a short note to himself in a round hand: *Prune pear trees*.
Then he filled the kettle, placing it on the hotplate of the
Rayburn, and picked up a yellow box containing cheesy cat
biscuits. Isaac Mewton was already on the table, a paw raised, the
adorable begging pose. Robert stroked her fur three times, head

to tail, then he offered four square biscuits and watched as she snaffled them. In seconds, her paw was raised again and she was making moon eyes. Robert shook his head fondly and turned away, busying himself with Earl Grey, a small pot, a china cup. He liked to do things properly. He glanced at the wall clock. It was almost four. Things were as they should be, on time, regulated.

'I'll treat myself to a fruit scone,' he told the cat before moving to a cupboard, lifting out a butter dish, a tin of freshly baked scones and a jar of strawberry jam. He placed a plate and a bronze knife at the table and settled himself down. He had just spread a perfectly even covering of butter on his scone, a neat teaspoonful of jam on top, when there was a sudden rapping at the window. Robert looked up, his expression composed as he smiled at a round-faced woman with tidy, well-cut hair. She was wearing a cream jumper with short sleeves and tiny gold earrings, and was waving frantically.

'Susan.' Robert stood politely, watching Susan make gestures, asking if she could come in. He'd have been able to hear her; the top window was open. Robert made his way to the back door and Susan bustled inside. 'I just called to say—'

'Come in,' Robert suggested. 'I was about to make a Victoria sponge...'

Susan spoke breathlessly. 'I really enjoyed the cake you made for the last meeting. It was so light. What's your secret?'

'Fresh eggs.' Robert smiled at the compliment. 'I whisk the whites to stiff peaks.'

'Oh, I bet you do,' Susan replied, licking her lips.

'I wonder,' Robert dithered. 'I'm just having a cup of tea.'

'Oh?'

'And I thought you might—'

'I might—'

'—want one too. And a fruit scone.'

'Oh?'

'With strawberry jam.'

'Jam?' Susan glanced over Robert's shoulder to where Isaac Mewton had clambered onto the table and was licking the buttered scone for all she was worth. 'Your scone...' she said.

Robert turned round, smiling. 'Oh, you monster, Isaac. Well, you may as well have that one, it seems you've won it.' He met Susan's eyes. 'Scone? And tea?'

'I don't mind if I do,' Susan said, sitting at the table, pleased with herself. 'Although I only came round to say how much I enjoyed the wonderful sponge.'

'Of course.'

'And to ask for the recipe. I mean – a man who bakes is so irresistible.'

'Of course.' Robert was pouring a second china cup of Earl Grey from the remains of the pot for one. There was just enough. He then placed a scone in front of Susan, and another bronze knife and spoon. 'Help yourself.'

Susan loaded butter on her knife, spreading it thickly on top of the scone, ladling jam before taking a hearty bite. 'Mmm.' She closed her eyes. 'So deliciously sweet. Like a kiss...'

'I have more.' Robert indicated the tin of scones, feeling anxious – he didn't mean kisses. He was puzzled by the way Susan was looking at him, one eyebrow arched as if she was waiting for something to happen.

'I'd better not.' Susan indicated her waistline. 'Although you're such a tempter, Robert,' she added, her skin blotching at the idea.

'Oh, perish the thought,' Robert said humbly, watching the scone crumble between his fingers.

Susan reached for her tea. 'You have it so nice here, in your cottage.'

'It's not difficult – I just look after myself,' Robert replied.

'Just yourself,' Susan said. 'All on your lonesome, and with so many incredible baked goods...'

'And Isaac Mewton.' Robert indicated the cat, who was swiping frantically at the half-eaten scone with her white paws.

'Of course,' Susan added. She pushed the last of the scone into her mouth. 'I seldom make scones. I'm all alone too... and desserts are so much better shared.'

'Yes, I was sorry about Gerald's – you know – passing,' Robert said delicately.

'Indeed.' Susan arranged her features to look sad. 'It was over a year ago. I'm coming to terms with it—' She took a breath. 'He went the way he'd have wanted, tending to his begonias.'

Robert nodded, as if he understood. 'A fine gardener, Gerald – I always said he grew the best blooms in Millbrook.'

'Oh, yes, but he couldn't grow beetroot. Now, your beetroots, Robert – they are firm and fine.'

Robert reached for the tin quickly. 'Another scone, Susan?'

Susan plunged in a hand and removed the largest scone. 'Just one more, then – and maybe another cup of tea.'

'I'll refill the kettle,' Robert said. 'Fresh and hot is always best.'

'Oh, it is,' Susan cooed. 'And maybe we can talk about the next get together. People are so keen to sample the refreshments – and I really think one meeting a week is not nearly enough. As secretary, I want to circulate an agenda in plenty of time. I'd love it if you'd bring a little jam along. No one makes better jam than you do, Robert.'

'With scones, of course,' Robert said hesitantly, spooning Earl Grey leaves into the pot. Susan crossed her legs, settling herself at the table. He shrugged – he had no idea what Susan wanted, so he tried a tentative smile. 'It would be my pleasure.'

* * *

Hattie spooned instant coffee into a mug. It was the third one she'd made for Bunty in the last hour, and it showed. Bunty was talking nineteen to the dozen, explaining her disastrous marriage and why leaving Sean was inevitable.

'Sean and I hadn't been right for ages. He doesn't pay me attention. He's simply not interested in having a wife. The nags – the horses, that's all he cares about. If I was a racing horse, he might give me a second look. But no, he's always at the betting shops. And the money he wastes, Hattie. I mean, he tells me I spend too much on make-up and clothes, but he's forever down the bookies with his brother, Niall, throwing heaps of money at a dead cert that's so knackered that it comes last wheezing at the post. As bad as each other, Sean and Niall are. If they aren't down the bookies, they're in the pub, buying everyone whiskey. And I'm standing between them like a spare part, looking for someone to talk to. I mean, what else is a girl supposed to do?'

Hattie shook her head. 'I don't know.'

'Anyway, I don't know if Sean loves me any more. That's the bottom line – so maybe it's time to call it a day. I'm not sure how I feel.'

'I suppose.' Hattie raised her newly neatened brows. If Bunty didn't love Sean, who was she targeting with her affection now?

'I don't know how you stuck Geoffrey for all those years,' Bunty remarked bluntly.

'Nor do I,' Hattie said honestly. 'I didn't love him.'

'I used to hate visiting you. Even Sean said Geoffrey was a bully. He treated you so badly.'

'You didn't visit often,' Hattie observed. 'I'd have liked the moral support.'

'Because of Geoffrey. He was rude and ignorant.' Bunty glugged half the coffee from her mug. 'But I'm here now. What did you say you were cooking for dinner?'

'Incarceration,' Hattie muttered. 'At the pleasure of Her Majesty for forty-nine years...'

'Pardon?'

'Marriage to Geoffrey. It was like being in solitary confinement. But I've woken up. It's taken me long enough to realise—' Hattie pressed her lips together. 'It'll never happen again. I'm my own woman now.'

'I'm pleased to hear it.' Bunty picked up her phone. 'You needed to change. When you were married to him, you'd become such a dish rag, a fuddy—'

A message came in with a ping, and her lips curved in a smile as she read it.

When can I call round, foxy lady? I can't wait... x

Bunty closed her eyes, imagining, then she began to thumb a reply.

Hattie coughed for attention. 'So, for dinner, we're going to get a takeaway. I'll drive you to Hurry 4 Curry and you can ring ahead and order what we both want.' She took a breath, intending to start how she meant to carry on. 'I'll buy the wine; you can get the takeaway. While you're here, everything is going to be shared, fifty–fifty.'

'Whatever – that's fine.' Bunty wasn't listening. She pressed send and the message was on its way.

Midnight – at the address I sent in Bodicote. I'll leave the front door unlocked xx

5

Later on, after a simple dinner of risotto, Robert was relaxing in the conservatory, his feet in socks raised on a stool as he read *The Complete Garden Expert*. The sun was setting beyond the field. The goats and chickens had been fed and he was listening to music and poring over the pages. He was enjoying the section on barbecues and leisure areas. He was toying with the idea of making a patio space for entertaining – ten, twenty people. He could start by inviting the gardening club around, bake pizza in a wood-fired oven. Robert didn't really like pizza, but the idea of curling woodsmoke, the aroma of sizzling dough, listening to friends' happy conversation gave him a warm feeling. Besides, he had made some elderberry wine last year and it might be nice to share it.

He closed his eyes, listening to Puccini's *O mio babbino caro* filtering from the smart speaker, imagining himself at the centre of a chattering throng, everyone sipping burgundy wine and helping themselves to a hearty slice of Pizza Boscaiola garnished with fresh basil. He could organise it this summer with a bit of judicious planning, if he wasn't too ambitious about the detail.

He reached out a hand and stroked Isaac Mewton, who was curled on his chest, purring rhythmically. Robert let the music soak into his skin, deep into his emotions, and he sighed.

Through the speaker, Montserrat Caballé hit a particularly high note with gusto and Isaac Mewton stiffened in shock and sprang for safety. Robert's eyes remained closed as he heard the sharp snap of the cat flap in the kitchen. He focused fully on the poignant aria in which the singer Lauretta begs her father to help her marry the love of her life. The music lifted his heart and Robert imagined a woman he once knew, a sweet twenty-something who taught at the same school when he was a young teacher. He always pictured Cynthia Taylor in the same way: the serene face of an angel, wearing a flowery frock, surrounded by her class of six-year-olds who stared in rapt attention as if she were their Madonna. Of course, Robert wasn't sure the image had ever been accurate, but he'd watched her once through the classroom window and he'd loved her for her gentle voice. Given the care she bestowed on children, how much more might she have loved and cherished him?

Of course, Cynthia had never known the depth of his affection: he'd never got round to telling her. She had arrived one day in the staffroom, showing everyone an engagement ring, murmuring about a boyfriend called David whom she was marrying during the summer holidays. Two years later, she left to have a baby and Robert never saw her again. He'd never mentioned how he felt. And after Cynthia, no other woman could compare. They were all too confident or they somehow made him feel inadequate. Miss Cynthia Taylor, later Mrs Cynthia Manning, had been his only love.

There was a rapping sound and, at first, Robert assumed it was part of the orchestra, intermittent percussion, but then it became louder and Robert realised someone was banging on the conservatory window. He sat up, looking at a broad-shouldered athletic figure who was visible in the fading light. She was tall, with blonde curls and an enthusiastic smile, wearing pale shorts over tanned legs. He gave a small wave. It was Angela Pollock from the gardening club, a chirpy woman in her sixties who had bought a cottage in the village last spring. She hadn't visited him at home before; she was a divorcee, living alone, not far from The Pig and Pickle Inn. She'd only spoken to him once to ask about the best way to stop insects from eating her broccoli. Robert had been happy to explain, at length, to everyone in the room. He wondered what she wanted as she waved frantically. He tugged open the sliding door. 'Hello. Can I be of service?'

'Well, yes – well, I hope so. You see,' she said breathlessly, 'I hope you don't mind, um, Robert, but I was talking to Susan Joyce today about your delightful cake – the one you shared at the gardening club last time we all met.'

'Oh, I see.' Robert ushered her inside and pulled the door almost closed; he didn't want to leave it open as a draught was blowing in, but he felt suddenly awkward.

Angela rubbed her hands together then pushed back her curls. Her face was flushed. 'Well—' She paused for a moment, listening to the music, and her eyes shone. 'Oh, I love opera. Verdi, isn't it?'

'Puccini.'

'Puccini, yes, I meant to say that.' Angela fiddled with her hair again. 'Anyway, Susan said you have lots of wonderful jam and you use your home-made jam in the middle of the sponges and tonight I realised I'd run out of, erm, jam, so – I wondered if you could possibly – sell me some – jam.'

'Oh.' Robert was confused. 'Well, I do have rather a lot. I don't usually sell it though. Do you want to see it?'

'Oh, yes, I'd love to, well, if I may—'

'It's in the pantry.'

'Ah...'

'Follow me, please, Mrs Pollock.'

'Angela – call me Angie.'

'Angie.' Robert led the way into the kitchen, feeling glad that he had washed up from dinner. He continued to the walk-in pantry and stood back, allowing Angie to gaze at the rows of gleaming pots on the shelves. She caught her breath. There were so many types of jam from apple to quince, and beneath, several racks of wine, all corked and labelled. 'Oh, how wonderful...' Angie said. She glanced at Robert and looked away again. 'What an incredible selection.' She traced a finger across a shiny jar of jam, as if caressing a face. 'What's this one?'

'Blackcurrant and cassis.' Robert smiled. 'I add some liqueur and grated lemon rind. I find it goes incredibly well with scones – and crumpets.'

'Oh, I adore crumpets.' Angie licked her lips.

'And I make a nice marmalade with chunky pieces of stem ginger and a glug of Scotch whisky.'

'Oh, that's naughty. But so inviting,' Angie said hopefully. 'So, Robert—' She met his eyes. 'Would you sell me one of each – the marmalade and the blackcurrant?'

'I don't usually.' Robert shrugged. 'But I'll make you a gift of a jar of each. To say welcome to the village, belatedly.' He reached up and handed her two jars.

She took them eagerly, and placed a hand on his arm. 'Thank you – I'll enjoy these at breakfast time... and whenever I bite into a home-made jam-filled sponge cake, I'll think of you.' She had a sudden thought. 'I'll put some money in a children's charity, as payment. You know, Robert, you could go into business, what with your cakes and jam. You'd do very well, I'm sure.'

'Oh, I'm retired now,' Robert said by way of an excuse.

'Me too. It's the time of our lives to do something new, exciting,' Angie exclaimed and offered Robert a look that unnerved him slightly. He realised he was standing in the dimly lit pantry with a woman he hardly knew.

'Well, I hope you'll enjoy the jam, Mrs – Angie.'

'Oh, I will. And I was thinking, I might look into keeping bees, as a hobby. Maybe you could show me how to – make honey?'

Robert shrugged. 'I'd have to read up on it.' He led the way from the pantry, through the kitchen and into the conservatory. Montserrat Caballé was still singing sweetly. He faced the woman in shorts. She was breathing quite heavily. He wondered what to say, so he decided on politeness. 'It was so nice of you to visit.'

'All my pleasure.' Angie flourished the jam and said, 'I have jam.'

'Quite.' Robert was puzzled. 'Well, I was going to have an early night.'

'Oh?' Angie raised an eyebrow.

Robert indicated his book. 'Reading often helps me wind down before bedtime.'

'Oh, me too,' Angie agreed.

'Well, I'll say goodnight.'

Angie seemed disappointed. Robert opened the sliding door and she stepped outside. 'Thank you, Robert. Until next time.'

'Indeed.' Robert was about to close the door. Angie popped her head round and said, 'I'll think of you while I'm enjoying all the – sexy jam.' Then she disappeared.

Robert shook his head. 'Sexy jam?' He had no idea what she meant 'It's just boiled fruit and sugar and a bit of imagination.' He thought about his words. 'I suppose that's sexy nowadays. I've no idea.' He returned to his seat and picked up the book, raised his feet onto the footstool, and closed his eyes. Women confused him. He wondered if life with Cynthia Taylor would have been as perfect and as simple as he'd imagined. Probably not, he concluded.

But he'd noticed that the women in the gardening club looked at him strangely; they'd started to behave in a different way. They seemed – he searched for a word – frisky? Flirtatious? It had become worse since he'd taken the last cake to the club meeting. Robert decided that women had always been an enigma. That would never change.

* * *

Hattie brushed the new pixie cut, cleaned her teeth and face and emerged from the bathroom in a voluminous floral nightie to find Bunty waiting outside in a short dressing gown covered in red hearts, clutching an armful of bottles. 'I thought you'd be quicker in the bathroom,' Bunty grumbled. 'I need a long soak. I brought all my products.' She brandished the bottles again. 'I want to do my hair. And my nails.'

'Before bed?' Hattie was surprised.

'Ah.' Bunty seemed momentarily flustered, then she grinned. 'A girl should always look her best.'

Hattie said, 'I'll see you for breakfast tomorrow.'

Bunty paused. 'Oh, I might miss breakfast and sleep in late – it's been a long day.' She watched Hattie walk away towards her room and called, 'The curry was nice. And the wine.'

Hattie waved a hand. 'Sleep well.'

She heard a response that sounded like, 'I might or, then again, I might not.' She dismissed it as Bunty's nonsense; her sister would be fine in the second bedroom. It was comfortable, there was a nice double bed, space in the built-in wardrobe for her things. The burning question was, how long did she intend to stay?

Hattie snuggled beneath the duvet, her mind still buzzing. An hour ago, they'd sat across the table from each other, Bunty swigging wine and eating curried chicken as if she belonged there. Hattie had asked her directly. 'How long do you intend to stay?'

Bunty had laughed loudly and said something about not wanting to be a burden, then she'd waited pointedly for Hattie to tell her she wasn't a burden, which Hattie had determinedly refused to. Hattie had waited even longer and Bunty had laughed again, then finally she'd stretched her limbs, announced that she was far too tired to talk about it and they'd discuss it tomorrow. Then she'd launched into a speech about family and how she and Hattie had always been so close when they were younger. Hattie had frowned; in her recollection of things, Bunty had done as she pleased, and Hattie had always been the one who was left to sort out her mistakes.

Hattie rolled over in bed and wriggled cold toes. Should she let Bunty stay as long as she wished? They were family, Bunty had nowhere else to go. But she knew what would happen: Bunty would take over the entire house. Hattie's tidy bungalow would become an extension of Bunty's bedroom, shoes everywhere, dirty clothes, empty cups. Bunty would never wash up or clean anything – it would always be the same excuse: she'd do it later. Then Hattie would have to cook, pay for everything, organise everything. No, Hattie was determined to be strong. She'd tell Bunty she'd put her up for a month gladly. She was welcome to stay – she was family. But then Hattie would like her independence back, thank you very much, and Bunty could decide what she intended to do. That would be fair enough.

Hattie could hear Bunty in the bathroom across the hall. She was singing, splashing in the bath. She sounded happy. Hattie wondered what had really happened with Sean, and if Bunty would change her mind and go back to him in Ballycotton. Hattie began to plan how they'd spend time together. They could go to the cinema, pop out for coffee, go shopping, as most sisters did. They would be good for each other: Bunty was outgoing and confident, Hattie was sensible. It might work out well. She decided that tomorrow she'd wear the new jeans she'd bought – and the kinky boots. She'd show Bunty that she could be cool too.

Hattie smiled at the thought of being cool. She didn't really know what cool was. She rolled over again, reached for her book, a historical romance, and flicked through the pages. She'd read for an hour, then she'd go to sleep. Tomorrow would be an interesting day. It was filled with promise.

6

Hattie was dreaming. It was a mixed-up kind of dream in which she was lying on the couch at the beautician's. Whale song was playing gently and Bunty was smoothing cream on her face. Hattie was enjoying the massage as Bunty related stories of her husband, Sean, and how she lived with him for forty-nine years and it was worse than being in prison. Hattie was surprised, about to speak, then Bunty placed a cool cloth over her eyes and Hattie couldn't see. She was in darkness, but in the dream, she was aware of Bunty moving around, pretending to busy herself with massage oil, then suddenly she picked up sharp scissors and rushed back to the couch, raising her weapon to plunge into Hattie's vulnerable, unsuspecting body. Hattie opened her eyes in alarm and froze.

Someone was moving around in the hall. She glanced at the clock by the side of the bed: it was past midnight. She remembered, and allowed herself a quiet sigh of relief. It was only Bunty, settling down. She rolled over, closed her eyes and hoped sleep would come. She'd like a nice dream this time, a romantic one. It had been years since she'd allowed herself any romantic thoughts – Geoffrey had put paid to any hope of affection – but now she allowed herself a moment's fantasy. She was wearing the jeans tucked into kinky boots; her pixie cut gleamed and she stood on a cliff top in sunglasses, looking out at rolling waves, the sunshine warm on her face. Suddenly she was on a cruise ship. A man stood behind her, his arms around her. He looked exactly like Robert Redford, blonde tousled hair, ice-blue eyes. He kissed her lightly, handed her a glass of champagne. Hattie smiled – yes, a handsome companion might have been nice.

She wrapped her arms around the pillow and began to drift off, then her bedroom door creaked tentatively. Hattie opened one eye, then the other. A burly shape was standing in the doorway, backlit from the hall. Hattie held her breath, both horrified and puzzled, as he lumbered into the room and began to remove his coat, his jumper, his shirt. She considered for a moment if he might have wandered into the wrong home. A bare-chested man was standing inches away from the bed, pulling off his trousers, hopping from one leg to the other as he tugged off jeans. His voice was guttural, a south-west accent. 'I'm here, sex kitten. Move over. Mr Lover Lover's arrived.'

He launched himself towards the bed and his arms were round her neck. A wet slobbery kiss landed on her forehead, breath that smelled of sausages and onions. Enough was enough. Hattie was more appalled than afraid. She reached out and grabbed the historical romance book on the bedside table and thwacked the man over the head with it. He yelled out loud. 'It's me, you daft bat. What are you playing at?'

Hattie flicked on the bedside lamp and stared at a man with a thatch of dark hair and a stubbly chin. The rest of him was very hairy too, as far as she could see – a broad chest, huge shoulders and arms. Hattie clenched her teeth. 'Who the hell are you?'

The man seemed as baffled. 'I might ask you the same question. Where's Bunty?'

'Bunty?' Hattie wriggled away from the overpowering stench of sausages and onions. She stared at the man; he wasn't bad-looking, but he was an intruder and this was her house. She wondered why she wasn't terrified and she realised the man looked more scared than she was. She raised her voice, indignant. 'How did you get in?'

'Bunty said she'd leave the front door unlocked—' The man suddenly seemed to realise he was only wearing his boxer shorts. He snatched the duvet from Hattie's hands and covered his chest. She snatched it back, covering her nightie. Then Bunty was in the room, laughing. 'You picked the wrong bedroom. I said the one opposite the bathroom...'

The man sat up. 'This one's opposite the bathroom.'

'Oh yes,' Bunty said. 'Well, this is my sister, Harriet. Sorry, Hattie – er – this is Jacko. Douggie Jackson. He's my boyfriend.'

Hattie frowned, staring from Bunty to Jacko, unimpressed. 'What's he doing here?'

'Ah.' Bunty came over to the end of the bed, picked up Jacko's hand as if it was something very precious and sat down. 'We met in Ballycotton. Jacko was on holiday...'

'I'm from Plymouth,' Jacko added with what he hoped was an endearing smile.

'And we hit it off straight away. Then Jacko went home and asked me to reconsider my options. Sean was at the betting shop all the time and he never seemed to notice me, so it just seemed the perfect time to follow my heart.'

'Here? To my house?' Hattie folded her arms.

'I came to see you, Hat – then I invited Jacko to join me – I didn't think you'd mind. I thought we'd try to make a go of it.'

Hattie tugged the duvet to her throat. 'He thinks he's staying here? No, Bunty.'

'I can't go back to Plymouth tonight,' Jacko complained. 'I've just driven up – it took me four hours.'

'Have you eaten, lovey?' Bunty cooed, kissing him tenderly.

'I stopped at a chippy – I had saveloys.' Jacko grunted. Hattie was surprised Bunty couldn't smell the overpowering sausage breath. She took over.

'Well, he can't stay here.'

'Oh, please, Hat.' Bunty pouted. 'Just for tonight.'

Jacko looked distraught. 'I can't sleep outside in the van. It's raining and I'm dog tired.'

'Right.' Hattie sat up straight in bed. 'This is what will happen. He can stay here for one night. Then tomorrow you and I will talk it over, Bunty.'

'Thanks, Hattie.' Bunty tugged Jacko's hand. 'Come on, I'll show you to my room – our room.'

Jacko looked wildly around, cast Hattie a thankful glance, picked up his discarded clothes and allowed himself to be shepherded away. In the hall, Hattie could hear him grumbling and Bunty sniggering, then the lights were turned off.

Hattie rolled over. It was too late now to summon the fantasy of Robert Redford handing her champagne on the cruise ship. If she kissed him, he'd probably taste of saveloys. Hattie decided sleep was the best option. Then tomorrow she'd give Bunty a piece of her mind at breakfast time and send Jacko packing by lunch. If Bunty wanted him so much, she'd be welcome to follow him back to Plymouth. She sighed deeply and tried to sleep. In the next room, she could hear Bunty whispering. Hattie rolled over again and pulled the duvet over her head.

* * *

The following morning, Hattie woke up at seven-thirty, showered, dressed in jeans and a pretty top, and made herself scrambled eggs. She'd need something substantial in order to make sure she said her piece. Bunty would have something up her sleeve, tears, pleas that she was in love, promises that they'd be no trouble, but Hattie was determined. Today Jacko would be on his way.

She was pouring a second cup of Earl Grey when Bunty wandered into the kitchen, a dressing gown loosely tied around her waist. Hattie recognised the fleecy hooded robe – it was hers. She frowned. 'Where's the short dressing gown with red hearts you were wearing yesterday?'

Bunty was momentarily puzzled, then she frowned. 'Oh, that one. I dropped nail varnish on it last night. I put it in the wicker basket in the bathroom. That's where you put your laundry, isn't it? I borrowed this one – you don't mind, do you, Hat?'

Hattie folded her arms. She minded a lot and it was her opportunity to say so. 'Bunty, you're not being fair.'

'Using your things?'

'Bringing that man here.'

Bunty's forehead crinkled with confusion. 'Can he stop for a few days?'

'No, he can't.'

'But this is home, Hattie – I've come to stay with you.'

'Then stay with him in Plymouth.'

'No,' Bunty said. 'We can't go there.'

'Why ever not?'

'His wife is there,' Bunty explained breathlessly. 'She'd be furious.'

Hattie breathed in sharply. 'He's married?'

'Well, sort of.'

'You can't be sort of married, Bunty. You are or you aren't.'

'He's left her – he doesn't love her.'

'Bunty.' Hattie covered her face with her hands. 'This isn't right. You know it isn't.'

'He says his marriage is over. We've just found each other – it's a new start for us both.' Bunty pleaded, 'Please let him stay – just for a couple of weeks.'

'Weeks?' Hattie said.

'We need time together – before we begin the rest of our lives.'

Hattie waved the idea away. 'You're being dramatic.'

'Not at all. I've left Sean and Jacko has left Marion. We just need time to get used to each other.'

'Not in my house.'

'Where else can we go?' Bunty said. 'You're my sister, Hattie. You are the only one I trust.'

'He can't stay here,' Hattie repeated, hoping that she sounded strong.

'But I need your help – we both do.' Bunty lowered her voice. 'What if he's *the one*?'

'Oh, for goodness' sake,' Hattie said impatiently. Then the kitchen door opened and Douggie Jackson walked in wearing a pink dressing gown tied at the waist that gaped at the chest, showing straggly hairs. He gave a sheepish look. 'I found this in the bathroom.'

'It's mine.' Hattie grimaced.

'I'll put it in the wash basket when I've had a bath.' He offered Hattie his most charming smile. 'It was a long drive yesterday. But – is that scrambled eggs you've just made? You wouldn't knock me up a plateful, would you, love? And I'm sure Bunty would like some too. Have you got any strong coffee? The stronger the better, first thing. I need the caffeine.' He glanced at Bunty and winked suggestively.

Hattie wasn't sure she'd heard him right. 'Are you asking me to cook you breakfast?'

'And one for Bunty.' Jacko leaned over and gave Bunty a lingering kiss. 'We need to keep our strength up.'

Hattie made an appalled face – she couldn't help it. Then she stood up slowly and deliberately. She thought of the forty-nine years she'd lived with domineering Geoffrey, and how the bungalow was peaceful and calm now. She'd put her foot down firmly.

'I'm going into town to do some shopping. Then on the way back, I'll pop in to see my neighbour, Glenys. When I return, I'd like you to have made yourself breakfast and cleared the dishes.' She glanced pointedly at Bunty. 'Then I'd like you to have washed both dressing gowns on an eco-wash, and packed your case ready to leave this afternoon. I don't care where you go, Plymouth, Ballycotton, Timbuktu, I really don't mind but, Bunty, I'd like you and Jacko to be on your way to a hotel somewhere when I get back. This is my home, and I want it back, please. Now, if you don't mind—' Hattie glared at Bunty, who was hanging her head like a scolded child, and at Jacko, who gaped, open-mouthed. Clearly he'd never been spoken to in this way in his life. She said a curt 'Good morning,' and reached for her bag and keys, whisking herself towards the door and out into the sunshine, feeling quite pleased with herself.

As she turned to close the door, she heard Jacko call out, 'Would you bring me a bag of cheese and onion crisps back with you, love – and a copy of the *Daily Mail*?'

Hattie ignored him and marched towards the car, feeling confident in her new jeans, hoping they'd be gone when she came back. Striding along in the tight leather boots that came just above her knee gave her a sense of swagger, new-found power and independence. She noticed Jacko's white van parked next to hers in the drive – D Jackson, Plumber – and was determined that her mood wouldn't sink.

She spent an hour in Banbury, treating herself to an expensive hydrating face mask made from natural clay in a new health shop and a vanilla latte in a café she'd never dared go into because it was always full of cool-looking people, then she stopped off at the newsagent's and bought a magazine on mindfulness. She glanced at the *Daily Mail* and decided she wouldn't buy Jacko a copy, or a bag of crisps. In all honesty, she felt a bit mean. She'd have happily put Bunty up for a few weeks and she was quite anxious about where she'd go, particularly since she didn't appear to know Jacko well. But she couldn't agree to having them both.

When she arrived back at the bungalow, she was a little surprised to see that the van, D Jackson, Plumber, hadn't moved. She thought about calling in at Glenys's for a cuppa; perhaps Bunty and Jacko would be gone by the time they'd had a chat, but Hattie knew Glenys would ask about the owner of the plumber's van, find out that Bunty was staying with her uninvited married lover, and tell Hattie she was a pushover. Glenys wasn't afraid to speak her mind. So Hattie decided she'd go indoors, make sure Bunty had packed. She was determined that by the evening peace and calm would be resumed.

When she opened the door and walked into the kitchen, Hattie gasped. Bunty and Jacko were bustling round the table, laying out plates, cutlery, a bottle of wine. Hattie asked, 'What's this?'

'Oh,' Bunty said. 'We wanted to say thank you for – putting us up last night.'

'So we made you lunch...' Jacko beamed, waving his hands at the table, adorned with her best plates. There was salad, tomatoes, bread, ham, cooked chicken, eggs, cheese. In fact, they had raided the fridge and used most of the food. Plus, they'd opened her bottle of Gevrey-Chambertin, which she'd been saving for a special occasion. She placed her hands on her hips.

'Lunch – then you go.'

Jacko glanced towards Bunty a little shiftily. Bunty said, 'Shall we just eat first?'

'I don't normally have much for lunch.'

Bunty made a cute face. 'Well, I've made it specially.' She poured wine in one glass and took a gulp. 'Oh, this is heaven. You have to try this, Jacko.'

Jacko filled his glass to the brim then, as an afterthought, he poured some wine in Hattie's. He swallowed half, smacked his lips and muttered, 'Nice drop of plonk.'

Hattie pressed her lips together; it was sixty pounds a bottle, for a special occasion. She sat down.

'Shall we eat?' She sipped the wine carefully and felt courage building. 'Then afterwards, I'll help you both pack. And, Jacko – I wouldn't have any more wine if I were you. Otherwise, you won't be able to drive...'

7

'This is looking a bit rickety, Isaac. We need to do some repairs.'

Robert inspected the old five-bar gate to the chicken field. It was a delightful day. The sunshine was golden honey, illuminating emerald grass. Robert and Isaac Mewton had just collected eggs; now they were considering replacing the rotting wood of the old white gate at the top of the garden. The chickens scuttled around looking for shaded areas, bushes and cool dirt. Robert carried a wicker basket full of eggs, calling out, 'Watch your step, Princess Lay-a,' as a ginger chicken rushed between his feet, flapping briefly as she hurried away from Isaac, who was far more interested in swiping at a butterfly. They walked on towards the fenced goat enclosure and stepped inside, securing a second white gate behind them.

One of the goats rushed over, head down, and Robert scratched the hairy chin that was placed in his hand. 'Good morning, Vincent.' He knelt down and rubbed the goat's face tenderly. 'And how's Vincent Van Goat this morning? Oh, here's your brother, The Great Goatsby. How are you both doing? Do you fancy a snack?'

A second goat arrived, butting Robert's arm warmly as he reached into his pocket, holding out a carrot. The goats snaffled it, munching hungrily. Isaac watched, lying flat on her belly. Robert smiled. 'You wonder why I keep these two old wethers? You think they are useless, don't you, Isaac? But they do a great job for me. They are living weed-eaters, both of them chew non-stop – they clear out poison ivy, shrubs and bushes. That reminds me – I must get them some bits of pine tree – that's a natural de-wormer.'

Isaac rolled on her back, lifting her feet in the air, and Robert smiled. 'Yes, you're right, Isaac, it's time to go back. I want to make a pavlova. I have some strawberries that will go very nicely. I thought I might take it to the gardening club meeting at The Pig and Pickle – Susan's arranged an impromptu one for tonight, so I'd better get a move on.'

He handed the goats another carrot each and set off towards the white gate. 'The crowd at the gardening club look forward to my treats. It's not the same as the packet of digestives that the vicar brings. I quite enjoy cooking something for them. It's nice to be well received. And the numbers have increased recently. Angie Pollock has been a few times now. I wonder how she got on with the jam she came round for. And there was another new woman from Dawlish last time we met – what was her name? Jackie? Jill? I can't remember – she seemed nice. I suppose she'll be there – people are more interested in gardening in the summer. Of course – that explains why Susan has been arranging meetings more frequently. She was extremely keen on the last cake I took..' He paused, puzzled. 'The women especially seemed to be fasci-nated by my baking...'

Robert led the way back to the cottage, Isaac at his heels. He thought momentarily about his sisters, feeling a little guilty that he hadn't spoken to Bunty for a while. He usually rang Hattie on

Sunday evenings – he often wondered if she was a bit lonely – and last time they'd spoken, she'd sounded a little unsettled. He'd give her a call soon, find out how she was getting on.

Bunty was in Ballycotton, living her life as only Bunty could, at full pelt. He hadn't phoned her for a while. He'd tried several times over the last few months, but it was often quite difficult to get anyone at the other end to pick up. He remembered calling her on Christmas Day last year, and she'd had a house full of guests, all celebrating, wild music playing and sounds of people dancing. Bunty was a party animal, in many ways still a teenager at heart. He smiled affectionately; he and Hattie were happier with their own company.

He recalled Hattie's ex-husband, Geoffrey Bowen. He hadn't liked the man, even before Hattie married him. He was always a braggart, a bit of a bully, and he'd often goaded Robert about being single, about his love of peace and quiet, a good book. He'd been so critical of Hattie. Robert had told her quietly just before he left for Devon that he thought Geoffrey was rude and abusive. Hattie had agreed and said that he'd always been the same. Geoffrey had eroded the bubbly person Hattie naturally was, sapping her confidence. Robert was glad when Geoffrey left; Hattie was better alone.

Back in the kitchen, Robert separated eggs and beat the whites by hand. He was strong for a man of his age, his arms wiry from all the work in the garden. It gave him pleasure to see the eggs transform to fluffy peaks. He held the bowl upside down over his head as he'd seen cooks doing on TV to prove that the whites were firm. Nothing fell out, of course. Perfect. He smiled as he replaced the bowl on the worktop, checked the oven temperature. He heard a buzzing noise: his mobile phone was vibrating on the table. He picked it up.

'Hello, Francis, good to hear from you – Yes, I'll be there

tonight, of course. Seven o'clock. No, I hadn't forgotten I'd promised to bring a dessert, I'm just making a pavlova now. Who said that? Oh, Susan Joyce? Yes, of course I'll bring a batch of fruit scones – no, I'll make time. And Angie Pollock wants some too? And who? I don't know Rosemary Eagle, do I? Oh, all the way from Teignmouth because she's heard about my jam and scones? You're pulling my leg, Francis.' He was smiling. 'So, tonight's topic is fruit bushes. Well, drainage is a common problem. Pardon?' Robert nodded as he listened. 'Of course I'll give a little talk – magnesium deficiency, yes. The main symptom is a yellowing between the leaf veins in early summer – I'd be glad to, of course. No, I think The Pig and Pickle Inn is the perfect setting. I know Shelley always sells quite a lot of beer to the group... Oh, Prosecco, is it now? Well, I'll see you later, Francis. It might be nice to sit outside, yes. Thanks – bye.'

Robert smiled, an enigmatic twist of his lips. He noticed Isaac Mewton had curled up on a cushion at the base of the Rayburn and was watching him with interest. 'That was the vicar. I'd better get this pavlova baked, Isaac. I have to make a couple of batches of scones too, by special request. There might be a big turnout – no wonder Susan arranged another get together for tonight. It seems we have more ladies coming than ever.'

Isaac Mewton closed one eye, observing Robert steadily with the other: there was nothing new about the foolishness of human behaviour. Robert went back to his egg whites, humming to himself. Isaac closed her other eye and purred.

* * *

Hattie collected the dishes from the table and stacked them in the dishwasher. The lavish spread at lunch had been eaten, mostly by Jacko, who had also finished off the Gevrey-Chambertin and had taken himself off to the bedroom for a snooze, despite Hattie's insistence that they left after lunch. Bunty was sitting at the table, watching Hattie, fingering a thin silver necklace nervously.

'The thing is, Hat – if we could just stay for a day or two, we'd have time to find somewhere. I mean, hotels are expensive and although Jacko's still got his plumbing business, he's semi-retired now and he only has customers in Plymouth and that's where his wife is. She makes poor Jacko's life a misery and she doesn't know about me. Jacko told her he's doing a complete bathroom installation on the other side of the county, in Axminster.' Bunty was pleading. 'We want to make a go of it, Hattie.'

'I asked you to leave this afternoon. You can go somewhere else for a couple of weeks.'

'I've got no money. Sean and I have a joint account. He'd trace where I was if I withdrew anything – and he wants me back. He keeps texting and phoning. Jacko hasn't got much money either.'

Hattie sighed. 'I'll lend you something.'

'Can't we stay here?' Bunty thrust out a lip. 'Please – just for me?'

'Bunty.' Hattie's eyebrows shot up. 'You can't stay here with him.'

'I think I still love Sean...' Bunty's eyes filled with tears. 'That's the problem. I've thrown myself into this thing with Jacko. I've been hasty. But Sean wasn't really paying me any attention and we were arguing a lot. Then I met Jacko and he was nice to me. He gave me this necklace and told me I was the love of his life.' A tear drizzled down her cheek. 'So I took a chance. We've been planning this for a week now in secret – it had been all sexy phone messages but, now we're here...' Bunty lowered her voice. 'I don't know what to think. We've only known each other for a few days. He doesn't even look like I remember him.'

'Oh, Bunty. You'll have to be honest.' Hattie sighed. 'Tell him you've made a mistake. Tell him to go home to Plymouth.'

Bunty made a happy face. 'But it's quite exciting, a new relationship. He says he adores me. And I like his fun side, he's a real laugh.'

'Bunty,' Hattie said. 'You don't really love him, do you?' Bunty had always been impetuous, making the wrong decision in a hectic moment. 'Sean was good for you. He's steady, wise. I liked him.'

'I miss Sean.' Another tear fell. 'But you know – things haven't been right for all those years – since – you know what happened...'

'You and Sean should talk about your feelings, discuss it.'

'He can't – he's too hurt.'

'And what about you, Bunty? It's affecting you badly.'

'My heart's still – broken.'

'Go back to Sean.'

'Don't you like Jacko?'

'I don't know him.' Hattie sat down forlornly.

'Give me just a few days. I'm not sure I'm doing the right thing. I know I can be hot-headed. I'll know for sure by the end of the week.'

'The end of the week?' Hattie was horrified.

'Let us stay here. Just till then, Hat. Just so I can decide what to do with the rest of my life. I'm safe here. I don't really want to go off with Jacko, I don't know where we'd end up.'

Hattie shook her head. 'Bunty, this is blackmail.'

'Please – help me make the right decision. Just a few more days, and I'll be sure. I'll either leave with Jacko or I'll go back to Sean, I promise.'

Hattie lowered her voice. 'You *and* Jacko?'

Bunty showed her most pleading face. 'Please.'

'Oh – what else can I say? All right.' Hattie couldn't help herself. 'Just a few more days. Then promise me – he'll be gone and you'll – you'll have made your mind up.'

'I promise.' Bunty nodded with all her energy. 'I absolutely totally promise you.'

'I'm only doing it to keep you safe while you make the right choice.' Hattie said, hardly believing her own words. 'Right – before the end of this week, you and I will sit down and talk – you'll let me know what you want, Jacko or Sean or neither of them, and I'll support you.'

'Maybe it would suit me best, living as you do, Hat, by yourself. It might be just what I need.' Bunty pushed a hand through her hair. 'I need to take charge of my own life.'

'Yes, you do,' Hattie agreed sadly. Then there was a tapping at the door and she looked up. 'Oh, it's Glenys.'

Bunty was on her feet, opening the door, smiling. 'Oh, hello. Pleased to meet you. I'm Bunty, Hattie's sister.'

'Glenys.' Glenys held out a hand. 'I'm Hattie's neighbour. She didn't say you were coming to stay.'

Bunty ushered her inside. 'Well, she didn't know.' She winked at Hattie. 'I just turned up with my new man yesterday. I've left my husband. I was just talking to Hattie – I don't know whether to stick or twist.'

'Oh?' Glenys met Hattie's eyes, raised a quizzical brow. 'Is he here, the new man?'

'Resting.' Bunty grinned.

'Well.' Glenys folded her arms. 'It sounds like a soap opera.'

'Oh it is – I mean, his wife doesn't know he's left her yet, poor woman. Although he doesn't love her. Would you like a cup of something?' Bunty asked. 'It's all very romantic. I believe in horoscopes, you know, the stars telling us what's meant to be will be.'

'I don't,' Hattie said grimly. 'I think you make your own luck.'

'A cuppa would be nice,' Glenys said hesitantly, glancing towards Hattie.

Bunty placed an affectionate hand on Hattie's arm. 'And I'd love a coffee, Hat, if that's OK.' She sat down at the table, patting the seat next to her, urging Glenys to sit. 'You see, the problem is, I'm Aries, the ram. That makes me courageous, generous. What are you?'

'Oh, I'm Pisces.'

'The fish? Really? That makes you deeply emotional and sympathetic. That's why you're so interested in others. Now Hattie, she's a Virgo – she's practical, reliable and organised, but she's no romantic. Do you believe in soulmates, Glenys?'

Glenys was unsure. 'Well, my Bill works for the post office. He's a Scorpio.'

'So was Sean, my ex, a real Scorpio, passionate. Of course, he's only passionate about the horses nowadays, that's the problem. But I still have feelings for him. Now Jacko's an Aquarius, that makes him a little unpredictable, so I'm not sure how compatible we are... I wonder what my horoscope says about today. Shall I look on my phone?'

'Go on, then,' Glenys agreed. 'What does it say for Pisces?'

Hattie watched in amazement as Bunty clutched Glenys's hand, desperate for guidance from the stars. She clanged a teaspoon loudly as the kettle whistled, and sighed: she was annoyed with herself. Bunty and Jacko were staying for another week. How was she going to put up with them both for six more days? And worst of all, Hattie was sure that Bunty was on the verge of making the stupidest decision of her life, basing her choice completely on her horoscope.

It was up to her to help her sister come to her senses.

8

It was a beautiful evening, so balmy and warm that Francis suggested the gardening club members sat outside The Pig and Pickle. The beer garden was in full bloom, pale roses growing over awnings, the scent of honeysuckle heavy on the air, and Shelley had laid out a table with a cloth specially for the spread. There were sandwiches and quiches and, in pride of place, several plates of scones with jams and cream, and the enormous strawberry pavlova.

Twelve figures sat around wooden tables sipping drinks. Francis was in the process of welcoming new members. Rosemary from Teignmouth, wearing a linen suit, her legs neatly crossed, sipped a spritzer as she eyed the scones. On one side of Rosemary, Susan Joyce was drinking white wine and, on the other, Angie Pollock in shorts, guzzling Prosecco. Beside her was Jill Davies, clutching a full glass of wine, nervous because it was only her second visit to the gardening club. Robert was opposite, gazing at some notes he'd made about growing fruit bushes. Around the table were several older men, some with flat caps, one in round glasses, one in a trilby, and a robust woman in a spotted frock.

'So, welcome all,' Francis gushed, meeting each set of eyes, 'to the Millbrook gardening club, a special Saturday evening get together, thanks to Susan's organisational skills. Just think, this time last year, we were a small group of seven men and one lady who met irregularly.' He nodded towards the woman in the spotted frock. 'Now we are growing by the week – just like the crops in our gardens.' He grinned at his joke.

'That's more down to hard work and less down to God. The weather's been bloody terrible,' one of the men in a flat cap grunted.

'I'm sure the Lord plays his part unseen, Dennis,' Francis said reassuringly.

'I think it's mostly down to Robert's heavenly guidance.' Susan flashed him a smile. 'His tips on how to improve our crops are second to none.'

'What's wrong with looking it up on the Internet?' The man in round glasses suggested.

'Oh, you can't beat the real thing,' Angie piped up. 'Robert's jam is exquisite. He gave me some the other night.' She shot a look at Susan.

'Ah, can we all sample your lovely jam, Robert?' Rosemary boomed confidently, patting his arm as if they were best friends. Robert jerked back, a little surprised; they'd never met before.

Jill folded her arms and muttered, 'I can't take my eyes off that strawberry pavlova.'

'Perfect with Prosecco.' Angie waved her glass enthusiastically.

'And the scones look so tempting,' Susan purred.

'Are we going to talk about fruit bushes?' the man in the trilby asked impatiently. 'I have dots on my leaves.'

His wife in the spotted frock raised her voice. 'That's on the agenda, George. Susan sent us all a copy.'

George pushed his trilby on firmly. 'I leave it to you to bring the agenda, Mary. I'm only interested in how I can get a better turnover on my raspberries and keep the bloody insects off.'

'I emailed most of the agendas.' Susan said. 'Do you have yours, Robert? I put it through your front door specially this morning – you weren't answering when I knocked.'

'I expect I was up the field picking fruit,' Robert murmured.

'Oh, and how are the animals, Vincent Van Goat? And The Great Goatsby?' Angie asked.

'And Isaac Mewton?' Susan added.

'Oh, what delightfully cute names.' Rosemary met Robert's gaze unashamedly. 'Such imagination you have, Robert – so fascinating.'

'I think so too.' Jill blushed, looking towards Angie for support. 'And Robert's bakes look mouth-wateringly tempting…'

'Can we get on with the meeting, Vicar?' one of the men in a cap asked hurriedly. 'I need another pint. And if we're not starting now, I'm off to the bar.'

'We'll start, then, shall we, Colin?' Francis said calmly, pushing a hand through his hair. 'So, because we have a new member and someone who's here for the second time—' Francis glanced at Jill and she blushed again '—can I ask for us to go round the table and introduce ourselves briefly? I'm Francis Baxter, the vicar of St Jude's, and I've been here in Millbrook for five years. I'm married to Sally, who teaches in Millbrook primary school – she's at home now with our teenage daughter, Tilda. So – who's next for introductions? George – would you like to say who you are?'

The man in the trilby tutted his disgust, then he said, 'George Tenby, pensioner, and this is Mary, wife.'

Mary opened her mouth to introduce herself, realised George had stolen her thunder and closed it again.

'Dennis Lyons, pensioner,' a man in a cap grunted, folding his arms. 'And general grumpy git.'

'Colin Bennett,' another man in a cap grunted. 'Pensioner and very thirsty beer drinker.' He banged his empty glass on the table just to make his point.

'Barry Butler, pensioner, landscape painter and gardener.' The man in the round gold-framed glasses beamed. 'I'm not the next John Constable, but I do enjoy playing around with water-colours.'

'Eric Mallory, ex police officer, now retired and enjoying life with my two dogs and my rather vast garden, with a terrible patchy lawn and a slimy fish pond,' the man in the dark navy cap said. 'Which I need to do so much work to improve, and my wife nags me perpetually about. Needless to say, Edie isn't here tonight. She prefers knitting to socialising.'

'Robert Parkin, ex head teacher,' Robert said quietly. 'I live in the smallholding at the end of the village.'

'And he makes delightful goodies for us all,' Susan added, clapping her hands. 'I'm Susan Joyce, widow, secretary of the gardening club and former medical receptionist.'

'Angie Pollock, tennis player and divorcee,' Angie said. 'Currently I work from home part-time, just for fun really, for a financial service company. I'm officially retired, but I'm a whizz with numbers.'

'Jill Davies from Dawlish. I'd heard wonderful things – so I came here tonight on the bus.' She glanced at Robert. 'I work at a newsagent's – but my real passion is history. I just love old books and libraries, and churches and villages like Millbrook. And the idea of growing things in gardens excites me beyond belief.'

Rosemary coughed abruptly. 'Rosemary Eagle. Rosie. I'm a

journalist for *The Teignmouth Chronicle* – I'm fascinated by anything newsworthy in Devon. I'm currently writing my own column.' Rosie leaned forward and scribbled something on a notepad. 'I've heard all about your wonderful garden, Robert. And I'm here to learn more about Millbrook's fabulous gardening club.' She waved her phone. 'I love this spread of food you've prepared, and the enthusiasm of the club members, and the expertise that you all seem to share so readily. In fact, I think there may be a lot more interest in this particular gardening club than any of you possibly realise.'

'Splendid.' Francis rubbed his hands. 'So, item one on our agenda – how to get the best from our fruit bushes.' He beamed towards Robert. 'If you wouldn't mind, Robert, perhaps you'd like to enlighten us all.'

'Lovely,' Susan said and Angie shot her an irritable look.

'Then can I have a pint?' Colin mumbled. 'I'm thirsty.'

'Or a slice of the pavlova?' Jill's cheeks pinked at the thought.

Robert stood up gravely, clearing his throat. 'Thank you, Francis. I'll be brief. Now... there are two types of raspberries: floricane, summer-fruiting, and primocane, autumn-fruiting. Floricanes produce all of their fruit in one go in early summer. Primocanes produce a slower crop from high summer right up to the first frosts. So, first you should choose a sheltered spot.'

'Bloody hell.' Dennis the grumpy git yawned a little too loudly. 'I just chuck a net over my bushes. It keeps the birds off.'

'Nets are always a good idea,' Robert began. He gazed around at his audience. Susan and Angie were leaning on their hands, watching him in awe. The men were fidgeting. Rosie took out her phone, her thumbs moving quickly. He took a breath. 'I could just make brief notes on fruit bushes—'

'I'd collect them from you, Robert,' Susan offered. 'I'll call round...'

'Time for a pint, I think.' Colin waved a hand. 'Over here, Shelley. Let's take a comfort break.'

'And can we try Robert's delicious pavlova with another Prosecco?' Angie sighed, wobbling a little in her chair.

'I'd like to take a group photograph,' Rosie said enthusiastically. 'If you'd all pose around the strawberry meringue and the scones. Just get in position with Robert in the centre, would you, please?'

Robert shuffled into position next to Francis. 'Had we better start on the refreshments a bit early?'

'I think it might be a wise move,' Francis replied under his breath.

Rosie snapped several photos on her phone and Shelley called from the bar. 'Time for more drinks? Shall I take orders?'

'Beer, please, Shelley,' Colin in the cap called out eagerly.

'Another pint of the same for me,' Dennis said.

'Splendid idea. And I'll have a pint of best beer and a couple of those lovely scones.' George in the trilby turned to his wife in the spotted frock. 'Another gin, Mary?'

* * *

That same evening, Hattie retired to her bedroom to read her mindfulness magazine. She'd left Bunty and Jacko in the living room watching television, laughing at a comedy show. Hattie watched the first five minutes of the programme and was frustrated that each line was greeted by canned laughter, and that the character of the harassed mum tolerated her feckless husband's bad habits. Hattie decided she'd read for a while, then have a bath before bed. She could still hear Jacko's loud ho-ho-ho booming from the living room. He was sprawled on the sofa, a beer in one hand, the other arm around Bunty, who rested her head on his shoulder. They were certainly making themselves at home. Hattie felt like an outsider in her own bungalow, creeping around, asking Jacko to wash his coffee cups, emptying the washing machine of their clothes. It felt almost as uncomfortable as it had when Geoffrey lived there.

She stretched out on the bed listening for their chuckles but they were quiet now. Hattie turned on the radio. A sixties hit that Bunty had always liked was playing, 'Daydream Believer'. Bunty had always got her way, that was the problem. Hattie wondered if she'd done the right thing, allowing them to stay. Had she been supportive to her sister, or a pushover? She wasn't sure. But she'd promised herself she'd put herself first and, indeed, the mindfulness magazine suggested that she should try to live in the moment. Hattie gazed at a photo of a woman smiling, sunshine melting across her face. The article told her to treat herself the way she would treat a good friend. Hattie wished she'd had such good advice years earlier.

As a teenager, she'd wanted to be a nurse, a midwife. She'd have been good at caring for others. Instead, her father had intervened: she needed a sensible job with sensible hours; she'd do secretarial training. Hattie had found a position at a car dealership, organising everything, working her way up over many years, becoming an indispensable PA. Every day had been about proving that she was punctual, reliable: she'd done everything before it was needed. 'What would we do without you, Mrs Bowen?' 'Oh, Mrs Bowen's worth her small weight in gold—' Then she'd return home, tired and unfulfilled, to Geoffrey, who'd nag her and make her feel even more unfulfilled. Hattie wished she'd known about mindfulness then.

She recalled the clay face mask she'd bought in town and it seemed as if now was the perfect opportunity to pamper herself. She'd run a steaming bath scented with sweet oils, slather the mask all over her face and neck and relax for twenty minutes.

Hattie undressed and shrugged on a kimono, the only dressing gown that wasn't hanging on the dryer, then she padded in bare feet to the bathroom and pushed the door open. She caught her breath. A hairy man was sitting in the bath, steam rising around him, a clay mask plastered to his face, his belly sticking out of the water like an island. Hattie said, 'Jacko?'

'Hello.' Jacko raised an eyebrow hopefully. 'Room in here for two...'

Hattie was appalled at his suggestion; twice appalled by the expensive clay smeared on his face. 'That's my face mask.'

'Oh, is it?' Jacko put a hand to his face as if to check. 'I found it and thought I'd give it a go. It did smell nice, but I thought it was just funny soap.'

'Read the label.' Hattie snatched the empty tube from the windowsill and waved it under his nose. 'It was my special face mask.'

Jacko winked. 'Bunty will get the benefit – I'll have skin like a baby's bum.'

Hattie slammed the bathroom door hard, ridding herself of the image of the man wallowing in rising steam. She retreated to her room, muttering to herself, 'The sooner he leaves, the better. And, if I have anything to do with it, Bunty will go straight back to Sean. He's an angel compared to that man in my bath.'

9

The following morning, Hattie opened the curtains to bright sunshine that illuminated the bedroom. She exhaled slowly, telling herself she was glad to be alive, living in the moment, then she went into the bathroom and scrubbed the ring of grime and clay from where Jacko had been wallowing last night. She heard voices in the kitchen, Bunty's tinkling laughter, and she could smell burned toast. She padded through in her kimono and found Bunty in shorts and a T-shirt and Jacko half naked, wearing baggy floral boxers. He waved a hand cheerily. 'Kettle's just boiled, Hatters...'

Hattie ignored him and leaned against the counter, watching the heat rise from the toaster, releasing the bread before it blackened any more. Then she made herself a cup of tea.

'Hattie, have you got any marmalade?' Bunty asked, her voice light. 'Jacko likes a bit of something sweet on his toast.'

'I certainly do,' Jacko said suggestively.

Hattie's back was still turned; she made a face, which she knew was a bit childish, but she was living in the moment and, right at this moment, he was annoying her. She replied sweetly. 'Robert makes the best jam.'

'He does.' Bunty stretched an arm above her head. 'Oh, I so miss Robert – it's been ages...'

'Who's Robert?' Jacko sounded jealous.

'My brother,' Bunty said.

'I never knew you had a brother.'

'There's a lot you two don't know about each other,' Hattie remarked quietly. 'It seems you have a wife though, Jacko. What's the state of play there? Are you still together?' She smiled sweetly. 'I'm asking for my sister.'

Jacko coughed into his fist. 'Marion's impossible to live with. She and I are done.'

'Does she know?' Hattie faced him, raising an eyebrow.

'I'm sure she does.'

'And does she know about Bunty?'

'Not yet.'

'And where does she think you are right now? A complete bathroom fitting in Axminster, wasn't it?'

Jacko's cheeks turned crimson. She detected a surliness in his tone. 'I'll tell the missus when I'm good and ready.'

'I'm sure you will. The thing is—' Hattie was just getting into her stride '—Bunty's always been a naïve soul and she's left a perfectly good husband. Right now, she's trusting you with her emotions, and you're not being honest. What I'm saying, Jacko, is – if you want a future with my sister, you ought to do things properly. You should tell your wife first, then you can approach my sister with your intentions, then you offer her an honourable relationship.'

Jacko laughed, a bit too loud. 'That's an old-fashioned attitude, Hattie. You should get with the times. Things aren't done that way now.'

Hattie gave him a wise look. 'They are in my house, Jacko. You have a phone, don't you? Call your wife, tell her the truth.'

'I'd rather talk to her face to face,' Jacko muttered.

'But you haven't done it at all,' Hattie said with a flourish.

Bunty gazed at her sister with shining eyes. 'Hattie has a point.'

Jacko rubbed his belly and reached for more toast, scraping butter over blackened bread.

Hattie tried again. 'Bunty is special, and, if you love her, you'd treat her with respect. *If* your intentions are to have a proper relationship with her.'

'We *are* having a proper relationship.' Jacko grunted, arching an eyebrow. Bunty fingered her thin necklace awkwardly; Hattie knew she was having second thoughts.

'Do you love her?' Hattie persisted.

'Yes, do you love me, Jacko?' Bunty said hopefully.

Jacko sniffed loudly. 'It's an adult relationship. I take each day as it comes.'

'I see.' Hattie finished her tea. 'Well, let me tell you exactly how each day comes in this house. You have several days to talk to your wife and sort out what you think your relationship with my sister is. And while you're here, I expect you to respect my home. That means you ask me when you want a bath and you clean up after yourself. It means that you keep your clothes in the bedroom, you don't borrow any of mine and you pay a visit to the supermarket for food tomorrow. *Mi casa* is definitely not *su casa*. You're a guest, and I expect you to behave properly while you're here. And, Jacko...'

Jacko gave her a scalded-hen look; he was well and truly chastised.

'If you can't make your mind up how you feel about Bunty over the next few days then I'd be very happy if you'd take yourself back to your wife. Bunty deserves better than being a bit on the side, with empty promises and no commitment. That may be your idea of relationships, but it went out with the ark. Women simply won't put up with being chattels any more.' She paused for effect. 'Have you got it?'

Jacko stood up, his face sullen. 'All right, all right, I've got it. I'll go and make myself useful somewhere.' He shuffled towards the door.

'The hall needs hoovering,' Hattie called after him.

Bunty scraped her chair and rushed over to her sister, her hands out as if she might clap. 'Oh, Hattie – I can't believe you said all that – and for me.'

'It was the right thing to say. He has a wife who knows nothing about you. And you've left a decent man for him. It's not good enough.'

Bunty squeezed Hattie's shoulder. 'Oh, thank you. You said everything I've been too nervous to say.'

Hattie wrapped an affectionate arm around Bunty. 'I was too scared for years to say what I wanted to Geoffrey. But things are changing, Bunty. The worm is turning.'

'It is.' Bunty said. 'So, I was thinking – I'm going to cook us all Sunday lunch today, Yorkshires, gravy, all the trimmings. We can all sit down like a family to eat at the table.'

'Why do you want to do that?' Hattie asked. She'd just given Jacko a piece of her mind – they certainly weren't one big family and she wasn't in the mood to watch him while he slobbered into his greens.

'I thought if Jacko could discover what a great cook I am and what a nice person you are, he might make that call to his wife and pick me.'

Hattie's eyes widened: Bunty hadn't understood at all. She was desperate to please Jacko, unsure if he was what she wanted but doing her best to endear herself to him in case. She was still childlike in her affections. Hattie recognised the old submissive behaviour in herself – she'd been that way throughout her marriage to Geoffrey, trying to be appealing. She wondered for a moment if it was a generational thing, if she'd been brought up that way. Younger women surely wouldn't be happy with being second best? She clamped her lips together. She wouldn't let Bunty go down the same route of subservience as she had in her marriage, currying affection, playing second fiddle. Hattie thought Jacko was selfish and lazy, and, in her opinion, Bunty was far too good for him. Bunty was making a fool of herself and Hattie had no intention of allowing it.

Robert wandered through the peaceful village of Millbrook, past the perfectly clipped village green and The Pig and Pickle Inn, its doors flung open wide, the heavy smell of hops lingering. He continued towards St Jude's church, crossing the road to push open the gate to the manse. Francis would be home from morning service by now and Robert had promised his wife, Sally, half a dozen eggs. She wanted to replicate the wonderful strawberry pavlova she'd heard about but not tasted.

Robert paused in the pretty garden, flowers clustering beneath the windows, which were flung wide to let the sunlight in. He knocked gently at the front door. The sound of a jangly guitar and thrashing drums burst from an upstairs window, followed by raucous screams. Robert was unsure if it was someone singing or swearing in anger – he decided the latter would be unlikely in the manse. Francis and Sally were quiet people. He knocked again, clutching the box of six eggs to his chest.

The guitar twanged again, a long note, and a voice began to sing.

'I'm rockin' in my grave,
Because I'm Satan's slave.'

Robert took a step back, not sure what he had heard. Drums crashed, the guitar reverberated discordantly and there it was again, a woman's voice, more of a snarl.

'Satan is the master
now and ever after,
I'm just rockin' in my grave
'cos I'm Satan's slave.'

'Well, I never,' Robert gasped. He was about to knock again, when the door opened and Francis appeared, wearing an apron, pink and blue daisies. He smiled apologetically. 'I'm helping to cook.'

Robert held out the six eggs tentatively. 'You might be needing these.'

'Oh, indeed – thank you.' Francis was delighted. 'That's so kind of you. I must say, I did enjoy our meeting yesterday. The gardening club is going from strength to strength.'

'It is.' Robert smiled. 'It's a shame we couldn't spend more time discussing fruit bushes though.'

'Oh, the club's becoming so popular – pulling in more punters than I had at Sunday service this morning.' Francis smiled sadly. 'It was just the usual crowd, all older people, a few single villagers and Eric and Edie Mallory. In fact, I was wondering...'

'What?' Robert grinned at Francis's hesitant expression.

'Well, if we offered a cream tea after the service, it might attract some people to give us a try, and then they might come again more regularly. I wonder if you might supply a batch of your fruit scones and some jam one Sunday – and possibly grace us with your presence.'

'Me?' Robert's forehead crinkled. 'I'm sure I could knock up a few scones, but I'm not much of a one for church services, except perhaps at Christmas.'

'But if you came along once in a while – the congregation would increase.'

'Would it?'

'Oh, Robert, you've surely noticed? God has given you a gift.'

Robert raised his hands in bashful excuse. 'Oh, I'm lucky to have my gardens, the orchard and the chickens—'

'I don't mean the garden,' Francis interrupted.

'Well, I can make a cake, scones, puddings, but then anyone could, with a recipe and an oven.'

'I don't mean the pavlova.'

Robert frowned. 'Then what do you mean?'

'You must be aware of it, Robert.'

'Aware of what?'

Francis lowered his voice confidentially. 'You're something of a – babe magnet – in Millbrook.'

'A what?' Robert said.

'Susan and Angie are competing over you, Jill is jittery around you, and Rosie the journalist couldn't take her eyes off you. Even my wife, Sally—' Francis paused, a little embarrassed. 'Even Sally can't stop talking about how wonderful you are.'

'Nonsense. It's just the scones and jam they enjoy.'

'It may be the key that unlocks their hearts, Robert, but they are all infatuated.'

'No, I don't think so—' Robert began then he and Francis gazed upwards as drums hammered and a thick voice snarled.

"Cos I'm Say-say-say-say-say-say-say-say-Satan's slave, I'm Say-

say-say-say-say-say-say-say-Satan's slave, I'm Say-say-say-say-say-say-say-say-Satan's slave.'

Francis said apologetically, 'I'm sorry. That's Tilda.'

'Your daughter?'

'She has a rock group. They are called Armpit. They're practising...' Francis winced. 'It's a bit inappropriate – on a Sunday – in a manse.'

Robert shrugged. 'I suppose it's creative – maybe it's a stage she's going through?'

'I wish she'd come out the other end soon. She's eighteen – she's just finished A levels...' Francis sighed. 'Now she's shaved the sides of her hair, dyed it inky black – Sally is distraught – and then there's the drummer.'

Robert listened while someone played a few frills and paradiddles from upstairs, smashing the cymbal several times. 'Drummer?'

'Her new boyfriend, Donkey.'

'Donkey?' Robert repeated.

'Donkey,' Francis said. 'Sally's taking Valium.'

'I can imagine.' Robert shrugged. 'Well, I'd better get back. I've got some pine wood for the goats – it's a natural de-wormer.'

'Good to know,' Francis murmured. 'Ah, right, I must finish cooking and prepare for the evening service. God calls...' He rolled his eyes towards heaven and another guitar chord boomed from the bedroom, followed by a second, then the rumble of a bass, playing one continuous note like a hammer to the brain. Francis looked momentarily proud. 'That's Tilda on bass and vocals.'

'Satan's – er – slave?' Robert said tactfully. 'I'll see you soon, Francis. And enjoy the eggs – Dora the eggs-plorer's very prolific at the moment.'

'Thank you,' Francis muttered and was gone, closing the door crisply. The music began upstairs again, drums battering from the window, a heavy bass note thrumming, a guitar wailing.

Robert turned to head back towards the smallholding, the music of Armpit resounding in his ears. His mind was full of anxiety, after what Francis had said. A babe magnet, indeed? All the women at the gardening club, desperate for his bakes?

The very thought petrified him.

10

Sunday lunch was a sombre affair. Bunty had done her best, taking a joint of beef from the freezer, using all the potatoes, baking crispy Yorkshires with the last of the eggs. It had been sweltering in the kitchen; Hattie would have been happy with a sandwich. But succulent aromas filled the air, and Hattie and Bunty sat down to eat. After being called twice, Jacko slunk in sulkily from the hall and plonked himself down, tucking into the food without meeting anyone's gaze.

Hattie took over. 'This is delicious, Bunty. Thank you.'

Bunty glanced towards Jacko proudly. 'I'm good at Sunday roasts.'

'The meat's a bit tough.' Jacko grunted.

'No, it isn't,' Hattie corrected him, thinking that Geoffrey would have said the same thing. 'It's melt-in-the-mouth.'

'Marion knows how I like my meat cooked best.' Jacko said and there was an uncomfortable moment of silence.

Hattie said, 'You can have Sunday dinner in Plymouth next week.'

Bunty wiped her eye as if there was a tear there. She pushed her plate away. 'I'm not really hungry.'

'Eat it up.' Hattie glared, turning her stare back towards Jacko. 'It would help matters if you were polite.'

Jacko sniffed and forced a smile. 'It must be the bit I ate first, the dried-up edge of the joint. The meat's perfect, Bunty love. And these Yorkshires are the best in the world.' He leaned over and patted her hand. 'You're a wonderful woman.'

Bunty picked up her fork and began to poke at the food. She had cheered up a bit.

Hattie frowned; Bunty was worth more than the sum of her cooking abilities. She sliced a carrot. 'So where have you been this morning, Jacko? You've been very quiet while Bunty and I were busy. Have you been asleep?'

'No, I've been—' Jacko looked around him. 'I've been taking a look at your old boiler.'

'My boiler?' Hattie said, surprised.

'It's very old – they don't make them like that any more. Anyway—' Jacko pushed meat into his mouth '—I noticed it's stuck in a cupboard right at the other end of the bungalow so it heats the bath all right but it takes a long time for the hot water to travel up here to the kitchen.'

'It's always been like that.' Hattie waved his words away. 'I just wait for it to come through the pipes. I'm in no hurry.'

'You need a modern boiler,' Jacko told her. 'One that does the job efficiently.'

'One day, perhaps – I don't need one yet.' Hattie chewed a piece of broccoli, considering the conversation done.

'The thing is – I've had a look at it.'

'Had a look?' Hattie eyed Jacko suspiciously. 'What do you mean, a look?'

'Well,' Jacko wiped his mouth on the back of his hand, 'I

thought I'd move it to the middle of the bungalow. That way it will provide water at both ends, at the same time.'

'I don't want the boiler moved,' Hattie said firmly. 'You can put it straight back.'

'It's very old and not fit for purpose.' Jacko tutted.

'He's a very good plumber,' Bunty added proudly. 'He'll do a good job.'

'The old boiler serves me perfectly well.' Hattie glared at Jacko. 'So please put it back where it was.'

'Ah, well,' Jacko began, then he shovelled a whole Yorkshire pudding into his mouth and said, 'I can't.'

'You can't what?' Hattie raised her voice.

'I can't put it back,' Jacko said, still chewing. 'It won't go.'

'Why won't it go?'

'It broke,' Jacko said simply.

'Then fix it.' Hattie felt her colour rising; she was becoming angry.

'It's not fixable.'

'It must be.'

'A part fell off – it snapped. I'd have to get a new one and I looked online on my phone.' Jacko avoided Hattie's eyes. 'Nowhere's open on a Sunday and it seems the part is obsolete anyway. So that's no good. You'll have to get a new one.'

'A new – what?' Hattie's teeth snapped together.

'A new boiler. I can put it in for you. I'll fit a modern one. I'll only charge you for the boiler and my labour.'

'You'll do no such thing,' Hattie spat. 'I want my old boiler back up and working and I don't intend to spend a penny—'

'Not possible.' Jacko shook his head. 'The old boiler's dead.'

'Oh dear.' Bunty gazed from Hattie to Jacko and back. 'I suppose we'll have to get a new one.'

'I can order one on Monday, fit it on Tuesday when it arrives –

all in all, it shouldn't cost you too much. I reckon I can do the whole package for—' He sucked air through his teeth '—three and a half grand.'

Bunty said, 'That's not too bad, is it, Hattie?'

Hattie ignored her. 'Do I have hot running water?' She glared at Jacko.

'Not exactly.'

'Do I or don't I?'

'Well, I can get it for you by Tuesday.'

'So, do I have hot water now?'

'Not hot. There's a bit of cold.'

'How do I have a bath? How do I wash dishes?' Hattie said. 'What are you going to do about it?'

Jacko shook his head as if it were a difficult question. 'Water is a precious commodity,' he said. 'We take it for granted in the Western world, especially when we haven't got it. Some countries have to get water from a communal well.'

'Don't you dare.' Hattie drew herself as tall as she could. 'Right. This is what's going to happen. Jacko, you can wash all the dishes in cold water. If you need it warm, you can boil a kettle. I'm going to my room for a lie-down, while I think about what I'm going to do next. But—'

He glanced at her, guilt settling around his eyes, displeasure around his mouth.

'You're going to sort this mess out. I didn't ask you to meddle with my boiler but I'm telling you that you're going to fix it.'

He shook his head miserably. 'You can't make me pay for a new boiler.'

'I haven't decided what I'll do yet. But I'll let you know when I do. Meanwhile, you can clean the dishes and put them away. I'm going to give this some thought.'

'What should I do?' Bunty asked, a little confused.

'You cooked dinner. You go and have a rest. Jacko can sort the kitchen out,' Hattie said and she swept from the room.

As she left the kitchen behind her, she thought she heard Jacko say, 'Your sister's a right bossy mare.'

Hattie couldn't help but laugh. She'd never been called a bossy mare in her life. And she had to admit – it felt good.

* * *

Robert was lost in thought as he wandered back home in the sunshine. He kept repeating the phrase, 'Babe... magnet...? Babe... magnet.' He understood what it meant; it was self-explanatory. It implied that good-looking women were drawn to him, they couldn't help but succumb to his charms. He laughed out loud. It was a ridiculous thought. Throughout his life, from being a bookish fourteen-year-old to the day he retired from teaching, women had been polite to him, respectful. Some had wanted to befriend him, or ask his advice. A raucous woman at a party in the seventies who was the worse for wear after a few glasses of cider had yelled at him that he had a lovely bottom and her friends had screeched with laughter. Robert had suspected they were ridiculing him. It hadn't made him feel good about himself. No, Francis was joking at best, or he'd made a mistake. Robert was no babe magnet. Women simply liked to share the fruits of his garden, the produce of his kitchen. That was all.

As he approached the smallholding, Isaac Mewton sauntered over to him, rubbing her head against his legs, looking up inquisitively as if she had something to say to him. Robert bent down, fondled the side of her face where whiskers sprouted. 'What is it, puss? Have you missed me?'

Robert glanced towards his drive and he realised what Isaac wanted. A white car was parked there, one of these sporty convertible models, open-topped. A woman was sitting inside, looking at something, perhaps her phone. Robert adjusted his metal-framed glasses on his nose and stared harder. She looked familiar. She wore a bright blouse, smart sunglasses and a head-scarf, which she took off, shaking fair hair loose. He'd definitely seen her before and as he approached she leaped from the car and waved enthusiastically. He walked across the drive, trying not to think of himself as a babe magnet, feeling awkward and off his guard. He held out a hand and realised he couldn't remember her name. 'Hello again.'

'Robert.' She clearly knew who he was. She took his hand, pressing his palm as if it were a masonic message. 'I simply had to come to see you after last night. I've thought of nothing else.'

He took in the blonde hair and the red lipstick. 'Oh?'

'The pavlova and the scones. Your spread was divine.'

'Ah.' Robert knew he'd seen her at the gardening club meeting. Her name was on the tip of his tongue. 'That's so kind.'

'Not at all. I was completely blown away. So much so that there will be an article in *The Chronicle* this week, and I wanted to tell you all about it.'

'That's nice.' Robert remembered her now. She was the journalist from Teignmouth; she'd taken photos of him surrounded by other members of the gardening club, standing by the refreshments. He searched in his head for her name but it wouldn't come. 'So?' he asked carefully. 'What can I do for you?'

She waved her phone. 'I'd absolutely love to take some more pics. Maybe you, surrounded by all your jams, or in the kitchen holding up a huge plate of scones, or perhaps in the field with your chickens and goats.'

'I don't see why not.' Robert was momentarily flattered. Yet another woman was complimenting his baking. It almost seemed too good to be true.

'And – do you have a panama hat perhaps? I want to promote you as an English gentleman living the good life in Devon, surrounded by animals and produce.'

'Promote?' The word almost troubled Robert – he hadn't thought of himself in need of promotion.

'In the article – well, I suppose I'd be promoting the gardening club.' The woman waved a hand to show that it wasn't important. 'My editor is very excited that we report on the best of the best across the Devon countryside and, it appears, Robert, you're the best.'

'Thank you, Miss—'

'Oh, please don't call me Ms Eagle. It's Rosemary. Rosie to my friends.' She met his eyes levelly. 'And I do hope we're becoming friends, Robert.'

Robert found himself staring at the smooth hair, the scarf, the bright blouse and yellow linen trousers. He assumed she was a babe, although he wasn't sure what the definition was. She was younger than him, confident, attractive. She must be a babe. He felt suddenly anxious, wondering if he really was a magnet. 'So – should I introduce you to the goats?'

Rosie Eagle looked around. 'It's a splendid afternoon. Maybe we can go and see the animals first, then perhaps you can lure me into your kitchen and show me your delicious stock of jams.'

'I have wine too, elderberry, blackberry—' Robert stammered. He had no idea why he was telling Rosie this. He wasn't intending to flirt – he simply felt awkward.

'Better and better,' Rosie threaded an arm through his. 'And I wouldn't say no if you wanted to tempt me to one of your scones when we've finished. I'm sure yours are the best in Devon – and beyond.' She met his eyes. 'So – would you like to show me around?'

'It would be my pleasure,' Robert said, believing it was the gallant thing to say. 'Let's start with the chickens, shall we?'

Robert escorted Rosie Eagle along the path towards the field in the distance. Isaac Mewton scooted behind, pausing to look over her shoulder; perhaps she'd felt the frisson in the air from the woman who was lurking at the bottom of the path beyond the gate, watching every detail carefully from behind sunglasses.

Susan Joyce's jaw was clenched, as were her hands, balled into fists. She'd showered, washed her hair, pulled on a pretty off-the-shoulder summer dress, sprayed herself in a cloud of Chanel and sauntered down to the smallholding to compliment Robert on his pavlova and ask him if they could make one together. He'd show her how to hold the whisk, his hand over hers, and she'd flourish under his guidance. But she'd been beaten to it. The damn reporter woman was here; she had poor unsuspecting Robert in her clutches, trying to lead him astray.

Susan felt her temper rise. The reporter, with her sporty car and her scarlet lipstick, her smooth talk and stylish clothes, was trying to seduce him. Susan wasn't going to let her steal Robert from under her nose, not after she'd played the game so patiently, keeping him in her sights for the last six months, arranging more and more gardening get-togethers. He was hers by rights, Susan thought crossly. She'd spotted his talents first, his gentleness, his culinary skills. She watched as the woman walked towards the field, clutching Robert's arm, her laughter tinkling like a pretty bell.

Susan gnashed her teeth, feeling fury boil.

'Right, Rosie Eagle, if you want him, you'll have to get past me,' she muttered. 'I'm not letting go of Robert that easily.'

11

Hattie stood in the hall, gazing despondently at her old boiler, the pieces spread out on the carpet, dismantled and useless. She was calm now. Bunty was resting in her room, reading a magazine; she looked emotionally exhausted and Hattie wasn't surprised. The more she saw of Jacko, the more she knew he wasn't a good match for sweet, trusting Bunty. Poor Bunty; she'd been carrying so much baggage for the last forty years. But Jacko wasn't the answer. Now Bunty had to realise for herself that Jacko was a poor choice compared to loyal Sean with his sense of humour and his devotion to all things Bunty, despite what she said about his penchant for betting on the horses. Bunty was in her seventies, for goodness' sake – it was time she figured things out for herself. It wasn't doing her any good, being protected at every step. So, to that end, Hattie had packed a case. She could hear Jacko in the kitchen, sighing and groaning as he collected the dishes. She wondered if he'd finish the job or leave them on the table. But that, Hattie thought, was not her problem.

She walked into the living room, over to the piano, picking up the photo of herself, Robert and Bunty in the 1950s, touching the childish faces lightly. Family, that was what was most important. She looked at the three children in black and white, Robert, Harriet and Elizabeth Parkin, so innocent, so unaware of what life would throw at them. Hattie wondered what she'd have thought if she'd known all those years ago where she'd be in her mid-seventies.

Hattie lifted up the lid of the old piano and pressed a key firmly, then she tried a chord. The notes jangled. She wriggled her fingers, waking up creaking joints, and began to play, Chopin: *Fantaisie-Impromptu* Op. 66. Her fingers touched the yellowing keys lightly, and she found that the music was returning to her. The dramatic opening chords crashed, then the fast-flowing fingers, the gorgeous array of tumbling notes. She could play it almost as well as she'd played so many years ago, confident, strong. Hattie paused, taking her fingers away, and found she was smiling. The music had lifted her spirit somehow; she'd played because she could, because she wanted to. She'd return to the piano; she'd play for herself, not for a critical teacher or to pass exams, or for her parents who wanted their daughter to sit up straight-backed on the stool and accomplish yet another étude. She'd play for pleasure because that was how life would be now, lived for the pure pleasure of it.

She approached Bunty's room, knocked lightly, then pushed the door ajar. The hideous smell hit her: the heavy stench of Jacko's socks, unwashed boxers. Bunty lay on the bed on her stomach reading the mindfulness magazine. She rolled over and smiled. 'Hi, Hattie – thanks for lending me this and, you know, what you said to Jacko earlier.'

Hattie chose her words. 'I think he needs to understand what you're worth. And you need to value yourself more than you do. He doesn't deserve you.'

Bunty's face creased. 'Do you think so?'

'It doesn't matter what I think.' Hattie left her words hanging on the air. 'What you think is important. So, you need to decide about him.'

'I do,' Bunty faltered. 'You know, I'm not sure that I did the right thing, leaving Sean.'

'It's your decision, and only yours to make.' Hattie made herself smile. 'Anyway, I'm off now, so you can spend quality time with Jacko and make your mind up once and for all.'

'You're off? Where?'

'I'll be away, just for a few days.'

'Hattie – don't leave me.'

'It's what you need – time to decide.'

'But not without you.'

'Why not?'

Bunty's face fell. 'I need you here.'

'You're a grown woman. You need to make your own mind up.'

'But – there's no hot water.'

'Jacko's a plumber.'

'Shall I get him to fix it?'

'No. I texted Graeme Towler who always does the job perfectly. He's a lovely man. He'll be here first thing on Tuesday. I've told him what I want him to do.' Hattie lifted an index finger. 'Jacko mustn't touch a thing.'

'So – what will we do while you're away?'

'Use the cold tap,' Hattie said. 'I'll be in touch.'

Bunty leaped from the bed and rushed over, enveloping her sister in a hug. 'Don't leave me—'

'I'll text you later.' Hattie placed a kiss on Bunty's head.

'You're right.' Bunty nodded. 'I've been silly, haven't I? I've taken advantage of your good nature, like I always do. And now you're making me stand on my own two feet.'

'Love you.' Hattie winked. She took a few steps towards the bedroom door. 'Bunty—'

'Hat?'

'Try not to let Jacko wreck my house.' She blew a kiss and was gone. In the hall, her case was packed, her handbag, her phone and car keys. It shouldn't take more than three hours if she drove steadily. She'd be at Robert's by teatime.

* * *

Two hours later, she was hunched in her silver Nissan Micra, staring at a line of stationary vehicles in front of her on the M5. She took the opportunity to glance at her phone, although she knew she shouldn't use it when she was driving but, in fact, she wasn't driving, she was parked on the motorway, kind of. There was no reply from Robert, although she'd messaged him that she was on her way as soon as she'd packed. She wondered if she should text Bunty and check that she was all right, but she decided against it. Bunty needed to be left alone to sort her own mess out. Hattie felt a bit guilty for leaving her in the lurch with Jacko and no hot water, but, as far as she could see, there was no other way. She looked at her WhatsApp conversation with Robert and realised she hadn't pressed *send*. No wonder she'd had no reply; he didn't know she was coming. She pressed *send* quickly, then wondered if she should type another message to say that she was stuck in traffic.

At that moment, the car in front of her shuffled forward; the lorry to her right loomed above her and released its air brakes with a breathy hiss before edging along. Hattie pressed the accelerator, moving less than a car length, then the queue stopped again. She sighed as a clear female voice on the radio announced that there was a delay just south of Bristol and all drivers were advised to avoid the M5. There had been an incident – the expected waiting time was well over an hour. Hattie reached for her phone. The least she could do was to let Robert know that she was on her way and that she would be very late.

* * *

Robert hadn't looked at his phone all afternoon. He'd been too busy escorting the delightful Rosie Eagle around his smallholding, introducing her to The Great Goatsby and Vincent Van Goat and the chickens, then taking her into the quiet temple of his pantry where they gazed at bottles of wine on racks and shining jars of jam on shelves. Then he had asked her if she'd like a cream tea, and she had almost bitten his hand off.

Now they were sitting in the conservatory nibbling vanilla scones laced with cream and blackcurrant jam with cassis, Isaac Mewton watching suspiciously from the chair arm. Rosie could hardly contain herself. 'I have to say, Robert – these scones are to Devon cream teas what orgasms are to *Fifty Shades of Grey*.'

'Do you like them?' he asked tentatively. 'The scones, I mean—'

'They are off the scale.' Rosie took another bite. 'I have never eaten such exquisite scones. Tell me,' she leaned forward, 'are these from recipes you've written down?'

'I start with a basic recipe, but I like to experiment. Vanilla scones, lemon scones, matcha and almond scones, I've even made Marmite scones with chives, and limoncello and blackcurrant, watercress and tomato with cheese. I'm working on an Arctic scone with ice cream in the centre.' He smiled. 'I like to mix it up.'

'You certainly do.' Rosie's eyes shone. 'And tell me, Robert – do you entertain? I mean – is there a space here in your wonderful garden where you give parties?'

'I'm working on it – I have a design in mind and I'm hoping someone will give me a good quotation and build it for me.' He smiled dreamily. 'A modest patio, a pizza oven beneath a shady tree – or a barbecue.'

'Glorious,' Rosie said. 'A blazing chimenea or a fire pit, some nice seating. Oh, I'd love to help you design that.' Rosie's expression was suddenly serious. 'Just think, Robert. You could get the whole village involved, do cookery demonstrations, charity events.' She clasped her hands together. 'Let's make plans.'

'Do you think so?' Robert asked, a little anxiously.

'Yes, yes, yes,' Rosie yelled. 'Let's do it now, me and you. We were made for this moment. Come along – we don't have time to waste.'

She whirled round excitedly to see Susan Joyce standing at the patio door watching them, her arms folded and her chin tucked in, looking decidedly unhappy. Rosie suddenly burst into peals of laughter. 'Hello. I remember you from the gardening club. You're another one of Robert's fan club.'

'I'm Susan – a very good friend of Robert's.' Susan turned to speak to Robert. 'Hello, Robert. I didn't realise you had company.' She flushed, not able to hide the fact that she'd been watching all afternoon, waiting for the right moment to make her presence felt. 'I popped round to see if you had any jam I could steal for my scones. I remember the last time we were in your larder, there was a particularly nice chilli jam and I wanted to try something – hot.' She licked her lips. 'If you can find the time to get a pot for me, but I can see you're busy.' She shot Rosie a sharp look.

'Oh, no, I've got what I came here for.' Rosie stood up coolly, brushing crumbs from the yellow trousers, sauntering over to Robert, kissing his cheek. 'But I'll be back soon, and we'll finish talking about – you know what. The article in *The Chronicle* is bound to be a success and my readers will demand more and more news of you.' She clutched her phone. 'I have all I need for the time being but – don't forget my offer. I'm full of garden design ideas. A social area – maybe a pagoda, some tasteful decking.' She winked. 'I'll see myself to the car. Thanks for this afternoon, Robert, it was truly grrrrreat.' She held up tiger claws, then she smiled at Susan briefly. 'Nice to see you again.'

They watched her go and Susan reached out an arm, placing it on Robert's shoulder, tenderly brushing a crumb from his cheek. 'Are you all right?' She gazed into his eyes, her own anxious.

'I think so, yes.' Robert was unsure.

'Women like that – I know the type.' Susan shivered. 'Predatory.'

'Really?' Robert looked alarmed. 'She said she wanted to see the goats – she took some photos.'

'Take my word for it, Robert – I've met her sort,' Susan said. 'What they say they want is not what they really want. She won't be happy until she's sucked your blood dry like a vampire.'

'Oh?' Robert was worried. 'I thought she seemed very nice.'

'Man-eater.' Susan came closer, her breath warm on Robert's neck. 'It's a good job you have me to protect you.' She fixed her eyes on his. 'Now, about that hot chilli jam...'

12

Susan was unwilling to leave. Robert gave her two pots of jam, refused payment and showed her to the door but Susan installed herself in the conservatory, asking if there was any chance that he would teach her how to make meringues. Robert glanced anxiously at the wall clock: it was half past four. He asked politely if they might make meringues another day – in fact, perhaps the whole gardening club would like a demonstration. He could just about fit a dozen people in the kitchen if they stood close together. Susan demanded to know if the reporter woman from *The Chronicle* had been eating scones and when Robert admitted that yes, she had, Susan asked if there was just a teensy one left for her. Robert obliged, and Susan nibbled at the scone for half an hour, asking questions about why Rosie Eagle had visited and if Robert found pushy woman attractive.

Robert was a little uncomfortable. Susan was wearing a summer dress that revealed her décolletage and he was trying not to stare. He knew it was rude to gawp but the dress hung from her shoulders, exposing a lot of salmon flesh. Susan had caught the sun and the red tan sat on her skin like a rash. She was not an unattractive woman; she had a pretty, round face with dimples; her hair was smooth. Pearl earrings shone from her lobes, and today she smelled like a floral bouquet of rose and jasmine, not unpleasant although quite overpowering. Robert closed his eyes and inhaled. It was an intoxicating scent. Then he opened them again and noticed it was past five o'clock. He wished Susan would leave; he'd made a cheese quiche for tea and it would be very tasty with a salad of rocket and tomatoes from his garden. But Susan was still talking.

'There are so many new people at the club now, and new isn't always good. I liked the gardening club more when it was smaller, intimate, just a few villagers, not outsiders from Dawlish or Teignmouth – what do you think, Robert?'

Robert didn't know. 'Rosie suggested we could meet here, at my house. I'd been thinking of putting a patio down at the side of the house, a pergola, an entertaining area.'

'Oh – Rosie suggested it, did she? You're on first-name terms already.'

'No, I'd been thinking that I might make the most of the space, use it for entertaining.'

Susan leaned forward deliberately. 'Intimacy is best though, Robert. A romantic arbour, roses, a kissing seat.'

'Do you think so?'

'Oh, yes,' Susan said. 'I can just imagine you and me, a plate of sandwiches on the wooden tray between us, a wobbly summer trifle, lashings of cream. The sun sinking beyond the goat field...' She sighed. 'Yes, a party for two might be just perfect.'

'The thing is,' Robert said, 'I'd imagined a barbecue.'

'Of course: leaping flames, sizzling coals, one steak, one plate, two forks.' Susan agreed. 'A dollop of lip-smacking horseradish.'

'Rosie mentioned that we could stage demonstrations.'

'Much nicer to be just one-to-one in your kitchen though,

Robert – don't you think?' Susan ignored any reference to the reporter as she popped the last morsel of scone into her mouth; she'd made it last for thirty-five minutes.

Robert stretched his legs, sprang towards her and whisked the plate from her fingers. 'So, Susan—'

'When can we make a date, so that you can teach me to make a crispy meringue with a soft centre? I'm free on Mondays – oh.' She gave a light laugh. 'That's tomorrow. Shall I come round early?'

Isaac Mewton decided it was time to help out. She brushed against Robert's legs, mewing adorably. Robert gave a light cough. 'Isaac wants her dinner. Do excuse me.' He moved to the conservatory door. 'I'll get back to you on the meringues, if I may. I know Angie Pollock said she'd like help to make some and Jill, the lady from Dawlish, said the same thing.' He smiled kindly. 'Perhaps I could show you all at the same time? We could have a sort of cooking class here.'

Susan made a sour face. That was not in her plans. 'I always learn better when I have my teacher to myself.' She stood up and made a small swaying movement so that her dress swished. Robert inhaled the swirl of floral perfume again. 'Let's find a mutually convenient time, shall we, Robert?' She snatched up the chilli jam. 'Well, I'll think of you when I'm eating this – hot stuff.' She swirled towards the conservatory door. 'Until next time...' She gave a little wave and was gone.

Robert frowned. He'd had a lot of female company recently but women still confused him. They seemed to say one thing and imply another. He recalled Angie Pollard had called his jam sexy; Rosie had talked about orgasms and Susan had used the phrase hot stuff. Robert was perplexed. Women were an unknown land that he'd seldom visited and he didn't know where to buy a map. He sighed and rummaged in his pocket for his phone. He'd left it somewhere – the kitchen perhaps, he wasn't sure, he'd hardly looked at it all day. Isaac rubbed her head against his ankles again and he bent down.

'You're the only female who says what she means, Isaac. Oh, I don't know. Let's find you a nice bit of dinner, shall we?'

Isaac purred and frisked after Robert in the direction of the kitchen.

* * *

Susan walked sullenly through the gate and towards the narrow road that led back to the village. She didn't understand Robert. He was, to put it mildly, a bit thick. She'd turned up in her best most revealing dress and made all the right noises, and he just didn't seem to realise that she wanted to take their relationship to the next level. She wondered if she'd need to resort to desperate measures. Almost at once, plans floated into her imagination – a feigned twisted ankle, and he'd have to hold her leg lovingly and apply a bandage. Or she could ask to see the goats, fall in the mud, and ask to use his shower. Perhaps he'd join her, James Bond style. And if not, she'd emerge in a fluffy towel that might accidentally slip.

Susan snorted. What did she have to do to get Robert to pay her any attention? She was suddenly troubled; he'd spent a long time showing Rosie-*The-Chronicle*-woman around his smallhold-ing. Perhaps she was weaselling a place in his heart? And Susan suspected Angie Pollock of doing the same, and the shy woman from Dawlish who'd spent the whole time at the gardening club simpering and blushing. Susan was suddenly resolute. Robert was hers. She just needed to up her game. She'd go home, watch *Love Island* on catch-up TV and hatch a plan.

Just then, she saw a silver Nissan Micra chugging past her,

slowing down, turning into Robert's drive. Susan followed the car's movement like an eagle observing prey. She'd noticed a confident-looking woman driver with a smooth pixie cut. Susan was shocked: no wonder Robert was so anxious to get rid of her – another one of his secret harem was arriving for a liaison.

Susan scuttled back to the gate and peered in, hiding behind the hedge, watching as the car slowed down and the woman slid out. She had nicely fitted jeans, leather boots; she was certainly bang on trend. Susan fidgeted with her low neckline and watched frantically as the door opened and Robert rushed out, his arms in the air, whirling the woman into an embrace, watching her reciprocate with equal gusto. To Susan's horror, Robert draped an arm around the woman and led her into his house. The woman hugged Robert's waist, leaning her head against his shoulder.

Susan was furious. 'Right, Robert,' she muttered beneath her breath. 'I'll show you who is the hottest totty in Millbrook. You just wait...'

* * *

'You didn't say you were coming.' Robert was delighted to see Hattie.

'I messaged. The journey was awful.'

'Oh, I'm just so glad to see you, Hat. Life has become a bit surreal recently and I'm hoping you can shed some light. But anyway, let's have supper, I'll open a bottle of elderflower champagne and you and I can set the world to rights.'

Hattie sat at the table in the kitchen. 'It's so nice to eat simply and calmly. You've no idea how refreshing it is to be here.'

Robert bustled in the larder. 'I have a three-cheese quiche with chives, watercress, rocket salad, fresh tomatoes, home-made sourdough.'

'Heaven.' Hattie sighed. 'Can I stay here for a few days?'

'Of course – why? What's wrong?' Robert sliced the quiche neatly.

'It's purgatory at home – Bunty's turned up in Bodicote with a new man.'

'She's left Sean? I thought they were good together.'

'And so did I. The new bloke, Jacko, is not good for Bunty. He's used to women running around after him.'

'So why did you leave them in your house?'

'If I'm not there to mediate, Bunty will soon see him for the lazy man he is and return to her senses.'

'I hope so. Poor Bunty. She's never been right since...' Robert placed a bowl of salad on the table, tomatoes that gleamed like rubies. Hattie felt herself begin to relax.

'This is just so – normal.'

'It's lovely to have you here. I've missed spending time with you.'

'Me too.' Hattie accepted the glass of sparkling elderflower. She took a sip. 'Mmm. Delicious. So, I'll tell you all about Bunty and the plumber from hell later. But first – how are you?'

'It's funny you should ask.' Robert lifted his fork. 'I'm a bit baffled, to tell you the truth.'

'Baffled? Why?'

'It's the gardening club.'

'What about the gardening club? Oh, this quiche is delicious.'

'Well – good – you see, lots of women have started to turn up to all the club meetings and they keep asking me for sexy jam and making remarks about my scones that I don't even want to repeat.'

Hattie burst out laughing. 'Oh, Robert, you've always been a bit of a heart-throb.'

'I haven't.' Robert was astonished. 'How do you know that?'

'I've seen it since you were a teenager, all sorts of girls and woman fawning over you, competing for your attention.'

'Why didn't you tell me?' Robert asked.

'I just thought you didn't like any of them,' Hattie said.

'I don't know if I do or not, Hattie – it's all a bit overwhelming.' Robert pierced a radish. 'There's Susan, who's attractive but – she frightens me, to tell you the truth, she's so flirtatious. Rosie's a reporter and isn't afraid to speak her mind, and Angie wears shorts so short I don't know where to look, and Jill hardly says a word but blushes all the time.'

'It sounds difficult,' Hattie said.

'The vicar tells me they have ulterior motives – they keep calling round here for scones and jam – and I can't get them to leave.'

Hattie continued to eat. 'Well, you *are* an exceptional baker.'

'I'm glad you're here – I need some sisterly advice.'

'Then I'm just in time.' Hattie grinned. 'Can I stay until Friday?'

'Stay as long as you like. You could stay until Sunday and meet Francis the vicar. You'd like the church in Millbrook – it's old and beautifully preserved. Have you been in there?'

'Once, years ago. Geoffrey was with me. He said the place was cold and godless. I remember a thirteenth-century building with an old tower and spire, and wooden pews and a glorious pipe organ. I'd have loved to have a go.'

'Francis's struggling to bring in numbers for his Sunday services. He asked me if I'd provide refreshments to coax a congregation in.'

Hattie held out her plate for a second slice of quiche. 'I can see why – your food is a crowd-pleaser.'

Robert was delighted. 'There's summer pudding with mixed berries for dessert.'

'Glorious.'

'Then we can sit in the conservatory,' Robert suggested, 'and listen to Puccini and put our feet up.'

Hattie closed her eyes. 'You've no idea how much I need this break, Robert. Thank you so much for letting me stay.'

'No, thank you,' Robert said, exhaling slowly. 'I really don't know what to do about all this interest from these well-meaning women. I think you might have arrived just in time to save me from a fate worse than death...'

13

On Monday morning, Bunty woke to the sound of a buzz saw. She opened her eyes. Jacko was lying beside her, hogging three quarters of the bed and all of the duvet, his face crumpled as he snored. He threw a heavy arm over her and mumbled something affectionate, although she wasn't sure if he'd said 'my deario' or 'Marion'. His breath smelled of onions. Bunty wriggled away, shrugging into Hattie's blue dressing gown, making for the bathroom, stepping over discarded clothes heaped at intervals like camel droppings. The hall was still littered with bits of broken boiler, oily rags, spanners and screwdrivers. Jacko had tried to fix the old boiler again yesterday, ranting at Hattie's tight-fistedness, not letting him replace it with a new one. There had been an argument – Bunty had stuck up for her sister and sulked, then Jacko had eventually apologised. Supper had been an awkward affair, conversation monosyllabic.

Bunty stood in the doorway of the bathroom. She needed a shower but there was no hot water. She sniffed her own skin and wrinkled her nose: she needed a long, perfumed bath. She thought briefly of Hattie, who'd texted last night to say she was staying with Robert in Devon and they had just shared a delicious summer pudding packed with fresh berries. The crackers and cheese she'd made for Jacko had been dull in comparison. Jacko had said he'd eat at the chippy tonight. Bunty wasn't looking forward to it.

She spotted a pair of Hattie's slippers, big grey fluffy things, and pushed her feet into them. She thought for a moment about what to do, then she slipped out of the front door and rapped at Glenys's. The weather was warm, but Bunty tugged the wrap around herself and shivered. Her legs were goose flesh. The door opened and Glenys stood in the gap, staring. 'Are you all right?'

'Yes.' Bunty took a breath. 'Look, I know it's a bit cheeky but – our hot water's not working and – I don't suppose I could have a bath?'

'Hattie's not home?' Glenys frowned. She'd noticed Hattie's car pull away yesterday. 'Well, I suppose you could have a shower. Bill got a new one put in last year. It's instant – and really scalding hot.'

'Oh, yes, please.' Bunty almost swooned at the thought. She was inside, glancing around Glenys's neat hall, the moss-green carpet, the photos of Glenys and Bill, of their children, the tidy rack of coats. Glenys was watching her.

'So, Bunty – what's your place like in Ireland? Cork, is it?'

'Oh, it's nowhere near as tidy as this,' Bunty said. 'We have an old Aga that doesn't work half the time, and a rickety staircase and cobwebs and dust – but it's home.' Bunty's words were out before she realised it and she felt more than a twinge of nostalgia. 'Well, it *was* home.'

'And where's home now?' Glenys asked pointedly. She seemed clearly a little put out by Bunty's request for a bath.

Bunty shrugged. 'I haven't made my mind up. Jacko's from

Plymouth but we can't exactly stay there because of his... you know who. Hattie's been so good to us.'

'She has.' Glenys folded her arms. 'Where is she now? I notice her car has gone...' Her face was suspicious, as if Bunty and Jacko might have bumped Hattie off and buried her in the garden.

'She's at Robert's – he's our brother. He's in Devon.'

'Why has she gone there?'

'For a break,' Bunty said guiltily. 'She's giving us some space.'

'And what did you say happened to your bath?'

'Jacko tried to fix the old boiler – well, it wasn't actually broken but – it is now.' Bunty shivered. 'We only have cold water.'

'What's this master plumber doing?' Glenys sniffed. 'Have you had breakfast?'

'He's still asleep and – no, I came straight here. I smell – not very pleasant,' Bunty said apologetically.

Glenys didn't disagree. 'Go on, you have a shower. It's down the hall on the left. Use the shower gel. It's toffee scented and it's lovely. Meanwhile, I'll put a couple of croissants in the oven and make a pot of coffee, shall I?'

Bunty looked as if she'd kiss her. 'Oh, Glenys, that's so kind.'

'Hattie's a good neighbour. I count her as a friend,' Glenys said by way of explanation. 'Go on, before you freeze to death.'

Bunty scuttled away gratefully, finding the room with the power shower, pressing the hot-water switch and staring at the steam rising in the cubicle as if it were a miracle. She dropped the dressing gown on the tiled floor, stepped into the heat and sighed – ahhh! – like the Bisto kid from the advert.

Forty minutes later, she was damp, swathed in Hattie's dressing gown, perched on a stool in Glenys's kitchen, nibbling a croissant and sipping sweet black coffee. She met Glenys's inquisitive gaze thankfully. 'This is the life. Thank you.'

'So,' Glenys asked with interest. 'How's the life next door?'

Bunty thought for a moment, then said, 'Not great.'

'Oh? I thought it was a new romance? Wasn't he Aquarius – a little unpredictable?'

Bunty shrugged uncomfortably. 'I rushed into it a bit. I thought he was exciting and fun and that he adored me.'

'And?' Glenys urged her to continue.

'I met him while he was on holiday with some friends from Plymouth. A boys' outing. He was in the pub where I was with Sean and we got talking and Sean was too busy chatting so we met up a couple of times in secret. When we left each other and he said he wanted us to be together for ever – he bought me this.' Bunty fingered the thin necklace with a tiny metal heart pendant. 'He told me it symbolised love.'

'Did he tell you about his wife?'

'He said they led separate lives and he was going to leave her anyway.' Bunty shook her head. 'I thought when he met me here it would be like a dream, we'd find our own place and—'

'What about your husband? Sean, is it?'

'He's texted me a few times. The last text...' Bunty's eyes shone with tears. 'The last text said that I can take all the time I need but he'll love me forever.'

Glenys's expression was one of an admonishing teacher. 'And Sean's what? Scorpio – passionate and faithful, like my Bill. We've been married for almost forty years, Bunty, and many's the time I wondered, is the grass greener elsewhere? But the answer comes back straight away. No, it isn't. Bill and I have been through thick and thin, we know each other, we care for each other.'

Bunty nodded.

'Is it like that for you and this Jacko?' Glenys asked.

Bunty shook her head.

'And is it like that for you and Sean?'

Bunty nodded slowly. 'What am I doing? Glenys, have I made an awful mistake?'

'What do you think?' Glenys said.

Bunty reached for another croissant. 'Sean treated me like a princess, when he wasn't obsessing with the horses. And he's funny and sweet. I thought Jacko was like that, but he seems to think women are servants and he was so rude about Hattie yesterday and I was really hurt. He called her an old battleaxe.'

Glenys clearly disapproved. 'That's awful. What did you say?'

'I told him he was ungrateful. Hattie had been kind to him, allowing him to stay in her bungalow as a guest and he'd meddled with the boiler and broken it. Then he said he was doing her a favour and she was a sour-faced witch, not like me, sweet and sexy, and I told him he was an intolerant narrow-minded chauvinist.'

Glenys said, 'Well done. What did he say to that?'

'He said they were big words from someone with a small brain and he'd take care of me forever if I trusted him, and that was my problem, I'd been treated so badly by my family and the men in my life that I had to start again from the beginning and learn how to love a real man.'

'So what did you say?'

'Well, I thought about it. I've been married three times. The first two times I was immature, I made bad choices. The third time, Sean was my rock. Then I fell into Jacko's arms because he promised me so much.'

'That he can't deliver?'

'Yes, you're right.' Bunty agreed. 'I'll give it a few more days.'

'Why?' Glenys asked.

'I promised Hattie—'

'The man's a misogynist,' Glenys said.

'I expect he's up and about now. He'll be wanting breakfast.

I'd better go back.' Bunty reached for her coffee and drank the last mouthful. 'Can I pop in tomorrow, Glenys? Just for a chat? It really helps – I feel stronger, talking to people like you and Hattie.'

'Things happen for us all at different times in our lives,' Glenys said philosophically. 'This may be your time to grow and learn, Bunty. It's never too late.'

'I hope so,' Bunty muttered. 'I think I might be seeing the light. It's taken me a long time…'

'Come in for a shower – and a croissant,' Glenys offered. 'About this time tomorrow. You can tell me how things are going with your Plymouth plumber.'

'I will,' Bunty said sadly. 'He's not a bad man. He's just made mistakes too. And I'm wondering if one of them wasn't leaving his wife.' She stood up, her face determined. 'I think I'll ask him straight. I think he misses her. Maybe he'll agree with me.'

'Maybe he will.' Glenys moved to the door, opening it for Bunty. 'Life teaches us every day. And do you know what I truly believe, Bunty?'

Bunty's eyes were round with new hope. 'What do you believe?'

Glenys smiled. 'Yesterday is not ours to recover, but tomorrow is ours to win or lose.'

'You're so right,' Bunty said, fingering the necklace. 'That's my new motto from now on. I'll keep it in mind.' Then she was gone into the brightness and Glenys stood in the doorway, shaking her head.

* * *

Hattie walked through syrupy sunshine towards the free-roaming chickens, carrying a shallow basket of grain. Robert was still in the kitchen, washing up breakfast dishes, making a batch of muffins, and Hattie was enjoying the quiet peace of wandering through daisies towards the chickens. She threw feed to them as they clustered around her ankles, smiling as a fluffy ginger one rushed between her feet. Hattie spoke soothingly. 'Hello – you must be Princess Lay-a. Robert said you'd be first in the corn queue.'

She let herself into the field and gazed over the hedgerows towards Millbrook. In the distance she could see the tall church spire, a group of houses nestling around the village green, trees and rolling farmlands beyond. It was a beautiful view that helped her be mindful, to realise that she could enjoy each moment, accepting the best that nature offered. She thought about what she'd do while she was in Devon. She'd enjoy the simple life on the smallholding; she'd help Robert in the garden and the kitchen. He seemed permanently busy making batches of treats, tending his vegetable patch and his fruit bushes. He certainly could use another pair of hands. She had ideas of her own too; she wanted to make a few bottles of mint lemonade, some wholemeal rolls, tomato soup with Robert's fresh basil.

She also wanted to explore the village. Robert had said there were houses dating back to medieval times, an old baker's shop now converted into the beautiful home where Eric and Edie Mallory lived, the charming manse with its tangled flower gardens, and a row of cottages opposite the pub that apparently dated back to George II. Hattie thought it might be nice to meet some of the villagers. Robert had mentioned some of them at supper last night, and they seemed a good crowd, even if one or two of the women were a little forward with Robert.

Shelley at The Pig and Pickle sounded lovely, as did George and Mary Tenby, whom Robert suggested they invite to dinner one night, and Dennis Lyons was apparently charming although he referred to himself as a grumpy git. Also, Robert said, Colin Bennett was a generous sort of bloke, Barry Butler was a shy but good-hearted man, a landscape painter, and Hattie would enjoy his stunning pictures of Dartmoor, the tors and the rocks.

Hattie was excited by Robert's plan to reorganise part of the garden area into an entertaining space. The idea of a pizza oven, a barbecue and a fire pit appealed to her. It would be fun to help him plan it.

She felt a gentle pressure against her leg and gazed down to find an old goat nuzzling her knees as a second one looked up hopefully. She found the carrots in her pocket and allowed the eager goats to munch from her fingers. She ruffled the hoary head of one of the goats and thought momentarily of Jacko. She hoped he wasn't ruining her home, taking more of her appliances to pieces. Most worrying was how Bunty was managing – not that she wasn't capable, but Hattie hoped Jacko wasn't bullying her into decisions she might later regret. Hattie wouldn't interfere, but she'd give her sister a call tomorrow, just to check. She retraced her footsteps back to the cottage. She'd make the lemonade now; there was fresh mint in the herb garden. It would be ready in time for lunch.

She noticed an athletic woman with curly hair bounding along the path towards the house, dressed in bright shorts. Robert stood at the door greeting her tentatively and Hattie noticed how close to him the woman positioned herself, how she caressed his shoulder. Robert took a step back, retreating anxiously into the house, returning with a pot of something that he handed to the woman, who seemed reluctant to leave. Hattie smiled. She'd better rescue Robert. He clearly needed a sister to save him from the constant devotion of all the gardening groupies.

14

Before Hattie reached the house, the woman in shorts jogged away. Robert was standing in the doorway, bemused. 'That was Angie Pollock from the village. She said my jam was luscious.' He couldn't understand it. 'She wanted to come in and watch me make a batch of scones but I said I was a bit busy and she said she'd be back.'

'That was sensible of you,' Hattie said. 'She looks nice enough. Don't you like her?'

'I don't like all this attention.' Robert was confused. 'Just before she left, Angie patted me on the arm and said something most odd...'

'What did she say?' Hattie covered a smile.

'I told her I was going to be busy, I intended to mow the lawns today and she said that she was sure I'd flattened some grass in my time.' He scratched his head. 'Whatever did she mean?'

'I've no idea.' Hattie thought that was the simplest reply. 'So while you're mowing, I might make some lemonade with some of your glorious mint, then I think I'll have a stroll into Millbrook. Why don't you come with me?'

'I could. Hattie, do you think all these ladies will give me a bit of space now you're here?'

'It might help, who knows?' Hattie said. 'It can't do any harm. Oh – look.' She pointed to a white van that was driving towards the house. 'You don't think this is your fan club, coming to sample your summer pudding?'

Robert was mystified. 'I'm not expecting anyone.'

They watched as the van came to a halt. The name on the side said Georgescu and Dunn, Builders. Two men clambered out in jeans and light shirts, one tall, the other shorter and much younger. The older, lean one held out a hand. 'Hello, I'm Danut and this is Joey. Rosie Eagle asked us to call in and we were passing, on the way to another job in Newton Abbot...'

'Did she?' Robert frowned. 'Why would she do that?'

'We're builders from Teignmouth,' Danut explained. 'We've done quite a lot of work on Rosie and Alex's property.'

'Who's Alex?' Robert asked.

'Alex Eagle, Rosie's husband.'

Robert looked around as if hoping for help. 'I didn't know she was married.'

'Oh, we've done several jobs for the Eagles – nice people – Joey and I have worked inside their house and outside. Recently, we rebuilt a patio area and put in paving, then we built an outdoor stone oven and a canopy. She asked us to pop in and do a quotation for you, so here we are.'

'Oh?' Robert wasn't sure what to say. 'That was nice of her.'

'Where would you like us to start?' Danut asked.

Hattie offered the builders a warm smile. 'I suppose a quotation would be useful. Shall we show them the space, Robert, you tell them what you want, and we can discuss it?'

'That's a good idea,' Robert said, beckoning Danut and Joey to follow him into the garden, past the vegetable patch to open

grass and a border of flowers. 'I want to make a place for entertaining.'

Danut nodded thoughtfully. 'It's a useful area, reasonable
space. We could do something quite impressive here. Tell me,
what would be the main reasons for using it? Parties? How many
people are we talking about roughly?'

'Fifteen people, perhaps twenty – I could do some cookery
demonstrations, invite the local gardening club, other people in
the village, do wine tastings and cream teas.'

'So, space for seating, a table or two, a small barbecue
maybe?' Danut asked.

'With a canopy for when the weather turns?' Joey added.

'And coloured lights.' Hattie clapped her hands. 'So that the
balmy afternoons could drift into warm evenings of music and
conversation.'

'It sounds delightful,' Robert said, imagining. 'Can you do
that?'

'We can do various versions of it, depending on what you
want the end product to look like.' Danut pulled out a booklet
from his jacket pocket. 'Let me take some notes and sketch some
designs.'

* * *

In the bungalow in Bodicote, Bunty was pushing the vacuum
cleaner along the hall carpet and into the bedrooms. Jacko's
clothes were rotating in the washing machine on the eco-wash.
She was determined to make Hattie's house gleam. She'd got up
early, had a shower, a coffee and croissant at Glenys's and had a
long chat about Sean and her old life in Ireland. She'd talked
enthusiastically about how she'd always been made to feel part of
the O'Connor family and the Ballycotton community; there was

Sean's brother, Niall, and his wife, Maeve, his sisters Biddy and Nora and their husbands, Bryan and Pat, all their children, the neighbours and friends. Her eyes had shone as she'd told Glenys that a Ballycotton party was really something to behold. Her time there was filled with fond memories, she admitted as she wiped a tear from her eye, but what upset her most was the thought that she'd never enjoy another evening around the piano in The Hole in the Wall, singing, arms around each other, that delicious warm feeling of belonging. She missed it, and it hurt her more than she realised.

Jacko was out for a drive in the van; he'd promised to bring back warm pies for lunch. He wanted to buy a copy of the *Mail* to keep up with the news. He'd grumbled that Oxfordshire was a dull, flat county and he'd hate to live there, then he'd disappeared, calling back that he'd bring her something sweet. She had a horrible feeling he was referring to himself.

She shoved the vacuum cleaner along, singing, skirting around the beautiful old piano near the window. She paused to pick up a framed photograph of herself, Hattie and Robert as children. Tears sprang to her eyes immediately, and she knew why. Things had changed beyond all she had hoped for. She'd been a confident child, indulged for her prettiness so much that she'd made the most of it. She was always Bunty, not Elizabeth, a childish name, a nickname that hinted at the ringlets and dimples. As she'd grown, men had found her cuteness appealing and she'd simply continued behaving the same way, always getting what she wanted. But that was the problem – she didn't know what she wanted. As soon as she had something she thought she'd craved more than life itself, its importance seemed to dwindle.

She replaced the photo and lifted the piano lid, touching the keys, listening to the harsh sound. She'd had no musical ability, although she could sing a bit and make people smile; Robert had shown an interest in the trumpet as a child, but Hattie had been the talented one, reaching grade eight piano. Their father had grumbled about the waste of money – she'd never be a concert pianist so what was the point? The days had long gone since musical skill attracted a husband. Harriet would be better off using her fingers to learn to type, he'd said with a grunt, puffing on his pipe.

Bunty turned away and glanced at the wall clock. It was almost twelve o'clock. Jacko would be back soon. Bunty wasn't sure she wanted a pie for lunch. She'd been reading Hattie's mindfulness magazine. Eating mindfully meant nourishing the physical and emotional senses, thoughtfully experiencing the food that gave strength and goodness. A pie wouldn't have been her first choice. Bunty needed to learn to live in the moment, to relish her life. She wasn't relishing her time with Jacko, if she was honest.

Her phone vibrated in her jeans pocket and she pulled it out to read a text. It was Sean – he'd messaged a lot when she left, but he hadn't messaged since Sunday morning and Bunty had been afraid to approach him first. She'd been hoping he'd call or message.

Then she read his words:

if it's space you want darlin then ill give it to you ill not stand in the way of what you want now - ive been an eejit to lose you i hope life treats you well bunt all my best love always sean

Bunty stared at the phone in horror. He'd decided to let her go. She reread the message with tears in her eyes, realising that separation was not what she wanted. She hoped he'd give her his attention, beg her to come back with declarations of everlasting love and the promise that he'd stay away from the horses and devote himself to her for ever.

She'd been a fool.

She typed:

I love you sean

and the words blurred through her tears. She wondered if she should send it or if she should wait. If only Hattie were here to advise her. Then she heard the front door click and a voice called, 'Grab some plates, Bunty, and bring them in here, quick. I've got pies and chips and a few beers. There's snooker on TV this afternoon. I thought we'd have a session.'

Bunty's heart sank. Pies and chips and snooker weren't her idea of mindfulness; she'd be bored beyond belief. The message was unsent. She pushed the phone into her pocket, let the vacuum cleaner nozzle slip from her hand and slunk to the kitchen like a chastised cat, passing Jacko in the hall with a plastic bag in his hands and a newspaper under his arm. He barely acknowledged her as he eagerly hurried to the living room. She found plates, beer glasses, wiped her eyes on her sleeve, and she took a breath.

'Coming, Jacko,' she called, making her voice cheerful, but she could already hear the buzz of the television. The cloying smell of chips clung to the air. She carried the tray into the living room where Jacko was already engrossed, his eyes on the screen, his feet up on the sofa, tucking into chips in paper and swigging ale from the can.

* * *

Hattie poured sparkling lemonade, laced with fresh mint, into two glasses and served herself salad. She beamed at Robert. 'This lettuce was in the ground half an hour ago. I wonder what Bunty's having.'

Robert sliced bread. 'Poor Bunty. Her new man sounds awful.'

'Jacko's having a mid-life crisis,' Hattie said sympathetically. 'I don't think he's a bad person – he's just unhappy and selfish. He's a bull in a china shop.'

'He should go back to his wife and Bunty should talk to Sean.' Robert shook his head. 'I hope she sees the light.'

'I hope they aren't wrecking my bungalow.' Hattie thought about her precious piano. She wished Robert had one. She'd like to practise. She watched her brother slicing tomatoes and smiled fondly. 'It was nice to hear Danut and Joey's ideas for an outdoor area.'

Robert looked up mistily. 'A sleek fire pit, a canopy, seating areas – blooms everywhere, lavender plants, outdoor lighting. I have to say, I could imagine it all.'

'Can you afford it?' Hattie asked.

'It depends on what Danut quotes – he said he'd cost it all out and email me. But imagine, Hattie, how much fun we could have.'

'We?' Hattie grinned. 'I'm going back home in a few days.'

He leaned across the table. 'But you'd come down more often? You'd stay for long weekends and we'd have barbecues and parties and – oh, we'd have such fun.'

'I don't see why not,' Hattie said. 'It doesn't take too long to get here, although the traffic was awful.'

'Oxfordshire's miles from the ocean,' Robert said. 'We could go into Dawlish later, walk on the seafront, eat chips.'

Hattie agreed. 'That sounds good. The bite of the breeze, the whisper of the sea, the salt and vinegar tang of a too-hot chip held in the fingers. Delicious.'

'We'll go later,' Robert said excitedly. 'Make an evening of it.'

'Wonderful!' Hattie said.

'I want to get the garden mowed and the weeding done after lunch,' Robert mused.

Hattie forked a nasturtium leaf and allowed the peppery flavour to explode on her tongue. 'This afternoon I'm going to walk into Millbrook, maybe pop in the little shop for a few treats and enjoy the stroll in the sunshine.'

'Perfect.' Robert grinned and Hattie thought he looked more relaxed than he had when she'd arrived. He caught her eye. 'I do like having you to stay. I'm not sure I'll let you go on Friday.' He winked, helped himself to more lemonade and went back to buttering bread.

15

Hattie ambled into Millbrook, past the old row of cottages with hanging baskets, past The Pig and Pickle, past St Jude's church and Millbrook County Primary. She watched for a moment as children screamed and ran around the playground. In the far corner, a little girl stood alone, watching everyone else. Hattie remembered her own childhood. That would have been her, watching, wondering how to join in. Hattie continued on towards the post office and went inside, gazing at postcards of Dawlish seafront, a train curving around the coast, the ocean rolling in, the rocky coastline. She was looking forward to walking to the seafront this evening with Robert.

She chose two postcards – she'd send one to Bunty and one to Glenys. Hattie bought stamps at the counter, withdrew some money, and selected a pretty notebook and a pen in case she wanted to write anything down.

On the way back, Hattie paused by St Jude's church, gazing beyond the stone wall. It was clearly an old building, also stone built, with its high tower and crenellated turrets and the arched windows. The church door was ajar, inviting newcomers. The churchyard was well kept, the grass neatly mown. Many gravestones were sunken, leaning at angles like misshapen teeth; many more were crusted with lichen, the names and dates on the engraving invisible.

Across the road was the old manse, the gate ajar, the garden crammed with wild flowers. Loud music came from the bedroom window upstairs. Hattie stopped to listen; there was a frantic drumbeat, a whining guitar, a thrumming loud bass and then a female voice singing wildly.

'*My father's a bragger,*
My mother's a nagger
I'll stop their talk
With a rusty dagger...'

Hattie covered a smile. The music stopped abruptly and there was a moment's quiet, then the same riff began, the same words, louder and faster. Hattie raised an eyebrow.

A woman in a spotted dress walked across the road to stand next to her. She was probably the same age as Hattie. She arranged her face in an expression of displeasure and indicated the music in the manse with a nod of her head. 'That's Tilda Baxter, the vicar's daughter...'

'Ah.' Hattie didn't know how to reply.

'She's eighteen. Her punk-rock band is called Armpit.'

'Oh, that's nice.' Hattie turned to the open window where Tilda was repeating the verse about annihilating her parents with even more gusto. She said, 'Tilda's very good.'

The woman looked surprised. 'Is she?'

'Tuneful voice, strong, lots of self-belief,' Hattie observed.

The woman examined Hattie's face to see if she was joking. She found no humour there, so she said, 'I'm Mary Tenby. My husband George and I have lived in Millbrook for years. Are you visiting or are you new to the area? I saw you looking at our beautiful church.'

'I'm just staying in the smallholding for a few days with Robert.'

'Oh?'

Hattie held out a hand. 'I'm Harriet, but please call me Hattie.'

Mary looked very pleased with her new information as she shook Hattie's hand in both of hers. 'So, Robert has a guest? How are you finding it at the smallholding?'

'It's lovely,' Hattie said.

'And so is Robert.' Mary smiled. 'I shouldn't say – I'm a married woman and George thinks I'm mad as it is – but Robert is quite a hit with the local ladies.'

'Is he?'

'Oh yes – he's an incredible cook, you know. He brings treats to the gardening club. The pavlova he brought was to die for. But his scones – oh, Hattie – get him to make some for you, with his strawberry jam and clotted cream. We had a reporter at the last club meeting at the pub – Rosemary something from *The Teignmouth Chronicle* – and she was very taken with him. She's writing an article – it will be out tomorrow. We're all looking forward to reading what she had to say – and she took lots of photos of us.'

'I can't wait to see it,' Hattie said.

'Well, it's nice that you're staying here for a few days. Where are you from?'

'Oxfordshire,' Hattie began.

'Didn't Robert live near there as a boy? I can't remember. Are you an old friend?' Mary winked. 'Well, you'll have a lovely time at Robert's – we have the weather for it. We had a lot of rain a week or so ago but it seems to have perked up and remembered it's summer.' Mary didn't stop for breath so Hattie had no time to enlighten her that she and Robert were siblings. Mary indicated the church. 'St Jude's is quite special. I'm a regular churchgoer, one of Francis's flock, so I know the church like the back of my hand. Do you want a tour?'

'Oh – that's so kind,' Hattie said. 'I don't want to be a nuisance.'

'Not at all. I'd only be home arranging the flowers or feeding the fish. Follow me.' Mary flourished an arm. 'Let's go inside. It will be cooler in there.'

Mary led the way through the entrance in the stone wall and up to the church door, tugging the metal handle, scraping the uneven step. Hattie crept inside; the air was cold, the ceilings high. She gazed at the rows of wooden pews, the tiled floor, the arched windows filled with stained glass, gorgeous colours. Then she noticed a wooden organ and she gasped. 'Oh, how beautiful.'

'It is,' Mary agreed. 'Francis's wife, Sally, usually plays it on a Sunday for the hymns. She's not happy doing it, she has no real talent, but we've no other musicians in our congregation.'

'Do you think I could – have a go?' Hattie stepped up to the organ and sat down on the stool, touching the stops with her fingers, pressing lightly on the keys. 'Would it be all right?'

'Oh, I don't know.' Mary tutted. 'It's not a toy. I mean – there are all these pipes. You have to be an expert to play it. And it's incredibly difficult to master – it takes years.'

'Oh, I played one a long time ago. I practised a bit in a church as a teenager.' Hattie pressed a switch, and there was an eerie hissing sound. Then she pushed buttons, and began to touch her feet against the pedalboard. She moved her fingers lightly across the keys and echoing notes suddenly filled the church. Mary frowned as Hattie played the introduction to Cat Stevens' version of the hymn 'Morning Has Broken', the beautiful piano piece played by Rick Wakeman. The music echoed around the church, soaring to the rafters, resonating against the walls. Then Hattie stopped and there was silence.

Mary looked at her, amazed. 'That was just incredible. Do you know anything else?'

'I have one or two tunes in my repertoire.' Hattie stretched her fingers and launched into 'Joyful, Joyful, We Adore Thee' followed by 'When I Survey the Wondrous Cross'. The air in the church vibrated with pure sounds of devotion. Mary was listening, open-mouthed. Hattie played 'Amazing Grace' simply because she could. She was just warming up; the organ gave out a rich, magnificent tone, the timbre of angelic trumpets. Hattie saw the delight on Mary's flushed face, so she carried on. She whizzed through Procul Harum's 'A Whiter Shade of Pale' and then banged out Ray Manzarek's jazzy keyboard introduction to The Doors' 'Light my Fire'.

When Hattie stopped, she heard light clapping and she whirled round to see a slim man with an amazed expression and a slimmer teenage girl dressed in black, with dark tresses shaved at the sides. They were both applauding.

Hattie stood up, all apologies. 'Oh – I didn't mean to intrude.'

Francis Baxter held out a hand, smiling warmly. 'Not at all. I'm Francis, the vicar, and this is my daughter, Tilda. That was truly incredible. All the hymns and a few keyboard solos, played just how the Lord intended them to be played, with devotion.'

'I'm Hattie.' Hattie shook his hand. 'I can do Chopin, Beethoven... Emerson, Lake & Palmer,' she offered, almost as an excuse.

'Cool.' Tilda Baxter ruffled her hair. 'Loved the last one you played – that funky stuff.'

'Hattie's here for a while, with Robert at the smallholding,' Mary explained.

'Oh, really?' Francis was interested. 'Are you staying long?'

'Until Friday,' Hattie said.

'Oh, that's a shame. I'd invite you to play here on Saturday. Jennie Ward is having her baby christened, little Max is six months old, and I'm sure she'd have loved some music during the service.'

'Oh, well, I'm sorry,' Hattie said.

'Can I invite you back to the manse? Tea and biscuits?' Francis offered warmly.

'I'd better get back to Robert.' Hattie still felt awkward, having been discovered belting out music on the vicar's old pipe organ without asking.

Mary butted in. 'I'm sure what Robert has to offer is much tastier.'

'We're going into Dawlish for chips,' Hattie said.

'Pure decadence.' Francis gave an indulgent smile.

'Can we have chips?' Tilda asked.

'We'd better let Hattie go back – we don't want Robert worrying where she is,' Francis told his daughter.

Hattie was glad of the excuse to mutter a quick, 'Well, nice to have met you all,' before she fled through the open church door into the sunshine and down the road, her heart thumping and her fingers tingling with the excitement of having played for an audience, of sorts. The organ had rumbled, the music had risen like a prayer, and she had been caught in the majesty of it all.

It had been wonderful and she had loved every moment.

* * *

Bunty was not enjoying watching the snooker with Jacko. Two greasy plates had been abandoned on the floor, covered with residual smears of ketchup, chips and gravy, and six beer cans had been emptied and crushed on top. Bunty had drunk one, making it last; Jacko had guzzled the other five in quick succession as he'd watched the snooker frame by frame. They'd hardly spoken. Bunty wondered what they'd do this evening. She thought that she might cook some soup from scratch, but there was nothing in the fridge except for an old piece of cheese and a yogurt. She folded her arms and snuggled down into the hug of the armchair. There was no room for her on the sofa; Jacko had his feet up and his socks off.

Then his phone played the Crazy Frog ringtone, and Jacko snatched it from his pocket and leaped up as if scorched. 'Oh, hello, love,' he muttered and indicated wild-eyed to Bunty that he'd take the phone call outside. She heard his voice in the hall. 'Yes, I'm still in Axminster – the bathroom installation job is a bit harder than I thought...'

Bunty picked up the remote and turned the sound down, straining her ears to listen. Jacko was talking in a hushed voice, wheedling. 'The thing is, Marion, it's not quite the plumbing job I thought it was, too many complications, no, it won't pay well. I'm sorry I even came – well, I'll be home soon, yes, I promise – oh, no, before then, I hope. I know it must be horrible sleeping alone. Oh, yes – me too, of course. Not much longer, eh – Mr Lover Lover will be back with his little foxy lady before you know it.'

Bunty turned the sound back on, louder, watching the screen, a man bending over a snooker table potting a pink ball. She wasn't really interested in the game; she didn't understand the rules. Ah, wasn't that the truth about life? She could still hear Jacko pleading and cajoling from the hall, the rise and fall of his voice, stilted laughter. Poor Marion, Bunty thought. She was welcome to Jacko. He probably still loved her, he'd probably never stopped, despite his protestations to the contrary. She'd let him go back. Bunty would find the right moment to tell him later.

It wasn't working; she'd made the mistake of her life. And, Bunty thought grimly as she picked up greasy plates, balled chip papers and empty beer cans, the sooner, the better. It was time to put things right.

16

Hattie and Robert walked arm in arm along the sea wall in Dawlish. A train shuddered by, clattering noisily against the tracks before it disappeared into the distance, leaving behind the sound of whispering waves, the open view to Exmouth across the Exe estuary.

'We could walk as far as the Warren,' Robert suggested. 'It's about thirty minutes from here. The sand is soft and we have good shoes.'

'Can we buy chips on the way?' Hattie asked. She squeezed his arm. 'We came here once when we were kids, remember? Dad and Mum rented a caravan near Dawlish Warren for a week. I recognise the view from here – nothing has changed.'

'It was in the fifties.' Robert's eyes misted. 'I remember they took us for a cream tea. And we played tennis on a tarmac court and I grazed my knee.'

'Bunty fell in love with a boy from Birmingham who was staying in one of the other caravans. She cried all the way back to Banbury and said she'd write to him every day. Of course, she'd forgotten about him by the time we'd unpacked.' Hattie gave a half-laugh. 'I wonder how she's getting on with Jacko.'

'You were right to leave them to their own devices – we can ring her tomorrow, check she's all right.' Robert seemed lost in his own thoughts.

'Are you still thinking about the quotation for the patio?' Hattie asked gently.

'Yes,' Robert said. 'I might accept it. Danut emailed me earlier – that's very efficient of him. And his estimate was competitive.'

'How do you know it's competitive? Shouldn't you get another quote for comparison? And how do you know they are any good?' Hattie asked. 'Perhaps they have no other customers.'

'I looked at their website. It's all five stars.'

Hattie was unconvinced. 'Maybe their relatives write all their reviews.' She wondered if she sounded like Geoffrey, cynical, sour.

'But Rosie Eagle recommended them.' Robert looked hopeful. 'And Danut said he and Joey could make a start next week – they had another job fall through. I could have it all done for August.'

'That would be nice,' Hattie agreed. '*The Chronicle* is out tomorrow – there's an article on you.'

'On the gardening club,' Robert insisted.

'But Rosie came to visit you in particular.'

'Mmm.' Robert knitted his brows. 'I was a bit mystified about why she came round to the house. She was very keen to see the pantry and the goats, which are nothing to do with the gardening group.'

'We'll get a copy of the paper first thing. I can't wait to see what she's written,' Hattie said. 'And you should have a think about the builders' estimate overnight. If you're still sure tomorrow, you can give them a ring.'

Robert gazed into the distance, across the blue curve of the bay, beyond rows of cream and pink cottages, the frothing ocean. For a moment, he was lost in dreams. 'It's strange how life turns out, isn't it, Hat?'

'It is.' She clutched his arm protectively. 'What are you thinking about, Robert?'

'I came to live here – I took a chance leaving Bodicote. I can express myself here – in the garden, the kitchen. And I love being part of the gardening club – they respect me.'

'I'm sure they do.' Hattie gazed into the distance. 'I miss you though.'

'I miss you too. I don't know how you could have stayed with Geoffrey for all those years. He wasn't a nice man. I used to listen to how he spoke to you, so judgemental. Do you know, once or twice, I could have punched him in the nose.'

'I wish you had,' Hattie said. 'Actually, I wish I'd punched him – although I've never been a believer in violence.'

'Nor have I,' Robert muttered.

'Perhaps we're allowed one mistake in life,' Hattie mused. 'Mine lasted forty-nine years. But I'm moving forward now.' She took a breath. 'Bunty's made a few mistakes, but I think Jacko is her worst.'

'My biggest mistake was being too introspective. I never looked outside myself to see if anyone else was looking. I just assumed they weren't, you know, because I was a bit boring. I didn't think I could possibly be – attractive or loveable.'

'It's never too late,' Hattie teased. 'You'd make someone a lovely companion. They'd never want for scones or jam. And from what I hear, the gardening club women are queueing up.'

Robert looked sad. 'I'd like to be loved for me, though, not my baking. I wonder if anyone will ever look beyond the scones and see me for the man I am.'

Hattie felt suddenly protective. 'Oh, Robert. You're a

wonderful man. And I'm so proud of you, living the life you want, with your animals, garden, hobbies – and now a new entertaining area. People in the village like you. You have friends. I have nobody except for a few ladies at yoga and Glenys next door, who's lovely but – I'm on my own a lot.'

'Me too. I've got used to my own company,' Robert admitted. 'Do you think we've wasted our lives, Hattie?'

'No, not at all. We aren't dead yet. I've lived through a whole marriage hating each day. But I'm trying to change.'

'Oh, I try to enjoy each new challenge, all the time,' Robert said. 'As I whip egg whites for a pavlova or stir jam or stroke Isaac Mewton's fur or collect one of Princess Lay-a's eggs, I remind myself how lucky I am.'

'So do I now.' Hattie's eyes swept across the sandy beach, the steel-grey ocean, the stretch of the Warren ahead. 'Life is a treasure, and we'll help ourselves to the riches.'

'We're like pirates.' Robert grinned. 'It may have taken us until our mid-seventies to realise it, but I think we have found what we were looking for – happiness, peace, belief in ourselves.'

'And chips?' Hattie suggested. 'I'm starving. Let's go and buy ourselves a fish supper and we can be mindful about each salty bite.'

Robert met her eyes. 'I'm glad you came to stay, Hattie. It's good to share time with you. I don't think I ever realised what a wonderful sister I had...'

'I don't think I really knew myself,' Hattie muttered. 'Right, there's a chip shop ahead. What's it to be? Cod?'

'I have this thing about mushy peas,' Robert admitted quietly. 'I might push the boat out – since I'm going to be living in the moment from now on – and get myself two portions.'

* * *

The following morning was a drizzly Tuesday. The greasy smell of chip paper still clung to the air as Bunty rushed to the door in Hattie's dressing gown, which was now a little grubby. Someone had been knocking for several minutes, and Jacko was fast asleep. The wall clock said it was well past ten. Bunty opened the door and stared through the crack at a man with spiky hair and a wide smile. She was confused. 'Hello?'

'You must be Hattie's sister? She said you'd be here to let me in.' The man's expression was confident, as if Bunty ought to know him. 'Graeme Towler.' He pointed a thumb at Jacko's van, parked next to his. 'Unless you've already got another plumber on the job?'

'Oh – oh, no.' Bunty realised who she was talking to. She tugged the dressing gown across her chest. 'Hattie said you were coming. Are you going to fix the... the broken boiler?'

'I've done her a deal on a new combi boiler. Apparently the old one can't be repaired.' He winked. 'I'll just get my stuff out the van. Any chance of a cup of tea? Milk, one sugar?'

'Oh, yes, I – I'll leave the door open and – be with you directly.' Bunty scuttled to the bedroom, tugging on clothes, Hattie's slippers. She muttered to a stirring Jacko, 'The plumber's here.'

Jacko mumbled something that might have been an expletive and rolled over. Bunty was on her way to the kitchen. Graeme Towler was already kneeling in the hall, his bag at his feet. Bunty busied herself with the kettle, a mug for her and one for the plumber. She thought again – she'd get Jacko one too.

She carried a mug of steaming tea into the hall just as Jacko emerged from the bedroom, his hair tangled, his eyes half closed and bleary. He was wearing an unbuttoned shirt and boxers, stumbling into the bathroom, turning on taps. As she handed the mug to Graeme Towler, Bunty heard Jacko yell, 'I forgot – there's no bloody hot water.'

'There will be by the end of the day.' Graeme grinned. He spoke to Bunty. 'I've been doing the plumbing jobs in Hattie's house for years, back to when I was an apprentice and she was married to the grumpy man who was always reading his newspaper. I like Hattie. She's a good sort.' He went back to working on the boiler, his face puzzled. 'I don't know who she got to work on this boiler, though. It's been bodged. A complete amateur.'

'Mmm.' Bunty passed him the mug of tea just as Jacko ambled past on bare feet, scowling.

'It's nothing I can't sort.' Graeme waved a spanner. 'But I've never seen anything like it – the bloke who broke this was ham-fisted. You used to get a lot of cowboys in the profession once, but I thought they'd all retired. We're all on the Gas Safe Register now. I've no idea how this numpty ever got a job.'

Jacko wandered back towards the kitchen, still half dressed. 'Any chance of some fried eggs?'

'We're out of eggs and bread – you need to go to the supermarket,' Bunty called back.

'This new boiler will be easy to fit.' Graeme was busy with his spanner and blowtorch. 'It's a straightforward job for someone who knows what he's doing.'

Bunty watched him work for a moment, deft hands, calm movements. She asked, 'How long have you been – plumbing?'

'Twenty years, man and boy,' Graeme said. 'I've never seen anything as bad as this though. I've no idea how that part came to be broken. It's twisted. It must have been wrenched off by a bungler. Never mind, you'll have a lovely new boiler and hot water by teatime, I should think.'

'Oh, thank you,' Bunty was delighted. 'Well, I'll hang on for my bath.'

'You'll notice the difference, too.' Graeme said. 'Cheaper bills, better water flow, more efficient.'

'Ahhh.' Bunty was not sure what to say or do next. She thought about vacuuming the living room again or collecting some clothes for the washing machine. She gazed at the bedroom, where Jacko was. He was making a lot of noise, moving around, grumbling. She didn't feel inclined to go in there and talk to him. She opted for the kitchen.

She opened cupboards, but there was nothing much to eat. Some flour, some sugar, a packet of chocolate biscuits. She looked in the fridge; there was a piece of cheese, a yogurt. She'd eat the yogurt. Or perhaps she'd go next door to see Glenys. There would be a cup of coffee with her name on it. And she could do with a chat to someone who was sympathetic. Bunty opened the lid of the yogurt and stuck in her spoon. It was plain, bitter, no fruit.

Then Jacko was standing in the kitchen, wearing his jacket, clutching a holdall. He put it on the ground and shuffled his feet. 'Er, Bunty.' His face was miserable; Bunty recalled one of Sean's expressions, a face like a smacked bum. That was exactly how Jacko looked. 'I don't suppose you could lend me some money?'

'No, I haven't got any.' Bunty held out her hands as if to prove it. 'Are you going to the supermarket?'

Jacko looked at the ceiling for an answer, then at his boots. 'What about your sister?'

'What about Hattie?'

'Has she got any?'

'Any what?'

'Money? Does she keep any loose in the house? A piggy bank? That sort of thing? Loose cash?'

Bunty was almost lost for words. 'You want to take Hattie's money?'

'The thing is – I'm off now – and I'm a bit skint.'

'Off?' Bunty was confused.

'I need to buy petrol – and food.'

'Off?' Bunty said. The penny had dropped. 'As in off back to Plymouth?'

'Er – I think so, yes.' Jacko moved his feet in a little dance. 'It's for the best.'

Bunty waited to feel upset, but the first feeling she registered was relief. 'Back to Marion?'

'I'm sorry,' Jacko said, but he wasn't.

Nor was Bunty. 'Ah – right – well.'

'It isn't working.' He tried a hang-dog face.

'It isn't.' Bunty stood up straight. 'No, I don't have any money. And I'm not letting you look round the bungalow for any of Hattie's.'

'I don't suppose—' Jacko pulled a face, '—the plumber in there might lend you a few quid?'

'No,' Bunty replied. She liked the sound of her voice, stronger, in charge. She folded her arms. 'You'll be able to get back home somehow, I'm sure.'

'Do you have anything to eat?' Jacko tried.

Bunty remembered the chocolate biscuits in the cupboard. She plucked them from the shelf and pushed them into his hand. 'Have these.' Immediately, she wondered what she'd eat herself.

'Right, well, that's it, I suppose, then.' Jacko looked at the door, his means of escape.

Bunty stared at him. She wasn't about to make it easier by saying something kind to offer closure. She opted to say nothing.

'So I'll say...' Jacko ummed and ahhed. 'Goodbye, Bunty and – and I'm sorry it didn't work but – it was nice while it lasted.'

'It was a mistake, Jacko. Our brief mistake. That's all.' Bunty narrowed her eyes. She felt some new strength fill her lungs. 'Now off you toddle back home and hug Marion and tell her how you missed her. And tell her that the bathroom installation in Axminster came to nothing.'

Jacko was alarmed. 'You don't have her number, do you?'

'No. I wouldn't do anything like that anyway.' Bunty shook her head. 'But you need to treat her with respect in the future. You go home, Jacko. Chalk it up to experience. And I'll do the same.'

'I will,' Jacko said, shifting awkwardly. For a moment he looked as if he'd kiss her cheek. He thought better of it and plunged towards the door in a quick movement, closing it crisply. Bunty listened; she could hear the low chug of his van, the acceleration of his engine as he pulled away. Then he was gone.

Bunty asked herself how she felt and the answer came immediately. Hungry. And foolish. She had been extremely foolish, and she was a long way from home with no idea what to do next.

She thought about rushing next door, begging Glenys for advice. Or she could ring Hattie, burst into tears, and ask her for sympathy and help. She wished she could ring Sean and say how sorry she was, but she had burned that bridge. She didn't deserve him. Besides, she couldn't slink back to Ballycotton with her tail between her legs and admit how stupid she'd been. She felt too embarrassed.

She heard Graeme Towler murmur from the hall. 'I'll be all done by the end of the day. You'll have plenty of hot water then.'

Bunty nodded. She wondered if she was all done too. And in hot water. She called back, 'I'll get the kettle on. You deserve another cuppa.'

Bunty stood in the kitchen and for the first time in her life, she realised she was on her own. A tear slithered down her cheek, then a second. But it was not because Jacko had left. The house felt calmer without him already. It was because she was ashamed of what she'd done, of who she was. She'd left Sean and he'd given her his blessing, told her to follow her heart. She didn't deserve him, not while she was so fickle, so weak. She'd been immature for too long, depending on others, and now life had presented her with an opportunity to step up. She'd seize it with both hands. She'd become a person who stood on her own two feet. One who deserved respect.

The problem was, Bunty had depended on everyone else for seventy years – she hadn't a clue where to start.

17

'Robert, look.' Hattie stood outside the post office, staring at *The Teignmouth Chronicle*, opened at the middle page. 'There's a picture of you and the gardening group. And another of you standing in the field with the goats.'

He stood at her shoulder and read the headline. '*Millbrook Man Leaves No Scone Unturned.* Article by Rosie Eagle, Community Reporter.' He frowned. 'What does she mean by that, No Scone Unturned? Is it supposed to be a pun or a misprint?'

'I'll read it to you,' Hattie said eagerly. 'She says, "*Members of the Millbrook Gardening Club don't just meet every so often for advice about weeds and aphids and blight on fruit bushes from local expert, Robert Parkin. They congregate around the table to sample his delicious baking. Local smallholder Robert is something of a celebrity, due to his incredible skills in the kitchen. Not only does he make mouth-watering jams, sponge cakes and meringues, but he is developing a reputation as something of a scone king. Former medical receptionist and gardening club secretary Susan Joyce says, 'Robert's scones are second to none. I believe he makes the most delicious scones in the south-west.' And the proof, apparently, is in the eating...*"'

'Really?' Robert scratched his head. 'That's a bit of a strange accolade.'

'She goes on. "*So,* The Chronicle *wants to know. Are there any better scones than Robert's anywhere in the south-west? Millbrook Gardening Club think not. Do you know of anyone whose scones are more scrumptious and crumblier than Robert's? If so, Rosie Eagle would like to hear from you.*"'

'She didn't tell me she was going to write that,' Robert said uneasily. 'What if she starts a scone war?'

Hattie chuckled. 'It won't come to that. You'll just be asked to send a few recipes in, I suppose. Look – she's written more – "*Robert believes variety is the spice of life – he bakes vanilla scones, lemon scones, matcha and almond scones. He turns out batches of Marmite scones with chives, and limoncello and blackcurrant, watercress and tomato with cheese. Is there no end to his talents?*"'

'Crikey.' Robert gasped.

'"*But, according to the members of the Millbrook community, there's nothing better than the taste of his fruit scones smothered with jam and cream. Mind you, Robert is a strict believer in the Devon scone – cream first. Are there any Cornish bakers out there who would like to add their ten penn'orth?*"'

'I never said anything about that,' Robert began.

'She's quoted you,' Hattie replied. '"*Robert said, 'I don't hold with this jam-first nonsense like they have in Cornwall.'*"'

'I said nothing of the sort.' Robert was horrified.

'Well, that's given me an appetite.' Hattie grinned. 'I haven't sampled a scone since I've been here. What do you say, we'll go home and make a cream tea for this afternoon?'

'We could bake a batch together.' Robert folded the newspaper and pushed it under his arm. 'We could try something new – I've always wanted to make fresh raspberry and white chocolate scones. What do you think?'

'The raspberries are still fresh on the bush.' Hattie linked her arm through his. 'I think that would be a great way to spend the morning...'

An hour later, 'Che gelida manina' from Puccini's *La Bohème* was blasting through the smart speaker while Robert added a glug of fizzy lemonade to his batter. 'It makes the scones lighter,' he told Hattie proudly. 'Cream makes them richer and arranging your scones side by side, just touching one another, helps them rise evenly, and higher.' He patted her arm. 'Have you washed the raspberries? I'm ready to stir them in.'

Hattie watched carefully while Robert went about his work. He cut the dough in triangles, explaining that, a bit later on, she could melt white chocolate to drizzle over the scones when they were cool. Then he popped them in the oven and they sat down together at the table with a cup of tea.

'I'm going to make pumpkin scones in the autumn,' Robert said. 'With ginger and mixed spice.'

'You could serve them on your new patio on bonfire night,' Hattie exclaimed. 'That would be lovely for the community.'

'Oh, not a bonfire and fireworks though – I have Isaac to think of, and the animals.'

On cue, Isaac Mewton bounded into the kitchen and sprang on Hattie's knee. Robert smiled. 'She has no loyalty – she loves you now.'

'She slept on my bed last night.'

'By the way—' Robert looked momentarily guilty '—I rang Georgescu and Dunn earlier and accepted their quote – I asked them when they can start. They'll be round here the day after tomorrow.'

'That's wonderful.'

'You don't think I should have got a second quote?' Robert asked. 'I'm just so excited about getting the work done.'

'Of course.' Hattie was about to reach for her tea when her phone buzzed on the table. She picked it up. 'Oh, it's a text from Bunty. She says the water will be back on in the bungalow later and she's looking forward to a hot bath. I'll go online and pay Graeme when he invoices me.'

'That's good.'

'And Jacko's gone.'

'Is that good?'

'Bunty thinks so.' Hattie read the message again. 'She wants to stop on at the bungalow for a bit to get her bearings. She hasn't told Sean that she's kicked Jacko out – I don't even know if Sean's aware that she had a fling with him – she hasn't said – but she's not ready to go home. She can stay as long as she likes. I'll head back in a few days.'

'It'll be good for her, having her own space for a while.' Robert frowned. 'Is she all right?'

'She says she's never felt better.' Hattie thumbed a message. 'I've told her to make herself at home. She can even have my appointment at the beautician's for a hot stones massage.'

'Hot scones?' Robert put a hand to his ear. 'Yes, they should be rising nicely – I'll check them in a moment.'

There was a hammering at the front door. Hattie leaped up. 'I'll go.' Isaac Mewton sprang from her knee and followed her.

Robert bent over, his hands in oven gloves, and eased two trays of triangular scones from the heat. Steam and the heavenly aroma of baking swirled around his head. He touched a scone with a fingertip and muttered, 'Not long now...' before returning them lovingly to the oven.

Then Hattie appeared in the kitchen, a line of people following her, all smiling. Francis Baxter led the way, holding a copy of *The Chronicle* in the air. Behind him, Susan Joyce scurried in, closely followed by Angie Pollock, Mary Tenby and her husband George wearing a trilby hat. Hattie threw out a hand, almost in apology. 'Robert – you had a queue at the door.'

Robert turned, his face surprised. 'Hello. How can I help?'

Francis brandished the newspaper. 'I've just read this article by Rosemary Eagle, and I was on my way down here to congratulate you when I bumped into Susan, then Angie, then George and Mary. We've all read what she wrote about your baking.'

'She certainly sings your praises, Robert,' Angie said, beating Susan to it, who sniffed deeply.

'I smell more scones. What delicious offerings have you made?'

'Raspberry.' Robert looked around, a little perplexed. 'Hattie was going to cover them with white chocolate before they are devoured.'

'Oh, to be covered in white chocolate,' Angie purred. 'And devoured.'

'They smell divine.' Susan spoke up, positioning herself in front of Angie. 'I'd love a nibble.'

'They aren't out of the oven yet,' Hattie said, covering a smile.

'We haven't been introduced,' Susan said a little too loudly. 'I'm Susan, the club secretary and a close friend of Robert.'

'Oh, Hattie and I know each other already,' Mary interrupted. 'We spent some time in the church. I showed her round.'

'And she plays the organ sublimely,' Francis added. 'I'd love her to stay on until the weekend and play for a christening and for Sunday service.'

'So why are you here, Hattie?' Angie asked, narrowing her eyes.

'And can we sample the scones soon?' George asked. 'They smell so good.'

'Which is why I came straight over,' Francis said, animated. 'I phoned *The Chronicle* to agree with them about how wonderful your scones are, Robert, and I had a fascinating talk with the editor. Apparently, she's been inundated with requests from readers for your recipes. Rosie Eagle is going to speak to you about her ideas to put you "out there" – that's what she said. The editor was suggesting all sorts of wild ideas based on your baking. She even considered a "Devon Cream Tease" column, where you feed a scone to a blindfolded young woman each week who will guess the flavours.'

'I'll volunteer—' Susan butted in.

'And so will I,' Angie added.

'I'll test a scone or two.' Mary folded her arms.

'And I'll do it – why does it have to be women?' George Tenby grunted.

'No, that sort of thing's not for me,' Robert said firmly.

Francis intervened. 'Oh, I think Rosie wants to promote a zingy, popular column, capitalising on the popularity of baking. Baking is sexy, apparently.'

'Is it?' Robert was puzzled.

'So – off the back of the article – what do you think about boosting Sunday service with some sexy baking? Is it hare-brained? Can it work?' He was breathless with excitement. 'I'm going to put an ad in *The Chronicle* – but only if you agree, Robert.' He waved his hand, emphasising each word. '"Come to St Jude's in Millbrook – sing with us and enjoy a cream tea." You know the sort of thing, "let he who is without sin eat the first scone."'

Hattie smiled. 'That's quite a lot of scones you're asking Robert to bake.'

'I thought we could form a team – you know, under Robert's direction, if we do it a second or third time,' Francis offered. 'We have so many offers of help.'

Susan took Robert's arm affectionately. 'I'll help.'

Angie linked herself onto the other. 'I'll certainly help.'

'And I'll bake too, if I can,' Francis said. 'And Sally will, and Tilda. In fact, we can get the whole gardening club involved.' He looked hopefully at Hattie. 'Might you help out too?'

'I suppose it depends on how long you are staying,' Angie remarked pointedly.

'And who are you? How do you know Robert?' Susan asked.

'I'm Robert's sister,' Hattie said firmly. 'So, if you want to be of assistance, why don't *you*—' she pointed to Angie and Susan '— get the kettle on and make tea for everyone? Mary, you put plates out and your husband can help. I'll get the raspberry scones and, when they've cooled, I'll drizzle some white chocolate over them, and we'll all sit down and share a cream tea. Then—' She took a breath. 'Then Robert, and only Robert, will decide what he's going to do about this baking situation. After all, the newspaper is just putting ideas out there.' She smiled. 'But it sounds like a real opportunity to bring the community together, doesn't it?'

* * *

Later that evening, Bunty sat in the bath, submerged in bubbles up to her nose. She was feeling better. The hot water was wonderful, the bungalow was clean and Jacko was gone. She'd changed the bedding, vacuumed the carpets; no sign of Jacko remained now. She'd thrown his one discarded smelly sock in the bin, replacing the lid with a clang. He was in the past.

Earlier, she'd taken a bus to the superstore in town and bought food, hauling it back in recyclable bags she'd found in a cupboard in the kitchen. She'd paid with her bank card. Sean would know where she was now, but it didn't matter. Her eyes were closed, and, in her imagination, she was writing in the blank greetings card she'd bought in the supermarket, a glossy one with a picture of a horse running wildly across a mountainous land-scape. Sean loved horses, and she had no intention of texting him with such an important message. She'd send the card in the post. She was working out how to phrase what she needed to say. She'd got as far as *Dear Sean*. The rest was much more difficult.

She knew what she wouldn't say: she wouldn't tell him she loved him, although she did, she was sure of it. She wouldn't mention everything they'd been through together, not yet, although there was so much. She wouldn't say she was longing to be home again, in his arms, although she knew that she was. She'd simply tell him she needed a bit of time by herself, to sort herself out. She wanted to be the best person she could be now. Then, if he'd have her, she'd go back to Ballycotton, back to the O'Connor family, their parties, the laughs and the craic. Back to loyal Sean, who loved her so much he'd forgive her. And if he wouldn't, she'd take the next step by herself.

She'd be stronger, wiser and ready.

18

The last of the weak evening sun streamed in through the kitchen window, a slice of fading light illuminating the empty plates and scattered crumbs on the table. The scones had all been eaten, every last morsel. The cream dish was empty and two pots of jam had been consumed. The group was still talking animatedly.

Francis rubbed his hands. 'So it's all agreed, then, for this Sunday? We'll leave no scone unturned.' He smiled at his joke, although he'd stolen it from *The Chronicle*. 'We'll have a batch of twenty-four plain scones, three jars of strawberry jam and lots of clotted cream, and I'll ask Sally to help serve them in the vestry after evensong with pots of tea.'

'Which I'm making, using the urn we've borrowed from the WI,' Mary interrupted.

'And we're serving on proper china plates, which we've borrowed from The Pig and Pickle,' Susan added, with a nod to Angie. 'With paper napkins.'

'We'll give everyone who turns up for the service one of Robert's scones each, split in two and topped with cream followed by jam,' Angie agreed.

'The proper way – the Devon way,' Mary said emphatically.

'And you'll contact Rosie Eagle from *The Chronicle* to ask her to report on the event?' George said to Francis, who nodded in agreement.

'I'll do that,' Susan offered. 'I'm club secretary.'

'And this will be just a one-off on Sunday evening, to test the water,' Robert said hesitantly. 'If your congregation increases, Francis, we'll sit down again and decide what happens next.'

'Oh, of course.' Francis looked happier than he had in a long time. 'Hattie – you'll stay on and play the organ for us? That will help no end, having proper, uplifting music...' He looked around him awkwardly, embarrassed to be criticising Sally's playing.

'I will,' Hattie said. 'Bunty's still in my bungalow, by herself...' She gave Robert a knowing look. 'So I can stay a little longer. I'm happy to play for the christening on Saturday afternoon, too, if it helps – just to keep my hand in.'

'Oh, wonderful.' Francis clapped his hands. 'I'm sure Jennie Ward will be glad to pay you a fee, and we can agree on the music she wants for baby Max.'

'No fee, please,' Hattie said. 'It's just a pleasure to play that beautiful church organ. I wouldn't mind staying on afterwards for an hour to run through the hymns you want on Sunday, just to make sure.'

'Sally will be relieved she doesn't have to play,' Francis said. He spoke to himself. 'So will the congregation.'

'And at the crack of dawn on Sunday morning, we'll come round here to bake the scones with you, Robert.' Susan beamed.

'Oh yes – I'll be here, bright and bushy-tailed,' Angie added.

'I'm not sure I'll need so many people in the kitchen,' Robert said hesitantly. 'Hattie and I can manage. It's only twenty-four scones.'

'But even if we just watch,' Susan offered gleefully. 'We might pick up some tips.'

'George and I will wash up,' Mary offered. George shot her a look that meant he wasn't keen.

'We have a dishwasher, dear,' George said. 'So does Robert.'

'It needs loading – and unloading,' Mary insisted.

'And we'll reconvene in The Pig and Pickle on Monday night to discuss how things went and plan ahead,' Francis said hopefully.

'I'll put the item at the top of the agenda,' Susan suggested, plucking a notepad from her bag and scribbling.

'It's hardly gardening club business,' Robert said anxiously.

'I disagree,' Susan said. 'Besides, that reporter woman can come along and we can get her to help with publicity for the gardening club.'

'Publicity?' Robert was unsure.

'Don't worry about *The Chronicle*.' Hattie patted Robert's arm. 'You might just offer Rosie a recipe a week for the summer. One a week for five weeks, to keep her happy. It will all blow over.'

'Oh, and my patio might be done by then.' Robert leaned forward. 'At the end of August, we can meet here for pizza, a barbecue.'

'I'll put that on the agenda too,' Susan said, scribbling furiously. 'The gardening club summer bash at Robert's. We can all bring fresh produce from our gardens for the barbecue.'

Angie waved a finger for attention. 'And we'll make batches of scones – because we'll have all learned Robert's wonderful techniques for making the crumbliest, sexiest—'

'Right,' Robert said abruptly. 'I think we have everything organised. Francis?' He turned to the vicar. 'I'll leave all the organisation to you and we'll reconvene here for the baking on Sunday morning.'

'Thank you so much, Robert,' Francis said, his face filled with gratitude. 'Oh, just imagine, the church will be full of people desperate to worship God and eat scones. Things are as they should be.'

'I hope the church won't be full.' Hattie imagined the church crammed with queues of people demanding cream teas. 'We're only planning to make twenty-four scones.'

'"And He rained down on them manna to eat and gave them the grain of heaven. Man ate of the bread of the angels; He sent them food in abundance,"' Francis said, his eyes dreamy. 'Psalm 78, verses 24 and 25. Scones are the new bread of heaven.' He raised a finger. 'I hope this will be our first cream tea of many in St Jude's. We'll start modestly and watch the numbers increase.' He smiled, full of hope. '"Large streams from little fountains flow, tall oaks from little acorns grow."'

* * *

On Wednesday afternoon, Bunty stood in Hattie's spotless kitchen putting the finishing touches to lunch. She was cooking a special meal for two, fettuccine, a fresh salad, and she'd serve it up with a glass of white wine each, just the one. The Chardonnay was chilling in the fridge, and she'd made a Basque cheesecake for dessert. She wanted to say thank you. She was pleased with herself; the bungalow was clean and pleasant now, the kitchen smelling of cooking and sweet peas from the front garden. The room was filled with sunshine streaming through the open window. She stirred cream into the fettuccine alfredo, one of Sean's favourites, with extra parmesan and butter. It smelled delicious. She thought of Sean as she added ground black pepper: she hadn't written the card for him yet. She'd tried twice, opening it up, hovering her pen over the blank page, but the right words wouldn't come. She'd try again later.

There was a light knock at the door and Bunty rushed to open it. Glenys stood smiling on the step and Bunty ushered her inside. 'Lovely to see you. Lunch is almost ready – please sit down. I have wine in the fridge.'

'Oh, how civilised is this!' Glenys was delighted. 'I didn't expect such a fuss. I never had lunch with Hattie in all the years we've been neighbours.'

'I want to treat you – you were so kind to me over the difficult days when I had no water and not a clue what to do.' Bunty fussed as Glenys sat down, placing a napkin in front of her, whisking the vase of sweet peas away onto the worktop to make space for the plates. 'I don't know what I'd have done without the hot shower and the coffees and croissants. Not to mention the good advice.'

Glenys watched as Bunty placed a leafy salad on the table, a bowl of tomatoes, a dish filled with steamy fettuccine. 'This looks gorgeous.'

'I hope so.' Bunty turned to the fridge, whisked out a bottle and sat down. 'I wanted to say thank you properly.'

'Well, I'll have just the one glass.' Glenys watched as Bunty poured Chardonnay. 'I never drink at lunchtime.'

'Nor do I.' Bunty laughed lightly. 'Well, I did when I lived in Ballycotton. Sean and I used to have a swift one in The Hole in the Wall sometimes...' She paused, misty-eyed.

Glenys helped herself to fettuccine. 'Will you go back to him now you've—?'

'Split up with Jacko?' Bunty shrugged. 'He was such a mistake. I don't know what I was thinking. It was a moment's madness.'

'You and Jacko are definitely over?'

'I couldn't get rid of him quick enough. And he was just as

keen to leave. We weren't suited. I learned that much – Aries and Aquarius just don't match. I'm better with my faithful old Scorpio. Or – like this month's horoscope says – "Rams are very good at flying solo". Jacko was a wild foolish fling, nothing more. I was just being silly, hoping for attention. I learned a lesson I should have learned fifty years ago.'

'And now?' Glenys asked.

'Maybe I need to be by myself for a while.'

'Doesn't your husband want you back?'

'I'm going to send him a card.' Bunty was glad she had Glenys to confide in. 'I'll pour my heart out and apologise.'

'Will he accept it?'

'I'm not sure.'

Glenys lifted her fork. 'Do you have children?'

Bunty shook her head.

'It's funny – none of you have children, do you? Mine are all grown and flown, four of them. But neither you nor your sister had any?'

Bunty closed her eyes for a moment. 'I think Hattie would have been a great mother, but Geoffrey didn't want children. And my brother never married.'

'And you? Didn't you want a baby?'

'I had one.' Bunty swigged from her glass. 'Sorry, but I can't talk about it.' She gulped again. 'Sean and I have been through a lot. Maybe I should just go home to Ballycotton.'

'Oh? Is that where you're heading next?' Glenys showed her most sympathetic face, encouraging Bunty to go on. 'I'd be sorry to see you leave.'

'I might not – for a while.' Bunty was unsure. 'I want to be a better person when I go back, if I do. I don't want Sean to feel I'm going to him because I have no other option. I want to choose him. I want him to choose me. Because we care, not because it's convenient or because we have history. Does that make sense?'

'I suppose so.' Glenys wasn't sure. 'And when's Hattie back from Devon?'

'I spoke to her earlier.' Bunty reached for the wine glass. 'She's staying with Robert until after the weekend, so I suppose she'll be there for another week. It gives me time to work out what's best for me and Sean.' Bunty lifted her glass in celebration. 'To have more lunches like this. And I have Hattie's appointment for a hot stones massage tomorrow. I'm going to take advantage of being by myself, get to know myself better.'

'You make it sound so nice.' Glenys was halfway through her glass of wine. 'We can go into Banbury together tomorrow. I have an appointment at Cloud Nine too – a hydro facial.' She forked more fettuccine, closing her eyes for a moment. 'I'm going to enjoy having you as a neighbour, Bunty.'

'I'm going to make the best of it.' Bunty picked up the bottle of Chardonnay. 'More wine?' She'd already forgotten she'd only intended to have one.

'I don't mind if I do.' Glenys had forgotten too.

Bunty refilled both glasses and held hers up. The sun made the wine in the glass gleam like gold. 'Here's to the future, Glenys. May it be filled with wonderful things.'

19

Hattie gazed at the plate where just a few crumbs remained of her light lunch, a crusty cheese sandwich with cucumber and rocket, home grown. She put the empty lemonade glass and the plate to one side and stretched out in the sunshine, gazing towards the garden.

She felt a fleeting glow of pride: Robert had made such a wonderful life for himself in Millbrook. Hattie thought she'd keep the clippings from *The Chronicle* to send to Bunty. She held out her hands, extending the fingers one at a time. It was good to keep them exercised. She was looking forward to playing the organ on Saturday: she'd agreed last night over the phone that she'd play 'This Little Light of Mine' for baby Max's christening, and his mother Jennie had been so delighted she'd burst into tears. Hattie wondered if she'd have time to go to St Jude's and practise later on. She intended to be note perfect, to include lots of frills.

She glanced at her phone; there were no messages. She hoped Bunty was all right, that she wasn't feeling too down after the fiasco with Jacko. Her texts were cheerful; knowing Bunty as she did, she'd bounce back quickly. A rattling noise made her look up; a van was hurtling along the drive, dragging a full trailer. It came to an abrupt halt and two men clambered out and started to unload. Hattie looked around for Robert; he was probably still in the field with the goats. She approached the men as one of them plonked a cement mixer on the grass and clambered back on the trailer, leaping into a digger, starting the noisy engine, reversing. The other man held a clipboard and said, 'Parkin?'

'You're parking where?' Hattie was confused.

'Robert Parkin?' The man watched the digger reverse, then his companion leaped out. Hattie stared back at him – she was clearly not Robert Parkin. 'Delivery for Parkin – a digger, a roller and a cement mixer.'

'To do the patio?' Hattie asked. 'He's not doing it by himself.'

The second man was unloading a ride-on roller, steering it down the ramp.

'We've been instructed to deliver machinery today. We're the hire company. Sign here.' He thrust the clipboard in front of her and handed her the pen. At the top of the sheet was the name T&S Hire Solutions. She frowned. 'What am I signing?'

'That the equipment has arrived safely.' The man's face held no expression.

'But how do I know it's safe? I haven't seen it working.' Hattie sighed. 'Oh, very well.' She signed her name, *H A Bowen*, and wondered briefly if she should have signed *Parkin*. It was ridiculous to keep Geoffrey's name now: she'd managed to rid herself of the rest of him. The men were back in the van without another word, accelerating, dragging the empty trailer away. She watched it bounce along the drive and disappear through the gate. Then Robert was by her side, his voice excited. 'Oh, they've arrived? That's wonderful.'

'You were expecting all this?'

'And a skip. That's coming today too.' Robert clasped his hands. 'Danut and Joey are starting first thing tomorrow.' He waved a hand around the garden. 'They are going to dig all this up, put the patio in and make areas for sitting and for the outdoor oven.'

'Won't they make a mess?'

'Oh, Danut will only work on this area – the rest of the garden and the orchard will be fine.'

'It'll be noisy,' Hattie said.

'No gain without pain.' Robert winked. 'And just imagine how nice it will look when it's done. I'm really looking forward to it. They've promised it will be ready by mid-August.'

'That's quick work,' Hattie muttered.

'Rosie says they are really efficient.' Robert wrapped an affectionate arm around her. 'It'll be wonderful, Hat. Don't worry.'

* * *

Hattie couldn't sleep. It was past two. She'd hardly nodded off since she'd come to bed four hours ago. She wondered if she should have had a hot drink before coming up, milk or chamomile tea always helped her sleep. Her feet felt numb and she wriggled them slightly. Isaac Mewton was asleep on top of them, purring. She threw an arm outside the duvet and it was too cold. She snuggled back in again and closed her eyes but her mind was filled with nonsense. The problem was, almost fifty years with Geoffrey had made her a worrier.

She was thinking about the bungalow in Bodicote, hoping Bunty hadn't left the back door unlocked. The estate was fairly safe, but you never knew – someone might sneak in and then what would happen? She'd read of such things in the newspapers: burglary, vandalism, murder. She told herself everything would be fine. Then she wondered if she should have phoned Sean to put his mind at rest over Bunty, offered her support. She liked Sean and she didn't want him to think that she didn't care. But they'd never been particularly close, Ballycotton was a long way away and, besides, Geoffrey had never been a fan of Sean and wouldn't travel to Ireland.

Hattie envied Sean's warmth, his sense of humour, the way he looked at her sister with affection. Perhaps she'd send him a brief email tomorrow and say she wished him the best. But she could hear Geoffrey's voice as if he were next to her in the bed, a grumbling monotone. 'Keep out of it, woman. No one wants an old busybody poking her fussy nose in.' She shivered. The memory of him still had the power to make her cringe.

Hattie forced herself to think of other things. Playing the organ in church was going to be a real thrill on Saturday and Sunday. She imagined herself pressing the stoppers, making heavenly music for a rousing choir. Then she'd hit a bum note, it would echo through the church, people would laugh. 'Whatever made you think you'd be any good? Look at your ugly hands. You've got fingers like fried sausages.' It was Geoffrey again. Hattie willed him away. She was at Robert's now. It was bad enough hearing his menacing voice in the bungalow – now she'd brought it with her to Millbrook.

Hattie reached out a hand and patted Isaac Mewton, who rolled over so that she could rub her belly. She ruffled the fur for a moment, enjoying the warmth and the rhythmic sound, then she snuggled back into the comfort of the bed and listened to the wind buffeting the windowpane. It was soothing, like a calm breath. Hattie tried to copy, exhaling, inhaling, allowing worries to drift away. What did the teacher say at yoga? 'Inhale courage, exhale fear.' She closed her eyes but sleep would not come for hours.

Then, as dawn began to tint the sky orange, she fell into a heavy slumber.

* * *

Robert was outside in wellingtons and gardening clothes hoeing the vegetable patch as the white van marked Georgescu and Dunn parked in the drive and the two builders ambled over, smiles on their faces. Danut shook Robert's hand, Joey standing behind him, hands in pockets. 'Right, we're ready to start. We'll peg the area out based on what we discussed, check that's what you want, then we'll level the ground up this morning. Do you want to keep the spare turf?' Danut looked around him. 'Is there an area in the chicken field where the hens have scratched? You might want to patch it in.'

'Great idea.' Robert rubbed his chin. 'I'll recycle it up there.'

'Then, after lunch, we'll put hardcore down – that's being delivered this morning – then start on a concrete base to lay the slabs on.'

'Sounds good.' Robert stared upwards. 'The weather looks ideal for outdoor building.'

'The forecast is perfect for the rest of the week and beyond,' Danut said. 'Joey and me, we'll make a start now, shall we?'

'Would you like a cup of tea and a scone later?' Robert offered.

Joey grinned. 'I read about your baking in *The Chronicle*.'

'Rosie Eagle's article.' Danut put his hand in his pocket and brought out chewing gum, offering it round. 'You're a celebrity in these parts.'

'Scones it is – round about lunchtime?' Robert declined the chewing gum. It stuck in his fillings.

'After one will do nicely,' Danut said, turning to wave to a small lorry with a crane on the back that was speeding through the gate. 'Here's our hardcore now. We'll crack on.'

'Right,' Robert said. He thought that Danut and Joey seemed confident about their work, so he headed towards the chickens. He'd collect a few eggs and make Hattie breakfast. She was sleeping in late today: it was past nine and she was usually up with the lark.

* * *

Hattie woke up to the loud repetitive sound of a chugging engine below the window and the harsh scraping of a shovel. She shook her head – her thoughts were still muddled; it felt as if she'd only just fallen asleep, but it was well past nine. Isaac Mewton had disappeared, probably outside chasing butterflies or sparrows. She peered through the window and saw the builders on a large patch of garden wearing ear defenders, shovelling gravel. The sound of a diesel engine rumbled loudly as the turf was scooped up in a mechanical shovel and swung round, depositing the grass and earth tightly rolled and stacked in a pile. She peered around the garden towards the fruit bushes and the orchard, hoping to catch sight of Robert.

Hattie slid out of bed in her nightie and wandered barefoot into the kitchen. It was cool there, the room deserted. She bustled around, filling the kettle, placing a teabag in a mug, wondering what to do. Even from the kitchen, the rumble in the garden was deafening and it was likely to continue all day. Hattie felt tired out – she'd hardly slept. Robert was nowhere to be seen. She poured hot water on the teabag and sat at the table, taking comforting sips.

Her phone pinged. It was a message from Bunty, attaching a photo of herself and Glenys seated at Hattie's table in the bungalow, wine glasses raised, a half-eaten cheesecake in the centre. Hattie examined the picture. Bunty's eyelids looked a little heavy, her eyes misty – and the bottle between her and Glenys was empty. Both women were smiling, as if they were having a whale of a time. Bunty had written a caption.

> I had a great lunch with our neighbour yesterday. I'm off to Cloud Nine today for a massage. Having a fab time here, Hattie. Hope you and Robert are too.

Hattie's immediate thought was to pack her things and go straight back to Bodicote. Perhaps Bunty was having too much fun – the bungalow would be in a mess, dirty dishes everywhere, unwashed undies on the bedroom floor. She paused; Bunty was taking her time, recovering from the mistake, learning to make good choices. She'd stay away.

Then Geoffrey's voice started up. She could see the sneer of his mouth, the blotched red of his cheeks 'You'd only be in the way, spoiling the fun like the sad old bag you are. You'd go back there with a face like a wet weekend and make everyone's life a misery.'

Hattie clutched her teacup, listening to the sound of the machinery rumble in the garden. The digger scraped and screeched as it lifted turf. Hattie took a deep breath. Robert was busy. Bunty was having fun. Hattie wasn't the old stick-in-the-mud Geoffrey always said that she was. She stood up.

'Sod you, Geoffrey,' she said out loud. 'Damn you. I've listened to you banging on for far too long. But not another word from you, never. I'm going out.'

Hattie placed her cup firmly on the table and made her way towards the stairs. She'd have a shower, get dressed and then she'd hit the town.

At least, she'd walk into Millbrook, go to The Pig and Pickle and order a small sherry. Because that was the sort of woman she was nowadays: independent, strong, one who sat alone in bars and drank sherry in the mornings. She was no longer browbeaten, timid Hattie Bowen. She was Hattie Parkin now.

And Geoffrey could stick that in his pipe and smoke it for the rest of his days.

20

It was almost eleven o'clock as Hattie walked into the village, her step sprightly. The sunlight seemed to illuminate every blade of grass; the blooms that hung from baskets outside little cottages were bright as jewels, the flowers in the garden nodding in the light breeze. Millbrook was like a painting, vibrant, winding from the path to the village green and beyond, past The Pig and Pickle to St Jude's. Hattie marvelled at how the view lifted her spirits.

There was someone sitting on the village green, an easel in front of him. A painter wearing a broad-brimmed hat and gold-framed glasses, his back turned, lifted his brush and swept it across the canvas. As Hattie approached, she noticed that he was painting the church in watercolour, and the surrounding frame of trees and greenery. She walked up behind him on quiet feet and glanced over his shoulder. He was good. His colours were a little more pastel than the real thing, but his attention to detail was wonderful. Hattie could see the shadow on the grey church tower. The flowers were vibrant dots, the gravestones silver in the sunlight. There was a shiny-feathered crow perched on the stone wall, its beak open. Hattie couldn't help herself. She pointed at the easel. 'That's incredible. I can see each leaf on the trees.'

The painter was deep in concentration and Hattie's voice made him leap in surprise. His knee jerked upwards and he knocked the easel over, sending paints and water flying onto the grass. He stood up, trousers damp, his face frozen in fear.

'Oh no...' Hattie leaped into action, rushing for the painting, holding it up. 'I hope there's no damage done.'

'Just my poor heart.' The painter placed a hand over his shirt. 'You gave me quite a jolt.'

'I'm so sorry.' Hattie waited for him to call her a silly old bag, as Geoffrey would have done, or a string of other derogatory nouns: crone, hag, harridan, witch, mutton, biddy, bint. She was used to all of them: Geoffrey used to refer to himself as a silver fox, a gentleman in his prime. Hattie put a hand to her head to chase away any memory of Geoffrey – she'd promised herself she would. She gazed at the painter instead, his wide-brimmed hat over brown eyes, and realised he was smiling.

'Please don't apologise,' he said. 'I'm afraid I become so absorbed in my work that I shut out everything around me.' He set up the easel and took the painting from her, repositioning it carefully.

'You're very good,' Hattie said.

'Oh, no, not at all,' the painter said modestly. 'Well, I'd like to become the next John Constable, but I think I've left things a little late. I'll be happy seeing my days out painting Devon in the sunshine.'

'Do you paint landscapes all over Devon?' Hattie asked.

'My favourite places are the moors, but I tend to paint from photos nowadays – it gets windy on Dartmoor and the cold is bitter. I'm too long in the tooth for sitting in Haytor car park all day. I like painting trees. I love the detail on the bark, the gnarly branches really appeal to me, the sense of time passing and the trees have always been around to watch the changes.' He paused. 'Oh, I'm going on, I'm sorry.'

'Not at all.'

'I seldom meet anyone who's interested in my paintings.'

'They are lovely.'

The painter thrust out a hand. There was a smear of blue on it. 'Barry Butler.' He smiled. 'I live in one of the old cottages you'd have passed on the way in.'

'Hattie – Parkin,' Hattie said. 'I'm Robert's sister. I'm staying for a few days.'

'Oh, how nice. Robert's a lovely chap. He's a real stalwart of the gardening club.' Barry raised an eyebrow. 'I suppose you know about his recent rise to fame as a baker.'

'The best scones in the south-west?' Hattie quoted the article in *The Chronicle*. 'He loves experimenting with recipes.' She noticed Barry pick up his brush and plunge it into his now half-full water pot. 'Anyway, nice to meet you. I'm sorry I made you jump.'

'Not at all.' Barry's face was all apologies. 'I'm sorry for being a numpty and dropping my paints all over the place. And I'm probably keeping you. You must have somewhere you're heading?'

'Only The Pig and Pickle,' Hattie replied, covering her mouth quickly: he'd think she was a lush, off to the pub straight after breakfast. She reminded herself that she hadn't eaten. She thought briefly about inviting Barry Butler to join her in the bar. It would be nice to talk about paintings over a small drink. And he seemed a pleasant man, placid, calm. His brow was creased in concentration as he touched the painting with his brush, adding a dollop of grey to the church. But it wasn't in her nature to be forward with men. With anybody. Hattie said, 'Well, I won't disturb you.' She watched him work for a moment and added, 'Lovely painting.'

'Thanks. It was nice to have met you.' Barry almost looked over his shoulder.

'You too,' Hattie replied and set off across the village green towards The Pig and Pickle. She couldn't help smiling – he'd certainly think her a racy woman, off to the pub by herself. She crossed the road. The doors were open and she could smell hops. Pop music was playing from inside. Hattie took a breath and walked in.

In contrast to the sunshine outside, the bar was dark and Hattie blinked to accustom her eyes to the sudden change. There were a couple of drinkers hunched over pints in the snug, but there was a window seat that was empty. From the vantage point, Hattie could look out onto the village green. A woman with a ponytail and faded jeans approached her. 'What can I get you?'

Hattie was momentarily taken aback. She'd thought she might have a sherry, but wasn't it an aperitif? Or a digestif? She wasn't sure – she wasn't much of a drinker. The words 'gin and tonic' came out of her mouth and she had no idea why.

'Coming up.' The woman lifted a turquoise bottle and said, 'Is this one all right?'

'Perfect,' Hattie said. She had no idea about the difference in brands. The woman with the ponytail placed a balloon glass in front of her and Hattie said, 'I don't suppose you have food?'

'The lunch service starts at midday, in ten minutes,' the woman answered. She saw Hattie's disappointment and said, 'If you want a cheese toastie, I can get one for you now.'

'That would be very nice.' Hattie opened her bag to pay.

'Are you new to the area?' the barmaid asked.

'I'm staying with Robert Parkin. He's my brother,' Hattie explained.

'I'm Shelley,' the barmaid said with a grin. 'Give Robert my best. His pavlova is to die for. We had some last weekend. They hold all the gardening club meetings here.'

Hattie took the glass and sat down in the window, sipping a mouthful of gin. It was refreshing, with a bit of a kick afterwards. She glanced through the window. Barry the painter was still there, absorbed in his watercolour. She took another sip.

'Robert's sister, eh? I didn't know he had a sister.' A voice called from the other end of the bar. Hattie looked up at a man in a flat cap, sitting in the gloom with a friend who also wore a cap. He looked a little like a bloodhound, permanently unhappy.

'He has two. I'm one of them,' Hattie replied cryptically.

'He's a dark horse, Robert. He keeps his cards close to his chest,' the first man in the cap said. 'We find out he can bake up a storm, then he's in the newspapers as the best thing since sliced bread, and now he has a sister.'

Hattie drank her gin. She had nothing to say.

'Leave her be, Dennis,' the other man in a cap said, scratching long sideburns. 'She's come in for a quiet tipple.'

'We can't let the lady drink alone.' The man called Dennis grunted. 'Where's Robert, then?'

'At home. The builders have arrived – they're sorting out the new patio,' Hattie explained briefly. 'I thought I'd take a walk, away from all the noise.'

'Which builder has he got?' Dennis asked.

'Georgescu and Dunn.'

'Oh, from Teignmouth,' Dennis replied. 'Didn't you know someone who used them for a patio, Colin?'

The other man lifted his cap and scratched his head. 'Tim from down the garage. They did his extension, in quick time too.'

Shelley arrived with a toasted sandwich, placing it in front of Hattie. She smiled. 'Enjoy.'

'I will.' Hattie picked up the toastie and took a bite. She was hungry.

'I'll have one of those, Shelley,' Dennis called. 'They smell nice.'

'Me too,' Colin added. 'And another pint for me, one for Den here and another G & T for the lady.'

'Hattie,' Hattie said, not realising that she should have said no instead. Hattie didn't want another gin, but Shelley was already at the optics. Dennis and Colin moved to the window seat, sitting down one either side of Hattie, clutching their half-finished pints.

'Hattie, is it? I'm Dennis Lyons, professional pensioner and generally grumpy git.' Dennis barked a small laugh. 'Pleased to meet you. Robert's a good friend of ours. We're all in the gardening club.'

'I'm Colin Bennett,' said Colin with the sideburns. 'Very thirsty beer drinker. And member of the gardening club too. Robert's an all-right bloke.'

Hattie looked from one face to the other. Dennis said, 'Don't let us keep you from your toastie, Hattie. Dig in.'

'Our grub will be here directly.' Colin reached for his glass. 'It's a nice day to be sitting in the snug with a drink.'

'Any day's nice to drink.' Dennis guffawed.

'Robert should have come along with you. We could have made a session of it,' Colin suggested. 'Mind, he's not much of a drinker.'

'Whereas you're drinking gin at midday. Hair of the dog, is it, Hattie?' Dennis asked, his face impressed.

'What? Oh, no – I'm just taking in the village.'

'And the best place to take it in from is the pub,' Colin agreed.

Hattie tried another bite of her sandwich, then a mouthful of gin.

'So – what do you think of Millbrook?' Dennis asked.

'Nice,' Hattie said through the mouthful.

'A bit quiet. Where are you from?' Colin asked.

'Oxfordshire.'

'It's too flat there,' Dennis said. 'I went once. Too many people – and all those old buildings, church spires, colleges.'

'That's Oxford.' Hattie was still chewing.

'Lots of farmland,' Colin said. 'Which bit are you from?'

'Banbury – a village just outside the town.'

'"Ride a cock horse to Banbury Cross,"' Dennis sang, swigging the last of his pint just as Shelley arrived with a tray, three drinks.

'Your toasties are on their way, Dennis. I believe there are free scones on Sunday evening at St Jude's?' Shelley asked Hattie. 'I heard Susan Joyce say that she and Robert were organising it with the vicar.'

'We're all organising it—' Hattie began.

'Free cream teas in exchange for a rousing chorus of "All Things Bright and Beautiful"?' Colin smacked his lips. 'Count me in.'

'I don't normally go to the church – too bloody cold in St Jude's. The wind blows right up my trouser legs,' Dennis grumbled.

'I'm only going for the scones – then I'll come straight here to warm up.' Colin rubbed his hands.

'Good idea. Anything free is worth turning up for,' Dennis muttered.

'I'll be back with the toasties,' Shelley trilled and turned to go.

'Great, Shelley, thanks.' Colin reached for his pint. 'And you can bring another two pints and a gin and tonic.'

'Oh no.' Hattie surveyed half a glass of gin and a new full one. 'I'm fine, really.'

'It's my round,' Colin protested. 'Nothing's better than a nice drink in the morning with friends, putting the world to rights.

Den and I come down here every day to chew the fat. It'll be your round next, Hattie.'

'So, Hattie—' Dennis reached forward and grabbed his new pint. 'It's good you're here. We could do with a fresh face, some new opinions on the world. Tell me – what are your thoughts on this bloody government of ours?'

21

Hattie stood in the middle of Millbrook, facing the church. Barry Butler the painter was no longer sitting on the village green. It was probably time for a siesta – it was almost two and the sun scorched overhead. Dennis and Colin were still hunched in the snug, drinking pints and arguing about strikes, the cost-of-living crisis and how the people running the country were out of touch. Hattie thought that both men were very opinionated, especially after so much beer, and that neither listened properly to the other's views, being happier to shout each other down. Hattie had drunk three gin and tonics, and two mouthfuls of a fourth. She'd told Dennis that he was somewhat to the right of Genghis Khan and that Colin was an armchair revolutionary who should get off his backside and do something instead of whingeing. She'd stunned them by speaking so frankly and surprised herself with her outspokenness. She wasn't used to drinking – or standing up to people.

Looking up and down the main street of Millbrook, the cool air in her face, Hattie felt the worse for the gins. She wondered what to do. She looked to the left: it was quite a walk back to

Robert's, three quarters of a mile – not a difficult stroll normally, but Hattie could hardly feel her feet. She looked to the right. St Jude's loomed above her. Churches were places of refuge, weren't they? She'd sit in one of the pews and have a short rest. Hattie set off towards the gate at a stumble.

She opened the wooden door to the church, twisting the antique handle, and stepped inside. The air was chilly; something fluttered high in the rafters and Hattie shivered. She moved towards the enclosed wooden pews, each with hassocks to kneel on and a knotty shelf holding small Bibles. But it was the organ that caught her eye and, before she knew it, Hattie was perched on the stool, pulling stoppers, touching keys. Flushed with the confidence of too much gin, Hattie started to play a boogie-woogie tune she remembered from somewhere, a Scott Joplin ragtime tune, 'The Entertainer', then 'Maple Leaf Rag'. It occurred to her that the music might be inappropriate for a church, but didn't all music celebrate the love of God? (Maybe not quite *all*, but certainly anything Hattie liked.)

She was showing off; she played Pachelbel's *Canon*, 'The Stars and Stripes', 'La Marseillaise' – each tune sounded impressive, resonating through the church, and Hattie was amazed at the fluidity of her fingers. On a roll, she launched into Beethoven's *Moonlight Sonata*, and couldn't believe how inspired she felt as she played it. The music floated to the rafters as if it were an offering to heaven. Hattie wondered with a smirk if she should drink gin more often. As she finished playing, the air in the church vibrated with the last note, then it was still.

'That was just amazing.' A quiet voice spoke behind her, and Hattie jumped, reminded instantly of how she'd surprised Barry Butler on the village green. She turned to see a young woman dressed in dark clothes, her black hair shorn at the sides. Hattie examined the smooth expressionless face, piercings in her nose and ears, one in her lower lip. 'I wish I could play like that.'

Hattie swivelled all the way round on the stool. 'Tilda, isn't it?' She was conscious that her breath smelled of gin.

'And you're Robert Parkin's sister?'

'Hattie.' Hattie extended a hand. The young woman took it, her fingers limp. Then she squeezed next to Hattie on the stool. Their shoulders touched and Hattie was surprised at Tilda's forwardness.

Tilda said, 'My parents made me learn piano when I was small. I gave it up. It was boring, the way the teacher taught me. He was a hundred and fifty years old, and I just did exercises every week.'

'But you're very musical – you play bass,' Hattie countered. 'You sing well.'

'You've heard me?' Tilda didn't seem surprised.

'I heard through the manse windows. Your band is good but your voice is particularly impressive.'

'Do you really think so?' Tilda played with an earring. 'Most people in Millbrook wouldn't agree.'

'It's a strong voice, tuneful,' Hattie said. 'Perhaps you need to expand your horizons?'

'Are you a professional?'

'Oh no.' Hattie was briefly reminded of what Geoffrey used to say about her infrequent efforts to play the piano. 'I'm just – getting my mojo back.'

'You're brilliant. Mum told me you're playing at Sunday service. She's so relieved she won't have to murder "Come, Ye Thankful People, Come" again this week.'

'I'm just staying for a few more days,' Hattie explained. 'I'm playing for a christening too.'

'Jennie Ward. She's two years older than me. Her kid's called

Max.' Tilda pushed a hand through her hair. 'I'm supposed to be going to university next year to do Chemical Engineering, but I've persuaded my parents to let me defer for a year. I want to see if I can make it with my band.'

'Armpit.' Hattie remembered.

'We're a three piece,' Tilda said eagerly. 'I think we're good enough. We've been together for three months. We'll be ready to start gigging soon, local pubs, then further afield, Bristol, Birmingham, London. We'll get noticed.'

'I hope it works out,' Hattie said.

'My boyfriend plays in the band too. He plays drums – he's called Donkey.'

'That's a strange name,' Hattie said.

'It's because he's well-hung,' Tilda replied simply and Hattie burst out laughing. If she hadn't drunk the gin, she mightn't have understood. Tilda shrugged. 'I wouldn't know. We've only been together for two weeks. Early days.'

'Of course,' Hattie agreed quickly.

'I don't suppose I could – ask a favour?'

'Why not?' Hattie sat up straight.

'Would you mind listening to me sing?' Tilda's smooth forehead puckered. 'Play something on the organ and you can – you can give me your honest opinion of my voice singing something else. I'd appreciate it.'

'All right.' Hattie wriggled her fingers. 'What shall I play?'

'Do you know "Fallin'" by Alicia Keys?'

Hattie shook her head.

'Lady Gaga's "Million Reasons"?'

Hattie shook her head again. 'What about "Let It Be"?'

'I'll give it a go,' Tilda said determinedly. 'I want your honest opinion, mind.'

'Of course,' Hattie promised.

Tilda took a deep breath, stood up straight and stared ahead, concentrating. She sang her way through 'Let It Be', 'Sweet Caroline', 'Crocodile Rock' and 'Crazy Little Thing Called Love'. Her voice was strong as she belted out each song over the organ; she was exhausted by the time Hattie stopped playing. She wiped a hand across her brow.

'What do you think, Hattie?'

Hattie was smiling. 'You have a strong voice – it's superb.'

'Really? You're not messing me?'

'It's perfect for Armpit, but you could diversify too.'

'Diversify how?'

'You have a pure voice, but there's also a great smoky quality to it. You could sing jazz, blues, but you could also perform solos in church.'

'Church?' Tilda shook her head. 'Nah. I'd feel daft.'

'Well, you shouldn't.' An idea flipped into Hattie's head. Three and a half gins had made her surprisingly sharp. 'Why don't you offer to sing at baby Max's christening on Saturday? Use one of your band's mics – I'll play for you. I bet you'd be amazed how well it goes down.'

'Really?' Tilda was unconvinced. 'What could I sing?'

'"Let It Be". Get your dad to talk it through with the mother – or ask her yourself. And maybe you could do "Crazy Little Thing Called Love" as well at the end, when the service is over.'

'Do you think I could?'

'It doesn't matter what I think,' Hattie said boldly. 'I've wasted years caring what others think. Don't you do the same. You're talented and young – get lots of experience in different areas, try it out, see what you think.'

'I might.' Tilda pulled her earring again. 'But people would laugh at how I look. I'd have to wear a dress or something.'

'Nonsense.' Hattie was surprised how little confidence Tilda had; when she sang, she seemed exactly the opposite, animated, strong. 'You're gorgeous as you are, and if people don't like it, ignore them. Isn't everyone equal in the eyes of God?'

Tilda suppressed a giggle. 'I'll ask my dad.' She threw her arms around Hattie suddenly, a spontaneous expression of affection. 'Thank you so much. You've really helped me.'

'Have I?' Hattie was surprised. She'd simply enjoyed playing the music.

'Is there anything I can do for you?' Tilda asked.

'You can point me in the direction of Robert's house,' Hattie said with a grin. 'I made the mistake of going into The Pig and Pickle for a toastie this morning and ended up drinking more gin than I should have.'

Tilda's eyes widened. 'Maximum respect.'

Hattie took the arm she was offered and allowed herself to be led to the wooden door, out into the blinding sunlight. She gazed beyond the village green, past the rows of cottages to Robert's house. It was almost four o'clock. The builders would be packing up soon, and she'd have a nap with Isaac Mewton until dusk then she'd cook supper with Robert. Life was good.

* * *

The same evening, Bunty found herself in the village hall in Bodicote, standing alongside eleven women, including Glenys, and three men. Bunty had never done yoga before. She was watching the yoga teacher, Kay, intently as she instructed the class on the positions. Bunty was impressed by Kay. She was flexible and fit in Lycra leggings, although she could only be ten years younger than Bunty. Her face was serene, as if yoga had made her mindful, as if she was always calm. Her voice, as she gave instructions, was soothing and gentle.

Bunty felt like a carthorse in comparison – she wished she had some of what Kay had. She'd spent all afternoon trying to express her feelings to Sean in the card but her head was muddled. She didn't know whether to make excuses for her stupidity or to beg him for forgiveness. She asked herself what Kay would do and decided she'd just write a simple message, *Thinking of you, Sean,* and leave the rest to the universe. Bunty wished she had faith in the universe. In truth, she had little faith in herself.

Kay said, 'We will now move to Vrikshasana, the tree position. It is a balancing pose, which will tone muscles, but it will also enable you to be centred, grounded.' She smiled as if the room were filled with sunshine, and Bunty felt suddenly encouraged. Next to her, Glenys was already sweeping her arms in the air, lifting one foot. On the other side, a large gentleman with a smooth head, wearing a voluminous grey tracksuit, was doing the same. Bunty tried to copy them and almost went sprawling.

Kay said, 'Your hands are in prayer position. You may wish to move them up above your head. Now bend one knee and tuck the leg under the other...' Kay showed her how and Bunty gazed around at the others in the group, arms raised, standing on one leg, tall proud trees centred and aligned. Bunty tried. She couldn't help wobbling. She put her foot down and tried again.

'On a metaphysical level, the tree pose helps us to achieve balance in other aspects of life,' Kay explained as she held the perfect pose.

'I need balance in other aspects of my life,' Bunty muttered between her teeth, raising her hands above her head, lifting a foot, tottering. Then she fell.

Arms in the air, she lunged for support against the large man in the tracksuit, and they flopped to the floor. Bunty landed on him, cushioned. He blurted a muffled swearword and Bunty clambered to her feet, apologising.

Kay smiled kindly. 'It takes time for us all to perfect the tree.'

Bunty shook her head. 'I'll never achieve balance. I'm too unstable.'

The large man muttered something rude in agreement and went to stand elsewhere.

At the end of the lesson, Bunty shuffled towards the yoga teacher. 'I'm sorry I fell over.'

'It's fine.' Kay's expression was without judgement. 'You're Hattie's sister, aren't you? Are you taking her place? She texted me she's away in Devon.'

'That's right,' Bunty said.

'Did you enjoy the practice?'

'I did. Only—' Bunty was speaking quickly, nervously.

'Only?'

'It made me realise how far behind I am.'

'Behind?' Kay's brown eyes were kind. 'We all progress at our own pace.'

'I just seem to be behind in everything. I've charged through life without thinking and – just like what happened here today – I'm stumbling all the time.'

'Keep up the practice,' Kay said. 'Move forward at your own rate.'

'One step forward, three backwards, that's me,' Bunty muttered. 'I'm a nightmare.'

'No one is judging.' Kay smiled. 'How long are you staying in Bodicote?'

'I'm not sure. I'd like to be here for a bit longer, although it's a bit lonely on my own at the bungalow. I suppose I could come to yoga next week.'

'That would be nice. And – here.' Kay handed Bunty a business card, a silhouette of a woman stretching, the name Kay Weston, yoga teacher. 'Give me a ring. I don't live far from you. Come round for a cup of tea and a chat.'

'I'd like that,' Bunty said. 'I'm trying to be more mindful, to live in the present.'

'Aren't we all?' Kay agreed. 'The yoga will help. And self-acceptance and letting go.'

'Letting go?' Bunty felt a sudden jolt. She'd let go of Jacko. Was it now time to let go of Sean? Was it time to let go of the one thing that she'd never allowed herself to mention, the memory locked so deep she couldn't bear to think of it although every day it came to her. She pushed the image away, as she always did.

'Thanks, Kay,' Bunty said quickly, clutching the card. 'I'll give you a ring. I'll look forward to a cup of tea.'

She was on her way into the cloakroom, to find her shoes and pick up her bag, avoiding the disgruntled expression of the man in the grey tracksuit, hurrying towards Glenys, who was waving. Bunty's head was full of jumbled thoughts. Yes, Kay was right. It was time to let go.

22

Robert made a muffled sound of amazement as he sipped his whisky, gazing through the conservatory window towards the evening sunset. 'How many gins did you say you'd had in The Pig and Pickle, Hattie?'

'Too many.' Hattie covered a smile. 'I thought I'd live a little. After all, gin loosens the tongue and I was quite happy to tell Dennis and Colin that their opinions on politics were extreme – and quite unsubstantiated.' She sipped from the glass. 'This sloe gin you've made is delicious.'

'I was worried about you,' Robert said. 'You weren't back and it was gone four. Danut and Joey were packing up when you staggered home. Goodness knows what they thought—'

'I don't care if they think I'm a lush. I'll do as I please. I allowed myself a brief practice in the church, on the organ. Then I got talking to Tilda about music. She's very nice,' Hattie said. She noticed Robert's smile. 'What?'

'You've settled into life in Millbrook. You're drinking gin with the locals, hanging out with punk rockers.'

'Scaring the local landscape artist half to death?' Hattie

exhaled, proud of herself. 'Not the fuddy-duddy you thought I was, am I?'

'Oh, Hat.' Robert looked sorry for himself. 'I only meant – well, life with that dreadful man was doing you no favours. He was grinding you down, taking away the person you were.'

'No one stood up for me.' Hattie frowned. 'You kept your distance more than I'd have liked.'

'You're right – I did. Geoffrey was intimidating – he always made me feel in the way. He made the most terrible comments when I was around, asking why I never got married, and did I have a guilty secret he ought to know about,' Robert admitted. 'But you're right – I should have said something.'

'So should I.' Hattie gazed into the glass, enjoying the light reflecting through purple liquid. 'Looking back, I never really understood why I didn't.'

'How did things get so – bad?' Robert asked.

'I thought I was in love with him before we married. When we met, he was dashing, polite, flattering. He could be moody though – he made me want to please him, just to see him smile. Then he told me we'd get married, buy the bungalow together, settle down. He even worked out our joint earnings on a cigarette packet to see what mortgage we could get. I should have known then – he wasn't very romantic.'

'Hat, that's awful.'

'I went along with things. Just like Mum did – I let him take the lead. That was a mistake.'

Robert nodded. 'Our parents were traditional.'

'Geoffrey and I were as well. Ridiculously so. I put up with him for so long and now I can't believe I wasted all that time.' Hattie's face was calm. 'He decided what we were doing, even down to what I cooked for tea. I left him once, you know.'

'Did you?'

'I did. It was an ordinary day – I was doing his washing and there was a smudge of sticky red on his shirt collar. I knew he'd been – what's the phrase they use nowadays? – playing away.'

'What happened?'

'I got as far as the railway station with one suitcase. He came after me. He was carrying a bunch of cheap flowers and he apologised, said I was being a silly billy and I should come home where I belonged. So I went.' Hattie's eyes gleamed with the memory. 'I had nowhere else to go.'

'You could have come to me?'

'You had no idea how bad it was. Do you know, Robert, later that night I made his tea and he told me that I shouldn't worry about silly things like him flirting with the office girls and, anyway, if I was a proper wife and fulfilled his – you know – needs, he'd feel less inclined to stray.'

'He said that?'

'I just settled for a quiet life. It was easier than fighting back.' Hattie nodded. 'I suppose that makes me a bit of a wimp.'

'It makes you a martyr in a horrible marriage.' Robert squeezed a fist. 'I should have stepped up. I'm your brother.'

'I ought to have shown a bit of spirit too – but Geoffrey was controlling. He'd push me too far and then he'd be kind and apologetic. He'd even tell me how I was feeling, as if he knew better than I did. We never used words like coercive control years ago – it was just about wives responding to what was expected in those days. It was a lot of rubbish, really.' Hattie finished her drink. 'But it's never too late. When Geoffrey and I divorced, I felt like a bird escaping through an open window. I realised I'd been locked in and stifled for so long. And now I'm learning to fly.' She stretched her legs. 'I even bought kinky boots.'

'Kinky?' Robert was horrified.

Hattie laughed. 'I'll be staying out after midnight and snogging men in the street next.'

'Doing what?' Robert sat up, his face serious.

'Don't worry,' Hattie said calmly. 'You know, I'm enjoying staying here with you.'

'Stay longer.' Robert lifted his glass. 'It's great having you here. The outdoor kitchen will be ready for August. The builders are doing a great job on the patio – you can watch the progress with me. We have a gardening club meeting too. Stay for two weeks, more – stay as long as you like.'

Hattie wrinkled her nose. 'I have Bunty to think of. We'll see how she's getting on at the weekend. She'll be ready to go back to Ballycotton, I suppose. Then I should go home.'

'What for?' Robert's eyebrows shot up. 'We're having fun. Do you know, Hattie, I never realised you were such great company.'

'I'm your sister, Robert.' Hattie laughed. 'You must have realised—'

'How silly of me to waste so many years being a stick-in-the-mud. And that's what I've been.' Robert's face was dejected.

'Not at all, you're a local sex symbol.' Hattie held out her glass for a top-up. 'Babe magnet, isn't that right?'

'I do seem to be – it snuck up on me that the gardening club has – a gaggle of groupies – who want to sample my baked goods...' Robert eased himself from the sofa and reached for the decanter. 'Perhaps time hasn't passed us by, Hattie – not completely.'

'It certainly hasn't, Robert.' Hattie watched him fill her glass. 'Cheers to that, every day of the week.'

* * *

On Friday afternoon, Bunty was sipping tea from a pottery mug, listening intently as Kay leaned forward from her cross-legged position on the carpet. 'We have to love ourselves, Bunty, accept ourselves for the good person we are. Only then can we allow others into our lives.'

Bunty looked around Kay's living room, the mandala tapestry on the wall, the reiki symbols, the poster of yoga positions. 'But how do we do that?'

Kay's face held a gentle expression; she was sure of what she was about to say. 'We have to start from a position of non-judgement, of patience, of not striving for things we can't have, things that don't matter. We live in the moment, we breathe in acceptance and as we exhale, we release tension and negativity – we let it go.'

'That's what I want to do,' Bunty said eagerly. 'I can't return to Sean as the person I am now, not after the mistakes I've made, the things I've done. If I return at all. I'll just repeat the same behaviour. Kay, how can I change?'

'Take your time. Be gentle with yourself. You need to be as kind to yourself as you would be to your own child.'

'My own child.' Bunty bit her lip. 'I think if I'd – if things had turned out differently, I'd be a better person.'

'You are a good person right now. Accept who you are. Love the good in yourself and allow yourself to grow and develop.' Kay reached out an arm, pressed Bunty's wrist. 'There are things we can't change in our past. And the things we can change will flow from us gently if we don't force them.'

Bunty wasn't sure what the last comment meant. She gazed around at Kay's room, the pale walls, the soft lighting, the simple furnishings. 'Your house is so calm.'

'It's where I feel safe, comfortable and not easily distracted.' Kay smiled again and Bunty thought her face shone with peace.

'The bungalow where I'm staying – Hattie's home – is still as it was when Geoffrey left it. Apart from Hattie's piano, it still feels like Geoffrey's house – the cold walls, the impersonal furniture that looks like it's in a shop window but has no character. It's not a home, it's a clean space. And there's tension everywhere – I often feel scared to sit down.'

Kay shrugged. 'A home is just a temporary place, but it's important because it's where we relax. It should support us to be the people we want to be, in a place of warmth and solace where we can welcome others.'

'Warmth and solace,' Bunty repeated. 'You're right. A place where we can be ourselves... a home.'

'Exactly,' Kay replied.

Bunty sipped her tea thoughtfully. She had an idea. There was a DIY shop just down the road – she'd pass it on her way back to the bungalow.

An hour later, she had spread old newspaper on the carpet in Hattie's living room, moved the sofa back and she was sloshing paint on the walls. She had two pots of emulsion – Sizzling Heart Red and Purple Blush. The room would be warmer and vibrant, she thought – Hattie would be much more at home with it than the bland magnolia on every wall.

Bunty turned up the music on the radio, waving her brush against the walls as Creedence Clearwater Revival sang 'Bad Moon Rising'. She felt her spirits lift; it was nice to be doing something positive for Hattie. She'd finish the job over the weekend. On Monday she'd paint Hattie's bedroom a beautiful sunshine yellow – she'd seen the perfect colour in the DIY shop: Sunshine Dazzle. Then she'd persuade Glenys to go into town with her and buy a few modern prints. She'd seen just the type of thing that would cheer up Hattie's home. Vermeer's *Girl with a Pearl Earring*, blowing a huge balloon of pink bubble gum, and the *Mona Lisa* with muscled male arms, carrying toilet rolls. Bunty was sure it would make Hattie smile much more than the boring print of the yellow wicker chair on tiles that she had over her bed.

Half a wall was covered in purple paint – the other half was still pale. It was hard going, much slower than she'd thought, and Bunty was bored. The idea that she had three and a half more walls to do was worrying. Plus, she wasn't sure how she was going to paint round the windows with the curtains still up. She thought of Kay, who'd been inspirational – perhaps Kay would suggest that this was the universe challenging her to work hard in order to do a kindness for her sister and repay her with love. Bunty decided she'd finish the first wall and stop for coffee and a biscuit. She wondered if it wouldn't have been easier to buy a huge embroidered mandala and pin it over the magnolia wall.

She loaded the brush with paint and slapped it onto the wall; she hoped more paint would make the job quicker. A purple gobbet splattered on the newspaper, some of it dangerously close to the carpet. Bunty would deal with it later; she filled her brush again and moved up on tiptoe to reach higher. She needed to stand on a chair – she hoped she'd be safe.

There was a loud knock on the front door and Bunty paused. She'd finish the brush load and answer it – it might be the postman, or Glenys. She waved the brush against a swathe of magnolia wall and felt despondent – she could still see pale paint beneath the purple. She'd have to do a second coat. It would take ages.

The rapping on the door became louder and Bunty placed her brush carefully over the top of the paint tin. She was just about to move to the door when she heard a loud shout, followed by another. She edged towards the hall and peeped around the door. Through the stained glass in the door frame, she could see a tall man. He banged again as if he was hitting the door with his fist and then she heard an expletive, something that could have been, 'Where the hell are you?' Bunty watched as the man turned and walked away.

It was Jacko, he'd come back for her – she was sure of it. His wife had found out, she'd thrown him out and he'd returned to be with her. Bunty had no intention of going back to him. It had been a mistake and she felt foolish: now here he was again, haunting her. If she edged to the window, she'd see his white van, D Jackson, Plumber, parked at the kerbside. But she didn't want to see him. He sounded desperate – or angry.

She moved back to the wall, grabbing the paintbrush as a weapon, deciding that if he came back to the door and tried to get in, she'd thrust it at him, paint him purple. She was shaking. Bunty was annoyed with herself. She'd made some silly mistakes in her life, but she'd learned from this one. She sidled back to the front door and made sure that it was locked and bolted. On quiet feet, she went back to the living room, holding her breath, and dipped her brush in the pot. She'd make Hattie's house look beautiful and then, over the weekend, she'd write in Sean's card and post it.

On Monday she'd paint Hattie's bedroom Sunshine Dazzle, she'd text Hattie that she'd enjoyed her stay in Bodicote and say that the house was ready for when she wanted to come back from Devon.

Then she'd phone Sean and tell him she was desperate to come home.

23

On Sunday morning, Hattie and Robert walked to St Jude's church carrying plates of scones beneath tea towels and a variety of jams in pretty pots. Behind them, Susan and Angie were clutching another large plate each. The sky was dark, overcast and brooding. A wind whipped their ankles and lifted the cloths from the plate as if peeping at the scones beneath. Robert was undeterred. 'We made thirty-six scones this morning. That's more than we planned. Will there be enough?'

'What if there are too many?' Angie fretted. 'Francis says there are seldom more than twelve people on a good Sunday at church and—' she glanced at the sky '—this doesn't look like a good day.'

'The plain and the fruit ones will go down well, and people might like the lemon zest ones, but I can't imagine Dennis Lyons tucking into the ginger ones. And Dennis won't come to church.' Susan's teeth snapped together. 'He's the self-appointed grump of the village. He has no time for God. He has no time for anyone.'

'Perhaps the cream teas will make all the difference?' Hattie said.

'I did enjoy making them.' Susan gazed adoringly at Robert. 'You're such a good instructor – calm, clear, unflustered.'

'And you have such good hands.' Angie gazed at him too, and sighed.

'Robert makes the best scones,' Hattie agreed.

Robert was in good spirits. 'If we have any left I'll take them down the pub. I'm sure Shelley will get rid of them – a pint of best bitter and a scone. It could become a thing...'

'It will all be fine,' Hattie agreed. 'Lots of people at little Max's christening yesterday promised they'd come – Jennie said she'd bring the baby.'

'Oh, not a squealing baby at a church service?' Susan grimaced. 'That will put the congregation off.'

'Francis will welcome everyone,' Robert said.

'Jennie's mother will come, and her aunt,' Hattie persisted.

'I forgot to ask last night when you said how much you enjoyed the christening,' Robert said, 'how did you find playing the organ – were you nervous?'

'Not really. Francis's service was beautiful,' Hattie said. 'I'm sure I heard someone sobbing when I played "Let it Be" and Tilda sang. I played "Crazy Little Thing Called Love" at the end, and quite a few people asked me if I was playing the organ today and if I was staying on in the village.'

'And are you?' Susan asked, her face inquisitive. 'Staying on?'

'Only for a day or so.' Hattie shrugged. 'I'll be here tomorrow, for the gardening club meeting. I'll go back to Bodicote on Tuesday or Wednesday – I want to see how my sister's getting on. She's living in my bungalow.'

'You could stay a bit longer, Hat,' Robert said quietly. 'The patio will take another two weeks, three maybe. It would be nice if you'd stay until then.'

Angie gazed upwards. 'It's going to rain.' They had reached

the stone wall that surrounded the church. 'I swear I felt a drop just then. Let's get inside.'

Susan was still thinking about Hattie's words, about the christening. 'I can't imagine Tilda Baxter singing at the service – did she have all the piercings in her face and ears, and all that spiky black hair sticking up? It's hardly appropriate.'

'Why not?' Hattie asked. 'She has a beautiful voice. The congregation really appreciated it.'

The wooden door was open, and inside the church vestibule a long table had been set up. Sally and Francis were busily setting out china plates, tiered cake stands and pots of cream. Francis was visibly nervous; his hands shook as he accepted the plates of scones. 'Oh, I hope this won't be embarrassing. All these cream teas and only half a dozen in the congregation.'

Sally arranged scones neatly. 'They smell heavenly.' She glanced at Robert. 'And all this jam. It would be nice if there was a scone or two left over at the end, Francis – so we could try them too.'

'I made extra.' Robert glanced at his watch. 'What time does the congregation start to arrive, Francis?'

'Just about now.' Francis glanced towards the door to see if anyone was there, but, so far, the church was empty. 'We start at eleven on the dot. My plan was to serve the scones as people leave. Usually, George and Mary Tenby arrive on time, Edie and Eric Mallory, then there are a few stragglers.'

'Shall I play something?' Hattie offered. 'At least the church will be filled with music...'

'Will you?' Francis looked relieved.

'My pleasure,' Hattie said. She was enjoying playing the church organ now; during the christening, she'd gained confidence. So many people had been impressed by her playing – she was getting into her stride.

She perched on the seat, pulled out the stops, placed her feet on the pedals, and soon she was playing 'Jesu, Joy of Man's Desiring'. She glanced across to where Francis was watching her, a hand over his heart, smiling benignly. He mouthed 'Bach' and closed his eyes in rapture.

Hattie closed her eyes too, and let the music flow through her fingers. She felt the sound swell in the church, lifting high to the rafters. She allowed the notes to fill her ears and her head, and she felt uplifted. When she opened her eyes, Mary Tenby was waving to her from the pews, George at her side. Edie and Eric Mallory had arrived, shaking Francis's hand. The church started to fill, there were ten, fifteen people. A woman in sensible clothes placed herself behind the trestle table, organising cups and saucers. Another woman, businesslike in a suit, was effusively welcoming people and, in between, messaging on her phone. Colin Bennett ambled in with Dennis Lyons, who appeared grumpy as ever. Then another man stood alone in the doorway, looking around. His eyes met Hattie's. It was Barry Butler, the landscape painter who Hattie had met on the village green. He raised a hand in greeting and Hattie smiled back, launching into the Trumpet Voluntary.

* * *

Bunty was sitting in bed, slurping coffee from a mug, trying to decide what to write in the card. She'd written *Dear Sean* and was stuck – she didn't know whether to write *I miss you,* or *how are you?* or *I'm sorry*. Nothing felt right. She gazed at her phone – it was past ten and she still felt exhausted. She'd spent the whole of Saturday until past midnight painting the second coat, but it was done now and, she had to say, the living room looked very vibrant in purple and red. She hoped Hattie would love it. The DIY shop was open on Sunday mornings so she planned to pop down and buy some paint and decorate the bedroom a bright shade of lemon. Tomorrow she'd buy the pictures and make the house look perfect, her gift to Hattie. By next weekend she'd be back in Ballycotton.

Bunty eased herself out of bed. Her back ached, her arms too. She'd worked hard on the walls and her muscles were complaining. She struggled into a dressing gown and tried to decide whether to have a bath or make breakfast. She paused to listen: there was a light knock on the door. Her first thoughts were that Jacko had come back again.

She tiptoed into the hall and the gentle rap came again. Through the painted glass, Bunty could glimpse a slight figure: it was not Jacko this time. She opened the door to see Glenys smiling.

Bunty breathed out with relief. 'Hello.'

Glenys took in the dressing gown, the untidy hair. 'You've needed that lie-in, by the looks of you. Late night?'

'Yes – I've been decorating for Hattie. Are you busy tomorrow? I wondered if we could go into town and buy some pictures.'

'Why not? We could get lunch somewhere. And there's yoga again on Tuesday – Kay will be so pleased to see you there.' Glenys's hand was behind her back. 'Anyway – I came round to give you these. They arrived yesterday and the delivery driver couldn't get you to come to the door.'

'I've been painting with the music turned up.'

'So—' Glenys produced a huge bunch of roses and gypsophila. 'These must be for you.'

Bunty took the bouquet carefully, as if she were handling a time bomb. 'There's no sender's name. But they are beautiful.' She was suddenly anxious. 'Oh, here's a message – *"Why don't we try again?"*.' She gasped. 'It must be from Jacko.'

Glenys leaned forward. 'Oh dear. You don't want to see him?'

'No.' The bouquet shook in Bunty's hand. 'He was here the day before yesterday, banging on the door, really insistent. He must have driven all the way from Plymouth. I wouldn't let him in.'

'Do you think he'll come back?'

'Who knows?' Bunty shuddered. 'I don't want to speak to him.' She decided she'd finish the card, post it tomorrow. Perhaps a text to Sean might be easier, but it would be less of a grand gesture. She wondered if she should send him flowers. She looked at the bouquet. 'These weren't cheap.'

'He must want you back a great deal.'

Bunty groaned. 'I've been so stupid. I'll put these in water – hopefully, Jacko won't come round again. But if he does, I won't let him in.'

Glenys leaned forward. 'I'll ask my Bill to keep an eye out for him. If he starts causing a scene, Bill will tell him to move on. And if I see him, I'll do the same – and call the police.'

'Thank you, Glenys.' Bunty exhaled. 'It's so good to know someone's looking out for me. Well – I'd better grab a shower. Then I'm off down the DIY shop to get more paint.' She waved the flowers.

'I won't keep you.' Glenys turned away. 'But I'll call for you tomorrow, mid-morning. And...' she tapped her nose '... I'll keep an eye out for the amorous plumber.'

Bunty shuddered. 'Thank you, Glenys, and do say thanks to your Bill.' She closed the door and put the bouquet to her nose. The smell was heavenly. Her mind moved quickly. She rushed to the kitchen and bent down, rummaging in the cupboard, pulling out the largest frying pan. She clutched it in her fist, raising it in challenge. If Jacko wouldn't take no for an answer, she was ready to defend herself.

* * *

The church was crammed; every seat in every pew was taken and voices soared as one in a chorus of 'Come, Ye Thankful People, Come'. Robert looked across to where Hattie's fingers drummed on the keyboard. Her eyes were closed and she swayed with enjoyment. He couldn't remember when he'd seen her face so relaxed, so composed. The rich swell of singing filled the church. Then there was silence, and Francis's low voice echoed in a prayer of thanks. There was a muttered 'Amen,' then Francis said, 'We are serving cream teas in the vestibule for anyone who would like to stay on and join us.'

Robert glanced across to where Sally was waiting, flanked by Susan and Angie, who were vying for the best position in front of the cake stands. Jill Davies from Dawlish hovered behind them, trying to be helpful. Mary Tenby was filling a teapot from an urn. Robert stood up quickly; he should be helping them. A glance around the congregation told him they did not have enough scones. A rough count of heads meant that there were at least fifty people there, even if he didn't count himself, Francis and the helpers.

A hand touched his elbow and he swivelled round to gaze into the smiling face of Rosie Eagle. She was standing next to a small woman who wore a beret and a raincoat, black-rimmed glasses. Rosie patted Robert's arm. 'What a good turnout, Robert. I'm writing a report for *The Chronicle*. How Devon cream teas saved a community in Millbrook.'

Robert was flustered. 'We might have to give everyone half a scone each – there are more people here than I'd counted on.'

'That's good news. Then we'd better get to the front of the queue.' Rosie smiled. She turned to her companion. 'You must be keen to sample Robert's scones, Geraldine.'

'Oh, I am.' Geraldine glanced at Robert and her eyes glinted. 'I've heard all about these famous Devon scones.'

Robert was unsure of her tone. She certainly wasn't auditioning for his fan club. He offered a placatory smile. 'Do try a lemon zest scone with the raspberry jam... it's a new recipe of mine.'

'I'm not easily impressed, mind you.' Geraldine pressed her lips together. 'Let's say I'm a bit of an expert on cream teas.' She turned to Rosie. 'Lead on, then, Rosie. I'll let you know my verdict – I'll give a score out of ten.'

Rosie winked at Robert. 'I'm sure you'll get top marks. Robert's scones would melt the hardest heart.'

'Not mine.' Geraldine grunted, pushing forward to the front of the queue. Robert thought she was quite rude. Then Hattie was at his side.

'Everyone has half a scone and extra jam and cream.' Hattie grinned. 'The crowd seem happy.'

'I hope that will be enough,' Robert said hesitantly, rubbing his eyes behind the metal frames.

'Just look.' Hattie indicated the queue that had formed in the vestibule, people sitting in pews tucking into scones, cream first, topped with jam. He could hear sounds of contentment, chewing. Barry was sitting alone, finishing the crumbs on a plate on his knee, Colin and Dennis in the pew in front of him, munching quietly. Susan and Angie were very busy; Mary clanking teaspoons in cups, Sally and Francis talking to delighted members of the congregation. Francis's face shone with new light as they promised to return next week as long as there were cream teas afterwards. Even Tilda was there, slouching against a pillar with a slim young man in a black leather jacket and jeans, and a ponytail.

Robert watched as Hattie moved eagerly to talk to Barry

Butler. He heard her say, 'I hope you enjoyed the cream tea?' He watched as Barry glanced up, his eyes meeting Hattie's, and a smile crossed his face.

Robert edged towards the vestibule where Susan was busy serving Rosie and her guest with scones. Geraldine's face was arranged in displeasure. Rosie took a huge bite. 'My fruit scone and raspberry jam is heaven. Tell me, Geraldine, aren't these the best you've had?'

'Hmm, I'd say not.' Geraldine chewed as if it were torture. 'The ginger ones are a bit excessive. Too much spice, as if he's trying too hard. No, Rosie, I disagree. They are nice enough, good texture, light, but nothing special.'

'You're wrong,' Rosie argued firmly. 'Robert's scones are sublime. He's filled the church today on reputation alone. His baking is second to none throughout the south-west.'

'Throughout Devon, perhaps – I'll give you that much,' Geraldine said emphatically, wiping crumbs from her mouth. 'But Devon's hardly the whole of the south-west. Oh no.' She turned on her heel. 'I think there are better scones out there, and I plan to prove it. I'll call you tomorrow morning first thing, Rosie. There's an opportunity here, for both of us. I think we can say quite firmly that we have a cultural disagreement here, and our readers will love it. I can't wait to put into print my proposal for what's going to happen next.'

And with that she turned on her heel and marched outside. The rain had started to pour and was splashing on the cobbles. Robert stared after her, a frown on his face, wondering what had just happened.

24

Robert was still troubled on Monday evening as he prepared to go to the gardening club meeting. Hattie watched him lift a tray of scones from the oven, his face creased in doubt. 'I've made some savoury ones – rosemary with Cheddar cheese. Do you think the people at the club will like them as a change from sweet scones?'

'They smell wonderful,' Hattie said. 'Who are you trying to impress? You're taking them to the meeting out of the goodness of your heart. You have a fan club of so many devoted women who come along just to sample your baking.' She smiled slowly. 'Are they who you're baking all these new recipes for? You've no need.'

'It was something that happened after the church service,' Robert said. 'There was a woman there with Rosie, the reporter – I've never seen her before – and she was quite critical of the ginger ones. She said I was trying too hard.'

'Robert, you don't need to listen to the voice of one critic. Everyone loves your scones.'

'But she had the air of someone important.' Robert hovered over the warm scones. 'She told Rosie she intended to prove that there were better scones than mine.'

'That's nonsense.' Hattie laughed. 'It's just a matter of taste, it's subjective. I wouldn't worry – just let people enjoy your baking. And if it's stressing you, you're under no obligation to take food to the meeting at all. The gardening club can get a packet of biscuits from the supermarket.'

'Oh, but I enjoy it – I was going to make a batch of mini quiches too.'

'You don't think you're becoming a bit – obsessive?' Hattie asked fondly.

'I've just got used to taking nibbles.'

'It's become more than nibbles.'

'I like the praise, if I'm honest.' Robert was aghast. 'What am I without my baking? Just an ordinary man.'

'Robert – you're lovely, everyone adores you.'

'But it's because of the cakes and meringues and cream teas. I mean, I've just been ordinary Robert Parkin all my life; a quiet, harmless man no one really noticed. But now people love my baking – I feel like a local hero.' Robert seemed troubled. 'Hattie, do you think I'm being silly?'

'I think it's a lovely hobby and you shouldn't allow yourself to be worried by it,' Hattie said simply. 'Just bring a batch of nice scones and let everyone enjoy the meeting. Francis is delighted. He got a great turnout in church, which was what he wanted. He'll ask you to bake scones every week but I don't think you should – there should be a village rota. It's fine to have refreshments after church, but I'm sure Sally can make sandwiches one week and Susan knows how to make scones, Angie too. And Colin and Dennis can throw a few biscuit trays together.'

'Do you think so?' Robert asked.

'I don't like to see you so stressed...'

'You're right.' Robert took a breath. 'I've let the woman who criticised my ginger scones get to me. Why do we do that, Hat?

I'm happy, basking in the fact that I'm making others happy with my baking, and then one person comes along and puts a spoke in the wheels, and I disregard all the nice comments and worry about her single criticism. I don't even know her.'

'You know how these people can be – they are unhappy in their own lives so they feel better by criticising others.' Hattie placed an arm on Robert's shoulder. 'Let's have a cup of tea and try one of your rosemary scones – they smell gorgeous. Then we'll get organised for the meeting tonight.'

Robert smiled. 'Thanks, Hattie.' He placed an affectionate arm around her. 'Do you have to go back this week? I like having you here. Stay on until the weekend, perhaps?'

'I ought to go home,' Hattie said. 'Bunty messaged last night and said that she's thinking of going to Ballycotton soon. I'd like to see her before she leaves. Besides—' she met Robert's eyes '— goodness knows what she's been up to while I've been away. I dread to think what kind of state my bungalow's in...'

* * *

Bunty surveyed the sunshine-yellow paint in Hattie's bedroom, the music still blaring from the radio. She'd been listening to sounds of the seventies and Blondie was playing, 'Heart of Glass'. Bunty wondered if her heart was shattered. She didn't feel too bad, in limbo. The walls were almost dry now so she closed the windows. The strong smell had virtually gone. She'd put another coat on tomorrow and then she'd be finished. Hattie would love her vibrant new home. Earlier, in town, Bunty had bought several prints that she was sure would make the bungalow a really modern home. Along with the pink-bubble-gum-blowing *Girl with a Pearl Earring* and the muscular *Mona Lisa* carrying loo rolls, she'd also bought a print of a huge postage stamp with the outline of Queen Elizabeth II complete with crown and necklace, but the face was a moustachioed Freddie Mercury. Bunty thought it was hilarious and hoped Hattie would love it.

She picked up the addressed envelope on the piano, took out the card and read what she'd written.

I'm yours if you'll have me back, Sean. Your Bunty x

It was brief, to the point, but she hoped that would be enough. She'd post it now – it was almost seven o'clock – and it would go off in tomorrow's post. She hoped he'd receive it on Wednesday, message her immediately and beg her to come home, and she'd be back in Ballycotton by the weekend. On Sunday, they'd throw a party for her in The Hole in the Wall – all the O'Connor family would be there to welcome her back, and she'd be forgiven. It was what she wanted more than anything now.

Bunty stood in the hall, tugging on her jacket, checking her handbag for her purse and her keys. The Stranglers' 'No More Heroes' was blaring from the radio. A sudden knocking sound jolted her from her thoughts and she looked towards the door; the silhouetted frame of a large man filling the space behind the glass loomed ominously. She caught her breath; it was Jacko, she was sure of it. She stood against the wall: she wouldn't be visible if she didn't move. The knocking came again, this time more insistent. Bunty made a dash for the kitchen. She checked that the back door was locked, then she reached for the frying pan, which she'd left on the worktop, the handle towards her hand, ready to be grabbed. She seized it and stood in the doorway between the kitchen and the hall, breathing deeply.

A voice shouted, 'I can hear music – I know you're in there.' The voice was gruff, but Bunty was sure that was what he said. It was best to say nothing – he'd go away soon if she didn't engage in conversation.

The Stranglers became a different song, 'Da Ya Think I'm Sexy?' by Rod Stewart. Bunty closed her eyes. No, she didn't think Jacko was sexy – she couldn't believe she ever had. It had been flattery – he'd shown her attention – and she'd been plain foolish. The door rattled, as if someone was trying to put keys in the keyhole or shake it open. She raised the frying pan above her head. If Jacko managed to get in, although goodness knew where he'd have found a key, she'd hit him with the frying pan and ask questions afterwards. Bunty could imagine her explaining to the police. 'He came in to kill me so I killed him first.' Her heart was thumping.

The door rattled again and she heard the voice mutter something that sounded like a threat, a low grunt. Then the voice became smoother, more cajoling. She heard a few words. 'Still love – good together – I'll be back.' There was no further noise except for Rod's gravelly plaintive whine and the sound of Bunty's teeth chattering as she lowered the frying pan from the attack position. She didn't want to see Jacko again. She was furious with herself.

Bunty grabbed her phone from her pocket and checked messages. There weren't any since her conversation with Hattie earlier that morning. Bunty thumbed for Jacko's contact details and blocked him. At least he wouldn't be able to call.

She tiptoed to the living-room window, peering outside. There was no one there, no white van parked by the kerb. No one at all. He had gone. She rushed around the bungalow, whisking all the curtains closed, turning off the music. She hoped he wouldn't come back.

Bunty decided she'd make herself a coffee, pour something alcoholic and medicinal in it to calm her nerves and read a book, have an early night. She'd post Sean's card tomorrow – she'd ask Glenys to come with her. In truth, she was feeling decidedly edgy.

* * *

Around the table in The Pig and Pickle, Francis had been gushing for fifteen minutes. 'I can't believe the turnout at St Jude's, and it's all down to Robert and Hattie and the team. Thank you all so much for the delicious cream teas and also for the delightful organ playing, Hattie. Do you know, we had fifty-four members of the congregation and, as everyone left, there were so many comments about the refreshments and the wonderful music.' He sighed. 'It felt like Millbrook was a real community again.'

'And people were actually smiling,' Sally said. 'I haven't seen that in church in ages.'

Rosie crossed her legs. 'I'm doing an article this week in *The Chronicle* about it.' She looked pleased with herself. 'Before long, you'll have a congregation of people from all over the county on a Sunday.'

'How will we feed them all?' Susan asked.

'Indeed,' Hattie added. 'It's hardly loaves and fishes.'

'We'll all chip in.' Susan glanced at Robert.

'With Robert as our head chef?' Angie suggested.

'Perhaps others could provide refreshments?' Hattie said protectively. 'What about you, Dennis – or Colin?'

'I can't cook toast,' Dennis said grumpily.

'I can buy a packet of digestives,' Colin offered.

'That's hardly the same,' Mary Tenby said to her husband, George.

'I'll help Robert – if he'll teach me,' Jill from Dawlish whispered shyly. 'I'd like that.'

'We certainly need to keep the momentum going,' Francis said.

'Why don't we use the manse kitchen next time?' Sally murmured.

'You can all come round to ours and use the kitchen.' Eric Mallory took off his dark cap and wiped his brow. 'Edie isn't much of a baker, though.'

Edie elbowed him in the ribs indignantly. 'I can make an upside-down cake.'

'I'll have a go at making some scones.' Barry Butler glanced at Hattie hopefully. 'If anyone would be kind enough to help me.'

'We'll make it a village effort,' Francis said emphatically. 'After all, we are a strong community. Robert, we value your lead on this, but I have to say, you aren't expected to come up with the goods every Sunday and if you do bake, you'll be supported by the whole team. I won't expect you to produce what you did yesterday for every Sunday – although the cream teas were second to none.'

'Thank you,' Robert said humbly. 'I'd appreciate that. In terms of what cakes or scones to bake – I want to avoid unpopular choices. Apparently, someone didn't like the ginger ones yesterday.'

'Oh, I loved them,' Susan gushed.

'They were my favourite.' Angie leaned forward aggressively. 'Who said they didn't like them?'

'Can I say something, please?' Rosie Eagle looked up from where she was thumbing a message on her phone.

'Of course.' Francis beamed. 'May I say, though, that I appreciate all your publicity, Rosie. You've really put Millbrook on the map.'

'I have, and that seems to have caused a slight problem.'

'Problem?' Francis's eyebrows shot up. 'How can that be?'

'Geraldine Fielding, who came to the service yesterday, is being very vocal about her opinions. She was the one who was being critical of your baking, Robert. She's a reporter and she's quite incensed by my comments about you being the best in the south-west.'

'Oh?' Robert said nervously. 'Well, I don't claim to be anything special.'

'Oh, you are special,' Susan said.

'Very special,' Angie added.

'Very special indeed,' Jill from Dawlish repeated.

'And that's the problem.' Rosie folded her arms. 'Geraldine's a reporter for *The Cornish Anchor*. And she insists that the best scones in the south-west are made in Cornwall.'

'That's rubbish,' Mary retorted.

Dennis grunted. 'She should put her money where her mouth is.'

'She's going to.' Rosie smiled as she rubbed her hands together. 'Geraldine thinks she knows someone who is a better baker – she wants a public competition, a great scone showdown. So – I was hoping – are you up for it, Robert? My paper will back you and – it's incredible publicity.'

'Really?' Robert was unsure. 'What will I have to do?'

'Bake a cream tea. Oh...' Rosie's face took on a dreamy look. 'I can see it now – Robert from Devon wins the Great South-West Scone War... It will be a perfect opportunity to show how we shine, and we'll invite the TV cameras, get a top chef to judge. And *The Teignmouth Chronicle* will sponsor the whole thing.' She smiled, a moment of triumph. 'It appears that there are going to be sizzling Scone Wars in the south-west this summer and the whole thing will happen live on TV.'

25

Robert gripped a glass of whisky, his legs up on the sofa, staring at the conservatory clock. Isaac Mewton was asleep on his legs, purring loudly. He said, 'I don't know what to do, Hat – I can't make my mind up.'

Hattie sipped cocoa. 'You don't have to do it. Just tell Rosie you don't want to.'

'But I might want to.'

'Then do it.'

'But I might not.'

'Sleep on it tonight,' Hattie said kindly. 'You can make your mind up tomorrow...'

'The thing is—' Robert shifted nervously '—I'd love to win. I think my baking is good enough. And there's so much support in the village. It would be nice to win – it'd be an accomplishment. And Rosie said we'd be doing the competition for charity.'

'For the Devon Air Ambulance – and the St Ives RNLI.'

'So – we'd raise money. And it's in three weeks so we might be able to do it here, on my new patio. What a way to break it in.'

Hattie sat back in her seat. 'Then say you'll do it. Ring Rosie tomorrow and say you've decided.'

'But what if I lose?'

'Someone has to.'

'But it's Devon against Cornwall and I'll be representing Devon. What if I let the county down and everyone hates me?'

'They won't hate you. You can tell them you don't want to compete.'

'But...' Robert gulped whisky. 'All my life I've hidden my light under a bushel. I ought to be brave and show what I'm made of.'

'Then say yes.'

'But if I lose, I'll feel awful – I'll be embarrassed.'

'You won't lose,' Hattie said firmly. 'And if you did, you could be gracious in defeat knowing that your cream teas are the best in Devon.'

'I don't know.' He stared into the distance, then he said, 'Are you going home next week?'

'I've decided to drive back on Wednesday,' Hattie muttered. 'I've promised Barry I'd visit him tomorrow. He wants to show me some of his landscapes.'

Robert raised an eyebrow. 'Barry Butler?'

'He seems a nice man. He invited me round for a light lunch. It's probably coffee and a sandwich – not everyone has your baking skills, Robert.'

'I didn't know you knew him.'

'I don't.'

'So why has he invited you?'

'I spoke to him in church yesterday. I almost frightened him to death when he was painting on the village green. He probably thinks I'm weird.'

'Why did you accept his invitation, then?' Robert's tone was almost accusing. 'I mean – you will be all right on your own, won't you?'

'Is he a serial killer?'

'No, he's a quiet man. He keeps himself to himself.'

'The worst sort.' Hattie met Robert's eyes and winked. 'Oh, Robert. You and I have spent all our lives being good and quiet and sensible. Let's take a few risks.'

'How do you mean?'

'I'll go and have lunch with Barry and tell him how lovely his paintings are. He might open the door wearing nothing but a bow tie and a smile and try to seduce me but...'

'Hattie!'

'The chances are we'll just sit at his dining table and talk about the weather and how nice his painting of Haytor Rock is and then I'll come home. But you and I need to stop holding back.'

'Oh?'

'Go for it, Robert. Take a risk. Enjoy the thrill of the competition. It doesn't matter how it ends – the journey is the exciting part.'

'Do you think so?'

'I do. I gave Geoffrey forty-nine years and he reduced me to a shell of the woman I could have been. But no more.' Hattie offered a wry smile. 'I'm having lunch with Barry tomorrow. Perhaps we'll have a fling – you know, snogging and such like. Now that would be good for my morale.'

Robert made a sad snuffling sound. 'It would be good for anyone's morale.'

'Or we might make each other laugh. We might talk art and literature and music and philosophy. We might be best friends forever. Or we might hate each other. But I won't know if I don't go.'

'I see,' Robert said slowly. 'So – you think I ought to do the competition?'

'Yes, I do,' Hattie said. 'How else will you know if you'll win or not?'

'But you're going back home,' Robert began.

'I'll come back to visit and support you,' Hattie promised. She finished her cocoa. 'I'll be here for you. Think about it tonight, Robert. Then tomorrow you can give Rosie a ring and tell her your decision.'

'All right.' Robert stared into his empty glass, shifting slightly, hoping not to disturb Isaac Mewton who was purring like a traction engine. 'I suppose I ought to take more risks. I'm just afraid of looking like a loser.'

'Everyone feels the same,' Hattie said. 'But the thing is, Robert, the biggest risk is not taking any risk at all. And if we don't make mistakes and get things wrong – how will we know we're alive?'

Robert watched her shuffle to her feet, cup in hand, towards the kitchen. She mumbled, 'Goodnight, Robert. Sleep well.'

'Goodnight, Hat,' he whispered. He'd never realised how wonderful she was but, at this moment, he was filled with affection and admiration: Hattie was the best sister in the world. He just wished she weren't going home so soon.

* * *

Bunty squeezed her eyes closed and tried to sleep. But there it was, the sound again, as if someone was pushing the front door. She told herself she was being silly – it was the wind bumping against the front of the house, it was just nerves. She glanced at her phone. No messages – not Hattie or Robert, not Sean. She was on her own.

She could smell paint, a light whiff of it on the air from the adjacent bedroom. The house felt alien and she wished she were back home in Ballycotton where the cottage smelled of scented candles and baking bread. She'd be comfortable there, tucked up in her warm room, Sean in her arms, snoring like a penny whistle, up and down. Now she was by herself, the bed was too quiet, the sheet too cold against her skin. For a moment, Bunty thought that was what she deserved from now on – loneliness, sadness. Then she heard it again, a rattling sound. The front door.

It was past midnight. Surely Jacko wouldn't come now. But then it was exactly when he would come. He probably had no hotel booked. He needed somewhere to sleep. She listened so hard her ears rang with the silence. There it was again, a scuffle. Bunty exhaled; she'd locked and bolted the door before she came to bed.

She reached down to the carpet and her fingers touched the frying pan, curling round the handle. She lifted it as she swung her feet out of bed and padded to the doorway, peering into the hall. Holding her breath, conscious of her heart bumping hard, she gripped the pan, ready to swing it if she needed to. Then she heard the flip of the letter box, a light click. She waited for a moment, peering into the darkness. Bunty didn't want to turn on the light, so she crawled towards the door, feeling with the flat of her hand. Her fingers touched something that felt like paper – an envelope. She snatched it up and crawled back to the bedroom, using her phone as a torch.

The envelope was crisp, neat, no name on the front. She opened it with shaking fingers: inside there was a note and two tickets for The Mill Arts Centre in Banbury to see Dark Circles Contemporary Dance. The note, in round handwriting, proclaimed:

Dinner for two and an evening of culture... I'll call round
tomorrow at six. Be ready.

Jacko was trying to woo her with dinner and a dance troupe!
She couldn't believe it. He'd stop at nothing. She snuggled deep
beneath the covers and pressed buttons on her phone, looking for
train times. Bunty blinked as the website revealed itself and a
plan began to form. She couldn't stay at Hattie's any longer. It was
all becoming too dangerous. She wondered where Jacko was
staying – she imagined him sleeping in the back of the plumber's
van on a mattress, waking at eight and going to a greasy spoon for
a fried breakfast. She wondered if he had a suitcase full of
clothes, what he'd wear to treat her to dinner and a show. But it
didn't matter. She would never find out. She closed her eyes and
willed sleep to come.

The following morning, Bunty crept out of bed at nine, showered and packed all her belongings. She felt fretful; every time a
car passed, looking up to see if it was a white van. She told herself
that Jacko wouldn't call round until six. She sat hunched at the
table drinking coffee, booking a train ticket on her phone. She'd
get a taxi to Banbury, then take the lunchtime train.

Knuckles rapped at the back door and Bunty looked up; a
slight figure stood outside in the bright sunshine. Bunty opened
the door a crack, smiled with relief when she saw Glenys and
ushered her inside.

'I called round – we're going to yoga this morning,
remember?'

'I can't go,' Bunty said quickly.

'Kay will be disappointed.'

'Tell her I'm sorry – I'm leaving today – I have to get away.'

'Why?'

Bunty thrust the envelope with tickets into Glenys's hands.

'Do you and Bill like contemporary dance? Can you use these tickets?'

Glenys frowned. 'Where did these come from?' She examined the note. 'A dinner date?'

'Jacko put them through the letter box late last night.'

'Jacko?' Glenys shook her head. 'Is he a dance fan?'

'It's his idea of being romantic, cultured, I suppose.' Bunty shuddered. 'I just booked a train ticket. The taxi is coming at ten past eleven.'

'I'll be sorry to see you go.'

'Me too.' Bunty rushed over and enveloped Glenys in a hug. 'Thanks for everything you've done.'

'When's Hattie back? Shall I keep an eye on the house?'

'Please…' Bunty nodded energetically. 'I'll text her when I'm on the train to tell her what's happening.' She caught her breath. 'I just have to get out of here as soon as I can.' She pulled a face. 'I'm just being melodramatic again. I ought to show some back-bone and stay and tell Jacko to leave me alone, to go back to Plymouth.'

'I can see why you'd want to rush off,' Glenys said kindly. 'No, you go on – I'll keep an eye on everything here. And if I see Jacko at the door – I'll ask Bill to go out and have a word with him, tell him you've gone home.'

'I've blocked him on my phone.' Bunty's face was sad. 'I'm sorry it ended like this. I've been so stupid.' She took a breath. 'Do tell him I'm really truly sorry. Tell him to go back to his wife and try again. I've made such a mess of things.'

Glenys hugged her again. 'Onwards and upwards, as my mother used to say.' She took a step back. 'I'll get off to yoga now. I'll tell Kay that you're leaving.'

'Kay was nice. She said so many helpful things about mind-fulness and taking control of my own life. I'll never forget. And you've been supportive, Glenys.' Bunty felt tears prick her eyes. 'I'm so grateful, I really am.'

'Good luck with everything, Bunty. No doubt you'll be down again to visit Hattie at some point, and we'll catch up then.' Glenys reached out an arm, patted Bunty's shoulder. 'Bring Sean with you when you come. It would be nice to meet him. Sean's a Scorpio – he's your soulmate.'

'He is,' Bunty said sadly. She watched Glenys disappear down the path, her yoga bag in her hand. The glossy horse card she'd written so carefully was inside her case, packed away with her things, unsent.

Bunty wasn't sure if she'd ever send it now.

26

Hattie marched along the road into Millbrook, her tummy bubbling with excitement. She'd left Robert in the garden talking about patio slabs, canopies and seating areas with Danut and Joey while Isaac Mewton tried to dismember a leaf. She sauntered past them all in her best summer frock, sprayed in a haze of sweet perfume, on her way to have lunch at Barry Butler's cottage. She hadn't told Robert just how excited she was – she'd tried her best to maintain an aura of composure, to hide her racing pulse. It was important to look calm on the outside. In truth, it was her first date since her early twenties, when she'd met Geoffrey, and that hadn't ended well. She was out of practice and seriously nervous.

But Geoffrey could go to hell – she promised herself that he was the last thing on her mind today. Her step was sprightly – she was a new woman, enjoying life, ready for a date with a landscape artist. Barry had invited her for lunch at twelve-thirty and she was neither early nor late as she walked towards the green door of Crimble Cottage. She tapped the knocker and felt her breathing kick up yet another notch towards rapid. She exhaled, practising what she'd learned at yoga: she'd appear serene.

She was about to knock again when the door opened and Barry peered out anxiously, a tea towel draped over his shoulder. 'Oh, it's you – good,' he said and Hattie wondered who else he was expecting. 'Come in – come in.'

His gaze landed nervously on her floral frock and away, suddenly awkward. Hattie followed him into the hall. She breathed deeply: inhale courage, exhale fear. Inhale courage.

She paused to linger by some of the paintings on the wall, trees with hefty roots, thick slabs of grey rocks and brooding skies, but Barry was forging ahead, turning into the kitchen, where he realised he was wearing a tea towel. He placed it shyly on the worktop before hurrying out of the back door towards a patio table.

'Shoo – shoo, Monster.' He waved his hand kindly at a fat black cat who was on the patio table attacking the pastry crust of a quiche.

Hattie paused to look around the little garden, the lawn newly mowed, borders of bright shrubs, a rustic wooden pergola with a patio table beneath. Although it was lunchtime, little twinkling lights gleamed like jewels, threaded around the pergola, and water bubbled gently from a water feature, cascading down three stone bowls. Two plates and two glasses were arranged on the table, shining cutlery, napkins, a bottle of water and a bottle of wine. There were quiche, salads, crusty bread, something that might have been pâté, a butter dish.

Barry waved a hand. 'Won't you sit – please?'

Hattie spoke her thoughts aloud. 'You've gone to a lot of trouble.'

'Oh, no, no.'

'I just expected a sandwich and a tour of your paintings.'

'Oh, I hope you're not disappointed.'

'Not at all, I didn't mean—'

They stared at each other in silence, both wondering what to say, if they had got it wrong already. Then Hattie sat down and said, 'Thank you.'

Barry seated himself opposite. 'Wine?'

'A small glass. I don't usually drink at lunchtimes,' Hattie began, remembering how she'd sauntered into The Pig and Pickle Inn after almost frightening him witless on the village green.

'No, nor me,' Barry said, embarrassed, as if Hattie would think he was a regular boozer. 'It's a special occasion.'

'Oh, I hope I haven't put you to any trouble.'

'No trouble. I'm no cook – I hope the quiche is all right. I made it from scratch. I've never made one from scratch before.'

'Oh, I'm sure it will be lovely.' Hattie gazed at the thick crust, the sinking middle, the half-moon bite the cat had taken from the side.

Barry hacked a huge slab and dropped it on her plate upside down. 'Sorry – it wasn't meant to fall.'

'Oh, please, don't worry.' Hattie paused. 'Barry—' She took a breath. It was time they stopped apologising and fretting. 'I'm so glad you invited me to lunch. It's nice to get away from Robert, talking about his patio plans with Danut.' She put a hand to her mouth. She hadn't meant to imply that being with Robert was dull or that visiting Barry was a temporary improvement in her boring routine. She dug into the quiche, smiling for all she was worth, biting down on the crust. She felt something crack in her mouth and hoped she hadn't broken a tooth. She smiled more and said, 'I love wholemeal pastry.'

'It's not wholemeal,' Barry said. 'It's supposed to be shortcrust – it's a recipe I found online – Brie cheese, salmon...'

'It's lovely.' Hattie couldn't taste salmon or Brie. She took a glug of wine as Barry passed the salad bowl, almost knocking her glass from her hand.

'Salad?'

'Thank you.'

'I can't cook like Robert does – I don't usually cook at all.'

'Oh?' Hattie scooped dry leaves onto her plate and looked around for salad dressing. She found none. 'What do you eat normally?'

'Meals for one,' Barry replied without thinking. 'In the microwave.'

'Ah.' Hattie nodded as if she understood. 'Some of them can be quite – nice...' Now she was being patronising.

'Most of them aren't – but it's probably my cooking. I never get the timing right and I either incinerate everything or it has a frozen centre.' He said haplessly. 'I can do peas...'

'It can be so hard by yourself.' Hattie met his eyes sympathetically, her fork in the air.

'It is.' Barry's gaze was sad; Hattie noticed he had the brownest eyes, large and round, as he blinked slowly. They were honest, soulful eyes, a little like a cow's, Hattie thought, but very attractive. She'd been staring too long. He'd said something to her but she hadn't heard. 'Pardon?'

'Are you a – a widow?' Barry asked.

'No, I'm an escapee,' she replied quickly.

'A—?' Barry put a hand to his ear as if he'd heard 'escaped pea'.

'My husband left, and I was glad he did,' Hattie said honestly. 'I was silly to stay with him for so long. I was in the biggest rut. I had the Grand Canyon of all marriages.'

'Where is he now?'

'Happily shacked up with Linda from the bowling club.'

Hattie waved a fork. The quiche was quite pleasant once you'd got past the crust. 'And good riddance.' She wondered if she was coming across as blasé, callous even, so she added, 'I do wish him all the best.'

'Ah.' Barry put a fist against his chest in a 'Me Tarzan' gesture. 'I'm a widower.'

'I'm sorry,' Hattie said quickly, hoping she hadn't offended him in some way by making light of her own marriage.

Barry lifted a leaf from his plate and studied it. 'Anne was my world. She died five years ago. Short illness.'

Hattie was about to say 'I'm sorry' again, but she placed a hand over her mouth and thought for a while. 'It must be difficult being suddenly alone once you've loved someone all your life.'

'She got me started on the painting. When we retired, we both took it up as a hobby. She dragged me out and we bought brushes and watercolours, then we took the car all over Devon and sat in the sunshine, working on the landscapes.'

'That's so sweet.'

'She was a better painter than I'll ever be.'

'Do you have any of her work on your walls?'

'I keep Anne's pictures upstairs in the spare room. I still feel a bit wobbly when I look at them, even now.'

Hattie was suddenly filled with admiration for Barry; he'd been devoted to his wife. Such a man was remarkable, in her opinion. She said, 'You must miss her very much. You're lucky to have had someone you cared so much about.'

'I was.'

'I don't think I ever loved Geoffrey, even when we were first together. I just thought that's what I had to do, meet someone, marry them, keep the house tidy, work hard.'

'That's very sad,' Barry agreed. 'At least I knew how it was to love someone. I'm sorry you missed out on that.'

'I did.' Hattie waved her fork determinedly. 'But do you know, Barry, I've recently woken up to the fact that life is for living. Each day should be positive and enjoyable. It's no good looking back. Those times are in the past.' She thought about Barry and his beloved Anne and tried again. 'In your case, the past is a treasure chest of sweet memories and they will be in your heart forever.'

'But—' Barry pushed the salad leaf into his mouth '—we have to live for now. Anne would want me to enjoy life. And right now, I'm enjoying lunch with a – a very nice companion – even if the pastry is a bit like chewing pebbles.'

'I've developed quite a liking for the quiche,' Hattie said.

'Good. Because I tried my hand at making Bakewell tart for pudding – with the same pastry.'

'I look forward to it.' Hattie smiled. 'And I'll enjoy looking at some of your wonderful landscapes.'

'It would be my pleasure to show you round.' Barry's eyes shone. 'Thank you for having lunch with me, Hattie.'

'It's my pleasure – I mean, it's just a pleasant lunch.'

'No, it's more than that. It's an oasis in my usually arid day. It's a delight to talk, to spend time with someone who makes me smile.'

'I couldn't agree more.' Hattie held out her glass. 'I'll drink to that.'

Barry misunderstood and picked up the wine bottle, thinking that she'd asked for a refill. He topped the glass up to the brim, then topped up his own. 'Cheers, to spending time,' he said, his face now relaxed.

Hattie sipped a mouthful, reminding herself sternly that this would definitely be her last glass. She didn't want to totter back home to Robert again. Goodness knew what he'd think of her, tipsy twice in one week.

Oh, who cared? she thought. It was good wine. She was

starting to enjoy herself. Barry was nice company; the conversation was starting to flow. They'd finish off the whole bottle and to hell with the consequences.

* * *

Robert waved a hand cheerily as Danut and Joey pulled away from the drive in a puff of black smoke, leaving the beginnings of the new patio behind them, the ground dug and levelled. It was after five o'clock and Hattie still wasn't home. Robert wondered if he should walk up to Crimble Cottage and knock at the door. He imagined Barry answering in his boxer shorts, hair tousled, Robert stammering, 'Do you have my sister in there?' Hattie would appear over his shoulder wearing a fluffy towel. No, Robert told himself sternly, he was being silly. Hattie wasn't a teenager. She'd do as she pleased.

Then it occurred to him that she might have been hit by a truck on the way home. Very few trucks passed through Millbrook; a bus called in three times a day. He was worrying for nothing – he could always text her. Briefly Robert wondered what she'd like for her evening meal. She probably had something substantial for lunch, so he'd cook a nice quiche for supper.

He felt something brush against his legs and he looked down at Isaac Mewton, whose job it was to remind him that it was time to feed the animals. He wandered through the garden, past the orchard and into the field where the chickens strutted, pecking at the soil. He gazed affectionately as Princess Lay-a rushed past his legs, flapping her wings. Vincent Van Goat and The Great Goatsby rubbed their heads against his knees in protest: they were hungry. The grass was a little damp; Robert was glad he'd worn his wellingtons. He inhaled the sweet smell and was filled with happiness for his life. He patted Vincent's gnarled head and watched as Isaac Mewton turned to lead the way back to the house.

It was then that he saw a red saloon car accelerating along the drive. He didn't recognise the vehicle – it looked to him like a Skoda Octavia, and Robert didn't know anyone who drove one. At first, he wondered if someone had given Hattie a lift home, then he noticed the taxi sign painted on the side, Albany Taxis. He stared harder, wondering who'd come to visit; then he caught his breath as a woman wriggled from the passenger seat, waving her arms, calling, 'Robert – Robert. It's me.'

He waved back, hardly able to believe his eyes. The red taxi reversed away, and Robert rushed forward to where Bunty was smiling, hands on hips, a suitcase at her feet. 'I've come to stay, Robert. Where's Hattie? Get the kettle on – I'm parched.'

27

Hattie wandered back to Robert's house, thinking that she probably should have texted him she'd be late. She'd lost track of time. After lunch, Barry gave her a grand tour of his paintings in the downstairs rooms, then he took her upstairs where he kept Anne's watercolours. He was hesitant, unsure about showing her his late wife's work, but it was a gesture of trust.

Hattie was fascinated, and it wasn't down to the three small glasses of wine she'd enjoyed with lunch. Barry's paintings demonstrated a good eye for detail: he knew the landscape of Devon so well. He was nervous as he pointed out to Hattie beautifully captured paintings of Wistman's Wood, Clapper Bridge and Lydford Gorge. Then they sat in the garden, drinking tea and talking. Hattie had never told anyone about her marriage to Geoffrey without feeling foolish, but discussing it with Barry was therapy: she even found some of Geoffrey's controlling behaviour ridiculously funny. She wasn't sure whether it was the wine or whether it was Barry, but they laughed until their eyes watered.

Barry asked her when she was going back to Bodicote and she replied without thinking. 'At the weekend, probably.' She was instantly surprised: she'd intended to return the next day, but she was in no rush – she liked Barry and he'd already hinted that he'd like to see her again. Hattie was sure Robert wouldn't mind. So, as she left, she invited Barry to lunch the following day in The Pig and Pickle. She found herself smiling as she walked along the drive towards Robert's front door – he'd left it open for her, and she wandered inside.

She found him in the kitchen, lifting a large quiche from the oven. Isaac Mewton rubbed against her shins purring as she said, 'That smells nice.'

'I wonder, Hattie...' Robert gave her a searching look and Hattie wondered if he was checking to see if she was sober. 'Could you give me a hand? I've got a potato and chive salad in the fridge, and there's some crusty bread, and I need to make a leafy salad with rocket and tomatoes and—'

'This is a big spread for the two of us,' Hattie said. 'The quiche smells nice.' She remembered the one Barry had made for lunch and the way they had both picked over their food, preferring conversation, looking into each other's eyes.

'It's goat's cheese, spinach and sun-dried tomato.' Robert was bustling around. 'And I thought we'd have lemonade.' He rolled his eyes to the ceiling. 'Bunty's here.'

'Bunty's where?' Hattie frowned.

'Upstairs in the bath – or making herself comfortable in the third bedroom, I'm not sure – she's been ages. She turned up late this afternoon and said she was seeking refuge.'

'Refuge?'

'Apparently Jacko has been calling at the bungalow.'

'I thought he'd gone?'

Robert shook his head. 'He's been back at night, it seems, trying to get in. He gave her flowers, posted tickets for a dance show and invited her to dinner.'

'Jacko did that?' Hattie couldn't believe it.

'Bunty says he's obsessed – she's blocked him on her phone.'

Hattie found she was whispering. 'Why didn't she go back to Sean?'

Robert was whispering too. 'He messaged her a while ago and told her he loved her but that she was free to follow her own path.'

'So, is that what she wants, to be on her own?'

'No, she wants him back, but she wants him to ask her to go back with him.'

'Can't she just go to Ballycotton and apologise?'

'No, it seems…' Robert took five glasses from a cupboard. 'She feels she's let him down. She wants him to forgive her.'

'I'm sure he will – he thinks the world of her.'

'Apparently, she's got a card to post to him. I don't know why she can't just ring him and say sorry but—'

'Why have you put five glasses out?' Hattie asked. 'I thought there was me, you and Bunty for supper?'

'Ah.' Robert looked uncomfortable. 'We have guests. Rosie Eagle rang me this afternoon and asked if she could call round – she has something she needs to discuss with me. So I invited her to dinner.'

'With her husband?'

'No, she's – she's bringing that Geraldine woman.'

'The one who said your ginger scones were too spicy?'

'Yes – they'll be here in twenty minutes, which is why I need your help, Hat.'

'Right.' Hattie launched herself towards the fridge, taking out a salad, potatoes. 'Why have you invited her here when she criticised your cooking?'

'Pride, I guess,' Robert said. 'And I wanted our meeting to be civilised. Rosie wants to discuss that darned competition – she said it was very important – so I wanted the solidarity of you with me. Oh, sorry, Hattie – I should have asked,' Robert remembered. 'How was lunch with Barry Butler?'

'Civilised.' Hattie chose to use Robert's word. 'I'm treating him to lunch in the pub tomorrow by way of reciprocating. I'll go back home at the weekend.'

'You could stay until Sunday afternoon – Francis would be delighted if you'd play the church organ again. And Sally's organising a potluck lunch for the congregation on the village green. Everyone in the gardening club is taking a contribution. I'm baking a pavlova.'

'I might stay until then.' Hattie started to cut bread as Bunty appeared in the doorway, her hair damp.

'Hattie.' Bunty rushed into her sister's arms, hugging her. Hattie could smell bath oil – it had a familiar scent. It was her own favourite, Citrus Celebration; Bunty had borrowed it. Hattie hugged her back. Typical Bunty. But she was so glad to see her.

'You look wonderful – different...' Bunty held her sister at arm's length. 'Robert said you'd been having lunch with a friend you'd met in the village. Did you have fun?'

'Yes, it was – very pleasant.' Hattie winked at Robert, grateful that he'd told Bunty that Hattie had met *a friend* and not *a man* – Bunty would have been frantic with questions. An hour ago she'd been standing at the doorway at Crimble Cottage, giving Barry a kiss on the cheek as their noses collided awkwardly. Barry's brown eyes shone as he said how much he had enjoyed spending time with her.

She tugged her thoughts into the present. 'So – are we eating in here, Robert?'

'I thought so – it's a bit dusty in the garden with all the building work. It's going well though – Danut says he'll have the patio stones down next week and put some edging round. Then he'll build the pergola.'

Bunty clapped her hands. 'Doesn't it sound fabulous? It will look lovely.' She sat down at the table and reached for a piece of crusty bread that Hattie had just sliced. 'When are the guests arriving? I'm starving.' Isaac Mewton sprang onto her knee and she offered her a small dot of butter on the end of her finger. The cat's little pink tongue licked frantically and she began to purr.

Robert rearranged the cutlery nervously. 'Any moment, I guess.' He looked from Hattie to Bunty. 'So – should I say yes to this cream-tea contest thing?'

'It's entirely up to you,' Hattie said.

'But you said it might be on TV? That's exciting,' Bunty added.

'Rosie mentioned it...' Robert said.

'And it's for charity,' Hattie reminded him.

'You'd be famous.' Bunty reached for a second piece of bread. Isaac swiped at her hand and she gave her another knob of butter.

Hattie said, 'You have to be sure about it, though. Don't let yourself be persuaded to do something you don't want to.'

'I want to. Part of me is competitive. And I take your point about the result not being as important as the taking part but—' Robert hovered over the quiche, moving his hands to the salad as if he were conjuring a spell. 'What if I'm humiliated?'

'You won't be – it's not possible,' Bunty almost shouted.

'Listen to what Rosie says – make up your mind then,' Hattie said.

Then a loud knock at the front door made Robert jump. 'Here she is.'

'Rosie?' Hattie asked.

'And that terrifying woman, Geraldine.' Robert bustled from his seat and rushed to the door as if propelled.

He returned a few seconds later, Rosie behind him beaming and calling, 'Hello.'

A few steps behind, Geraldine stood in her beret and raincoat, arms folded, her face disapproving. She said, 'Thank you for inviting me to supper,' as if she didn't mean a word of it.

'You remember Geraldine Fielding?' Rosie's grin widened.

'I'm from *The Cornish Anchor*. I'm a senior reporter. I wanted to talk to you about the arrangements for the Scone Wars.'

'Scone Wars?' Robert repeated.

'Like *Game of Scones*?' Bunty thought it was hilarious. 'Jon Snow against the Night King. Or *Star Wars: the Clone Wars*. Han Solo against Jabba the Hutt – oh no, I don't think they were they in that film together.'

'What does any of that mean?' Robert was confused.

Rosie indicated the table. 'The spread looks lovely – shall we sit down?'

Bunty was already seated, Isaac on her knee. Chairs scraped and everyone sat down as Robert coughed formally. 'This is my sister Bunty, and my sister Hattie.'

Geraldine nodded curtly, accepting the slice of quiche Robert popped on her plate. She helped herself to potato salad. 'So, Rosie, shall we put our proposal to Robert?'

Robert's hand shook as he handed Rosie a plate containing a delicate slice of quiche. 'The competition? Is it on? Have you found another baker?'

Geraldine was already munching, her elbows tucked in. 'We have.'

'Both *The Chronicle* and *The Anchor* will be sponsors. I've spoken to the television people, and also we have a merchandise company involved who will make button badges, car stickers, T-shirts with slogans...'

'*Cornish Cream Tease* with a huge picture of a jammy scone,' Geraldine said.

'*Game of Scones South West.*' Rosie grinned. '*Devon knows they are delicious.*'

'*Jam first – the proper job...*' Geraldine said.

'*The REAL cream tea from gorgeous Devon,*' Rosie suggested.

Robert nibbled his quiche. 'And this is a fundraiser?'

'For the air ambulance and the lifeboats,' Rosie said. 'The TV channel will run a slot every night for a week, a brief chat with someone famous representing Devon or Cornwall, with scones in the studio and a big push to buy merch online. The money will go to the charities. Then on the Saturday afternoon, Robert, you'll be part of the preview show that will go out live, with the competition itself being on the Sunday. It will be called Scone Wars. Can you imagine – the Final Frontier: Devon against Cornwall.'

'Where will it be?' Bunty asked, offering Isaac a morsel of quiche.

'We haven't decided.' Geraldine's plate was almost clean. 'Perhaps a lovely Cornish beach?'

'It's summertime so we could put up a tent in the grounds of Castle Drogo,' Rosie offered.

'You could hold the competition here – in the garden,' Hattie said.

'That's hardly neutral territory.' Geraldine was horrified.

'We'll discuss venue later – this is a lovely quiche, by the way, Robert,' Rosie said quickly.

'And who will be my – challenger?' Robert asked quietly.

'Well, there is someone.' Rosie tore a slice of crusty bread.

'A very well-known Cornish cook who runs a tea shop near Padstow – cream teas are on the menu there every day.' Geraldine was gleeful. She helped herself to more quiche.

'Plain scones, the odd fruit one.' Rosie shook her head. 'No variety – nothing like Robert's flavours.'

'That's not important,' Geraldine insisted.

'It is,' Rosie countered. The two women locked eyes for a moment, daggers drawn, then Rosie turned to Robert, her face sweet again. 'So, this is the format of the competition. You'll both be asked to make three batches of scones, all different flavours, determined by you, to be served with the cream and jam or topping of your choice – as long as it's local.'

'It won't be hard for you, Robert,' Hattie said encouragingly.

'Or for our Cornish competitor,' Geraldine retorted.

'So – what do you say, Robert?' Rosie glanced at Geraldine. 'I'm quietly confident.'

'Not quiet enough,' Geraldine muttered.

'When can I meet the other competitor?' Robert asked. 'I mean, it would be nice to meet him before the competition.'

'*Her.*' Geraldine met his eyes. 'She's called Tressy Carew and she's very keen to meet you too.'

'Why doesn't she come to the potluck after church on Sunday – on the village green?' Hattie suggested. 'Does she have an entourage? Robert has an entourage...' She imagined Susan, Angie and Jill clad in T-shirts with Robert's face on and a slogan that proclaimed *Devon Scone King*.

'Oh, is there a potluck? I'll be there.' Bunty dabbed her mouth.

'I'll ask her and let you know, Rosie.' Geraldine held out her plate. 'May I have some more quiche, Robert... just a smidgin?'

Rosie winked in Robert's direction. 'Once you've met Tressy we can ask you both to confirm that you'll compete. Then it's all systems go. We have a date set for the Scone Wars competition – two weeks on Saturday. And we'll get a famous TV chef who will turn up as neutral judge. That will draw the crowds.'

'I'll decide on Sunday then,' Robert said hesitantly. 'Since it's for charity...'

'Oh, it's so much more than that.' Geraldine's eyes glinted. 'For years, there have been fierce scone wars between Cornwall and Devon. The age-old argument, jam first or cream first. But this is even bigger – whose scones are best, Cornwall's or Devon's? Who can produce the tastiest cream tea in the south-west? And now we have the opportunity to decide – once and for all.'

28

Hattie sat in the pub with Barry Butler, enjoying scampi, chips and peas. Hattie was drinking white wine but she'd promised herself she'd only have one glass. Barry had a pint of mild and it seemed to have calmed his nerves. He was listening to her relate the story of last night's supper with the two reporters, although she omitted to tell him they'd eaten quiche. She didn't want him to feel bad about the one he'd made specially.

'So – Robert's going to accept the challenge?' Barry asked.

'I think so,' Hattie said. 'It will be quite a spectacle. I think it could be fun – and a real boost for his confidence.'

'I was thinking about that – losing might be difficult.' Barry raised an eyebrow. 'That's why I paint just for myself – I'd never go on one of those landscape artist competitions.'

'Oh, but you're talented enough to enter a competition,' Hattie said kindly.

Barry shook his head. 'I don't know about that, but I'm sure Robert's in with a chance of winning. And if it raises money for a good cause, so much the better.'

'It will.' Hattie noticed Barry was staring. 'What is it? Do I have ketchup on my nose?'

'No.' He laughed, the awkward chuckle of a man who wasn't used to women's company. 'I was just thinking how nice this is – spending time, having lunch.'

'It is.'

'Sharing, having another person to talk to, to confide in.'

'We all need that, Barry. I know when I was in the bungalow by myself for the last year, I was kind of trapped in one space and I lost the enthusiasm to venture outside much.'

'I know what you mean.' Barry toyed with his food. 'Since Anne died, I have a lot less get up and go, and I try my hardest to force myself to go outside the four walls because they remind me of her all the time. Not that I want to forget her – I don't – but it's the sadness that comes with it.'

'And the loneliness.' Hattie agreed. 'Geoffrey turned me into a person I wasn't, a fuddy-duddy with no confidence in myself. Life with him was unbearable and, by myself, it was lonely. I was a shadow.'

'I can hardly imagine that,' Barry said. 'But it's so important to get outside our comfortable space and push ourselves.'

'I agree. That's why I'm trying to persuade Robert to do the Scone Wars competition.'

'He's going to do it, then?' A voice boomed from behind Hattie's shoulder and Dennis Lyons brought his full pint to the table, plonked it down and dropped into a seat next to Hattie. 'I heard from Francis that Robert was going to do a baking competition against the whole of Cornwall. That might be fun. I could organise a sweep.'

Colin Bennett sat down next to Barry. 'Nice to see you again, Hattie. I enjoyed our last political debate. Barry – we don't see you often in The Pig and Pickle.'

Barry indicated his plate. 'I'm having lunch.'

'And it looks good,' Dennis said. 'I was going to order the pie but the scampi looks appetising. Shelley's pies can be a bit dry some days.'

'My pies aren't dry.' Shelley was at his shoulder with another pint of beer. 'You're a grumpy git, Dennis.'

'I am.' Dennis seemed pleased with the compliment. 'Get Barry and Hattie another drink, will you?'

'Oh no,' Hattie protested. 'I don't want—'

'I insist,' Dennis said, making a grandiose gesture with his arm.

'We'll both have lemonade,' Barry said quickly, catching Hattie's eye.

'So,' Colin said quickly. 'What do you think of the tomato shortage? Apparently, there's been a heatwave in Europe and the tomatoes aren't getting through. It might be more to do with Brexit.'

'It's canned tomatoes that are the trouble,' Dennis argued. 'And if they put it out on the telly that there's a shortage, everyone buys in bulk and that's why there are none on the shelves.' He turned to Hattie. 'I don't suppose Robert has any going spare? I'm partial to fresh tomatoes.'

Colin took a slurp of his pint. 'They aren't what they used to be years ago, tomatoes. It's the fertiliser they use.'

'And global warming – that affects the taste of them – and they grow too big,' Dennis said. 'Big tomatoes taste of nothing but water.'

Hattie smiled. 'I'm sure Robert wouldn't mind letting you have a bag of tomatoes from his greenhouse.'

'And a lettuce?' Colin asked hopefully. 'The slugs have had all of mine.'

'My beetroots have shrivelled up completely.' Dennis grunted.

'Mind you, they never cook up properly. Like brown bullets. You wouldn't have any fresh beetroot, would you, Hattie?'

Barry put his knife and fork down. 'There's some ice cream in my freezer, Hattie – and I've a few strawberries. We could take dessert at Crimble Cottage.'

'Lovely,' Hattie said.

'Oh, that would be nice.' Dennis swallowed beer. 'I'm partial to a nice bit of ice cream.'

'And strawberries,' Colin added. 'Can you hang on till we've had our pies?'

'I thought we were having scampi? The pastry on those pies can be a bit hard,' Dennis said. 'Like concrete.'

'Hattie,' a familiar voice trilled and Hattie swivelled round to see Bunty standing, hands on hips, smiling. 'Robert said I'd find you here.' She glanced at the plates. 'Are you having lunch? The scampi looks nice.'

'This is Bunty, my sister,' Hattie blurted.

'Pleased to meet you.' Dennis doffed his cap. 'Can I get you a drink?'

'Yes, what are you drinking, Bunty?' Colin asked.

'Well, if you're buying, I'd love a G & T.' Bunty settled herself at the table. 'This is nice.'

'Shelley,' Dennis called out. 'Can you get me a G & T and three scampi and chips?' He turned to Bunty. 'You'll join us for a spot of lunch?'

'I'd be delighted.' Bunty beamed.

A voice from behind the bar yelled back. 'Coming up, Dennis.'

Bunty placed her elbows on the table. 'So, Hattie – are you going to introduce us?'

'Bunty – this is Colin, Dennis and Barry.'

Bunty turned her best smile on Barry. 'Pleased to meet you.'

She swivelled round to Colin and Dennis. 'Well, I think I'm going to like being here in Millbrook. Pub lunches and gin and tonic? Lovely.'

'Are you staying with Robert?' Colin asked. 'He must have a houseful.'

'I suppose you're here for the Scone Wars competition?' Dennis wondered.

'No, I just popped out to post a letter,' Bunty said, misunderstanding, waving the envelope containing the horse card. It was addressed to Sean O'Connor.

Hattie looked at her plate, almost finished, and placed her cutlery down neatly. Then she whisked the envelope from Bunty's fingers. 'I fancy a stroll after that lunch.' She turned to Barry. 'Just as far as the post office. Would you like to come along?'

Bunty looked anxious. 'Are you coming back?'

'As soon as—' Hattie indicated the letter. 'A stroll after a meal is good for the stomach.'

'It is,' Barry agreed, standing up. 'We won't be long.'

Outside, the sunlight was blindingly bright and Hattie blinked for a moment. Then she said, 'I hope you don't mind, Barry. I just wanted to make sure we didn't get involved in an all-day drinking session.'

'I'm with you on that one,' Barry said. 'Colin and Dennis like their beer.'

'I know.' Hattie recalled the lunch she had shared with them, drinking and debating politics. 'Bunty will enjoy their company. She'll give them a hard time if she disagrees with them. She likes a banter. By the time we're back, they'll have eaten.'

'I'll gladly invite them all round for ice cream,' Barry said hesitantly.

'And strawberries. But they can drink tea,' Hattie said defiantly. She accepted the arm that Barry offered. 'It's five minutes' walk to the post office.'

'And ten coming back,' Barry suggested. 'We might linger to gaze at the flowers in the gardens.'

'Or we could even pop in the church. I could do with a bit of practice on the organ for Sunday.'

'You're stopping until Sunday?' Barry was delighted. 'Then I think a bit of practice might be a perfect way to spend fifteen minutes.'

They walked on to St Jude's, Hattie with her arm through Barry's, clutching Bunty's card to Sean in the other. The wooden door was wide open. A sound from inside made them pause; it was a voice, singing to a strumming guitar. Hattie listened for a while; it was an expressive contralto voice singing a jazzy song.

Barry raised an eyebrow. 'That's really very good.'

'It is,' Hattie said. 'Let's go in and listen.'

* * *

Robert was sitting in the conservatory listening to Dusty Springfield sing 'Wishin' and Hopin''. Robert wished that Hattie and Bunty were around; the house felt quiet without them, although outside he could hear the repetitive sound of Danut and Joey shouting to each other, joking as they clanked spades, the rumble of a concrete mixer. They were making good progress on the patio. Robert, however, was making poor progress; he was scribbling on a notepad, trying to work out what to bake in the Scone Wars competition.

He'd written *plain scones* and crossed it out and written *vanilla* instead; the sweetness of the vanilla might complement the cream, and a bitter blackcurrant jam would cut through it. Then he thought he'd make lemon zest scones with blackberry jam – but that was too similar to blackcurrant. He needed an unusual flavour, one that would make the judge gasp with surprise and admiration. He thought about coconut scones with lemon curd, or rocky road scones with marshmallow sprinkles. Perhaps pumpkin and lemonade scones served with cinnamon sugar and cream cheese. But cinnamon was spice and Geraldine had said his ginger scones were too spicy. He crossed the whole page out with one sweep of the pen and wished he had someone to talk to.

Isaac Mewton leaped onto his knee and he stroked her from head to tail. She arched her back and he scratched her chin and whiskers until she rolled over, purring. He smiled. 'Have you been on the catnip again, Isaac?' He sighed. 'I wish it worked on humans. I feel down in the dumps.'

Dusty's mezzo-soprano voice was singing 'I Close My Eyes and Count to Ten'. Robert closed his eyes and wondered if he ought to say no to Rosie Eagle. The competition was already causing him far too much stress. He'd save himself a lot of bother if he just refused. He breathed in and out deeply; it would be easy once he'd said no.

Something buzzed in his pocket and he pulled out his phone. It was a number he didn't recognise. 'Hello?'

A voice sweet as sugar fizzed in his ear. 'Hello? Is that Mr Robert Parkin?'

The r's were rounded, furry, warm and friendly – Robert recalled the word rhoticity, which described the purring r-sound perfectly. He was intrigued.

'Yes, I'm Robert.'

'I'm Tressy Carew from Padstow. I got your number from Rosie. I hope you don't mind me ringing.'

Robert hesitated for a moment, and then it dawned on him. 'The Cornish scone lady?'

'If you like.' Tressy sounded a little offended. 'I haven't said I'll do it yet.'

'Nor have I,' Robert replied honestly.

'Oh, and why's that?' Tressy's voice dripped like honey. Robert trusted her instantly, although he had no idea why.

'I just don't really like – competitions. I mean – the ladies from the newspapers want me to do it – and I love baking – and I'd like to raise money for charity.'

'Exactly,' Tressy said. 'I just don't like this business of who comes first and who is second being such a big deal. Devon is Devon. Cornwall is Cornwall. Scones is scones. It don't matter.'

'You're right,' Robert agreed. 'So – I'm not sure what to do.'

'Nor am I.' Tressy lowered her voice. 'That Geraldine from *The Cornish Anchor* is a bit pushy. And the other one – your Rosie Eagle – she smiles a bit too much for my liking. I don't trust either of them as far as I can throw 'em.'

'Ah,' Robert said. 'I hadn't thought of it like that.'

'So – they've asked me to come up to the potluck thing on Sunday and I've said yes I will but—'

'But?' Robert asked, anxiously. He was already looking forward to meeting Tressy.

'I'd like to see you first. On my own terms.'

'Oh?'

'Without the two women sticking their noses in, if you take my meaning. So...'

'So?' Robert asked.

'I'm driving up from Padstow and I know where Millbrook is, so I wondered if I could meet you first, around nine in the morning, so's we could have a chat together and sort it all out, me and you?'

'Would you like to come for breakfast?' Robert asked quickly. He hoped she'd say yes.

'Well, no, I won't, if it's all the same to you. It'd mean eating your food and that would put us on unequal footing if I do the competition. I'd know your cooking and you wouldn't know mine.'

'Oh, I suppose it would.'

'Although there's nothing stopping you coming to my tea shop in Padstow and having a cream tea, you know, in disguise.'

'Oh, I wouldn't do that,' Robert said.

'No, 'course not – that'd be proper sneaky. Well...' Tressy took a breath. 'Then I'll see you on Sunday morning and we'll have a cup of tea together and a talk and we'll decide what we're doing about this cream-tea business.'

'Scone Wars.'

'Exactly. Well. Nice to talk to you, Robert. I'll see you dreckly on Sunday.'

'Yes, on Sunday, directly,' Robert replied, but Tressy had hung up. Robert gazed down at where Isaac Mewton was purring on his knees, at the notepad with all the scone choices crossed out, and he closed his eyes and let Dusty Springfield's husky voice take him to a calm and wonderful place.

He exhaled as he relaxed and wondered what Tressy Carew looked like, hoping she was as lovely as she sounded.

29

Hattie led the way into the church, Barry at her shoulder. The music became louder as they approached; Tilda Baxter was sitting in a pew with a dark-haired man who was playing guitar. Hattie stood at a respectful distance, listening until the song finished. It resonated high in the rafters, the delicate guitar, the soulful rich voice, Amy Winehouse's 'You Know I'm No Good'. When they had finished, Hattie clapped and Barry followed suit. The sound of their applause echoed thinly off the walls. Tilda looked up; she'd been unaware she had an audience. She said, 'Hattie – good to see you. Have you met Donkey?'

Hattie shook his hand. 'I thought you were the band's drummer.'

'He's our band's best drummer and our best guitarist too. Skinny Norm plays guitar with us, and Donkey plays drums because no one else can do it.'

Donkey spoke in his quiet voice. 'I like to play lots of instruments. Music's all I do.' He smiled at Tilda. 'We're practising in here because the acoustics are good. Tilda's dad won't mind – he says the house of God belongs to us all.'

'I really think your voice is exceptional, Tilda,' Hattie said.

'Thanks,' Tilda replied shyly. 'Donkey thinks we should diversify – me and him, acoustic gigs in jazz clubs. I don't know.'

'It's all experience,' Donkey murmured. 'Tilda's taking a gap year and it makes sense to fill it with improving our music. We have time to gig as Armpit and to do our own stuff.'

'You're giving it your best shot, and that's what's important.' Hattie agreed.

Donkey smiled politely. 'I came to the Sunday service to hear you play the organ. Tilda said you were good. She's not wrong. Are you classically trained?'

'Grade eight piano as a teenager.' Hattie smiled. 'I have an old piano. I didn't practise for years – my ex-husband was very critical of my playing. But now he's gone, I'm getting my mojo back.'

'Keep it coming.' Donkey turned to Barry. 'Do you play?'

'No.' Barry shrugged. 'They gave me a set of drums in the Boys' Brigade, but that was sixty years ago.'

'I don't suppose—' Tilda's face was tight with thought. 'Have you got any spare time now?'

'A little.' Hattie held up Bunty's card. 'I'm only posting a letter.'

'Could you come across to the manse?' Tilda was suddenly excited. 'We have keyboards up there. I don't suppose you fancy a jam?'

Hattie smiled. 'Jamming's not something I've ever done, except between scones. Why not?' She saw Tilda's puzzled expression. 'I'd love to play with you. I'm sure we can spare half an hour. What do you think, Barry?'

Barry was grinning with enthusiasm. 'Definitely. Our lemonades will still be in The Pig and Pickle when we've finished...'

* * *

Bunty, Dennis and Colin had eaten dessert and the table was full of glasses when Hattie and Barry stepped into the darkness of the snug. Bunty thumped her fist on the table. 'You really don't know what you're talking about, Dennis.'

'I'm just saying,' Dennis protested. 'We've all got too PC nowadays. In the old days you said what you liked and no one took offence. You can't compliment a lady any more. I mean, if I said you have lovely legs, Bunty, you'd probably call me sexist. That's silly.'

'You do have nice legs.' Colin clutched his pint glass.

'You're not listening.' Bunty leaned forward. 'Women are more than the sum of their body parts and we've never been comfortable with it, it's just that we were marginalised. We need to be embraced as people.'

'Embraced?' Dennis lifted his eyebrows suggestively. 'It's a long time since I embraced a lovely woman.'

'So why can't you have a conversation with my face?' Bunty countered. 'You've spent the best part of the last half-hour addressing my boobs.'

'Have I?' Dennis swayed a little. 'To be honest, I can hardly see straight. I think this is my fifth pint.'

Bunty swivelled round. 'Hattie – I thought you'd got lost.'

'Sorry.' Hattie sat down next to Bunty. 'You seem to be enjoying yourself.'

'I'm explaining wokeness to Dennis and Colin.'

'Wokeness – isn't that a town in Essex?' Colin joked.

'It's not funny,' Bunty insisted. 'No matter what your age is, you can keep educating yourself. It's what we should all do and you two—' Bunty pointed a finger, '—are both straight out of the Dark Ages.'

'I do like your sister, Hattie – in fact, I like both of Robert's sisters...' Dennis said, his eyelids drooping as he swayed from side to side. 'Or all four of them.'

'Anyway, Barry, you two have been gone a long time. You said fifteen minutes, but it's been over an hour.' Colin winked. 'What have you been up to, or shouldn't I ask?'

'We've had a wonderful time, and it's none of your business,' Hattie said sweetly as she reached for the now flat lemonade and took a sip. 'We posted your card, Bunty, then we went to the manse for a jam session with Armpit – or at least, two thirds of an armpit. Tilda has a nice set of keyboards.'

'I had a go on the drums.' Barry couldn't help smiling. 'I was getting quite good by the time I left.'

'We played The Stranglers, The Doors, Manfred Mann. We even composed something – we called it the "Scone Wars Blues". It was fantastic fun.' Hattie smiled. 'But it's almost three o'clock, Bunty. We should be getting back to Robert.' She turned to Colin and Dennis. 'Will you both be at church on Sunday? I'm playing the organ.'

'We'll have to, if we want to share the potluck lunch on the green.' Dennis's glass was empty.

'We wouldn't miss the food,' Colin agreed.

Hattie kissed Barry's cheek briefly. 'Right – I'm going to take Bunty home. I'll text you, Barry.'

'Great.' Barry's dark brown eyes met hers. 'And we'll take those kids up on their offer of another jam session soon.'

'We will.' Hattie helped Bunty to her feet. 'OK – let's get you home, Bunty.'

'I only had the one gin...' Bunty protested. 'I had lemonade after that. I'm stone-cold sober – unlike these two reprobates.' She held out a hand, bumping a fist against Colin's and then Dennis's. 'It was good to meet you both. I enjoyed our chat – and I hope you both learned something. You badly need a woman's point of view.' She turned back to Hattie. 'Right, let's get back to the homestead. There are goats to feed and chickens to tend. In case you haven't noticed – I'm a reformed woman.'

They walked home together, and Bunty linked her arm through Hattie's. 'I gave grumpy Dennis a piece of my mind. Do you know, he was saying that if a man whistles at a woman and shouts things about her appearance, she should take it as a compliment. I tried to explain that unsolicited attention was harassment.'

'I don't suppose he understood that?'

'Dennis was banging on about gender identity – he was mocking people's choices and then Colin said he might identify as a pint of best bitter and he laughed. I gave them both a piece of my mind. Hattie—' Bunty took a breath. 'I've had that trivialising, sexist behaviour all my life, being judged for being a pretty little girl, a cute teenager, an attractive woman, and I was stupid – I simpered and searched for compliments like they meant something important. Then when I married Sean, I realised what a proper companion was; he's a soulmate. I suppose we both let our marriage get a little stale – Sean spent a bit too much time with Niall and the horses, I went back to my stupid teenage ways and looked for attention, then Jacko came along at just the wrong time and flattered me. I was so wrong.'

Hattie made a sound of agreement. 'We live and learn. I put up with a man who tried to control me for years. It was easy to be a mouse, to hide and say nothing, but all the time Geoffrey was eroding my confidence, I could hear a little voice in my head say, you ought to leave him, Hattie. I kept thinking, one day, I will. I wonder if Linda from the bowling club hadn't come along, if I'd still be married, listening to him grind me down.'

'Oh, Hattie.' Bunty tugged her sister closer as they walked.

'I'm so annoyed with myself for being such a fool. It's taken me such a long time to come to my senses.'

'We should be kind to ourselves,' Hattie said. 'We start off from childhood where we're taught that, as girls, we are somehow less than boys – that's certainly how it was when we were growing up, although I hope it's better now. But there are enough people in the world who love to criticise and give us a hard time – we don't want to make things worse for ourselves by being self-critical. I'm being good to myself now, finding who I am again and enjoying every moment.'

'Mindfulness.' Bunty smiled. 'You're right – I'm very good at blaming myself, but I've turned over a page. I suppose I had a chance of healing past hurts when Sean and I – you know – the thing that happened – but – oh, Hattie, I find it so hard to let that go.'

'It was a horrible time for you.' Hattie felt the warmth of Bunty's arm in hers. 'I don't suppose you ever get over something like that.'

'Sean and I never spoke about it. That's really the big wedge between us. It broke my heart and I never really got it back, not fully mended.'

'Will you go back to Sean?'

'I would, in a minute, but I want him to ask me. I'm the one who let him down. If he's had enough of me, then I'll understand. That's why I sent him the card.'

'He loves you.'

'I hope he does.' Bunty shuddered at the thought that he might not, now.

They turned into the drive leading to Robert's house. Bunty said, 'I love it here in Devon.'

'I thought you loved Ballycotton.'

'I do but – coming here, I feel like I've taken a breath and relaxed.'

'I know what you mean,' Hattie said. 'Robert likes us being here too. We restore the balance. I think he's a bit mystified by the Robert Parkin Fan Club of local ladies who all have the hots for his scones.'

'Hattie! Is that rude?' Bunty grinned.

'Robert is just Mr Nice Guy, Bunty – but he never had confidence in himself. As a head teacher he was totally professional – that's what he hid behind. And now school's out. But he was never Mr Lover Lover. He missed out on all that, and I think he's so lonely.'

Bunty winked. 'I can tell you've been spending time with a rock band – all these musical references.'

Hattie smiled. 'I'm making up for lost time. I was a seventy-something punk rocker this afternoon. And Barry too. He had a whale of a time.'

'Barry?' Bunty raised an eyebrow. They had reached the builders' van, and they strolled towards where Robert was watching Danut and Joey swing pickaxes into the ground. 'Are you and he—?'

'Barry's a friend,' Hattie explained firmly.

Bunty's eyebrow moved higher. 'But what sort of friend? A special one?'

Hattie didn't have time to answer. Robert turned to them, a smile on his face. 'The lads are making good progress. The slabs will go down sooner than expected.'

'The weather's been kind.' Danut lifted his pick. 'We'll get finished on schedule, early perhaps. It's looking good.'

His pick descended on the earth with a thwack. Joey copied, lifting the axe high, bringing it down with a thud. It pierced the hard ground and there was a pause while he raised it again. Then suddenly water was shooting in the air like a fountain, dripping down, covering Joey, soaking his hair and clothes. Danut stepped back quickly. Robert felt splashes against his face as Joey yelled in fright and water gushed along the ground, soaking into the earth.

Danut turned to Joey. 'You've put in a water feature.' He laughed. 'Well, that's torn it.'

'What's happened?' Robert looked up in horror as the water leaped higher.

Bunty grabbed Hattie's arm and asked, 'Is it serious?'

'No – not serious.' Danut grinned. 'But you'll need to turn your water off, Robert. My lovely assistant here has cut a hole in a water pipe.'

Joey was screaming, leaping out of the way of the spray. The ground was quickly turning to mud.

'Where is your stopcock?' Danut asked. Robert waved towards the gate. Danut ran across, screwdriver in hand, and bent over, opening the cast-iron cover. Joey stood shivering as water continued to spray and splatter.

Hattie watched, mouth open. 'So when our water is turned off – will it be turned off for long?'

Joey shivered. 'No – with a bit of luck we'll be able to fix it in an hour or so. These things happen.'

Danut was back. The water became a dribble, then it stopped. He picked up a shovel and started digging in the mud.

'The pipe should be deeper than two feet beneath the surface, but it isn't, and we've put an axe straight through it,' Danut said as he shovelled.

Joey picked up another shovel and began shifting sludgy earth. 'Oh, well. We ought to be able to fix this before teatime.'

'Good...' Robert sighed with relief. 'I have a nice piece of salmon that I wanted to steam for supper...'

'It will be no problem.' Danut dug deeper, piling mud to one side, then he paused abruptly. 'Oh, *that's* a problem though.'

'What is?' Robert stepped forward.

'Your house is old. You still have lead pipes.'

'Is that bad?' Bunty asked.

'No, I can fix it. But it is a bigger job. The best thing is to replace the lead with plastic pipes. I will need to buy the pipes and dig a trench from the water meter to the house. That will take another day.'

'Oh no.' Robert put a hand to his face.

'And no water until tomorrow afternoon at the earliest.'

'You're joking,' Bunty said.

'But that way you will have good pipes in the ground for many years,' Danut said. 'We won't charge for the labour – we broke the pipes.'

'Then you'd better do it.' Robert scratched his head. 'But what will we do for supper? And water?'

'We can go to the post office in Millbrook and buy bottled water,' Bunty suggested.

'But what about my steamed salmon?' Robert asked.

Hattie waved her phone. 'Leave it with me.'

30

'Impromptu parties are the absolute best,' Bunty said happily, raising a glass of fruit punch. 'And barbecues are so nice – sunshine, food, company, what's not to love?' She gazed around at the enormous lawn, perfectly trimmed shrubs and groomed fruit trees, the water feature of an elf peeing into a pool in a curved arc. In the corner of the garden, Tilda and Donkey were seated on a rug, playing their guitars, singing together. Robert was barbecuing salmon, flanked by Angie and Susan, who were competing furiously for his attention. A trestle table had been set up and several people were helping themselves to food. Bunty watched them as Susan and Angie waved long forks and tongs and she wondered if they were going to attack each other. She turned back to Hattie. 'It was very kind of Eric and Edie to let us use their beautiful garden.'

'It was Barry's idea,' Hattie said affectionately. She glanced towards Barry, who was talking to Eric Mallory. Eric was flanked by two well-behaved spaniels, who gazed up at him adoringly. His wife Edie was sitting on a bench, her knitting on her knee, talking to Francis and Sally Baxter. 'We thought we'd use Barry's garden,

then he mentioned that Eric and Edie had more space and a gas
barbecue – Robert's always loved barbecuing.'

'Our supper's grown into a party though – why are all the
others here?'

'Susan and Angie heard from Edie that there was a barbecue
and they were like rats up a drainpipe.' Hattie covered her smile
guiltily. 'They knew Robert was here, so they couldn't help themselves. Bees to a honeypot.' She gazed towards the barbecue,
where both women were leaning across Robert, their hands on
his arms, competing to taste the salmon. 'And Tilda wanted to
sing, so she turned up with Donkey. Francis brought salads and
bread... and Sally. It's just such a lovely community.' She pointed
towards the barbecue. 'Look, George and Mary Tenby are here –
they've brought more food.' Mary waved and held up a bottle of
wine. Hattie waved back.

'And look who else is here,' Bunty muttered as Dennis and
Colin hurried across, carrying a four-pack of beer between them.

'Bunty.' Dennis flung his arms around her. 'It's good to see you
again.'

'We heard there was free booze and food at Eric's, so we came
straight over.' Colin wrapped himself around her in a hug.
'Besides which, Dennis has a thing for you. He told me in the pub
that he thinks you're irresistible.'

'Me?' Dennis was suddenly embarrassed. 'It was you who said
Bunty's a bit of all right.'

'No, I never did.' Colin snatched one of the beers from
Dennis. 'You're the one with the hots.'

'I simply said she wasn't bad for her age.' Dennis grunted.

'Right – so, we need to discuss this again, boys.' Bunty put her
hands on her hips. 'What are you trying to say? That a woman
has a sell-by date? That she's only attractive before she has grey

hair and wrinkles? What's the sell-by date, then? Twenty-five? Thirty?'

Dennis gulped. 'We didn't mean—'

'It was you, Den – not me,' Colin stammered.

'And what about men?' Bunty was on a roll. 'What is their sell-by date, do you think? Sixty-five? Seventy-five? Are they like an old cheese, they get better as they mature? I think the only similarity between older men and cheese is the very strong smell.'

Hattie smiled and left Bunty to it. She wandered over to Barry, who turned to her with a gentle smile. 'Well, this is nice.'

'Eric and Edie have a lovely garden.'

'Eric had quite a good job in the police force years ago, and Edie was in the civil service. She's an interesting woman – she told me once that in the sixties, the average wage for a woman was ten pounds a week, less than half of what a man earned. She and Eric were the hub of this village years ago, apparently. Anne and I didn't move here until we retired.'

'What did you do, for a job?'

'I was a painter and decorator.' Barry grinned. 'I sloshed paint on walls with no idea that I'd enjoy doing it on a more delicate canvas.' His gold-framed glasses glinted. 'Anne was a secretary – she was very good at shorthand. Of course, no one does that now. And she was sacked as soon as they found out she was pregnant.' He shook his head. 'It's a good thing that times have changed.'

'How many children do you have, Barry?' Hattie was suddenly aware that she knew very little of him.

'Just the one – a son, Darren. He lives in Exeter with his family. They come over from time to time or I take the bus over there.' He spoke quietly. 'You don't have any children?'

'I'd have liked some, but Geoffrey said no. He said we'd have a better life without them.' Hattie laughed once. 'Yet life with Geoffrey couldn't have been worse. He'd have been a dreadful father. He was very controlling and he could say some nasty things.'

'He sounds horrible,' Barry said. 'The sort of man you'd dislike on first meeting.'

'I hope I never see him again.' Hattie smiled, but as ever she shook her head to push away the memories. 'I should have stood my ground more often. Still, that's best forgotten.' She gazed around. Bunty was talking animatedly with Dennis and Colin, who were both gaping at her, holding cans of beer, a mirror image of each other. Robert was unwrapping sardines with chermoula sauce in foil paper. 'Shall we go and rescue Robert?'

'Why not?' Barry reached for Hattie's arm. 'The fish smells wonderful.'

They arrived at the barbecue just as Susan and Angie were sampling fiery prawn and pepper skewers. Susan closed her eyes. 'Robert – this is heaven. So tender. Is there anything you can't cook?'

'You must come round to my house and show me how to cook like this.' Angie said breathily.

'Oh, it's very simple.' Robert was trying to ignore the way they pawed his arm. 'It's just a fish on the barbecue, a choice of flavourings – chillies, garlic, paprika, lemon juice, parsley.'

'You have a special touch, though,' Angie purred.

'Whatever you touch melts.' Susan gazed into his eyes. 'It's like magic.'

'Can we try some salmon?' Hattie asked and Robert placed a slice on her plate with a look of relief. She handed another fork to Barry and they took a bite each. 'It's good.'

'It is,' Barry agreed. 'I'm so glad we had a barbecue.'

'Robert has no water in his home,' Susan said simply. 'So – I've invited him round to my house to stay.'

'My place is closer,' Angie said emphatically. 'And more comfortable.'

'You'd be most welcome with me.' Susan ignored her. 'We'd have such a lovely time.'

Barry looked concerned. 'Is it going to be difficult to stay at Robert's? You have no water at all?'

'Thanks, Barry, but we'll be fine. There's plenty of bottled water and Danut will be able to fit new pipes tomorrow.' Hattie placed a gentle arm on Robert's and watched the relief spread across his face. 'It's all worked out rather well. Let's just enjoy this evening together. So, Susan, Angie, if you don't mind, I'm going to steal my brother from you. He's been doing all the cooking so I'm going to get him a huge portion of all the fish dishes and a glass of punch, then it's time for us to socialise.'

* * *

Robert was troubled, and he couldn't work out what was bothering him. He was up in the field, trying to fix the white gate, Isaac Mewton rubbing against his ankles. Hattie and Bunty had driven to Exeter to look round and do some shopping. He thought he'd leave them to it. He loved having them to stay, but it was nice to spend a few moments alone, thinking.

Perhaps that was it – today was Saturday and Hattie had said she'd go home after the church service tomorrow or on Monday. Robert was enjoying having her and Bunty to stay. They were good company. Hattie was wise and much stronger than he'd ever thought – he found himself turning to her for advice, asking her opinion. And Bunty was fun to be around; her laughter filled the house and she had a zany side, which he'd never appreciated before. He was also astonished by how bright she was; he'd heard about her discussions with Dennis and Colin, whom she'd tied up in knots. He wondered when she'd go back to Ballycotton, to Sean. He'd miss his sisters when they left.

But something else was scratching away at Robert's emotions like an itchy blanket. It wasn't the broken pipe: Danut and Joey had fixed it as promised. They'd done a superb job, fitted a modern pipe system and they were now back on track with the patio. That wasn't worrying him.

He wondered whether he was being a protective brother. Dennis and Colin certainly had started to demonstrate an increasing interest in Bunty, and they were a pair of old reprobates who spent most of their time in The Pig and Pickle. Robert wiped a hand across his forehead. Bunty could take care of herself. She wasn't worrying him – she was clearly in love with Sean. The mistake with Jacko had cost her dearly. Perhaps it was Hattie's friendship with Barry? Robert didn't know him particularly well – Barry spent most of his time painting, but from what Robert knew he was a decent type, he'd be respectful to Hattie. Robert laughed – he was so old-fashioned. Respectful indeed – what did he know about relationships and love? Nothing much at all.

That was it. That was what was bothering him – he had it now. He was due to meet Tressy Carew tomorrow and he had no idea what to say to her or how to behave. He couldn't be aloof and cool – he simply wasn't made that way. He couldn't be suave and confident. That wasn't his style either. He'd probably shuffle and stammer. Robert hadn't even mentioned her visit yet to Hattie or Bunty – he hadn't known how to say it, but if he was meeting Tressy at nine, he'd be happier if Hattie and Bunty weren't there. He wanted to talk to her by himself, or he'd be embarrassed, he'd let his sisters do the talking and come across as weak and incompetent. But he couldn't tell them that – what if they suspected that his heart had already started to beat too fast at the thought of meeting her? What if they teased him?

The thought of Tressy Carew troubled him more than he dared admit. He was imagining opening the front door to a small, sweet-faced woman who looked as appealing as she'd sounded on the phone. What if she was a six-feet-tall battleaxe? He'd be horrified. What if she brought her husband – what if she had one? He'd assumed she was his age, but what if she turned out to be thirty-five? He'd be so disappointed. He was being silly – he'd started to assume so much and he'd end up blaming himself.

Robert took a deep breath. He ought to ask Hattie and Bunty to help – the three of them should meet Tressy Carew together, and then he'd have a casual chat with her about the contest and they'd agree whether they wanted it to go ahead or not. Perhaps that would calm his racing pulse and he'd be able to behave normally. After all, he was an old man, a bachelor all his life. The local ladies in the gardening club were only fascinated by him because he could bake – what did that make him? Inoffensive, safe, stuffy. It was easy for them to make a fuss of him because he'd never offer them more than a buttered scone. If Tressy Carew was his age and attractive and as warm and sweet as she'd been on the phone, why ever would she show any interest in him?

Robert bent down and picked up Isaac Mewton, bringing her smooth fur to his face, and he sighed. He wondered if he would cry. All his life he'd wanted someone to love him; in all his years, he'd pretended he didn't. He kissed Isaac's fur. 'I'm just a silly man that no one really wants,' he said, his voice flat. 'I've missed my chance, Isaac. In truth, I never really had a chance. Even Cynthia Taylor never noticed me, not really.' The breath shuddered from his chest. 'I'm just a failure. I always have been and I always will be.' He tried a short laugh. 'I'm being silly, Isaac – I just spoke to the lady on the phone once and now I'm nervous about meeting her because she sounds so nice. How daft am I?'

Isaac wriggled and Robert put her four feet on the grass, watching as she sprang away. He turned towards the house with a heavy heart.

Tressy Carew would be here tomorrow morning at nine, and he had no idea what to say to her.

He was petrified with fear.

31

Hattie woke at seven o'clock on Sunday morning to hear muffled footsteps coming up the stairs. She sat up in bed blinking as Robert plodded into the room, holding a mug of tea, which he handed to her before plonking himself down on the end of the bed. Hattie waited for him to speak, but he put his head in his hands and sighed. Hattie touched his shoulder affectionately. 'Thanks for the tea.'

'I was up early.'

'Didn't you sleep well?'

Robert moved his shoulders. 'I always get up with the sun. I didn't bring Bunty any tea because she sleeps like a log. Besides, I'm all at sixes and sevens...'

Hattie slurped from the mug. 'Are you worried about today? The potluck? Rosie Eagle and the other newspaper woman? Isn't today when you make a decision and meet your opponent?'

Robert shuddered. 'Opponent?'

'The Cornish lady, Tressy something—'

'Carew,' Robert said. 'That's what I wanted to talk to you about. She rang me.'

'Doesn't that break the rules of the competition, chatting to the enemy?'

'She seems nice. The thing is – neither of us is sure we want to do the Scone Wars competition. She wants to discuss it with me.'

'That seems sensible. You can talk at the potluck.'

'With Rosie and Geraldine listening in? No.' Robert shook his head. 'She's coming round this morning at nine.'

'Oh, that's a good idea.'

'So we can talk to each other here. But I wondered if you and Bunty—'

'Would give you a bit of space? Of course.' Hattie thought for a moment. 'Bunty usually gets up at nine. We don't want her wandering into the kitchen in her pyjamas while you and Tressy have your heads together.'

'I see what you mean.' The image made Robert's hands shake. 'I was going to take her into the conservatory, where we'd have a bit of privacy.'

'Right. I'll wake Bunty up and offer to take her into Dawlish for breakfast. We'll find a café on the seafront and I'll buy her a bacon sandwich. If we're off the premises, you won't run the risk of interruption.'

'Oh, Hattie – thank you.' Robert's eyes shone with gratitude – she understood him perfectly. 'You're a star.'

'Leave it with me.' Hattie smiled. 'I'll finish this mug of tea and I'll get Bunty organised. You chat to Tressy and decide what you want to do about the contest, then you can present a united front to the reporters at the potluck.' She swung her legs out of bed. 'We have a plan.'

* * *

Just before nine, Hattie and Bunty were sitting in a pretty café on Dawlish seafront. There were two old sailors in the corner by the Welsh dresser ordering full English breakfasts, and a lone woman in a cream mackintosh sipping tea and reading *The Observer*. Hattie was examining the menu.

'They do gluten-free things here – even gluten-free cream teas. Do you think we should suggest that Robert tries something like that for the competition – a gluten-free cream tea, even a vegan one? That might be nice – the poor vegans miss out on so much.'

'Is he definitely going to do the competition?' Bunty picked up her phone and put it down again.

'That's what he's talking to his Cornish visitor about. He seemed very nervous.'

'Poor Robert.' Bunty moved her phone across the table, closer to the edge. 'If he's nervous now, he'll be terrified on TV.'

'I'm not sure he will,' Hattie said. 'I think he'll be fine while he's baking. He was the same when he was a teacher – he can appear efficient and cool and in control. I think he's just nervous with women.'

'I'm not surprised.' Bunty recalled the barbecue at Eric and Edie's. 'Susan and Angie can't keep their paws off him.'

'It certainly confuses him.' Hattie was thoughtful. She watched as Bunty picked her phone up again and checked for messages. 'Any news?'

'No.' Bunty shifted in her seat. 'I was hoping Sean might have got the card. I thought he'd text me.'

'The card should have arrived by now,' Hattie agreed.

'I keep checking to see if there's a message from him.' Bunty was clearly disappointed. 'Nothing so far. I suppose I should give him time but—'

'You thought he'd be straight back to you, begging you to come home.'

'Yes, I hoped he might.'

Hattie noticed a gleam in Bunty's eyes, the beginning of tears. 'Maybe you should text him. Or give him a call.'

'Maybe I should but – I want him to contact me first, so I know how the land lies between us. Am I being silly?'

'It's your decision,' Hattie said kindly. 'Maybe give him another day or two and then call him.'

'But what if he tells me he doesn't want me back?'

'Then you'll know for certain. That's better than not knowing at all.' Hattie leaned over and squeezed her sister's hand. 'It must have knocked him for six, you leaving as you did. I know he was very good about it, telling you to work things out for yourself, but – you should talk to him.'

'I will. In a day or two.'

'So what are you going to do meanwhile?' Hattie asked.

'I'll stay with Robert, at least until the competition is over. He's enjoying having us in Devon, he told me.' Bunty met her sister's eyes. 'What about you?'

'I was going to go back home tomorrow,' Hattie said.

'And what about Barry?'

'Barry's a friend.'

'Nothing more? Nothing romantic?' Bunty leaned forward.

'No, not yet.' Hattie was thoughtful. 'He might be if I was here for longer.'

'Then you should stay on.'

'Or it might be a good reason to go.' Hattie stifled a sigh. 'I'm a bit too long in the tooth for relationships.'

'I'd say just the opposite,' Bunty said quickly. 'After fifty years of bossy Geoffrey, you're ready for someone who's nice, who appreciates you.'

'I'm not sure.' Hattie gazed at the menu again. 'Maybe I'm too independent, too fond of my own company.'

'Or maybe you need someone to snuggle up with at night, someone who'll dance with you in the garden and tell you you're the most gorgeous person on two legs,' Bunty said mischievously.

Hattie ignored her. A waiter had arrived, a young man with a hopeful expression. She offered him a smile. 'I'll have a cup of tea and a muffin, please.'

The waiter turned to Bunty. 'Madam?'

'Sweet black coffee, full English, scrambled eggs, sausages, ketchup, beans, the works,' Bunty said with a flourish. 'At least one of us knows how to grab life by the—'

'Scruff,' Hattie said quickly, smiling as the waiter scuttled away. Bunty burst out laughing.

* * *

Robert hadn't stopped glancing at the clock for the last half-hour, his palms damp. It was five past nine – she was late. He saw his image reflected lightly in the glass of the conservatory; he was neat, in clean light trousers, a tidy shirt. He'd thought about putting on a tie, but that would have looked too formal. His pulse was racing as he thought about how he'd greet her. Should he shake her hand? Briefly, he wished he'd asked Hattie to stay – having another woman around might have made him feel less awkward. Isaac Mewton was dozing on Robert's comfy chair, purring. He glanced around to check that the room was tidy, plucking a thread from a cushion, putting it in his pocket. He asked the smart speaker to play Debussy's 'Clair de Lune' and wondered if it was too soporific. Perhaps Tressy liked pop.

A light knock on the door made him leap. His heart bumping against his ribs, he rushed to the door and flung it open. A small woman was standing in the doorway. She had pale hair, a green floral dress. She was around his age. But it was her face that caught his attention. Her eyes shone like brown buttons; her face was dimpled, her cheeks round. She smelled sweet and looked sweet, making Robert think of juicy apples. She held out a hand. 'Hello. You're Robert. Pleased to meet you. I'm Tressy.'

'Like apple pie,' Robert mumbled and immediately felt foolish.

'I beg your pardon?'

'I like them – apples – baking – I'm – I'm Robert Parkin,' he said quickly. She'd already told him she knew his name. 'Pleased to meet you. Won't you come in?'

Tressy bustled indoors. 'I'm properly thirsty, Robert. A cup of tea would be nice. The journey up here was ridiculous. The A30 was chocker. And on a Sunday too. It took me two hours and it was stop, start all the way.'

Robert led her into the kitchen. 'How do you take your tea?'

'You got any Cornish tea?'

Robert gazed at her. She was lovely. 'No, I have green, black, redcurrant, chamomile, or honey and apple.' He was conscious that his hands were trembling.

'That sounds nice. I'll try that.'

'Sweet apple,' Robert said again, conscious of how his fingers shook as he lifted the kettle and poured water into one of his best bone china mugs. He placed her tea on the table. It was too much of a risk to hand it to her – his nerves were shot. 'You can take the bag out when it's strong enough.' He was gibbering.

'Right.' Tressy took the teabag out and placed it on a plate. 'Shall we talk here?'

'I thought we'd go in the conservatory.'

'Lead on,' she told him, and Robert ambled towards the

conservatory where Debussy was blaring. Tressy smiled in recognition. '"Clair de Lune".'

'You like Debussy?' Robert gaped. He was in love.

'I like all the classics – I play them in the tea shop. Of course, Rachmaninov's my favourite but he gets a bit lively for most of my customers.' Tressy plonked herself in Robert's chair and began to stroke Isaac Mewton. 'Well, you're a little sweetheart, aren't you? What's your name, my handsome boy?' Isaac rolled over on her back and stuck her legs in the air, allowing her belly to be rubbed.

'Isaac Mewton – and she's a girl,' Robert said, feeling even more foolish.

Tressy brayed a laugh. 'I like you already, Robert. You're quite a character.'

'Oh,' he said and sat down clumsily on the opposite chair, spilling hot tea on his pale trousers, leaving a damp patch. He smiled, trying not to wince in pain.

'Well,' Tressy said. 'About this Scone Wars competition nonsense. What do you think of it all?'

Robert was still rubbing at the damp patch on his leg. 'I'm not sure.' Now he was sounding indecisive.

Tressy leaned forward. 'Do you think you can win?'

'I don't know.' Robert groaned inwardly. He was incapable of saying anything manly. She must think him a drip.

'No, I agree,' Tressy said. 'We don't know much about each other. I think we need to work together on this. I've heard you're a pretty good baker and you probably know that I bake every day and have done so since I was fifteen years old so that's fifty-seven years of non-stop cream teas.' She took a breath. 'I ought to retire and let someone else run the tea shop. But what else would I do with myself? There's only me and I'm used to the routine, day in,

day out. Although goodness knows I'm due a holiday. I don't
think I've taken one in twenty years.'

'You're not married?' Robert blurted.

'That's the first thing I asked the reporters about you.' Tressy
laughed. 'I didn't think you were – most wives do the baking
where I come from. Well, maybe the older ones, the traditional
ones. No, to answer your question, I never married, Robert. I lived
over the brush with a bloke once. Nine years of it. That was nine
years too long. Then I threw him out of my cottage for being a
miserable cuss.' She sipped tea. 'You?'

Robert shook his head. 'I was a teacher, then a head teacher. I
just worked hard. Then, before I knew it, it was time to retire.'

'I know exactly what you mean, Robert. Time flies by, don't it?
But I want you to know what you're up against if you take me on
with the baking. My scones are damned good, everyone says it. I
hear the same about yours too. But there are people who will
make it about something more than me and you – Geraldine and
Rosie want a war between Cornwall and Devon, so they look
good in their newspapers. I'm not so keen on that.'

'Nor am I,' Robert said. 'I've always been anti-war.'

'Me too – I'm a pacifist.' Tressy agreed. 'But I like you, Robert.
You're an interesting man and I think I'd enjoy baking with you.
Not for the competition but for love.'

'Love?' Robert's hand shook and the teacup wobbled.

'Precisely. Love of baking. There's nothing better than trying
out new recipes, watching someone enjoy eating up something
you've baked with your own two hands.'

'Oh, I agree,' Robert said.

'But I'm not going on the television and saying up with Cornwall, down with Devon, or any nonsense like that. I want to say
look, me and Robert are having fun, baking up a storm and
singing from the same hymn sheet.'

'Or recipe book,' Robert joked.

'Whatever.' Tressy shook her head. 'I want to say to the audiences, look, me and Robert are friends, we both love baking, and I'm not in the business of slagging off my Devon buddy just over a silly cream tea.'

Robert's eyes were shining. He'd given his heart away. 'My thoughts... exactly.'

'Right, then. Let's tell these reporters we'll do it for charity. Let them have their show. But you and me – we'll meet up at my place or yours and we'll share recipes and decide how we're going to play their little game. Then we'll know each other better and we won't care if you win or I win, because we'll be in it for the love of baking. The air ambulance and the lifeboats will get money, we'll get even better at what we do best because we'll share our experience, and then, when it comes to the competition, we'll both bake for the joy of it and we'll both feel like winners.'

Robert couldn't take his eyes off her. 'We'll spend time together – baking?'

'That's what I thought too. We won't tell Geraldine or the other one – we'll just share the love for what we do.'

'Love—' Robert agreed.

'And we'll have fun doing it. I think you're just the same as me, Robert. You're never happier than when you've got the oven warming and a light-as-air cake rising.'

'Oh yes,' Robert said.

'Good, then that's decided.' Tressy put her cup down and stood up quickly. 'So, I'm here for the potluck lunch on the green, but that's a few hours away. So, meanwhile, let's get to know each other better, shall we?'

'Yes, let's.' Robert stood up too, his cup still full of hot tea.

'Why don't you take me for a tour round your garden? I see

you're having some work done on the patio. That'll be nice when it's finished. And I believe you have chickens and some goats. I'd love to take a stroll up to the field and meet them and then you must tell me all their names...'

32

Hattie sat next to Barry on a rug, watching the activity on the village green. Everyone – fifty people at least – had emerged smiling from the church into the sunshine, although Hattie assumed the cheerfulness had more to do with the fresh air and the spread of food that Sally and Mary were serving than the service itself. Hattie had played the organ well and Tilda had sung 'Amazing Grace', her rich voice filling the entire roof and resonating off the walls. So many people she'd never met were congratulating her as she filed out of the large door behind the long queue and walked to the village green. Francis's smile was so wide it must have made his face ache. The green was a hive of activity, chatter, groups of people sharing food. Tilda and Donkey were talking animatedly to Edie and Eric, who were saying how much they had enjoyed the music.

Colin and Dennis were competing for Bunty's attention; she was drinking lemonade, trying to have a discussion with Rosie and Geraldine while they bounced like excited terriers at her elbow. Hattie heard her telling Rosie not to put Robert under any pressure – he'd make his own mind up about what type of scones he'd bake. Robert was talking to Tressy, his eyes only for her, but he was flanked by Angie and Susan, who'd placed themselves one at either side of him, arms folded like bodyguards, assessing the opposition. Tressy was oblivious, talking ten to the dozen about the tea room she owned in Padstow, inviting everyone to come over for a cream tea.

'No rivalry intended,' she said. 'You'd all be welcome to visit me, sit down and have tea and cake, whatever you fancy. After all, a competition is a competition, a scone is a scone and a cup of tea is a cup of tea. I don't intend to worry about the scone contest at all. Who wins don't matter – it's only for one day. A cream tea is for life.'

'For life,' Robert agreed, gazing at her as if she were a hallowed saint, his eyes shining.

Barry turned the same gleaming eyes in Hattie's direction. 'Are you having a good time?'

'I am.' She smiled. 'The food's lovely, and the company's nice. It's good to see the village coming together.'

'Robert seems to be making friends with the enemy.'

'He is.'

'And Dennis and Colin both seem to be in competition to talk to your sister.'

'Bunty's her own person. She won't put up with any of their nonsense.'

Barry placed a hand on Hattie's arm. 'You played beautifully in the church.'

'It's so much fun – I can't tell you how much I missed playing.' Hattie pushed away the memory of Geoffrey complaining that she had two left hands and her efforts at the piano made his neck ache with tension. 'I intend to keep playing. I have a piano at home – it's not a bad one. I'll practise a lot more when I get back.'

'But you like playing the organ too?'

'I do.' An idea occurred to Hattie. 'I might pop down to the local church, or even St Paul's in Banbury, and offer my services. Yes, you're right.' She smiled. 'I won't give it up.'

'So...' Barry took a breath. 'Do you think we might have the chance to play some more music with Tilda and Donkey? I had a lark playing the drums.'

'I don't know – they are busy with Armpit and other projects.' Hattie glanced over to where Tilda was talking to Rosie Eagle. 'I'm sure they are happier playing with people their own age.'

'Do you think so?' Barry was unsure. 'I thought it was so much fun.'

Hattie spoke quietly. 'I'm going home tomorrow, Barry.'

'Do you have to?'

'No, but...' She shrugged. 'I can't impose on Robert forever and – it was only meant to be for a few days while Bunty had my place in Bodicote to herself. Now she's here – I ought to go back.'

'What do you need to go home for?' Barry asked, his brown eyes round.

'Well, nothing really – it's my home. I have a nice neighbour, Glenys. I go to yoga with friends – sometimes I go to a beauty salon.'

Barry was perplexed. 'So, you don't need to go back yet.'

'No, but – I ought to go, I suppose.'

'Can you stay on?' Barry asked hopefully. 'I look forward to our time together.'

'Oh, I'll be back at some point.' Hattie tried to make her voice breezy. In truth, she wasn't sure quite why she intended to go back. She was enjoying herself too. 'Maybe I'll pop back for the Scone Wars, now Robert and Tressy have decided to do it.'

'Oh, they've definitely decided?'

'They'll have fun, Robert told me – and it's for charity. It's his decision. I hope he's sure about it. All those TV cameras? In his place I'd feel very flustered and stressed.'

'Tressy seems quite calm though.'

'Oh, she does,' Hattie agreed, glancing towards where Tressy was telling a crowd of people that she made cheese and potato scones on demand and they went down a storm.

Geraldine boomed, 'You should cook them for the competition. They'd be very on-trend.'

'Oh, I ain't trendy, not at all,' Tressy retorted with a grin. She turned to Robert. 'I've made myself clear. Robert and I are doing the baking competition in the spirit of friendship and harmony between Devon and Cornwall. If not, I ain't doing it at all.'

'Right,' Rosie agreed, then she raised her voice. 'Can I have everyone's attention? I have an announcement to make.'

'*We* have an announcement,' Geraldine corrected her.

'*The Teignmouth Chronicle*—'

'And *The Cornish Anchor*—'

'Would like you to know that Scone Wars will be held two weeks today.' Rosie beamed. 'And I'm delighted to say that the venue has been decided on the flip of a coin and the competition will be held here in Millbrook at Robert's house.'

'On the new patio,' Robert muttered.

'As hosts, *The Teignmouth Chronicle* will be all over it...' Rosie said.

'With a live pre-show scheduled for Saturday. And the judge on Sunday will be the TV chef Rocco Chiarello,' Geraldine added.

Mary Tenby placed a hand on her heart. 'He's so dishy.'

'The TV cameras will be there and selected members of the village will be invited to attend.'

'And a busload of people from Cornwall,' Geraldine butted in.

'The TV people will make an announcement each night of

the week during the news, leading up to the weekend, explaining to viewers how to donate for the lifeboats and the air ambulance, how to buy T-shirts and mugs.'

'Everyone on set will be wearing a Scone Wars T-shirt to promote the show and a cup will be presented to the winner.'

'And here's a special announcement,' Rosie said excitedly. 'I've just arranged for local singer Tilda Baxter to sing with her band while the judging is taking place.'

'Who?' Geraldine pulled a face.

'She'll play a jazz song.'

'But why isn't there a Cornish singer? I could find a good folk band.' Geraldine grunted.

'There won't be time,' Rosie said in a syrupy voice.

'Then I'll get a traditional Cornish shanty to play out at the end,' Geraldine grumbled.

'Whatever.' Rosie smiled at the assembled crowd. 'So, it's getting exciting – Scone Wars, and there can only be one winner.'

'Goodness me, that doesn't give you long, Robert...' Hattie looked at her brother's face. He looked like a rabbit caught in headlights.

She watched as Tressy took his arm and muttered, 'This is our show, Robert. Me and you baking and having a right good giggle. We'll have a great time.'

'Danut's promised the patio will be done – it's bang on schedule,' Robert said nervously.

'It'll all be tickety-boo,' Tressy soothed. 'Don't you worry yourself.'

Bunty was at Hattie's shoulder. 'Two weeks until the competition. That's exciting, isn't it?'

'I'm off home tomorrow,' Hattie said, glancing briefly at Barry, who looked sad. 'But I'll be back for Scone Wars.'

'I hope you like the new walls,' Bunty said with a grin. 'They are meant to be uplifting. And I've put up new framed posters too.'

'Walls?' Hattie frowned, confused.

'I wanted to say thanks for letting me stay and for looking after me when I made the awful mistake with Jacko, so I decorated the lounge and your bedroom. Those old magnolia walls were so depressing, but now it's bright and calm.'

Hattie nodded. Bunty was right: Geoffrey had left a year ago, but she'd been tiptoeing around as if he were still there. She tapped Bunty's hand affectionately. 'Thank you. I should have put my own stamp on the place now I live there by myself. It's my house – well, Geoffrey and I decided I'd live in it, but it belongs to us both until one of us – goes—'

'You didn't buy him out?' Bunty asked.

'No. We arranged in the divorce that the bungalow would continue to belong to us jointly and it was my place of residence. Not that I want anything to do with Geoffrey, but neither of us could afford to buy it outright, we have no children and Geoffrey is living with Linda so...' She shrugged – it didn't matter. 'I'm so glad you've brightened it up a bit. And new pictures, you say?'

'Bang up-to-date ones. You'll love it,' Bunty gushed. 'It's really modern. You'll feel at home straight away.'

'I look forward to seeing it tomorrow,' Hattie said. 'Thanks so much for being thoughtful.'

Hattie hugged Bunty. Barry looked on, saying nothing, his hands folded together, his expression sad. They were joined by Robert and Tressy.

'Well?' Tressy put her hands on her hips. 'What do you think about the scone showdown? It should be a lot of fun.'

'Tressy was marvellous,' Robert said, his face full of admiration. 'Rosie and Geraldine asked us if we wanted to do the competition, and she said they had to agree to some rules first.'

'I told them straight.' Tressy nodded firmly. 'I didn't want any of this big Cornwall versus Devon rubbish. No animosity. I insisted it should be here, despite what the reporter said about the toss of a coin – Robert will be much more comfortable in his own domain and my place is too small to accommodate all the people from the television.'

'Tressy and I are meeting next Sunday in Padstow at her tea room,' Robert said gently. 'We'll be able to use the kitchen there and do some baking together.'

'It'll be lovely,' Tressy said with a smile. 'Just me and Robert and a whole lot of scones.'

'Fabulous,' Bunty said. 'But you won't be able to make church. I've promised to do some refreshments for Sally after the service. I'm making boxties.'

'I'll come to church first and go straight afterwards,' Robert said, glancing at Tressy.

'What's a boxty?' Tressy asked. 'It sounds interesting and I'm always looking for new recipes.'

'Irish potato pancakes – Sean's favourite.' Bunty looked sad for a moment. 'I'm really good at them. I have the knack, just like a proper Irishwoman, Sean used to say. I promised to make a batch for after church. You can help me before you set off for Cornwall.'

'I'd love to,' Robert agreed. 'Besides, I wouldn't want to miss you playing the organ, Hat.'

'Oh, I won't be there,' Hattie explained. 'I'm going home tomorrow...' There was a moment's silence that stretched like elastic. Barry looked at his feet. Robert struggled for something to say.

Then Bunty said, 'No, you can't go yet. Just hang on until after the baking contest.'

'But that's two weeks away.'

Tressy butted in. 'I was hoping you'd come down to Padstow with Robert next week and I'd show you round my tea shop. Anyway, what have you got to go rushing off back to Oxfordshire for? Robert told me you've thrown your no-good husband out and you live by yourself so – why not stay where people want to share your company?' She met Hattie's eyes, her own gleaming. 'What do you say?'

'Well, I suppose – if you put it like that.' Hattie felt Barry reach for her hand.

'Stay a bit longer, Hat – just until after the baking contest,' Bunty urged, placing her other hand in Hattie's. 'It's so lovely for us all to be together.'

'Well...' Hattie breathed out. They were right. She'd be on her own in the bungalow, settling back into the old routine, and here she was in Millbrook, being welcomed. She squeezed both hands that held hers.

'All right, then. I'll stay...'

33

The following Saturday, Hattie and Bunty were seated outdoors in deckchairs, watching Robert tending his fruit bushes. Isaac Mewton sat on Bunty's knee, reaching up a paw or a pink tongue to steal the ice cream from Bunty's cone. The cat knew that Bunty was a soft touch; she'd dip her finger in the ice cream and offer it to Isaac to slurp. Hattie had a sketch pad in front of her and was attempting to draw Bunty's face.

'It's so hot.' Bunty yawned and Hattie held her pencil still for a moment. 'Scorching hot. It's like being in Ibiza.'

'I've never been to Ibiza,' Hattie remarked.

'Nor have I,' Bunty said sadly. 'Sean and I went to Tossa de Mar a few years ago. It was nice. We had a day in Barcelona.'

'You should go again, both of you.' Hattie stretched her legs and lifted her pencil, attempting to shade the flesh around Bunty's mouth.

'I haven't heard from Sean.' Bunty sighed. 'Perhaps I won't now.'

'Have you phoned him?'

Bunty's face clouded. 'No. I ought to.'

'So why don't you?'

'I don't know what to say.' Bunty wriggled her phone from her pocket.

'He's your husband – tell him you love him.'

Bunty was unsure. 'I've been so unfair.'

'Then say you're sorry.'

'What if he doesn't reply? What if it's over?'

'You won't know until you talk to him,' Hattie said emphatically.

'I'll message.' Bunty stared at the phone, her thumb pressing buttons. 'There – I've written it. "I love you, Sean. I'm sorry." Shall I press send?' Bunty's face was troubled.

'Yes,' Hattie said, her eyes wide. 'Do it now.'

'Oh – it's sent.' Bunty closed her eyes. 'It's done.' She paused for a moment. 'Do you think he'll text me straight back?'

'Put your phone down.' Hattie smiled. 'Don't keep looking at it. Finish your ice cream – it's dripping.'

'Is it?' Bunty placed the remainder of the cone in front of Isaac, who began licking furiously. 'Hattie – what if he doesn't respond?'

Hattie squeezed Bunty's hand. 'One step at a time.'

'I couldn't bear it.'

'Patience.'

'I was never patient – or sensible.' Bunty forced a smile. 'What are you sketching?'

'You.' Hattie showed her the picture. 'Barry said he'd like to take me out to Haytor to do some painting and he said doing a bit of sketching might ease me into being better at observation. What do you think?'

'It's not bad.' Bunty muttered. 'Do I look like that?'

'Like what?'

'Fat and old?' Bunty sighed. 'Oh, it's a lovely sketch, Hattie. It's just – I've messed things up and I'm feeling sorry for myself.'

'Then we need to get the old Bunty back.'

'I don't know who the old Bunty is.' Bunty shook her head. 'Dennis keeps asking for my phone number. Colin keeps asking me out for a drink. They both keep telling me not to trust the other one because he's an incorrigible old lech.' She smiled. 'I don't want either of them. I want Sean.'

Hattie said, 'You've realised that he's your soulmate.'

'And the universe is asking me to be patient,' Bunty agreed. 'It's time for me to learn to value what I have. You, Robert – Sean. I'm blessed.'

'You are.'

'And so are you, Hattie. You've got rid of Geoffrey, and Barry likes you.'

'He does.' Hattie put a hand to her head. 'We're going to Padstow tomorrow. I offered to drive Robert down to meet Tressy. He'll be a bag of nerves.'

'He likes her a lot,' Bunty murmured. 'And I think you like Barry a lot too.'

'I couldn't sleep last night. I was thinking about it, trying to work myself out,' Hattie admitted. 'I'll spend Sunday afternoon with him and next week. By the time the competition is over, I'll be sure how I feel about him. I'll just give myself time.'

'Maybe Sean's taking time too,' Bunty said sadly. 'Right, I'll give him until next Sunday too. If he doesn't reply to my text, I'll phone him straight and ask him how he feels. If he tells me it's over – well, I've tried, I've given him time and it's my own fault.'

'We have each other whatever. We're family.'

'We are.' Bunty stood up, letting Isaac fall to her feet. She called out, 'Robert, I'm making a cup of tea. Do you want one?'

Robert pushed his panama hat back onto his head and wandered over. 'Yes, please.' He took out a handkerchief and mopped his brow. 'Shall we take it in the conservatory? I'm boiling.'

'All right.' Hattie stood up. 'The patio is looking good.' She pointed to the level ground where half of the slabs had been placed down.

'Danut says there are a few more slabs to lay, then the grouting and some bordering, then we'll be ready for the seating and the pergola.' Robert looked nervous. 'You do think I've done the right thing, agreeing to this scone competition?'

'Most definitely,' Hattie said.

'Rosie Eagle rang this morning. She says that the merchandise is going well, the charities are making a lot of money already. And the TV crew will come here on Saturday to set up and to film a short interview with me and Tressy.'

'That's exciting.'

Robert was unsure. 'What if I make a fool of myself?'

'You couldn't do that,' Bunty said emphatically. 'You're a great baker. Your scones will be perfect.'

'No.' Robert lowered his voice confidentially. 'I don't mean the scones. I mean Tressy. She's – she's the nicest woman I've ever met. What if I behave like a buffoon? I – I like her.'

'Just enjoy being with her.' Hattie grabbed his arm. 'See what happens tomorrow afternoon when you're cooking together.'

'Like Hattie was saying to me earlier.' Bunty grinned. 'We just need to trust the universe, give ourselves time.'

'I don't trust myself not to behave like a babbling fool, that's the problem,' Robert said. 'Shall we go inside? I'm feeling all hot and bothered just talking about it. I think I need that cup of tea more than I thought.'

* * *

The following day was overcast, and the church was packed. Hattie was sure there were at least ninety people – she'd tried to count as she listened to Tilda singing 'My Sweet Lord' while Donkey played acoustic guitar. The church had been silent apart from Sally snuffling with emotion as she listened to her daughter's pure voice. Bunty was in the vestibule with Mary, who was making tea, and Dennis and Colin, who were elbowing each other to help Bunty pile warm buttered boxties onto plates while the congregation queued and chewed. Hattie looked for Robert, who was immediately by her side, munching a boxty. 'These are good. I must tell Tressy about them. Are we ready to go? I don't want to keep her waiting. I said we'd be at the tea room by two.'

'And we will.' Hattie examined Robert in pale jacket, panama hat and clean shirt and trousers. He was the quintessential English gentleman. But he was wearing too much Paco Rabanne. She wondered when he had bought it – she'd never smelled cologne on him before, so she said, 'That's a heavenly scent – it suits you.'

'Ah. Thanks. Can we go soon?' Robert said again, nervously.

'I'm just waiting for Barry,' Hattie replied. 'He's popped back to his cottage for some watercolours. We're going to try a bit of landscape painting while you're baking.'

'Oh?' Robert led the way to the door. 'Isn't it a bit cold?'

'We'll wrap up.' Hattie was outside. There was a stiff wind blowing from the coast. 'Perhaps it'll be warmer in Padstow.'

She indicated the silver Nissan Micra parked nearby. Barry was waiting there, a smile on his face and a bundle of art folders under his arm. He heaved a bag higher onto his shoulder, struggling with the weight of it. 'I'm all ready to go...'

'Good.' Hattie opened the car and was just about to jump in when she felt a light touch on her arm.

'Hattie.'

Hattie looked into Tilda's darkly outlined eyes, noticing the golden piercings, the blue-black hair. 'You sang beautifully in the church – like an angel.'

'Are you going somewhere now?' Tilda asked.

'Cornwall,' Hattie explained. 'Robert and his Cornish opponent are meeting.'

'Oh – can I talk to you sometime next week?' Tilda looked troubled.

'Is everything all right?' Hattie asked, her face concerned.

'Nothing I can't handle.' Tilda swept her fringe from her eyes with black nails. 'It'll keep. Can you pop round to the manse on Monday? Or Tuesday?'

'I'll text you.' Hattie pushed her phone into Tilda's hand. 'Give me your number.'

Tilda's fingers wriggled on the buttons and she handed the phone back. 'There. Message me and I'll message back.' She turned to go. 'Don't forget.'

'I won't,' Hattie called reassuringly but Tilda had rushed back into the church. Robert was moving from one foot to another.

'Will we be late?'

Hattie winked. 'I'll put my foot down.' She noticed his nervous expression. 'I'll have you there for two and then Barry and I can go on to...' She gazed at Barry for an answer.

'Trevone Bay, I thought, or St George's Cove. As long as we're warm enough.'

They were all inside the car and Hattie started the engine. 'I brought a jacket, a hat, and I borrowed a scarf from Robert.' She smiled as the car pulled away. 'I'm really looking forward to his.'

'Me too,' Barry agreed, leaning back in the passenger seat.

'So am I.' The sound of teeth chattering came from the seat behind as Robert shivered. 'But in all honesty, I'm scared to death.

I haven't been on a date with a lovely woman for nearly fifty years.'

They arrived at Tressy's tea room overlooking the harbour just before two, and Hattie dropped Robert off on The Strand, watching while he crossed the road and knocked on the blue door. Tressy answered almost immediately, dressed in a yellow print frock, whisking him inside with a wave to Hattie before she drove off along the North Quay Parade towards St George's Cove.

Robert hesitated inside the doorway, looking around at the empty tea room, blue chairs, cream walls, twinkling lights. His voice was thick with emotion as he whispered, 'You have it nice here.'

'It's a perfect position, on the harbour,' Tressy said simply. 'I worked hard for this place. It hasn't always been easy. There were times when business boomed and times when it was tough. During the pandemic, I kept people going with cups of tea and cream teas delivered to their houses. I just piled them up in boxes in my little car.'

'Beautiful,' Robert murmured, although he wasn't sure whether he was talking about the tea room, the idea of takeaway scones or Tressy herself, standing there in the yellow print frock, her face shining and dimpled as an apple. She smelled sweet as plucked fruit. He said it again. 'Beautiful.'

'Well. Let's go into the kitchen,' Tressy suggested. Robert was surprised that she took his hand and tugged him towards the back room. They stood in the small kitchen where everything gleamed, stainless-steel worktops, oven, fridge. She had laid out a pumpkin, fresh ginger, jars of preserved ginger, spices, sugar, flour. 'I thought we'd think about making some scones.'

Robert looked around, gaping. 'Oh?'

'Indeed,' Tressy said. 'A little birdie told me that when you met Geraldine, she was proper teasy when she first sampled your ginger scones.'

'Teasy?' Robert was unsure.

'Irritable – grumpy. Only—' Tressy lifted his hand in hers '—she's a proper teasy maid, that one, and I don't want her sniping remarks affecting your confidence when we do the actual baking, so I thought we'd make some ginger scones together and bake them to perfection, then we'll sit down and eat one each with a nice pot of tea.'

'You're just so lovely.' Robert couldn't help himself. 'I've never met anyone so kind.'

'I'm standing here thinking the same thing about you.' Tressy smiled.

'Oh?' Robert asked.

'So, my handsome.' Tressy met his eyes. 'This is our time. Shall we make the most of it? I feel a little bit like that nice lady in *Notting Hill* – the one in the bookshop, who comes in to tell Hugh Grant how she feels about him at the end of the film.'

'Notting Hill? I don't understand. We're in Padstow.' Robert was confused.

'We're exactly like them though – Julia Roberts, Hugh Grant.'

'How?'

'I'm just a girl – looking at a boy – hoping he'll give her a kiss.'

Robert was even more befuddled. 'What?'

'Oh, for goodness' sake.' Tressy laughed good-humouredly as she wound her arms around his neck. 'Come here, my handsome. We've got plenty of time to do some baking. But before we start on that – I was hoping we'd do a bit of kissing.'

'Oh.' Robert tugged her to him, feeling the warmth of the yellow print frock, inhaling the sweet smell of apple, and he pressed his lips against hers for all he was worth.

He didn't need to be asked twice. He was in heaven.

34

Hattie sat on a fold-out camping chair and attempted to place her canvas on the easel. Next to her, Barry was trying to do the same thing. The wind tugged at it, threatening to blow it over. Hattie frowned. 'Is this going to work?'

Barry fiddled with the watercolour paints in his bag. 'I've never been here before.'

The wind ruffled the sea, blowing light grains of sand towards them, golden sprinkles on their knees. Hattie asked, 'Did you and Anne paint seascapes often?'

'No.' Barry shook his head. 'We were more into Dartmoor – painting rocks and trees. I just thought...'

'What did you think?'

'I thought you'd like it here. You seem much more of a beach person.'

'Do I?' Hattie covered a smile. 'In what way?'

'Anne was shy. She always had her head in a book, or she was painting – she wouldn't say very much. Our life together was very quiet. You seem much more – outgoing, confident, a strong woman. Like the sea – powerful.'

Hattie's smile turned into a laugh. 'You wouldn't have said that if you'd seen me with Geoffrey. He made all the decisions. I was a timid mouse.'

'Really?' Barry was surprised. 'I see you as an independent woman.'

'I'm learning to be,' Hattie said. 'The problem with being strong is that coercive controlling husbands become louder and more determined to take the wind out of your sails. I found out quickly that the best thing to do was to keep a low profile.'

'That's dreadful.' Barry adjusted his gold-framed glasses; the wind was yanking them. 'Yet you stayed with him for so long.'

'I know – it seems ridiculous now I look back.' Hattie tugged her jacket around herself. 'I suppose I didn't want to fail. I just kept trying and trying with Geoffrey in case I could get something right once in a while. And he knew exactly how to play it – the odd compliment or small gift would keep me in place, trying again. Do you know, he'd often say, "Hattie, you're a good girl," and I'd be so pleased. Now I think about it, he was training me like people train dogs.' A strong gust blew and she put out a hand as the easel wobbled and the canvas fell forward. She stared towards the metal-grey sea, the surf rolling in with a whisper.

Barry said, 'Would you like to do something else?'

'Painting's going to be hard in this breeze,' Hattie agreed. 'And really, I'm not much of a painter.'

Barry sighed. 'I don't think watercolour painting at St George's Cove was my best idea.'

'So, offer me a better one,' Hattie challenged him.

'Well, how about a long walk across the cliffs?' he suggested. 'Then we can find a nice inn and get a warm drink and sit by a log fire. It's cold out here today and some of these little Cornish inns keep a fire in the grate all summer.'

'Perfect.' Hattie began to pack up her equipment. 'It's not a good day for painting the coastline.'

'It's not.' Barry's brown eyes shone. 'And I've learned a lesson. I was trying to recapture the past, suggesting we did things together that I did with Anne. I was wrong. We need to discover new things, you and I. I don't want to relive the past. I want to move forward, to see what we can discover together, a future...' He held out a hand. 'If you'll come with me.'

'I don't see why not.' Hattie placed her hand in his. 'Slowly, along life's path. One step at a time.'

'I'm all for that.' Barry smiled as they walked back towards the car.

* * *

Bunty wrapped the last five boxties in a paper towel and waved to Mary and Sally. 'I'm taking these home to warm up. I didn't get any lunch, we were so busy. I'll see you soon.'

'Before the competition, I hope,' Mary called. 'Come round to ours for a cuppa in the week.'

'Or we can get together at the manse,' Sally suggested. 'We ought to organise a gardening club meeting before the competition next Sunday to help Robert.'

'The patio will be finished by Thursday, Danut thinks,' Bunty called.

'Then on Friday, we should all move in and make the place look smart for the TV cameras. Robert shouldn't have to do it by himself,' Sally replied.

'It's already smart,' Bunty protested.

'Of course, but we can mow the lawn, trim hedges, maybe put a few new pots and shrubs around the patio, fairy lights – whatever Robert wants,' Sally offered.

'Plus we can set out a few deckchairs for the day, a couple of bistro tables, bring some fruit punch,' Mary added.

'So that he has the support of his friends in the village,' Sally said. 'Then he'll win, for Devon.'

'That sounds like a great idea,' Bunty agreed. 'We have plenty of time to chat to Robert in the week and ask him what he'd like us to do. I wonder how he's getting on – I hope he's having fun baking.'

'I'm sure he is. Well, I'd better get back to the manse,' Sally said. 'I promised Francis I'd give him a hand with tidying the rose bushes.'

'It's past three.' Mary gasped in horror. 'George will be watching cricket. The dog will need feeding and he never hears the poor thing yelping. George would let Tansy starve. I'd better get on.'

'I'll see you both.' Bunty was already on her way back to Robert's clutching her wrapped boxties. She glanced up at the sky as she increased her pace; the clouds were low, broodingly dark.

A voice from the doorway of The Pig and Pickle called her name and she glanced over her shoulder. Dennis was leaning against the doorpost, pint in hand. He shouted again. 'Bunty – come and join me. I've got a gin and tonic with your name on it.'

'Come on in,' a second voice followed. 'We can spend the afternoon putting the world to rights...'

Bunty swirled round, grinning. 'Thanks Colin, Dennis, but I'm busy.' She walked on, hearing the men groan behind her. She assumed they'd disappeared back into the snug. Then the first drop of rain fell with a fat plop on her nose and she walked faster, pushing her hands deep into her jacket pockets. Robert's place was in sight. She'd get home, put the kettle on and warm up the boxties. Her stomach was rumbling.

The skies opened and the rain fell, drenching her hair and

jacket. Bunty broke into a staccato run, head down to take the brunt of the shower, stumbling forwards through the gate and down the drive.

Then she stopped dead.

A green Peugeot 406 estate was parked outside the house. Bunty knew everything about the car, the number plate, the dent in the side door that someone had made in a car park when they parked too close and opened their door without thinking. She knew everything about the driver too. She'd bought him the black jacket he was wearing last Christmas. The cap he always wore was squashed on his head, flattening the curls that stuck up, that she loved to ruffle. He was sitting at the wheel, munching. He'd be eating honey-roasted peanuts. They were his favourites. The car door opened and a voice shouted, 'Bunty – you'll get soaked.'

She gasped, 'Sean,' then she was running as hard as she could and they were both drenched.

He tugged her into his arms. 'You'll be catching pneumonia. Come here, will you?' Then they were kissing.

She looked into his face. 'You're here.'

'I am.' The rain bounced off his cap. 'Will we go inside?'

Bunty rummaged in her handbag for the key Robert had given her. Sean took the damp paper parcel from her hands. 'What do you have here? Boxties. My favourites.'

'I made them for the church potluck.' They were in the hall. 'I'll warm them up for us.' Bunty shook the rain from her hair. Her face shone with the wetness. 'When did you arrive?'

'I got the overnight ferry. I drove all day. I just got here.'

'Why did you come?'

'How could I not?'

'I sent you a card.'

'That's how I knew you were here. The Devon postmark. I

knew you'd be at Robert's.' He grabbed her hand. 'I've been wanting to do this for weeks now.' Then she was in his arms again, his lips warm.

'I thought you didn't want me,' Bunty murmured. 'I behaved so badly.'

'It hurt me, Bunts – I thought I'd have to let you go because you asked me to. And he was no good, that Jacko. I played darts with him in The Hole in the Wall. He was a gobshite.'

'You knew? It was a silly mistake, Sean. I didn't love him.'

'I guessed it. He was an eejit. Not worth wasting another thought over. And he could peel an orange in his pocket – he never bought a single drink the whole time he was on holiday. I felt bad you'd gone off with him. I didn't think he'd treat you right. Besides...'

'Besides?' She met his eyes. Her own were filled with tears.

'Besides, I love you. I always will. You're my girl.'

'I'm sorry...' She took a breath. 'I sent you the card, but you didn't message me. Then I messaged again.'

'I got the card. You wrote you'd be mine if I'd have you so I wanted to come and get you straight away but—'

'But?' She stifled a smile. 'You thought you'd let me stew for a bit.'

'No, no, darlin', nothing like that but I needed a bit of time to get my head straight. I wanted to be sure you meant it. Then I got your text and you told me you loved me. I knew where you were – so I came to find you.'

They reached the kitchen and Bunty bustled around with the kettle, mugs. Sean looked around. 'I haven't been here for – what – eight years now.'

'It's been a while since we visited Robert.'

'I've been neglecting you,' Sean said quietly. 'That's why I'm here. I was hoping we could go away somewhere together. A second honeymoon – somewhere warm, just the two of us.'

'We should.' Bunty put a frying pan on heat to warm up the boxties.

Sean felt something brush against his leg. 'Ah, you're a friendly little fella.' He reached down to rub Isaac Mewton's furry ears.

'She's called Isaac.' Bunty placed a mug of hot tea in front of Sean. 'Here – get this down you.'

'Ahhh,' Sean sighed as he sipped tea. He took off his cap and laid it on the table, ruffling his curls. Bunty flipped the boxties. 'This is lovely.' He gazed at her. 'It's good to have you back.'

'Can we stay until Sunday? I'm sure Robert wouldn't mind.'

'Why would we do that?'

'Robert's in a big baking head-to-head with a Cornish woman - it's going to be on TV. We should support him.'

'Then we will.' Sean watched Bunty as she placed a plate next to him, grabbed one for herself and sat down. He took a bite. 'You make the best boxties. Even better than my own mother, bless her, and she made them just right.'

Bunty sipped her tea, munching, watching her husband as he chewed. She sighed. 'I'm so glad to have you back.'

He placed a hand over hers. 'I'm glad to be back.'

'I shouldn't have left.'

'I shouldn't have let you go.'

They were quiet for a moment, sipping, eating, aware that the rainwater still dripped from their hair. Then Bunty said, 'You know when it all started for me – when I lost it all a bit—'

'I do.'

'It was the same for you?'

'It was, Bunty.'

'We never spoke of it, not really.'

'We didn't.' Sean's grip tightened over Bunty's hand. 'It was over forty years ago, and we never talked it through as we should have.'

'It still breaks my heart. I think about him all the time.'

'I do too.'

'But, Sean – I was too hurt to say anything.'

'And I didn't want to hurt you more by bringing it up. I thought it was best to leave him where he was.'

'In the past?'

'Buried.'

'Sean...' Bunty felt the first tear fall. 'Can we talk about it now? Can we try?'

'I'll do my best. Talking about feelings isn't my thing.' Sean shook his head as if he was shaking away the memory, the pain. 'When you lose a child, it's easier to say nothing, to keep the hurt away.'

'But it just goes deeper.'

'It does.' Sean caught his breath. 'I still miss him today.'

'Him.' Bunty wiped her cheek with the back of her hand. 'You can't even say his name.'

'Daniel.' Sean closed his eyes tightly. 'Our Danny boy.'

'Oh, Sean, how we loved that little boy.' Bunty shuddered as the first sob came. 'He made us complete. He was our entire world.'

Sean's cheek was streaked with tears. 'He'd be forty-one now. He'd have had a family of his own, wife, kiddies – we'd be grandparents.'

Bunty nodded, swallowing hard. 'It broke my heart. It broke me in pieces.'

'I didn't know how to reach you, how to talk about it, Bunts.'

Her face contorted. 'So you said nothing, Sean. As if it hadn't happened. And for all these years you said nothing while it was killing me every day.'

He met her gaze, squeezing her hand in both of his. 'It was killing me too. But what else could I do? I thought it was best to just carry on. I'd be the joker, I'd make the lads laugh, I'd try to make you smile – but all the time I was pretending everything was fine, I could still see his little face in the cot.'

'We had him with us for three months. Three tiny months.' Bunty's breath shuddered. 'He looked like an angel when I found him that morning with his eyes closed. I thought he was asleep but, Sean, my heart had started thumping – it was as if I knew.'

'I heard you scream. I came straight away but there was nothing to be done.'

'The doctor said that, when she came out – there was nothing we could have done to prevent it, it was just one of those things.' Bunty's shoulders slumped. 'She even gave it a name, the doctor, as if it were a normal everyday thing – but it wasn't for me. She called it Sudden Infant...'

Bunty sobbed, out of control now, and Sean gazed at her, helpless, miserable. 'Bunty...'

She looked up, her eyes wild. 'You never mentioned him, in all those years, you never said how much you missed him.'

'I carried his little coffin.' Sean's face contorted. 'I helped put him in the ground. But I couldn't bring him back.'

'I needed you to talk to me, Sean – I needed you to tell me how you felt. I always loved you but the silence drove something between us.'

'I felt it too.' Sean was out of his chair, next to Bunty, his arms around her. 'You're all I have now, Bunts. I love you as much as I love life itself.'

Bunty buried her head in his chest. 'I know – and I've been stupid. Can you forgive me?'

'There's nothing to forgive.' Sean kissed the tears from her face. 'We'll try our best, we'll talk about everything, us, about Danny.'

'We'll mention him on his birthday.'

'Light a candle.'

Bunty took a breath. 'We'll be all right, Sean, won't we?'

He smoothed her hair with his fingers. 'We'll be dandy. We'll get even closer to each other now. Let's go away after Robert's cream-tea thing – take some time for us, to talk, heal, start again.'

Bunty smiled. 'Me and you.'

'Me and you, darlin',' Sean repeated. Then he gazed at the table. Isaac Mewton had lifted a boxty in her claw, nibbling it with her little teeth. Sean laughed. 'She knows what tastes good.'

'I'll put the pan on and make another batch.' Bunty wiped her face and stood up. 'Life goes on, Sean. I'm learning to make the best of every moment.'

35

The rain continued to pour for two days without a break. It was bouncing off the tarmac, forming puddles on the drive as Hattie set out to Millbrook. The work on the patio had stopped. Danut scratched his head and said that there was no way he could control the weather and the cream-tea competition should be held on the village green, that was all there was to it. Robert had been in a daze; he'd been that way since Hattie and Barry had picked him up from Tressy's tea rooms. He'd been going about his business in a dream, a smile on his face. On Monday evening, he'd even suggested watching *Notting Hill*, and he'd sat through the entire movie with his head on one side, grinning, while Bunty and Sean cooked supper.

Hattie pushed her hands in her pockets and thought about Bunty. She seemed happier since Sean arrived. They hugged a lot and there was a lot of kissing. Hattie snorted quietly – she was the only sensible one in the house. She and Barry had exchanged a peck on the cheek once or twice, nothing more. She liked him but she certainly wasn't rushing anything. The wind blew a strong gust and her hood tipped back, rain in her face.

She tugged the hood over her head as she approached Mill-brook. A car sloshed by, tyres squelching. It occurred to Hattie that by this time next week, she'd be back in her bungalow, prac-tising piano, going to yoga, having coffee with Glenys. She wondered how easy it would be to return to normality. She was happy in Millbrook; she liked the people there, she was popular. And Barry was lovely company; she'd really enjoyed their walk on the clifftop in Padstow.

She reached the manse and rang the bell. Sally Baxter answered it, almost breathless. 'Hattie, it's you! Come in. I've got the kettle on and there's some matcha shortbread in the oven. It's a recipe of Tilda's. She wants to talk to you.'

Hattie stepped inside. 'That's why I'm here – we texted...'

'But what about the baking competition?' Sally looked worried. 'What if it rains all week?'

'Rosie Eagle called round yesterday.' Hattie shook raindrops from her jacket. 'We've said we'll do Scone Wars on the village green under a big tent if the weather's really bad. Rosie said she hoped it would thunder – she said they'd be able to crank up the drama, you know, "The heavens are unhappy – Cornwall and Devon are at war and the scone is their weapon of choice..." But Robert and Tressy don't want that. They are—' Hattie stopped herself. She almost said that they were an item. It was true – she'd overheard Robert on the phone twice a day talking about baking to Tressy as if it was a term of endearment. 'They're friends.'

'That's nice,' Sally said as they reached the kitchen, spacious, with wooden cupboards and a tall Welsh dresser. Tilda was busy, placing mottled green biscuits on a pretty plate. She'd just boiled the kettle. 'Thanks for coming, Hattie. I'm just desperate to talk to you.'

'Oh?' Hattie sat down and accepted a biscuit, nibbling tenta-tively. She could taste almonds. 'Delicious.'

'Matcha biscuits. Healthy.' Tilda passed a mug of tea. 'So – I wanted to ask...'

'Ask away,' Hattie said, conscious that Sally had perched herself on a stool and was listening.

'Well, you know Armpit had been asked to play in the background at the competition on Sunday? Well, Rosie Eagle and the Cornish reporter – Geraldine – have had a falling out. Geraldine said Armpit aren't the sort of group you'd want on TV to represent the south-west, and Donkey said it didn't matter as we'd probably be edited out so you'd only see us for about two seconds, and then the band had a blazing row. Our guitarist Skinny Norm was very snobby about the baking competition – he said he didn't want to waste his talents on a lot of old people making biscuits.' Tilda stopped herself. 'Anyway, I think any air time on TV is a good thing and Donkey agrees with me, but the band has split up, Norm has gone off travelling - there's just me and Donkey now.'

'That's awful,' Sally said.

Tilda acknowledged her mother with a nod. 'So, Hattie, what do you think?'

'I think it's a perfect opportunity for you and Donkey to play together. He's a great guitarist and you can sing a jazz number.'

'Plus, Rosie thinks that's more "appropriate" if just Donkey and I perform.' Tilda used her fingers as inverted commas. 'She said we could play in the background on Saturday and we'd get more exposure – they are doing a bit of filming about the Scone Wars for publicity on Saturday, a kind of preview.'

'I know.'

'So, what do you think, Hattie?' Tilda asked again.

'I think you should sing "Black Coffee" – it's a really gutsy song and it would suit your voice and it fits with the baking theme – black coffee goes with everything – and you and Donkey should dress in black, him in a suit, you in a little black dress, but keeping your own style, you'd grab attention and sound fantastic.'

'That's what I think.' Tilda smiled, helping herself to a matcha shortbread. '"Black Coffee"'s a great choice of song. But Donkey and I wondered—'

'What do you need?' Hattie asked.

'Well – we wondered if you'd join our band – you could play keyboards – and maybe Barry would be able to do some light drums, you know, a soft sound with brushes or a bit of rhythm, nothing too hard.'

'I'm sure if we rehearse a few times, Barry and I could sound passable.'

'Passable?' Tilda laughed. 'It would make everything sound so much better. Say you'll do it, Hattie? You don't mind about being on TV? We might even be able to play our own composition, Scone Wars Blues.'

'I think it's a great opportunity,' Hattie agreed. She helped herself to another biscuit. 'And we should always seize opportunities with both hands. I'd be delighted to join Armpit – even if it's only for the weekend.'

* * *

By Wednesday morning, the rain had stopped and the sunshine made the grass glow like emeralds. Isaac Mewton was rolling on her back in the garden next to the rows of lettuce and radishes. Hattie rushed out after breakfast to rehearse with her new band, leaving Robert and Bunty standing outside with Danut and Joey. All four of them had their hands on their hips, shaking their heads as they stared at the patio. The ground where the slabs hadn't been placed yet was muddy, a dark red paste of earth. 'It'll be finished on Tuesday. That's the best I can do, Robert,' Danut said.

Robert shook his head sadly. 'Tressy and I were really looking forward to doing the competition here.'

'Didn't you say they had the village green as a backup?' Danut asked.

'The grass will be wet,' Bunty said.

'It'll have dried out by Saturday,' Joey said. 'And anyway, if they put up one of those big tents, no one will know the difference.'

'I will,' Robert muttered. 'I just imagined the tent over there, me and Tressy and a couple of cookers and fridges...' He pointed to a patch of grass. 'And the patio, full of guests, eating and drinking, bistro tables, deckchairs and in the background, my hens, the goats.'

'It can't be done, I'm sorry.' Danut was apologetic. 'Even if Joey and I worked a twelve-hour day, which we'd be prepared to do, the grouting still won't be finished in time.'

'That's a shame,' Bunty said. She turned as Sean came to stand next to her in vest and shorts.

'What's up?'

'The patio won't be ready, Sean,' Bunty said. 'Robert had set his heart on it.'

'So...' Sean scratched his curls beneath the cap. 'The problem is – all those patio slabs need laying, then the grouting needs doing, then a bit of edging and tidying.'

Danut nodded. 'That's the size of it. Joey and I won't finish until next week.'

'I'm going for a walk around the garden.' Robert sighed. 'I'll collect a few eggs and perhaps I'll make a sponge when I get back.' He pushed a hand over his face. 'I'll have to ring Tressy and tell her the competition is on the village green. She'll be so disappointed.'

Bunty grabbed Sean's arm. 'Don't ring her until we're back, Robert. Come on, Sean – grab the car keys.'

'Where are we going?'

'Down The Pig and Pickle.'

Robert shrugged. 'Not the best time to go for a pint, Bunty, but there you are – there's not much else to be done.' He turned to Danut. 'Thanks for everything you're doing. It's a shame we won't be finished, but there it is.'

Danut picked up his shovel. 'We'll do our best, Robert, but we've lost two days.'

'I know.' Robert held out his fingers. 'Come on, Isaac – let's go feed the chickens. Princess Lay-a will be hungry, and Hen Solo.'

Robert walked slowly towards the big field, Isaac trotting behind him, as Sean steered the Peugeot out of the drive and towards Millbrook. He and Bunty paused in the car park behind The Pig and Pickle. They could hear blues music coming from the manse through the open window, a chuntering guitar, lazy keyboard chords, a rich voice. Bunty led the way into the pub. 'Right – let's see who's in the snug.'

Inside, it was gloomy, a few yellow lights glimmering. Colin and Dennis were hunched over a table, pint glasses in their hands. Colin said, 'You have to admit, Dennis, Brexit has damaged the economy beyond repair...'

'But you can't deny that 52 per cent of the population voted for it.' Dennis thumped his fist on the table.

'Not quite fifty-two. Only 51.9 per cent of the voters were in favour of leaving.'

'That's still a majority, Colin. And a majority wins.'

'But 28 per cent of eligible voters didn't vote at all.'

'That's their lookout.'

Bunty stood watching them. Then she said, 'Sean, I'd like you to meet Dennis and Colin. They are good drinking buddies. Guys—'

Both Colin and Dennis looked at Bunty, then at Sean. She offered them a winning smile. 'This is my husband, Sean.'

'Sean,' Dennis grunted a greeting and went back to his pint.

'Are you stopping for a jar?' Colin offered. 'Shall I ask Shelley for a pint and a G & T?'

'Thanks, but the thing is,' Bunty said, 'we need some strong people to help Robert with the patio.'

'What's wrong with it?' Colin asked.

'It's been raining non-stop and now the patio won't be done in time,' Bunty explained.

'Unless we can get a few people to give us a hand,' Sean said.

Colin stood up, draining his glass. 'I've only had the one. I'll help Robert finish his patio.'

'And so will I,' Dennis agreed. 'Eric Mallory's a dab hand with a shovel, and Francis only really works on a Sunday.'

'I'll talk to Mary and Sally, see if they can help,' Bunty suggested. 'And I know a couple of other women who'd be very glad to join in.' She turned to Sean with a smile. 'I think the Mill-brook Gardening Club will be able to give Robert a hand.'

* * *

When Hattie returned to Robert's house later on that afternoon, she was surprised to see so many people working, sleeves rolled up. Danut and Joey had the cement mixer whirring, giving instructions. Mary Tenby was bringing out trays of tea. Sean leaned on his spade, his smile wide. 'We'll have this done by tomorrow.'

Edie, wearing jogging bottoms, and Eric waved trowels. 'We're really enjoying this,' Edie said. 'It's good to work together, share the experience, the sweat and the toil and the joy.'

'I've always fancied myself as a labourer's mate,' Eric proclaimed, wiping his brow with a clean handkerchief.

George Tenby agreed. 'This is such good exercise. And all in a good cause.' He paused to accept a mug of tea from his wife.

Sean was shovelling away, talking to Colin and Dennis about The Hole in the Wall in Ballycotton. Colin said, 'We'll have to come up one day, Sean – bring a busload from Millbrook, challenge your lads to a darts match.'

'It would be good craic,' Dennis exclaimed, proud that he was acquiring the Irish language.

Bunty winked at Sean, who grinned back. She and Sally were getting the hang of grouting, trowelling the sand and cement mix into the cracks between slabs, tamping it down.

'We're getting there.' Francis looked towards heaven, as if God would reward the efforts of the gardening club.

Hattie rolled up her sleeves. 'How can I help?'

'Grab a trowel – give us a hand putting in the grout.' Bunty grinned.

'Where's Robert?' Hattie looked around. 'Isn't he helping?'

'The gardening club took a majority decision,' Bunty explained. 'He was banned from working on the patio in case he damages his fingers before the competition. He's in the kitchen with a box of eggs, making sponge cakes for us all to share when we're finished. Sean told him to relax.' She gazed around. 'I can't imagine he's relaxed though. Susan and Angie and Jill have gone with him.'

36

Saturday was a hot, dry day. The patio gleamed with newness as the television crew worked through the morning, putting up a white marquee tent, rushing around organising electrics, tripods, microphones. Robert watched from a distance, Hattie and Bunty standing closely on either side of him. He said, 'The patio looks good.'

'The gardening club did so well,' Hattie remarked. 'Look at all the plants in pots, the little water feature. The pergola's glorious. It's going to be wonderful.'

'I hope so,' Robert murmured nervously. 'I have to do something. I can't stand still. I'm going to do some weeding, check the animals.' And with that he wandered off.

Rosie and Geraldine were bustling about, looking busy, clutching clipboards and talking to the crew in loud voices. Then Rosie rushed over to Hattie. 'We're live at four. There will be rehearsals from twelve. Can you get into whatever you're wearing...?'

'I was going to perform like this.' Hattie indicated her T-shirt, jeans and slippers. She saw Rosie's shocked expression and she added, 'Or I've got a lovely jumpsuit and kinky boots.'

Rosie wasn't sure if she was joking. 'When are the rest of the band coming?'

'They'll be here at any moment.'

'When's Rocco Chiarello arriving? I've seen his show on TV. He's very good,' Bunty said.

'Oh, Rocco will be here for the judging tomorrow. I just spoke to him on the phone. That reminds me – where's Robert? I need to talk to him and Tressy. She should be here by now. We need to start going through a few things.'

Bunty waved a hand. 'Robert's probably in conversation with Hen Solo and Jabba the Cluck.'

Rosie shook her head for a moment, mystified, then she rushed away, her clipboard in front of her. Hattie smiled. 'We shouldn't be so wicked.'

'A bit of mischief's great once in a while – it keeps us young,' Bunty suggested. 'I'm glad Robert is up the field with the animals. It's giving him time to calm down. And Sean's in the kitchen making some sausages and colcannon for lunch. Robert would have a fit if he saw the mess he's made. I'll go in and tidy up while you put the slap on and get dressed for the rehearsal.'

Hattie placed an affectionate arm around her sister. 'You and Sean are happy now? You seem very close.'

'We had a long talk about us and – and Danny. A few things that needed saying, but we worked it all through and now we're happier than ever.' Bunty's eyes glowed. 'He's a good man, a keeper.'

'And he loves you,' Hattie said gently. She was glad Bunty and Sean were back on track – they were good together. Hattie thought about herself, wondering if she and Barry could ever be so close. She shrugged – things would be what they'd be. But she intended to go home next week, and she'd invite him to visit her in the bungalow at some point. She decided that if she missed him when they were apart, it might help her to understand how she felt about him: feelings were complex, especially after Geoffrey. She wouldn't let Geoffrey spoil things but the thought of trusting someone still made her shudder. She caught sight of Tilda and Donkey walking up the drive hand in hand, very smartly dressed in black. She waved to them, thinking that she'd better go and change.

The rest of the morning was all about standing around and waiting, then someone called out, 'Armpit – can we have you here, please?'

Moments later, a camera was in Hattie's face and she was playing chords for all she was worth, until someone called out, 'Stop. Can we try that again?' Another camera focused on Tilda, who sang her heart out, completely calm and professional, unlike Barry, who kept whispering that he could hardly hold the new drum brushes as his hands were sweating.

Donkey leaned across and murmured, 'Totally natural, mate – just roll with it. You'll be fine by the fifth take.'

A woman whom Hattie recognised from TV, in a fitted dress and perfect make-up, her dark hair falling over one eye, practised her introductions in front of the camera. 'And from Devon, we welcome a local band. Put your hands together for Tilda Baxter's Armpit.' Then she stopped, covered her mouth. 'I can't say that, can I? Can we do it again, Peter?'

At half past one, there was a break when the set went quiet, people sat around talking, drinking from water bottles and flasks. Hattie and Robert were enjoying the cool of the kitchen, which was now pristine, sitting at the table eating the colcannon Sean had made.

Hattie said, 'Are you nervous, Robert?'

'About tomorrow?' He shook his head. 'No, I'm keeping calm.'

Bunty shivered. 'I'd be nervous. It's not just the cameras, it's all the viewers watching every detail and how bad I'd feel if I made a mistake.'

'I'm a bit anxious about the live filming this afternoon, the preview for tomorrow,' Hattie admitted. 'I don't think we'll make a mistake, but there's always the chance.'

Sean had cleaned his plate – there wasn't a scrap of potato or cabbage remaining. He said, 'So you're all right with the competition on Sunday, Robert? I mean, the usual baking shows on TV have three or more contestants. But with only two of you and one has to lose, I'd be worried, to tell you the truth.'

'Tressy and I have been talking about it,' Robert said quietly. 'We're both happy to lose because it means the other one will win.' His face was contented. 'As far as we're concerned, Scone Wars has brought us together and that's all that matters.'

'It's time,' a voice shouted from the hall. It was Tilda, who hurried into the kitchen. 'They're ready for us, Hattie.' She took in Hattie's clothes, the black jumpsuit, the heeled boots, and said, 'You look awesome.'

'Then let's get out there and show them what we can do,' Hattie said, full of new confidence. Bunty and Robert exchanged looks, both thinking the same thing – their sister had come a long way since Geoffrey.

Hattie wriggled on her seat, making sure that she was comfortable, then the presenter stared into the camera. 'And from Devon, we welcome the Tilda Baxter Band.'

Hattie launched into the chords for 'Black Coffee'. It was absolutely right that Tilda's voice was at the heart of the music. She glanced up as she played, watching Tilda perform, raunchy, sweet, at times vulnerable, at others powerful. Barry seemed more at ease with his drum brushes too and Donkey was completely oblivious, focusing on his guitar.

The music came to an end, and applause rang out from the crowd who'd assembled to watch. Then the presenter was glancing into the camera. 'Thank you.' She offered a professional smile. 'And now it's the Scone Wars moment you've all been waiting for. Time to meet our two contestants in the war of scones that will take place live on TV tomorrow. And they are both great bakers in their own right. From Millbrook in Devon, we have Robert Parkin.'

Robert smiled politely. 'Hello.'

'Robert, you used to be a head teacher?'

'Yes. I'm retired now.'

'So what started you off on the road to baking?' The presenter whirled back to the camera.

'It's a creative process and a scientific one at the same time. I enjoy it.' Robert thought for a moment. 'And it gives me great pleasure to see other people enjoy what I create.'

'Thanks, Robert.' The presenter moved to Tressy, who was staring, arms folded, into the camera, dressed in a pretty frock with a fairy-cake print. 'And, representing Cornwall in our Scone Wars tomorrow, we have Mrs Tressy Carew.'

'Miss,' Tressy said firmly. 'Or Ms. I don't mind which. But I'm definitely not a Mrs.'

'Tressy.' The presenter glossed over her error. 'How does it feel to be representing Cornwall tomorrow?'

'I'm very proud of being Cornish.' Tressy folded her arms. 'And I'm proud of my baking. I run a tea room in Padstow. My customers will tell you all about my cream teas, and how I've been baking for years.'

'And, Tressy—' the reporter's face was mischievous '—can you beat Robert, do you think? Can you win the baking competition for Cornwall?'

'To be honest I don't much care if I do or I don't.' Tressy laughed. 'It's not about the winning. It's about the competing. Robert and I both love baking and we make each other better bakers. So I don't really care much about what happens in the long run.'

'But this is about Cornish pride, Tressy.' The presenter was determined to make her point. 'Or Devon pride. It's about who puts what on the scone first, the jam or the cream.'

'I still don't reckon it matters all that much.' Tressy shrugged. 'Yes, it's tradition, I always put the jam on first and I always will. But there are wars all over the world and starvation and poverty, so I don't 'xpect it concerns people a great deal in the grand scheme of things whether it's jam or cream first on a scone.' The presenter was about to move the microphone away as Tressy grasped her hand. 'So Robert and I will just concentrate on enjoying our baking and we hope on the way we can give you some interesting flavours.'

'So can you give us any tasters?' The presenter laughed to emphasise her joke. 'A taster of some of the flavours you'll be baking tomorrow?'

'That'd be telling.' Tressy laughed. 'And as they say, if I told you I'd have to kill you.'

The presenter turned back to the camera. 'So as you can see, the tension's hotting up. In the Cornish corner, we have feisty Tressy from the tea shop in Padstow and in the Devon corner, we have Robert, serious and scientific. And top chef Rocco Chiarello will be taking time out from his popular TV show *Baking with Rocco* to judge. But who will win the Scone Wars? Tune in tomorrow afternoon at two o'clock and don't miss it. Devon or Cornwall? There can only be one victor.'

She held her smile until someone shouted, 'Cut!' Then she turned away as someone handed her a bottle of cold water.

She could be heard saying, 'Thank goodness that's over.'

Technicians were in action again, busy untangling electrics and tripods and wires. Rosie and Geraldine rushed around, Geraldine telling Tressy that she did Cornwall proud while Rosie grasped Robert's arm and told him he was sure to win. Tilda, Barry, Donkey and Hattie were packing up their instruments, pleased with their performances.

Bunty grabbed Sean's hand. 'I recorded the show when it went out live. Let's go in and see it. I can't wait to see Hattie – and Robert's interview.'

'Right you are,' Sean said. 'It should be good. That interviewer woman was a weapon though.'

'She was fierce,' Bunty agreed, then she called, 'Hattie, Robert – Tressy. We're going in to watch the recording. Are you coming?'

'Right behind you,' Hattie yelled.

'On our way,' Tressy muttered as she turned to Robert and grasped his arm, leading him away from the crowd. She lowered her voice. 'I think I'll stay over tonight.'

'Over?' Robert's eyes nearly popped out.

'Here, with you. That's all right, isn't it?'

'Oh.' Robert held his breath. The fourth bedroom was small; he'd put all sorts of junk in there, books, old records, magazines. 'Well, I'm sure I can tidy up and make space.'

'We'll talk about it dreckly.' Tressy's eyes twinkled. 'It makes sense. I can't be competing with all that traffic tomorrow morning on the A30, driving here from Padstow, and it would be nice to spend the time with you tonight.'

'It would.' Robert hesitated, unsure exactly what Tressy was suggesting.

'We'll go over the plan again, what we're going to bake on television tomorrow and discuss how we'll deal with all the palaver at the end when they announce the winner. Or...'

'Or?'

'Or we could just forget about it completely and take ourselves out for a nice dinner.'

'Dinner?' Robert repeated. 'That might be a thing...'

'Yes, let's all go out. I'd like to meet your family properly. I haven't met Bunty's husband yet and it would be fun if the six of us could all meet up as couples, somewhere where they serve tasty food and we could all talk and have a special time.' Tressy moved closer. 'Would you like that, Robert?'

'I'd like it very much,' he murmured.

'It's a good job I brought my suitcase and my pyjamas with me, then.' Tressy smiled. She glanced around at the film crew, bustling, rolling up cables and packing cameras. Rosie and Geraldine had their heads together, plotting. Tressy touched Robert's arm in a light caress. 'So, would it be all right if I went in and had a bath? I'm proper hot and bothered after all that talking on the television. And you can talk to your family and tell them I'm staying over...' She raised an eyebrow. 'Then we'll all put on our glad rags and go into Teignmouth or Dawlish and get ourselves a lovely dinner.'

Robert took her hands in his. 'I think that would be wonderful.'

'It would. And then after the Scone Wars is over and done with tomorrow – I might ask you if we can go out for another dinner, just the two of us, and then I'll ask if I can stay over another night. Just to wind down and get over the fuss of it all. What do you think to that, Robert?' Tressy stood on tiptoes and kissed Robert's lips.

'I think that would be heaven,' Robert said as he closed his eyes and kissed her back.

37

Hattie peered through the bedroom window. It was early, just after seven, but there were so many people in the garden scurrying like ants. There was activity inside the small marquee on the lawn next to the new patio – Hattie watched as a cooker was carried inside, and a huge white fridge. Two men were fixing fairy lights around the outside. She glanced towards Robert's drive, where lines of cars were parked. A small stage had been erected for the band to play. Her heart started to thump in anticipation – goodness knew how Robert must be feeling.

At least the weather would be fine. The sunshine was already strong, warming the dew on the grass. The garden sparkled; it would look good on the screen. Hattie smiled. She'd seen herself on the television yesterday when Bunty had played the recording back: she'd been moving her fingers across the keyboards behind Tilda's shoulder and her face had been visible for at least four seconds before the camera switched back to Tilda, who'd looked stunning. Television favoured the young.

Hattie tugged on her dressing gown and padded down to the kitchen. Tressy was already there, bustling about making tea. She handed Hattie a cup and she accepted it gratefully, glancing at Tressy in bare feet and pyjamas. Briefly she wondered where she'd slept, but she wouldn't ask.

Tressy said, 'Robert's up in the fields with the cameramen. I'm going to make him a proper Cornish breakfast – eggs, fried bread and beans, mushrooms and tomato, fried potato. I brought some hog's pudding with me too, so I'll cook some of that.'

'Hog's pudding?'

'Cornish delicacy.' Tressy smiled. 'No breakfast is complete without hog's pudding – I make my own from pork meat and fat, suet, bread, and oatmeal. Do you fancy some?'

'I think that might be a bit much for me first thing. I'll make some toast,' Hattie said politely.

'Robert will need a proper breakfast that will stick to his ribs today.' Tressy sipped from her mug. 'It's going to be hectic.'

'Is there anything I can do to help?' Hattie offered.

'You're doing it just by being so nice. Our dinner last night was lovely. And my Robert insisted on paying – that was dear of him, so I was thinking I might take him out tonight, just me and him.'

'I had a lovely time – Barry did too.' Hattie recalled the meal they'd shared together, the laughter as they sat in a pretty restaurant perched high on a cliff overlooking Dawlish beach before coming home in a taxi.

Tressy smiled as if she had a secret. 'Robert and I have some things to talk about.'

'Oh?'

'I've decided it's time for me to move on.'

'Ah...' Hattie said, even louder. If Tressy left Robert, he'd be devastated.

'I'll get someone to run the tea shop for me. Then Robert and

I can spend our time between Cornwall and Devon, having some fun in our retirement.'

Hattie breathed out in relief. 'He'd love that.'

'We both would.' Tressy lifted the frying pan. 'Well, I can't stand around gassing all day – I got breakfast to make and then, later, I got scones to bake.'

* * *

Hattie was too nervous to eat more than half a slice of toast. She showered, dressed and wandered out into the garden. There were people everywhere, television crew, technicians, almost everyone she knew from Millbrook and more. Susan, Angie and Jill wore special T-shirts with pictures of Robert on the front wearing a crown and the slogan Devon Scone King. Hattie wondered where they'd had them made. Everyone else was wearing the official Wars T-shirts, even Dennis and Colin, who'd arrived early to bag a good view and were sitting at a bistro table with cans of best bitter between them. A busload of Cornish supporters pulled up on the road outside and Francis was greeting them all, shaking hands and smiling.

Tilda and Donkey were tuning up, pausing to notice a black Jaguar come to a halt in the drive. Hattie assumed at first that it must be Rocco Chiarello, but the man who walked towards Tilda was not dark-haired and cheeky-faced. He was tall, in chinos, glasses, a ponytail. Tilda shook his hand and Donkey did the same. They appeared to be talking about music: Hattie overheard the man tell them to call him Guy and that he co-owned a recording company. Then Robert was at her side.

'Have you seen Tressy?'

Hattie nodded. 'She's in the shower, getting ready. Bunty's in her room doing yoga, Sean's over there, having a drink with

Dennis and Colin, and Rosie Eagle and Geraldine are going to collapse with nerves if they don't calm down. They are rushing around everywhere, clucking like your chickens.'

'Talking of which, I had to take the cameramen up into the field. They wanted some shots of the goats and the hens for part of the introduction.' Robert pointed. 'They are still there. I hope Vincent Van Goat doesn't damage their equipment – he's in a frisky mood this morning.' He glanced across to the new patio where Isaac Mewton was crouched down, watching the action. 'Isaac doesn't care. She's happy to be centre stage.' He squeezed Hattie's arm. 'Thank you.'

'What for?'

'Everything.' Robert's eyes crinkled with happiness. 'I've loved having you here. It's been tremendous. I'll miss you so much when you go back.'

'I think I'll be a frequent visitor.' Hattie smiled. 'I was talking to Barry. He'll visit me in Bodicote and I'll come down here. But we're taking things slowly.'

'Not like me and Tressy.' Robert's cheeks pinked. 'We're making up for lost time.'

'That's good. Oh?' Hattie tugged her phone from her pocket. 'Another missed call from an unknown number – that's the third one this morning.'

'A Sunday scam?' Robert looked worried.

'I'm not thinking about it until after the baking competition. We're playing our own composition live. "Scone Wars Blues".'

'You're an inspiration, Hat.' Robert looked at Hattie with pure affection. 'You'll be in the charts next.'

'That would be a thing.' Hattie indicated her clothes. 'I have the kinky boots, all ready to go.'

'Robert – you're here.' Rosie Eagle was breathless as she stated the obvious. 'Where's Tressy?'

'She'll be here in a—'

'Good. I've just had word that Rocco is minutes away.' Rosie said his name as if they were best friends. 'I need some publicity photos with the three of you for *The Chronicle*. And you'll need to do a short interview about the two charities, why we're supporting the air ambulance and the lifeboats. And some pictures of you and Tressy together, glaring at each other, holding wooden spoons as weapons, that kind of thing.'

'Oh, we won't do that,' Robert replied quickly. 'You can photograph us kissing if you like.'

Hattie was amazed at his new boldness and suddenly she relaxed. He'd be fine in the competition. She glanced around. Bunty and Sean were sharing another beer with Dennis and Colin. Barry was walking up the drive, waving his drumsticks, smiling. Hattie waved back as she watched a large car sweep through the gates. It slowed and a young man clambered out, confident, with dark hair, sunglasses, tight jeans. He was immediately swamped by Susan and Angie, leading a group of other women demanding selfies and signed T-shirts. Francis rushed over to offer a welcome as Rosie and Geraldine elbowed him out of the way, clutching Rocco Chiarello's hand. Hattie felt the phone buzz in her pocket. She ignored it and rushed over to meet Barry.

* * *

Then someone called out, 'We're live.' Hattie was hunched over the keyboards, crossing her fingers. She glanced over at Bunty, who raised both hands, her fingers crossed too, and smiled nervously. The presenter, whose name was Ananya Chainani, offered the camera her most professional expression. Her dark hair falling over one eye, she spoke smoothly. 'Welcome to Scone

Wars, the contest you've all been waiting for. This is the moment where two bakers from Devon and Cornwall will face off in an age-old rivalry.'

The cameras focused on Robert and Tressy, standing side by side in matching aprons, one with a green flag with a white cross, the word Devon and a picture of a scone with cream first, and the other with a black and white flag, the word Kernow and a scone with jam first. Tressy winked at Robert and he smiled.

Ananya Chainani continued. 'But first let me introduce you to our special guest, who's going to judge the cream teas and settle this scone war once and for all. Give a big West of England welcome to top celebrity chef and heart-throb, Rocco Chiarello.'

Rocco showed a pearly smile and began to talk to Ananya. Hattie heard him say words like 'flavour – texture – complementing the jam – presentation counts for so much...' But she was gazing at Robert, who was taking his place in the tent opposite Tressy. They both looked cool and focused. She hoped they'd be all right.

The competition was quickly under way. The first round was called, 'Plain with Jam'. Robert and Tressy needed to present a batch of their best simple scones, to be served with home-made jam of their choice. Rocco sat at a table, being filmed as he sampled them.

'Our Cornish Tressy has chosen to bake a plain scone with strawberry jam and clotted cream on top. I notice she dices her butter before mixing. And she has cool hands, touching the mixture as little as possible, with the lightest touch. Therefore...' he took a bite '... her scones have a crumbly texture, the jam's not too sweet, loaded with fruit, and the clotted cream offers a delicious balance. Robert from Devon, however, has chosen—' the camera closed in on a porcelain cake stand, three tiers of scones '—to add the cream first in the traditional way, but he's broken with convention by using raspberry jam, which I believe he makes himself, using the fruit from his garden.' He took a bite. 'Cream first. Delicious. I have to say, there's little to separate them both, but I'm going to award the points this first round to...' The crowd held their breath. 'To Tressy, as her scones were slightly lighter. Not much in it though.'

'Cornwall in the lead.' Ananya beamed and Hattie heard a voice screech from the audience. It was Geraldine, seated with other members of her newspaper, wearing matching Anchor T-shirts. Ananya continued, professional and full of excitement. 'The next round is for savoury scones. So let's see what our contestants have up their sleeves. It seems that Tressy is flavouring hers with hog's pudding, a Cornish speciality, and Robert is making a Devon blue cheese and walnut scone, his own recipe.'

Hattie shifted in her seat, wondering if she had time to sneak off to the loo. She looked across at Bunty, who had left Sean, Dennis and Colin at the table and was making her way to the house. Barry placed his hand on Hattie's, offering her a bottle of cold water. Hattie accepted it gratefully. Her seat at the keyboard was uncomfortable and she wished she'd brought a better cushion. It was hard to get a good view of what was going on inside the tent, but she could see Robert bobbing behind the cameras, mixing flour.

A slow hour passed and Hattie drank another bottle of water, then wriggled through the crowds to the house, feeling sorry for the queues at the Portaloo that had been placed at the edge of the drive. She returned ten minutes later with two soft cushions and as she took her place, Ananya Chainani said, 'So the second round goes to Devon. I can't wait to try one of Robert's blue cheese scones. One round each. The score is equal. Now we are poised for a big Scone Wars climax. This is the final round, the free choice. Tressy will make limoncello scones with champagne cream and Robert is going to make pumpkin and ginger, with lemon curd and cream cheese.'

'Boo.' A loud voice roared from where *The Cornish Anchor* were seated.

Geraldine stared across at Rosie, who was urging *The Teignmouth Chronicle* on, cheerleader style, punching the air, yelling, 'Go Devon, Go Devon.'

Hattie whispered to Barry. 'Geraldine upset Robert when she said his ginger scones tasted too spicy. It's plucky of him to make them again.'

Barry took her hand. 'I hope he wins.'

'He and Tressy don't mind either way.' She pointed towards the two newspaper factions, *The Anchor* and *The Chronicle*, who had started to hurl insults at each other. Geraldine and Rosie were shaking fists. 'They're the ones I'm most worried about.'

'I'm worried about playing the music just before the final judging,' Barry said. 'I don't want to mess up. I'm still getting used to my new role as a drummer.'

'The cameras will all be on Tilda and she'll shine,' Hattie murmured encouragingly. She looked up at where a cameraman was waving a hand. Tilda stood up, ruffled her hair, adjusting her position. 'I think we're on.'

'The scones are all cooked, the competition is all done, and the scores are equal,' Ananya Chainani said excitedly into the camera. 'So now our judge will settle himself at the table ready for the final adjudication. While he's getting comfortable and we try to calm our beating hearts, here's a song from hosting county Devon's Tilda Baxter Band, their own composition – "Scone Wars Blues".'

Donkey played a few guitar chords, Hattie and Barry coming in after the first notes, then Tilda's mesmerising voice filled the air. Hattie concentrated on her fingers, keeping them light on the notes. She glanced across at Barry, whose glasses shone and his smile filled his face. As Tilda sang, Isaac Mewton emerged from under a tree and stretched out in the sunshine.

'That was sublime – thank you,' Ananya said. 'But now it's time to see what Rocco thinks of the final batch of scones. This is the final heat in the Scone Wars.'

The cameras were back on Rocco, who sampled Robert's pumpkin scone, chewing, his face impressed. 'I've never tasted anything more delicious... the spice cuts through the richness of the lemon curd and cream cheese.' The audience held their breath. He took a mouthful of Tressy's scone. 'But the limoncello and champagne cream – pure decadence, a kiss in every mouthful.'

Someone sighed audibly. It was either Susan or Angie, who hadn't taken their eyes off Rocco for the entire show.

'So – will it be Cornwall – or will it be Devon in the Scone Wars?' Ananya asked the camera, as if it were the most important decision in the world. 'Will Robert from Devon emerge as the Cream Tea King? Or will Cornwall's Tressy steal his crown and become queen? For the final judgement – over to our heart-throb judge, Rocco Chiarello.'

Rocco was sitting on a mock throne, a crown on his head, legs crossed casually. A light table was on one side of him, holding two cake stands, Tressy's three batches of scones and Robert's. Tressy and Robert had been positioned behind Rocco and they were smiling, holding hands, as if the result was irrelevant.

'It's so difficult to choose a winner – both cream teas are the best I've tasted, ever,' Rocco said dramatically. He picked up a scone in each hand as if he were weighing them. 'Both are things of great beauty. But although it's the closest thing since time began, there has to be a winner. So...' Rocco lifted one scone then the other, dragging the tension out. 'The judge's decision is final, as they say, and the winner of the South-West Scone Wars is...'

The crowd was silent. Geraldine could be heard to whisper, 'Cornwall.' Rosie shot her a look, pure daggers. Robert and Tressy snuggled closer.

'The winner is...' Rocco said again as cameras zoomed onto Tressy's and Robert's faces, hoping for a glimpse of tension.

Then there was an almighty crash. Ananya yelled in fear and ran backwards, bumping into a cameraman. Rocco screamed and his crown slipped down over one eye. There was mayhem, people turning, moving backwards as Vincent Van Goat and The Great Goatsby knocked over the table and attacked the scones that rolled on the floor. Both goats rummaged around in the food, Vincent with a whole limoncello scone in his mouth, Goatsby snuffling at a pumpkin and ginger one. More scones were squashed under their hooves.

Tressy said, 'Shall we let the goats decide on the winner?'

'Look.' Robert smiled, pointing. The hens had joined them. 'Jabba the Cluck likes your limoncello best.'

'But Obi Wan Henobi prefers the ginger,' Tressy beamed. 'So, it must be a tie.'

Hattie stood up to get a better view of the animals wreaking havoc. 'The camera crew were filming up in the field earlier,' she murmured to Barry. 'Someone must have left the gate open.'

She gazed across to where Rocco's chin was covered with cream, his crown askew, Vincent Van Goat clambering all over him for the scone he was holding at arm's length, and Ananya was gushing into the camera, trying to restore order as she grinned widely. 'So the animals are the judges – and they think it's a tie – both scones are scoring highly with the goats – and the hens—'

Hattie noticed Isaac Mewton at Rocco's feet, licking cream;

Robert and Tressy were on camera, kissing, both wearing crowns. Bunty waved, laughing.

'Things couldn't have turned out better,' Hattie mouthed as she waved back, then she saw a car roll along the drive beyond Bunty's shoulder. It was an old Mercedes, a grey one. Hattie recognised the driver at the wheel immediately and her blood ran cold.

She stood up and a shiver passed over her skin, a terror as familiar as her own breath. She knew at once that she could either be afraid and silent or she could face her past and put this particular ghost to rest forever.

She clenched her teeth, muttered 'Geoffrey,' and began to march towards him.

38

Hattie had no idea what was propelling her forward as she hurtled towards the grey Mercedes but she marched like a woman possessed. Geoffrey clambered out and stood tall, arms folded. As soon as she saw him, the old feelings rushed back – discomfort, dislike, fear. But her feet pushed her on to face him, despite her heart thudding. There would be no stopping her now.

Geoffrey leaned forward, smooth in a grey linen suit and tie. 'I've been phoning you.'

'Wh-when?'

'All morning – six times.'

'Oh – I didn't recognise the number.'

'It's a new phone.'

They stared at each other. Hattie said, 'What do you want, Geoffrey?'

'I'm taking you home.'

Hattie stood her ground. 'I don't need a lift.'

'I mean – I'm *taking* you home,' Geoffrey said emphatically.

'I'm not ready to go. How did you know I was here?'

'I saw you on TV yesterday – on that ridiculous show.'

'You were watching the ridiculous show?' Hattie asked quietly.

'Playing in a band at your age, with some young singer who looks like a tart.'

Hattie took a shuddering breath. 'She does not look like a tart. Tilda looks lovely.'

Geoffrey glared, offering Hattie his don't-you-dare-disagree-with-me look. He said, 'I've been in the house.'

'My bungalow?'

'We own it jointly. Anyway, what you've done to the walls is dreadful. I've booked someone in to paint it back to the way it should be.'

'Bland?'

'What's got into you?' Geoffrey said irritably. 'Purple walls, bright yellow in our bedroom, at your age? And those cheap prints. Unbelievable.'

Hattie half smiled: Bunty's taste was clearly not Geoffrey's. She took a breath. 'Why were you in my house?'

'I sent you flowers. I even sent you tickets so that we could go to a show.' Geoffrey frowned and Hattie was reminded of the thundercloud that hovered over his brow, the threat of a storm.

'Why?'

'I wanted to take you out – for dinner. So that we could put things right again, back to how they were before the unnecessary divorce.'

'Why?' Hattie said again, her tone firm.

Geoffrey shifted his feet. 'I tried to use my keys to get in, but the door was bolted. Then later, I came back and the house was empty so I moved my things back in. I spoke to Glenys and she said you'd gone away and she wouldn't tell me where. I asked her husband to tell me where you'd gone – he should have understood, he's a man – but he was rude, to say the least.'

Hattie felt an immediate surge of warmth towards Glenys and Bill. She'd message Glenys to thank them later.

'Then I saw you on TV. I have to say, Hattie, I'm not at all pleased that you've been making a show of yourself like this.'

'It's none of your business.'

'I ought to tell you for your own good how foolish you looked in front of millions of people.'

Hattie examined him carefully, his clean suit, grey tie. Geoffrey looked foolish, frowning, miserable as ever. She spoke quietly. 'Why are you here?'

'I've told you – I'm taking you home.'

'Home?' Hattie was starting to feel uneasy. 'What do you mean, home?'

'Back to Bodicote – back to our bungalow.'

'Why?'

'I'm going to take proper care of you.' Geoffrey reached out a heavy hand and laid it on Hattie's shoulder. 'I've come back to you for good. You'll be all right now.'

'What?' Hattie took a few moments to process what Geoffrey had said, then she said, 'Has Linda thrown you out?'

'She's an objectionable woman.' Geoffrey's chin tucked in to make a double. 'Not like you. She's untidy, she's difficult, argumentative.'

'Not like me,' Hattie repeated, pulling back from him.

'No, exactly. You're a good little woman, clean, proper. You know your place.'

'And my place is – where?'

'With me. In our home.' He looked her up and down. 'What on earth are you wearing?'

'A jumpsuit and kinky boots.'

'Well. Go and pack your case and leave the fancy dress

behind. You won't be needing them.' Hattie hesitated and Geoffrey raised his voice. 'What are you waiting for?'

'I'm not coming.'

'Don't be silly – of course you're coming.'

'I'm not.'

Geoffrey's face became raspberry red. 'Get your things, Hattie, and don't waste time. We can get home at a reasonable hour if we're quick and then you can cook something for supper.'

Hattie took a breath. 'So, you're living in the bungalow now?'

'I am.' Geoffrey puffed out his chest. 'Our bungalow.'

'Then go back to it, and tomorrow you can put it on the market, sell it, we'll split the money. I'm staying here.'

'Hattie, I'm telling you—'

'No, you're not telling me, not any more.'

Geoffrey whirled as if he'd been slapped. 'What did you say?'

'I said no, I'm not coming.' Hattie stood her ground. 'And if you want me to say more, then here goes. You and I are divorced, and that's not ever going to change. We should have split up fifty years ago. You're a nasty, controlling man, Geoffrey. Linda saw sense long before I did and good for her. I don't want to see you again. I'll get a solicitor to negotiate for my half of the bungalow, so that it's properly sorted, for ever. And I'm keeping my piano.'

'Hattie – you're unwell. You need to see a doctor.'

'I'm not unwell. This is the most sensible and calm I've ever been, and the happiest. Now go away, Geoffrey. If I never see you again, it will be too soon.'

'You don't mean it. You're mistaken.' Geoffrey seemed to struggle with the next words. 'We can get married again. You'd like that, wouldn't you?' As a desperate afterthought, he added, 'I – I love you.'

'No, you don't.' Hattie realised that her heart was beating

normally; she was staring Geoffrey straight in the eyes; she wasn't afraid. 'You're not capable of love. You're a coward, a bully and a totally unpleasant man. I wasted fifty years of my life with you and I won't waste another second. Now go home. Sling your hook.'

Hattie realised she was not alone. Robert and Tressy stood at one shoulder, Bunty and Sean at the other. Barry placed himself behind her, his arm around her waist. Isaac Mewton rubbed against her ankles, coiling round her legs. 'Go on, Geoffrey. You're not welcome here.' Hattie spoke quietly but her tone was firm. 'Go away. And let's make this the last time our paths cross.'

'You'll regret it,' Geoffrey snarled.

'You're wrong.' Hattie shook her head. 'I won't.'

Geoffrey turned to Robert. 'I suppose this is your doing, Robert – putting ideas into her head? Hattie was a good girl before she came here, she—'

'Goodbye, Geoffrey,' Robert said, his voice hushed but firm. 'I watched you bully my sister for fifty years. I ought to have stood up for Hattie long ago, but I let her down. You've been a brute, a tyrant. I should have punched you on the nose and, I'm telling you, if you don't leave immediately, I'll do just that. It's long overdue, but it would give me great pleasure.'

'Hear, hear,' Tressy said, linking an arm through Robert's.

Geoffrey writhed like a snake, snarling, from one face to the other, then he turned on his heel. Hattie watched, shivering, as he wriggled into the Mercedes, started the engine and roared away.

She breathed a sigh of relief. 'I hope that's the last we see of him.'

'Good riddance,' Bunty said.

'Where will you go?' Barry took her hand tenderly. 'If you need somewhere...'

'I'll stay with Robert for now, if I may,' Hattie said slowly.

'Then when the bungalow's sold, I'll buy whatever I can afford near here.'

'What a lovely idea,' Robert agreed. 'Although you're welcome to stay as long as you wish.'

'Why don't we all go out for dinner and talk about it?' Tressy looked at Robert. 'I know we were going to go out by ourselves tonight, but there will be time for that tomorrow, or the day after. I think we need a family meal now somewhere nice – to talk about our success and to ask Hattie what she needs us all to do to support her.'

'I'd like it if we could all be together this evening,' Bunty said. 'Sean and I are off to Ballycotton tomorrow.'

'When we get home, we're going to plan a second honeymoon,' Sean added.

'Then let's all go out tonight.' Robert looked over his shoulder. Technicians were packing up; people had started to leave, Francis shaking their hands. Dennis and Colin were still hunched at the table, drinking beer. Tilda and Donkey were talking to Guy, the man with the ponytail, who apparently had a recording studio in London. They were in deep negotiation, and Hattie was sure she'd heard the words 'recording contract'. Rocco was signing more autographs for Susan, Angie and Jill from Dawlish, who were offering him parts of their body and indelible ink markers. Rosie and Geraldine were involved in a furious argument, the words 'jam first' and 'cream first' clearly audible.

'I'll book somewhere really nice for us all to go.'

'And it's on me this time.' Sean patted his T-shirt where a wallet might have been. 'It'd be a pleasure to treat you all – you've been so kind to my Bunty and me.'

'Thank you – then that's what we'll do,' Robert agreed. 'Give me a few minutes. I want to put the animals back in the field and give them some extra feed. After all – they've been the real stars of this competition...' He closed his eyes for a moment, his face suddenly calm. 'Thank goodness it's all over.'

* * *

Later that evening, Robert ordered a bottle of the best champagne and watched, smiling, as the waiter poured it into six crystal glasses. Hattie gazed out of the panoramic window at the sunset over the sea, the water glimmering crimson and gold. She felt exhausted but she was pleased with herself: standing up to Geoffrey had somehow helped her to decide what she wanted to do. She reached for Barry's hand and he met her eyes; he knew what she was thinking.

Bunty was guzzling champagne. 'We might go to Portugal. It's lovely there, apparently – I've never been. Or we might go further afield, the Caribbean.'

'Wherever you want, Bunts.' Sean wrapped an arm around her. 'You choose.'

'Cornwall's nice this time of year.' Tressy grinned mischievously. 'Lovely beaches – the best cream teas.' She winked at Robert, her face flushed with affection.

'I know – I'm off to stay there for a week, starting tomorrow.' Robert smiled. 'You'll be fine at the house, looking after the animals, won't you, Hattie?'

'I'll have plenty of help. The gardening club has promised to come round on Wednesday and do any tidying. Then Barry and I are having a barbecue for a few friends.' Hattie was still staring through the wide window at the glistening sea. 'I'm going to enjoy living here.'

'I hope so,' Barry murmured.

'We've been blessed with second chances, all of us,' Bunty

said. 'I'm not sure I deserve mine – I've been really stupid in the past.'

'We're just human.' Sean took her hand, kissing her fingers. 'Ah, I've always been a lucky man – I never really learned how to communicate properly with my lovely wife. But now I'm going to give it my best shot.'

'We'll live in the moment.' Bunty's eyes shone. 'It's all about now.'

'I'd never been in love,' Tressy said matter-of-factly, lifting her glass. 'It had never been anything I looked for. Why did I need a man? I was fine by myself. I had my tea shop, my health, my common sense. I didn't want some silly tuss holding me back and telling me what to do.' She glanced in Hattie's direction. 'I was proud of you this afternoon, maid. Telling that Geoffrey where to get off.'

'It was my moment to say what I felt.' Hattie smiled. The champagne fizzed on her tongue like happiness.

Tressy continued. 'No, I didn't look for love. Then I met Robert and it was love at first sight. I knew straight away that he was exactly what I wanted and I went for it.'

'And I'm so glad you did.' Robert took her hand in both of his. 'I'd believed I was too old for second chances. I'm not even sure I had a first chance. But Tressy, you were worth waiting for.'

'I never thought I'd have another shot at happiness either.' Barry smiled. 'But just this week I've walked on the cliff tops in Cornwall with Hattie, played the drums and been on television. I don't think you're ever too old to have fun.'

'I won't think about the past,' Hattie said firmly. 'I spent too long looking over my shoulder, worrying about what someone else wanted me to do. But never again.'

'Let's raise a glass to celebrate the end of Scone Wars,' Robert said mischievously with a glance at Tressy.

'To celebrate family and friendship,' Bunty added.

'And love.' Tressy's eyes sparkled.

'And the future,' Sean said.

Barry lifted his glass in a toast. 'To new beginnings.'

The sun sank behind the horizon and little lights glimmered in the bay. Six glasses chimed as Hattie said, 'Yes. To new beginnings. May every day we share be filled with possibilities...'

ACKNOWLEDGMENTS

Thanks always to my agent, Kiran Kataria, for her wisdom, professionalism and integrity. Huge thanks to Sarah Ritherdon who is the smartest, most encouraging editor anyone could wish for.

Thanks to Amanda Ridout, Nia Beynon, Marcela Torres, Claire Fenby, Jenna Houston, Rachel Gilbey and to the supportive family of Boldwood Books. And to everyone who has worked to make this book happen: designers, editors, technicians, magicians, voice actors, bloggers, fellow writers.

As always, thanks to Jan, Rog, Jan M, Helen, Ken, Trish, Lexy, Shaz, Gracie, Mya, Frank, Erika, Rich, Susie, Ian, Chrissie, Kathy N, Julie, Martin, Steve, Rose, Steve's Mum, Nik R, Pete O', Martin, Cath, Dawn, Slawka, Katie H, Jonno.

So much thanks to Peter, Avril and the Solitary Writers, my writing buddies.

Also, my neighbours – the best - and the local community, especially Jenny, Laura, Claire, Paul, Gary, Sophie and everyone at Bookshop by the Blackdowns.

Much thanks to the talented Ivor Abiks at Deep Studios.

Thanks to Ellen from Florida, Jo from Taunton, Norman, Angela, and Robin and Edward from Colorado.

So much love to my mum, who showed me the joy of reading, and to my dad, who proudly never read a thing.

Special love to our Tony and Kim.

Love always to Liam, Maddie, Caic, and to my soulmate, Big G.

Warmest thanks to my readers, wherever you are. You make this journey incredible.

ABOUT THE AUTHOR

Judy Leigh is the bestselling author of *A Grand Old Time* and *Five French Hens* and the doyenne of the 'it's never too late' genre of women's fiction. She has lived all over the UK from Liverpool to Cornwall, but currently resides in Somerset.

Sign up to Judy Leigh's mailing list here for news, competitions and updates on future books.

Visit Judy's website: https://judyleigh.com

Follow Judy on social media:

facebook.com/judyleighuk
x.com/judyleighwriter
instagram.com/judyrleigh
bookbub.com/authors/judy-leigh

ALSO BY JUDY LEIGH

Five French Hens

The Old Girls' Network

Heading Over the Hill

Chasing the Sun

Lil's Bus Trip

The Golden Girls' Getaway

A Year of Mr Maybes

The Highland Hens

The Golden Oldies' Book Club

The Silver Ladies Do Lunch

The Vintage Village Bake Off

The Morwenna Mutton Mysteries Series

Foul Play at Seal Bay

Bloodshed on the Boards

Boldwood

Boldwood Books is an award-winning fiction publishing company seeking out the best stories from around the world.

Find out more at www.boldwoodbooks.com

Join our reader community for brilliant books, competitions and offers!

Follow us
@BoldwoodBooks
@TheBoldBookClub

Sign up to our weekly deals newsletter

https://bit.ly/BoldwoodBNewsletter